The Molotov Box

The Molotov Box

Daniel Johnson

Library of Congress Control Number: 2010905703
ISBN: Hardcover   978-1-4500-8890-9
                 Softcover   978-1-4500-8889-3
                 Ebook   978-1-4500-8891-6

This book was printed in the United States of America.

To order additional copies of this book, contact:
Xlibris Corporation
1-888-795-4274
www.Xlibris.com
Orders@Xlibris.com
79842

Prologue

Overcast skies hid the setting sun, bringing early darkness and almost bearable temperatures to the dusty freight yard. In the distance the sound of heavy machinery could still be heard as the second shift prepared a stack train for its departure to California but the area around the little man in the tan suit appeared to be deserted.

Belatedly the man wished that he had left his jacket in the back seat of the cab waiting by the guard shack at the yard entrance, but now it remained on simply because it was one less item to worry with. A hot breeze was toying with his carefully constructed hairdo and he had to try to drape the thinning, overlong locks back across the top of his head using only the edge of a sleeve because his hands were full.

He was carrying a briefcase and consulting a page of instructions as he wandered the barren alleys between the rows of steel containers waiting their turn at new destinations. He had walked a long way from the entrance and his breathing was labored as he counted to himself.

" . . . *Trojka, Chetverka*," he mumbled in Russian as was his habit, and then paused.

There should have been five lines of the boxes stacked from one to three units high before he came to the one he was looking for. But there was a red Maersk forty-footer facing him broadside and there appeared to be two columns lengthwise behind it. Did that count as one row or two?

He caught a glimpse of white around the edge of the red container and walked another few paces. There was the Molotov Transport name and logo on a smaller box, a twenty-foot container with a jagged tear the size of a manhole cover near the corner closest to him. The little man looked around him as he stuffed the makeshift map back in his pocket and slowly approached the freight container. There was still no one else in sight.

The breach was in the shadows from the fading light so he removed a small flashlight from the briefcase and examined the hole in minute detail. Already he could see that the damage was not as bad as Ivan had feared. Obviously the secret could not have been compromised by this. Only the thin metal skin of the box had been mangled by the accident. He saw cardboard boxes through the opening so he knew someone would already have noted the discrepancy with the shipping manifest but that could be explained away.

One of the reinforcing ribs and a corner brace had been dislocated a few inches, but they were not separated from the structure. It should be possible to have the hole patched with a sheet of plywood and simply ship the box back to the warehouse where they could either repair it and place it back in service or retrieve its special cargo and destroy it according to the wishes of his employer. Ivan should have taken his advice and just arranged for a swift transfer. There was no need for this trip at all. He breathed a sigh of relief. There were some arrangements needed for the shipment but he should still be able to catch the late Northwest flight home.

The man in the tan suit had always been disdainful of the Americans and their obsession with electronic toys, but after seven years among them it was second nature for him to pull out his cell phone at every whim. He wanted to report the good news immediately to Miami. His finger was touching the first digit when he heard a metal-on-metal noise and stopped.

It had come from less than thirty meters away. Still grasping his phone and briefcase, he peered around the red container and saw an opening in the side of another light colored box where, according to his knowledge of these vehicles, there should have been none. As he watched, a man wearing a black t-shirt and jeans emerged from the portal, dropped quietly to the ground and closed the opening behind him with the same metallic sound. Their startled eyes met a moment later.

Black Shirt began to walk toward him with a halting, uncertain gait, smiling a little and looking around him as he came. Tan Suit reached into his coat pocket for his wallet. Who was this person? He hoped this would not become a problem—not that kind anyway. Bureaucracies he was well prepared to deal with alone but Sergei and Piotr were back in Florida where their physical skills could do him no good. But no, as far as he knew, only four—the real inner circle, it prided him to think—were aware of this particular secret. Neither Sergei nor Piotr was numbered among them.

"That is an unusual home you have there," Tan Suit said in what he hoped was a casually friendly voice, but it seemed to have the opposite effect as the smile left Black shirt's face as if it had been slapped and he paused for a moment and looked around again.

Tan suit put the briefcase down for a moment so that he could extract the proper credentials.

"I am authorized to be here," he said, reaching into a pocket and reflexively smoothing his few strands of hair again for the new acquaintance. Black Shirt began moving toward him again. *What is he doing here?* wondered the man in the tan suit. *Was he watching the Molotov container? Does he know somehow?*

"The freight container behind me and its cargo belongs to my . . ."

He was juggling the wallet and cell phone, while trying to display his identification properly for the stranger. The stranger said nothing and didn't halt until he was within arm's reach, much too close for such a casual encounter. It caused Tan Suit to halt his fumbling and look up into the new face. Even in the failing light, he could see that it was craggy and tan with an expression now of annoyance, perhaps confusion. The eyes in the dark face blinked several times as if trying to fight off the onset of a migraine.

Tan suit opened his mouth to begin explaining again but he didn't get very far.

Without any preamble or hint of warning the silent man in the black t-shirt struck several scientifically accurate blows in succession. For Tan Suit, there was only the blurred suggestion of motion, too fast even for pain. His knees suddenly folded beneath him like overcooked cabbage rolls. Before he could collapse, a powerful arm encircled his throat and breathing became impossible as he felt himself lifted bodily until he had a brief but panoramic view of the darkening sky. All the little man in the tan suit had time to experience was profound bewilderment; that and the flashing realization that the secret he had come so far to protect wasn't as important as he had thought.

Chapter 1

Gaby had just settled into a mindless but efficient routine of sorting e-mail into working folders when the muffled voice of her boss reminded her of the other reason she wanted to quit.

"Hey, Bah-*nahd*!" he brayed in his flat Boston accent from the adjacent office.

Tony Metcalf was Gabrielle Bernard's supervisor at the FBI. Among other annoyances, the man steadfastly refused to use the correct French pronunciation she preferred and had requested. Gaby didn't really know if he owned a dog, but if he did, and didn't care for it much, she imagined that this was the tone he used to call it.

Special Agent Bernard took a deep breath and let it out in a sigh at the video screen. She resisted the impulse to respond to this petty bit of rudeness with an answering bark of her own, but just barely. Finally she rose from her chair and walked around the corner into the open door of Counsel General attorney Paul Kramer, her office neighbor.

In some departments, evening shifts were just beginning but after six o'clock in this particular corner of the FBI headquarters building most of the chairs were empty and the mood was casual. Like the one Gaby occupied, this windowless office was so small that even with the back of his chair against the wall, Metcalf could rest a knee on the edge of Kramer's desk as he slouched in one of the visitor's chairs. He had loosened his tie and the collar of his ever-present white oxford cloth shirt but his attitude was as taut as ever.

Metcalf was a veteran of the Bureau who had risen the hard way. Over twenty years before, a freakish bit of luck and a kidnapping case in south Boston had allowed him to make the transition to the most respected law enforcement agency in America, but he was still an outsider. He was respected but not liked among his colleagues and consistently feared as a political rival. He was too short, too under-educated, too ambitious, too ethnic-looking and too accommodating to authority when it was expedient to his career. He just did not seem to fit the mold his peers liked to embrace, but he had managed by street smarts and ruthless tenacity to rise far enough that he no longer had to care about any but the very highest placed opinions at the Bureau. He was reputed to be very difficult to work for and he relished the reputation.

Gaby engineered a pale smile and said, "Yes, Assistant Director Metcalf? You bellowed?"

Kramer's face flickered a grin but Metcalf chose not to hear any sarcasm.

"Sit down," the AD said, indicating the remaining unoccupied seat.

"Agent Bernard," he began, "I need another legal opinion. It's a jurisdictional problem."

"That seems to be what I'm here for," she sighed, dropping into the other chair.

Gaby was doing a lot more lawyering than she had anticipated upon joining the Bureau as an agent. She made no secret of her desire for what she considered more suitable duty, but she was certainly an attorney by training and a good one.

"Let me run a scenario by you," Metcalf said.

Gaby nodded and stole a look at Paul Kramer. He was playing with a paperweight on his desk that had the FBI insignia encased in a glass hemisphere. He didn't seem to be aware that anyone else was present at the moment.

"A murder takes place in Memphis Tennessee," Metcalf began. "It happens in a freight yard. The victim is a foreign businessman, or seems to be. The method is very violent, very efficient, but involves no weapons. The body is left partly inside a freight container of some kind—a truck or whatever. Now, for reasons of my own, I want the Bureau to take over the investigation and for the operation to be run from Washington. What's the best way for me to do that?"

"I assume you are asking only about the jurisdictional part," Gaby said. "Once the Bureau is involved, you can pretty much horn in wherever you please, no?"

"True," Metcalf agreed.

"Okay, then." Gaby was staring at the fluorescent lights over Kramer's desk, deep in thought. By the time she lowered her gaze she had several ideas.

"You said foreign. Not a diplomat, I take it?"

"Hardly."

"What do you mean by that? This guy was connected?"

"Probably."

"No problem, then. RICO statutes will allow you . . ."

"No," Metcalf was shaking his head with impatience. Kramer was beaming at him and Gaby surmised that this was the answer he had already provided her boss.

"Don't want to use it in this case," Metcalf continued. "Anyway we're almost positive that his murder is not Mob related—and if it is, that won't help our—strategy."

Gaby paused, wrinkling an otherwise unlined brow in thought.

"Any other organizations? I assume he wasn't associated with terrorists or white supremacy groups—that kind of thing?"

"No, no chance."

"Okay then, tell me about the freight yard. Is it used by more than one carrier?"

"Yeah, I think so."

"Does it handle intermodal freight as well?"

"What the hell is intermodal freight?" Metcalf asked.

"You know. Those big boxes they put on trucks and then move to rail cars for long hauls—or ships for international destinations."

"I guess so. Maybe they do handle that kind of stuff. So what?"

"Well, it's pretty weak but Title 49 might work. It includes investigative powers for the Secretary of Transportation but that really bears more on code violations than criminal activity. You would have to show a connection between the crime and a conspiracy to violate one of the Title 49 statutes. Even then you might have to go in with an ICC inspector.

"The most supportable argument is one where you assert jurisdiction based on an assumption of a conspiracy to interdict interstate commerce at this particular location. There's a pretty good chance that one or more of the carriers represented at this yard is a subcontractor for the US Postal Service. That would improve your premise and also give you an excuse to push the local Bureau office out of the way, but as I said, it's pretty weak. Even so there shouldn't be much trouble about it. You know as well as I do that you would get no significant pushback from locals anyway and the burden placed on you for this kind of judgment is almost non-existent."

Metcalf turned to Paul Kramer with a satisfied look.

"I told you she would come up with something better."

Kramer grimaced. As an employee of OCG he reported to a different Assistant Director and was not required to be intimidated.

"It's not 'better' just different. You could accomplish the same thing by identifying the guy as organized crime and investigating the murder that way. It *is* true you know. Why would you want to complicate things?"

"The old man wants this low key all the way. I'm not sure we want to do it at all but the last thing I want is to call up the Memphis PD and tell them they've had a mob hit that they should ignore just because we say so. The Attorney General's office would be sure to hear about it. Bernard's way is better. You're just pissed off because I've got better lawyers working for me than you've got in OCG."

Kramer used a word to Metcalf that was not commonly heard in the J. Edgar Hoover Building.

"Next time feel free to bypass my department and consult your own," he added.

Kramer said it in a joking way but it was obvious that he really was irritated for several reasons, not the least of which was that he was one of the allegedly inferior OCG lawyers in question.

Gaby felt obligated to redirect the conversation and she had some lobbying to do anyway.

"I don't suppose this is a job you could give to me?"

"Don't make me laugh, Bernard," Metcalf replied. "No way you're ready for a field assignment. It's one thing to do the supporting research and quite another to run a proper field investigation. You got management issues and interagency issues besides the plain old street cop stuff. It takes brass balls to do it right and you don't have the credentials."

Metcalf smirked in a way that told her that his choice of metaphor was no accident. Gaby kept her composure only with conscious effort. The irony was that she knew Metcalf took this kind of liberty with her because he knew that she had too much pride to bring him up on harassment charges. It would be an admission of weakness—that she needed statutory support for something she couldn't control on her own. Also, even though there was no stated policy about it, a woman who blew that kind of whistle would be marked for the rest of her career. They wouldn't dare fire her of course and in fact she might even get a promotion out of it but the kind of field investigator role she was looking for would be forever lost.

"When I finished third in my class at the academy, the instructors made a point of telling us that anyone who graduated was more than prepared for any job in the FBI—even the five of us that had no balls, brass or otherwise."

Metcalf rolled his eyes.

"Don't go all Carrie Nations on me, Bernard. All I'm saying is you're not ready. Patience."

"Carrie *Nation* was a temperance worker not a suffragette," Gaby said.

Metcalf made a rude sound, but she wasn't letting go.

"Is there an assignment in this or not?"

Metcalf said, "As a matter of fact it's a kind of high profile gig. So what?"

"Then give it to me. You know I deserve a shot and I've been asking forever."

"I already told you my position, Bernard. Besides, I'm not making the assignment on this one. There's a stack of qualified personnel files on my desk right now and you're not in it. I'm going to deliver to the DD in the morning, he'll make a pick and that will be that. Besides, I can tell you I'm recommending Cannon for the job."

"Cannon? You're kidding. What are you trying to investigate, steroid use?"

"While you were smoking dope at Radcliffe, Cannon was becoming the youngest cop in Baltimore to make detective before he joined the Bureau."

"Yeah, yeah, yeah. Jesus, Tony. He's been filling out forms, counting reps in the gym and kissing your you-know-what to get an assignment, that's his contribution here."

"What the hell do you think you've been doing?" he asked. Gaby rejected the first two or three responses that came to her as being too incendiary.

"Besides," she said, "Are you afraid you'll get cold without his nose inserted?"

"Watch it, Bernard!"

"Okay, then at least put my folder in the stack. That's not asking too much."

Metcalf shrugged with a facial expression that was just as insulting as anything he had said out loud. Gaby sighed and looked over at Paul Kramer who was eyeing his paperweight again.

"What's all this about, anyway—the case, I mean?" she asked her boss.

"Like I told you, it's a murder."

"A murder we would normally never notice. And . . . ?"

"The Deputy Director has reasons, I'm sure."

"You're not going to tell me."

"Actually he hasn't told me everything yet. You obviously don't have a need to know any of it, but it seems to be some kind of international thing."

"International? In Memphis?"

Metcalf got up from his chair and walked slowly to the door while Gaby fumed.

"Then how about my transfer?" Gaby asked.

Metcalf just looked at her.

"If I need anything else from you on this, I'll let you know."

As he left, he gave the doorframe a high five for emphasis and said, "I'll talk to you later, Paul."

Gaby closed her eyes and waited until he had rounded at least two corners before swearing softly. She knew that kind of language was a bad habit, but didn't really work hard at overcoming it because she mistakenly thought it made her seem tougher.

When she opened her eyes Paul Kramer was staring directly into them. It made her uncomfortable. She began to apologize for swearing but the name Kramer had used for her boss a minute before was much nastier.

He smiled.

"Don't worry. If you really want that kind of assignment, you'll get it. It'll just take a little longer, that's all. What you ought to do is change your mind and come over to the Office of Counsel General with us. That's where you really belong. Or even somewhere else in the Justice Department. You are a hell of a lawyer. You won't find that kind of—uh—barrier over here."

"Thanks, Paul. And that 'better lawyer' comment he made—I never said anything to him that could be . . ."

Kramer waved her explanation away in dismissal.

"I know that. He just likes to rattle cages, that's all. Maybe he doesn't like me either. I can live with it."

"'Either'? So it's that obvious? Do you understand why he doesn't like me?"

He looked a little embarrassed, but Gaby just waited.

"Oh, Metcalf likes to play the tough guy, that's all. I wouldn't take it personally. The louder he talks, the less certain he is. That's why he's comforted by Cannon, but it's not personal."

"I think it's very personal. He came down here to ask a legal opinion and then called on me when he didn't like your answer. He has to know I'm smarter than Cannon on his best day. It's not an arm-wrestling contest. So what's wrong with me?"

"Not a thing . . ." Kramer began, a little too quickly and with a little too much emphasis.

Now a slight blush added to his look of discomfort. He was staring at his paperweight again.

In addition to her other qualities, Gaby Bernard was an extraordinarily beautiful woman. She was not unaware of the fact, and clearly neither was Paul Kramer. Moderately tall at just under five-foot nine, and blessed with finely chiseled features, deep chestnut toned hair and dark, expressive eyes, Gaby was immediately noticed wherever she went. Flattering though it was, she often found the attention inconvenient. It had begun to occur to her that it might even be career limiting.

"You know what I mean, Paul," she said with some embarrassment of her own.

"I guess so," he said, with a relieved expression. "Everybody in the Bureau isn't like Tony. And even he might come around given time."

"Yes but will I still be working here by then?" Gaby sighed.

She put her hands on the arms of her chair to get up and seemed to change her mind abruptly.

"Paul, can I ask your opinion?"

"Of course you can. Sure, Gaby. You know I'll be happy to help if I can."

She nodded toward the wall their two offices shared.

"In there on my word processor is a letter of resignation that I wrote up thirteen days ago. I told myself that I would give it two weeks to see if either my situation or my attitude changed, but tomorrow is the end of that and I feel worse than ever."

Kramer looked pained. He wrinkled his face and shifted around like the chair had suddenly become hard.

"It would be a shame if you did that, Gaby, really it would."

"We've talked before, Paul. You know I didn't come to Washington to practice law. I didn't have to leave New Orleans to do that. In fact my father's corporate practice would be high adventure compared to the kind of nit-picking bureaucratic nonsense I do every day."

The last syllable was crossing her lips when the ironic look appearing on Paul's face reminded her that she was talking about his job as well.

"Sorry. What I mean to say is, it's a perfectly fine career—challenging public service and all that but it's not why I became an agent. I've asked for field work at every opportunity for the last nineteen months. I feel like I've paid my dues but I'm not getting any closer. Am I just being unrealistic? What do you think?"

"Well, for one thing I'm pretty sure you're not quitting."

"Oh? And why is that?" she asked. Gaby interpreted his comment to mean that she was bluffing somehow—that this was only a display of childish petulance and her defenses went up immediately. Paul could sense it and he smiled at her hard expression.

"That's why! That's it right there. You're too competitive. I think you're just the kind of person who can't give up until you've won the game."

"Is that what you think of me, that it's just some shallow contest of wills?"

"But, I didn't mean anything bad . . ."

Paul couldn't maintain a steady gaze and looked down at the desktop again. He was a decade older than Gaby's thirty years but tended to be boyish and embarrassed when she was around.

"Okay, in a way, it is a contest. But I don't think there's anything shallow about you, Gaby."

"What then?"

"Even though he uses your legal advice on procedure, he'd love it if you would quit and you know it. That's why you're not going to do it."

Gaby rose from her chair.

"Don't take anything I said negatively, Gaby. I certainly didn't mean it that way. You asked my opinion."

"No, I understand."

"It's just that because of several factors it would take something unusual—a really lucky break to do what you're trying to do within the Bureau. Either that or a lot of patience. You really need that big break."

Gaby moved to the doorway wondering which factors he meant exactly.

"I was taught to make my own breaks, Paul."

She realized that she had made him the object of some misdirected anger and softened for a moment.

"But, I'm sure there's a lot of truth in what you say. Thanks anyway, Paul."

Gaby also sensed that Paul was working his way up to asking her out again so she quickly added, "See you tomorrow," and swung out of his doorway and into her own. She was in no mood for an office romance and besides; she had other things on her mind.

What was it he had said? It would take something 'really unusual'.

Gaby closed the office door and went immediately to the phone but when she picked up the receiver she paused with her index finger halfway to the keypad. She pinched her lower lip softly between her front teeth as she hesitated. She could get Karen to do it, she was sure of that. In addition to being the civil service version of a free spirit, Karen Elias was her best friend in the Bureau and more significantly at the moment, the administrator on the fourth floor where the offices of both Metcalf and Deputy Director Fallon were. It wasn't at all fair to ask something like that. Selfish. Unconscionable. *Something really unusual.*

Gaby hissed out another nasty word to the empty room. At the least she could be fired. She believed she could protect her friend if the worst came but she didn't want to lose her own job either. Not that way. She might be frustrated enough to quit, but the last thing she wanted was to go back home to New Orleans and try to explain another failure. Making your own luck was not for the faint of heart.

Quickly, like a plunge into icy water she dialed the four digits. She wasn't surprised that Karen was still on the job when most of the civil servants were at home having dinner.

"Hey, it's me," Gaby said into the receiver.

"Karen, I want to ask you something in absolute confidence. I need a favor. It's very important. It may really be my only chance but I know it's not fair to ask something like this."

There followed several mutual reassurances after which Gaby said, "Would you know how to go about finding my personnel folder?"

Chapter 2

Sunshine on swaying palm trees and relaxing vacationers on the beach outside filled the lobby's curved three-story windows with a picture postcard view. The pleasant vista was utterly wasted on one stocky man dressed in an open collared shirt and his only suit, a dark, heavy number he had worn from La Guardia that morning. He was there to do business. Carl "Lucky" Lucchesi rarely left the New York area even to ply his trade and until now he had not been called upon to murder anyone in Miami Beach.

Carl, who was called "Lucky" as a distortion of his surname rather than for any evident good fortune on his part, stood near the entry steps at a low wall of greenery separating the Fontainbleau's central traffic area from the lobby bar. His eyes darted from face to face in the pastel colored crowd. He expected to meet the head of the so-called Russian Mafia in North America but really didn't know who he was looking for. Their Godfather would recognize him, he had been told.

He stood next to a potted palm tree surveying faces and ogling a few of the more attractive hotel patrons. If he had had any degree of sensitivity at all he would have been self conscious of some of the looks he was getting from the guests. Instead he just stood as tall as he could and turned from time to time as he rejected the possibilities they presented.

After several minutes of diminishing interest, Lucky saw a tall man with short, wiry gray hair rise and nod in his direction from a table near the window. The man dropped a bill next to his glass and joined Lucky by the entrance. Nearby were two wary figures failing to be unobtrusive in their protective attention to the older man. Neither was quite as tall but similarly thin and sinewy in appearance. They sported light colored jackets whose purpose could only have been the concealment of weapons.

"I believe you are looking for me," the tall man said in crisp, unsullied English with a British lilt. When Lucky moved toward him the man offered his hand and said, "Mister Lucchesi, it is a pleasure to meet you. Please come with me."

Lucky adjusted his jacket with a shrug and moved with the little entourage into the dining area of The Steak House, just up another short flight of stairs from the lobby. A sign indicated that it was closed for remodeling. Two more tall, thin men with bored, hooded eyes waited for him and by gestures indicated that he was to be searched. It was a thorough job and he submitted without comment. One table by the floor-to-ceiling window had the protective plastic drop cloth removed and the first man waited for him there. Though the glass was tinted, the brilliant day prompted the Russian to don a pair of sunglasses with tortoise shell rims. Lucky didn't own a pair and he was left with the seat facing the glare.

"So, are you *the man?*" Lucchesi asked with some uncharacteristic nervousness and a squint when he was seated. The Russian organization had made itself into a formidable competitor in a relatively short time. Its leader in America would be a powerful individual indeed.

"My name is Ivan Balakova. The gentleman you expect will not be joining us, but I am authorized to act for him. I serve as advisor and in many other capacities."

Lucky shrugged his shoulders briefly.

"Okay, so you send me a couple grand and a ticket and you get Bruno's permission to talk to me and maybe we do a job together. So what is it, and why am I the lottery winner?"

"We have a very simple but important contract in mind. For various reasons we do not want our own people involved further. Also you may be uniquely qualified since you are somewhat acquainted with the target. The fee we have in mind is $200,000."

"American dollars?" he asked.

"Of course."

"Look, I don't do politicians, Mister—ah—Mister B."

Balakova smiled at his difficulty. He repeated his last name slowly, pronouncing each syllable separately.

"And no, Mr. Lucchesi, the object of our attention was an occasional employee of the old Gambino Family, but he is not a public figure. His absence will cause less than a ripple in the tide of our times."

Lucky pulled out a cigarette and lit it with the long flame of a gold Colibri that was a memento of a similar meeting some years before.

Asking permission simply wouldn't have occurred to him and his limited imagination was occupied with analyzing the opportunity. They weren't just giving him a six-figure cakewalk. There was something *wrong* with this arrangement. Also this guy talked like the first chaplain he had when he was sent up to Rahway in his youth. He was also a confusing asshole.

"Mister . . . Mister B, what say we cut this short? You know and I know that this is not enough money for the President and it's too damn much for some jamoke in the Bronx. We need to get right to it. Who is it? Did you tell Bruno when you asked if I could do a contract?"

The flat discs in Balakova's sunglasses were two depthless pools of ink. Lucky couldn't tell if he were expecting more information, considering his reply or just trying to rattle him with the wait.

"No. No, we didn't," the Russian said finally. "He is aware of some aspects of our request but not the identity." He waited another few seconds.

"We lost a low-level employee recently. He was in Memphis Tennessee to inspect the property of one of our commercial concerns.

"He was murdered by a professional assassin who, as far as we can tell, was acting on his own."

Lucky nodded once slowly.

"And you want me to take care of your vengeance. So who?"

"He is known by many names. I believe in some quarters men in your profession have been referred to as mechanics have they not?"

Lucky nodded again, even though the man's assumptions were not entirely true. He was a soldier for the Family, preeminent in his talent for violence, but the term 'mechanic' as Balakova was using it, implied a full time vocation as a murderer and this was largely a product of Hollywood imaginations.

"Within the Gambino family or its remnants, he is called simply *The Mechanic*, though they no longer have an exclusive lease on his services. You have heard of him?"

Lucchesi laughed out loud.

"Somebody's shinin' you, *Consiglieri*. I don't think there ever was no *capital M*—Mechanic and they don't even use the name no more. There was a movie back in the seventies with Charlie Bronson. That was about the time Castellano started using the name to scare faggots and old ladies. Any time he pushed a button on a guy they put out the word that *The Mechanic* did it.

"Castellano wanted the world to believe that he had the goddam *Angelo di Morte* on his payroll. It was the freakin' DiMeo crew. Shit! I haven't even heard the name in ten years." He laughed again, a short derisive expulsion of air.

Balakova opened a manila folder he had kept in his lap. "Yes, we now know that until this incident he was considered inactive and perhaps retired. This document is from an Atlanta Credit Repository. It is the working identity of this Mechanic.

"He has had many, but in this persona he is almost fifty years old. In truth he may even be a little older. He maintains at least the appearance of a job with . . . uh," he consulted the pages in the folder. " . . . Coastal Freight Consolidators at an office in Memphis, Tennessee. He was married over a dozen years ago to a woman whose previous name was Wallace and shortly thereafter seems to have given up his previous career. He has since lived a life which is extraordinary only in its pretensions to ordinariness. This is how he is known today."

He slid the open folder across the table toward Lucchesi, then leaned forward to retrieve it when Lucchesi made no move to pick it up.

"I don't get it. How could you know all this about him? If he's not just a bad joke, then he's a . . . he's . . ."

"Yes. Even if exaggerated, his successes are quite . . ."

"No, that's not what I mean . . ." Lucchesi interrupted.

After a brief and unsuccessful search for an ashtray Lucky tapped his cigarette in the direction of the carpeted floor and then scraped the ash into the nap with his shoe.

"Well, yeah if it's true he would have been good but everybody I know thinks the same thing that I do. Somebody would have taken him down a long time ago if they knew where to find him. He would have made a lot of enemies if he was for real." Lucky sniffed, "I guess I know 5 or 6 of them myself."

"The Interpol report told us that the Mechanic had eliminated our employee, but finding the name you see on those papers was much more difficult and expensive. In the past when the *Vor*, what you would call the *Capo di tutti capi* wanted to use his services he would call a number in Virginia and leave a message with his dispatcher who would make the arrangements."

Balakova continued the impassive scrutiny of his visitor. Lucky took a long drag, blowing the smoke at the ceiling some eighteen feet distant.

"At least now I know why the fee," he said more or less to himself. "If one of our guys had known he was for real they would have turned him in because he was competition, he was outside the Family and because we were sick of hearing all that living legend shit, but why should you push a button on him? Retired or not, he's freelance so there's no point in vendetta. Now that the cops know something about him they'll be all over the guy."

"The authorities have not learned the identity of The Mechanic nor are they likely to. As I indicated, our inquiry involved . . . unorthodox channels."

Lucchesi furrowed his brow as his eyes darted from side to side in an effort to understand the approach.

"Then you could tell them and they could bag him for you. The job would be easier in the joint and you could get it done for three cartons of Marlboros."

The Russian half-nodded in agreement. "They know only enough that they should be able to restrict his movements. That should allow you to complete our agreement and be on your way."

"I get it," Lucky said. "You're afraid of something he might tell the cops."

Balakova crossed his legs and brushed at the cuff of his expensive trousers. The crease was crooked and he straightened it. When he was done, it looked like the edge of a long razor and he seemed pleased with it for a moment.

Finally he said, "We are asking for your services in the usual tactical capacity, Mr. Lucchesi. I am not at liberty to talk of . . . strategies. If you refuse the contract, you may keep the honorarium you have already received for your silence in this matter and we can get on with the business of finding an acceptable contractor."

For his part, Lucky was still fidgety but he had a strong feel for the appropriate protocols to be followed on such occasions and he gave Balakova a look that would have intimidated most people.

"Don't get ahead of me, *Consiglieri*. Now, you said at first that I was familiar with this guy. How come?"

"It is known to us that you participated in an operation resulting in the death of two of my colleagues, Grigori Kasyanov and Yuri Kurzin. It was 1985 and we were at that time providing much of the product for your West Coast, at least to your family and also to the Gambinos, although Mr. Castellano was certainly unaware of it."

"Yeah . . ."

Unconsciously, Lucky's eyes made a quick trip to the exit and back.

"Calm yourself, Mister Lucchesi, we have long since leveled the accounts on that operation," he said.

"You were a part of the team that eliminated Kurzin in Los Angeles, I believe."

The assassin looked as if he still expected a late retribution.

"Hey, I was just a kid then. I swear, I thought he was KGB. In fact, they told me the guy I backed up was some kind of CIA loaner."

"Kurzin was KGB—among other things. So you do remember the incident?"

"Yeah. My guy had some special field piece mounted on that window. Put one through this guy Kurzin's throat at almost a quarter mile. Only fired once and started packing up his shit. I would have given him two more just to be sure. Kind of a hotdog move but it was a hell of a shot!"

"Do you remember his name—your temporary partner?"

"You're kidding! You telling me that was The Mechanic?"

Balakova nodded.

"Holy shit!" he said with a wry smile. Then, "No, I couldn't tell you his name. I figured it was fake, anyway."

"Quite right. It is of no particular importance since he probably never uses a name more than one time, but he has a very consistent mode of selecting his pseudonyms. On your job, he signed the hotel register as William Dukenfield."

"Yeah! That was it. Stupid name, Bill Dukenfield. How'd you know? So what's the deal with his fake names?"

"He is very professional in every other way. Quite subtle, even inscrutable. But from our experience, he always uses the birth name of a famous person who changed his name for one reason or another—usually a celebrity or film star. That particular selection once belonged to an early comic actor in the motion pictures who went by the name of W. C. Fields."

Lucchesi shook his head. "I'll be damned. I didn't know that."

"Not many would and if someone confronted him about it, he dismissed it as a joke of his parents. Still, it occasionally calls attention to him at a hotel or automobile rental counter and this is something one in his profession normally avoids. It is a silly and dangerous affectation—yes?"

"I wouldn't do it, if that's what you mean. Why does he do it?"

"Our informant is an agent of the US government who formerly dispatched the activities of the Mechanic. He told us of his belief that the man was, and presumably is, quite simply insane, psychotic in some unique way. The agent says that when he knew the man he was always 'in' one of these characters and that at those times he did not seem to remember any other life. He has scrupulously maintained that Memphis persona down to the smallest detail for over fifteen years, yet we know that it is a false one."

"So he's nuts?"

"As you say, he may have a fragile relationship with reality or it could be that he is simply more adept at deep-cover role playing. It is not important which interpretation is true. It has not hampered his efficiency. Fifty odd contracts in the two decades before his supposed retirement, says the controlling agent. The police associate him with only nine. Many of them were ruled suicides, accidents or naturally occurring medical events. There were others—not dispatched—that appear to be personal in nature—a hobby perhaps. We will provide you with whatever history you wish and assistance in other ways, perhaps even the participation of our informer. That is, if you agree to accept our task. Are you doing so, or do you need time to consider?"

Before Lucchesi could respond, Balakova continued.

"In fact, before you do, I should tell you that you would not be the first."

Lucky smiled with the left half of his mouth.

"Oh?" he said, expanding the syllable and waiting.

"For various reasons the decision to terminate the killer was made immediately upon discovery. The . . ."

"This guy in the freight car must have been pretty important to you for a—what did you call him? A low-level employee? So you already sent somebody?"

"When faced with more serious situations like this, we frequently call on our brethren from Chechnya. So we did in this case. They tend to have a particular brand of—uh—craziness, but they are faithful and relentless. We specified a team of two with whose work we were familiar.

"They seem to have been both over-zealous and clumsy. They chose the worst possible method; an explosion that resulted in the death of innocents in his family, his wife and daughter. Our operatives reported that the target was in his home at the time, yet his body was not recovered."

Balakova held his gaze steady. "Two days later their continued efforts apparently brought them in contact with this Mechanic and now they are also dead. I felt—we felt that you should know all of this, before we proceed."

Lucky was not unimpressed. If there really was a guy behind all those stories over the years he was damn good. He leaned back in his chair.

"Three dead guys already and a hot-shit living legend as a target. I'll need some extra for a deal like this," he said. "This ain't exactly a normal contract. The big number needs to be three."

"I understood that you didn't believe the legend."

Lucky blinked slowly and said, "You must have convinced me about a hundred grand worth."

Balakova smiled. He slid a thick white envelope across the wood veneer surface.

"If you will accept the retainer here, an additional amount will be sent to your room tonight with the balance due upon completion. Then we have reached acceptable terms?"

Lucky nodded and the Russian nudged the report a little toward the other side of the table. His posture softened marginally and he leaned back into the faux leather of the restaurant's chair. Now he was dealing with an employee.

"Even his 'real' name, that is the one on the credit report—is assumed from a child who died at age two months about fifty years in the past, but it was carefully selected. I'm sure you are aware . . ." only a slightly elevated eyebrow hinted at the mockery in his statement, "it was the given name of a well regarded English poet."

Lucky made a grunting sound in response. Balakova looked at him and considered for just a second.

Finally he said "So, Mister Lucchesi. There we are. Either he will be captured by law enforcement or he will make a mistake that will reveal his location to us. In any case, I shall require you to be available immediately to fulfill your agreement. I sincerely hope that I am being overly cautious and that this is the easiest fee you will ever earn."

Lucky got up slowly in response and took the proffered limp parting grip.

"You won't be sorry," he said, understanding that the interview was at an end. In moving away, he hesitated.

After another step, the killer stopped and turned back toward his host. It would be inaccurate to say that Lucky's mind raced, but the deep coruscations in his brow signaled a significant effort. The Russian noticed and waited.

"Mister Blva", his attempt at pronunciation faded into an unintelligible mumble. "Don't worry I'm not gonna get this guy or nothin' like that. That's no problem. To tell the truth, I ain't too sure that the guy you're sending me after is really The Mechanic, but whoever he is he's dead. Anyway, like I said, I never believed it myself, but you seem pretty sure and I'm . . . I'm kinda cautious by nature if you get my drift."

Balakova's smile held the beginnings of contempt.

"You sound as if you are concerned about your ability to overcome a man with his credentials."

"No, it ain't that. I know who I'm lookin' for and he don't know who's lookin'. That's plenty enough edge for me."

"What then?"

"When you send that package to my room, include in the name of somebody else in your outfit—somebody else who knows about me and has—uh, authorization. No offense intended—really, but this is a lot of money."

Balakova looked as if he was unsure if he should be offended.

"I don't understand," he said.

"I know he's just one guy and all that, but you had his old lady capped. Like I say, no offense, but if it was me and I got half a chance I'd be coming after you personally."

Lucky still feared that he might have crossed some line of propriety within Balakova's hierarchy but the Russian just smiled at him.

"As a matter of fact, Mister Lucchesi, I am counting on it."

Chapter 3

George's office meeting ran longer than expected and he had missed almost the entire game.

Alicia was in the on-deck circle taking awkward, but earnest slashes with her shiny aluminum bat. It was a broad interpretation of the controlled, level swing that they had been working on the previous evening. George was running in on the Home side of the field so he could see his little girl clearly almost from the time he got out of the car and he hesitated just a second as he took in the whole scene. At random times the sight of her could literally take his breath for a moment and this was both delightful and frightening. He smiled broadly and chuckled to himself.

The bill of Ally's cap was characteristically drawn too far down and he couldn't make out her full profile, but from the set of her jaw, she was sporting an adorably ferocious scowl. Sometimes it seemed to George that she matured, or at least grew, visibly in the space of a few hours.

The girl caught movement out of the corner of her eye and saw her Dad, late as always, making his way to the short set of bleachers on the same side of the field. Her face answered his immediately with an expression of delight. She waved at him with her fingers down by her side as if no one else could see and then turned back to the serious business at hand. A year or so away from puberty, Alicia did not yet understand on an emotional level that she would never play for the Atlanta Braves and this fact charmed and delighted her father to the core.

Still grinning, George Gordon aimed a kiss at his wife Valerie, or the diminutive, Val as he called her when he wasn't using one of a half-dozen pet names. He even took a moment to brush her cheek lightly and speak to her sister, Katherine. Kate returned his smile but when he glanced back, Val looked meaningfully at her watch and shook her head as she handed him the cap she had brought from home. Though his wife was the older of the two sisters, the first lines of middle age had barely smudged the beauty he remembered from their first meeting when a chance encounter at the supermarket had so changed the last fourteen years of his life.

Her clear green eyes momentarily acquired a little good-natured fire, but Val was accustomed to George's failings and an explanation would have been pointless. He did his best to look charming and contrite, shrugged and dropped his jacket and tie on the weathered wooden slab between the two sisters. There was no time to change shoes so he kicked up a small cloud of dust with his black wingtips hustling to the first base coaches' box. He raised a hand toward his neighbor on the other side of the field, but the man was deep in concentration and barely acknowledged George's arrival.

The head coach prowling the third base coach's box with the intensity of a recently captured animal was a transplanted northerner whose name was John Keathley. The fierce look and curt wave he received reminded George of the problem he had been putting off. Keathley was a dark, hulking man with an abundance of nervous energy. He was supposed to have played ball for a double-A franchise some years back but tended to be evasive in answering questions about his past. At the moment he was bellowing instructions in a New York accent, ostensibly to the player on second base, but louder than it needed to be.

The base runner singled out for his scorn at the moment was his own daughter, Jonie. There were no accusations of favoritism on John Keathley's team. In fact there had been accusations of a different sort, and that was the situation George had once more to put out of his mind for the moment so that he could pay attention to his job.

Charlie, a tall redheaded girl whose real name was either Charlotte or Charlene, George couldn't remember which, relinquished his accustomed post in the first base coaching box with a wave. He rolled up the sleeves of his white shirt and pulled the orange cap down over his eyes. Little Laura Kendall was at the plate and George clapped and called out encouragement for her. Like his Alicia, the girl was at the threshold of a time when most girls downgrade or forget completely the participative side of the athletic scene. Coltish, bony frames would soon beget long legs, gentle new curves and endless, if clumsy masculine attention. George's understanding of that imminent secret about his daughter and her friends only heightened his enjoyment of the moment.

He was barely settled when the waif-ish Kendall girl smacked one. She was so thin and insubstantial that when contact was made and the timing was a little off, you could see a recoil of her whole body, as if her mass and that of the softball had made a nearly equal collision. The blooper floated just over the shortstop's glove, which came completely off her hand when she jumped at it. The left fielder, who was no more than thirty feet off the infield, could most certainly have handled the soft fly ball had she not frozen in an attitude of stylized incompetence at the metallic clink of the bat. It rolled to a stop almost at her feet.

Laura rounded first base with a showy feint toward second. The tiny crowd reacted enthusiastically. St. Michael's was the major rival for Alicia's grade school at St. Anne, which was just outside of Memphis in an incorporated suburb. They affected grand rivalries and bitter hatred even though many of their parents socialized and the respective pastors had a regular racquetball game. Beating St. Michael's was a cherished goal not achieved in more than two years.

From the scoreboard, George gathered the information essential to his job. Laura had driven in the vivacious little round shaped girl who was their catcher, making the score nine to eight in favor of the visiting St Michael's team. It was the bottom of the fifth and final inning, the climax of a pitcher's duel by their standards. It brought Alicia to the plate with runners on first and third and two outs. Any kind of a hit would send them to extra innings.

"Come on, Ally, come on baby!" George shouted.

The opposing pitcher looked cool. She was Saint Michael's oldest player, a tall blonde who appeared to be maturing physically on a rather different schedule from the others. In George's opinion the little Amazon should have been sent to another league. Ally looked defiantly toward the mound as she strode to the plate.

"Time!" called Keathley.

He jogged gracefully in, spoke quickly in Ally's ear behind a cupped hand and returned when she nodded. The coaches and the teammates on the bench were vocal in their encouragement as the umpire made the sign meaning 'play ball'.

From the mound, the girl delivered a low arcing pitch accented with her shrill grunt. Probably less than forty miles an hour in velocity, it looked like a fireball to George, but it was outside.

"Ball one," said Pete Suliano, the chubby umpire standing behind her.

George saw John Keathley give the "take" sign repeatedly to Alicia and he unconsciously tugged his ear and then his belt buckle along with him when he repeated it.

Ally was left-handed so she was looking right at her head coach and nodding. Standing outside the box she took the smooth, level swing she had worked so hard on once again and stepped back in. The next pitch was high. Ally was a small girl and her hunched-over style made her a difficult target for opposing pitchers.

Again she stepped out and adjusted the batters helmet which was at least a size too large and looked down the third base line. Keathley gave the identical sign and kept up the fierce chatter. He was obviously betting that if she kept the bat on her shoulder she could draw a walk and load the bases. Sandy Perillo, who followed her in the lineup, was acknowledged by everyone but Ally to be the better hitter. Alicia took her stance and made a characteristic wiggle of her rear end as she dug in. George smiled. Everyone settled in, as tense as the situation and stakes allowed.

This time the pitcher was the one to call time out. She held her fielders glove and cap between her thighs while she drew a wandering shock of wheat colored hair back through the rubber band that secured her ponytail. Everyone else fidgeted, but she seemed to be in no hurry. George had time for several more unkind thoughts about her before she was finally ready.

This time the undersized Valkyrie was determined to get the ball in the strike zone. It floated tantalizingly in a higher arc and presented itself at the plate like a freshly scrubbed Prom date.

"Strike one!"

Alicia tossed her head back and aimed a pained expression at her father first and then her head coach. It had been just where she liked it—right at the top of the strike zone. She stomped around a bit theatrically, milking the situation until coach Keathley called out roughly to her to get back in the batter's box.

The pitcher was still tugging at her hair. Apparently something about it still wasn't right and it bothered her enough to throw ball three high and outside and then ball four a moment later in exactly the same spot.

But wait! The umpire had called a strike on the second one and the equivalent of a roar went up from the gathered parents and relatives.

Keathley exploded over the third base line and charged the few feet out to where Pete Suliano held court as the game's only official before George could even voice his own objection. Pete's daughter was now in high school and thus he had become eligible to fulfill these sacred, unbiased duties. When the man looked up from changing the little counter in his hand to 3 balls and 2 strikes, John Keathley's nose was inches from his own.

The coach's first two exclamations, while loud and irreverent were rather traditional in nature and delivered in a voice loud enough for everyone to hear. Without being specific, he questioned rhetorically whether Suliano was able to see the ball clearly enough to make a judgment as to its location and passing that qualification, was he sane enough to make that judgment known.

When Keathley lowered his voice, he took hold of the umpire's pad suspended in front of Suliano's chest. Turning him slightly by pulling on the straps, Coach Keathley began to speak softly into the umpire's ear. George had not reacted yet but when he saw the look on Suliano's face he ran quickly to his side. The opposing coach began to do the same but when he saw Keathley up close decided that twenty feet or so was near enough to offer his advice.

George arrived just in time to catch several words. They consisted of an assortment of vulgarities and the word 'kill'. George pushed the two men apart without resistance only because Keathley was finished with his message. George led him by the elbow back to the coach's box admonishing him for the hundredth time that season about the negative effects of temper on young minds. Roughly, the man pushed George's hand away but continued back to his station with his normal chatter of macho encouragement. Jonie tried to put in her two cents from third base but Keathley ordered her back in a voice that would almost have sent her by shock wave alone.

George returned past the pitcher's rubber where Suliano was trying to recover what dignity he could.

"He's crazy, George. I told you goddam it!" he said loudly enough for at least the pitcher to hear.

George patted him on the back and tried his best to control his own emotions and somehow transmit the feeling to Suliano. He downplayed it as a momentary aberration, but both men were aware that this sort of thing had been all but commonplace throughout the season. Nevertheless there was nothing to do but continue and finally Suliano began to nod his head with impatience rather than agreement. He felt humiliated and embarrassed and at this point he just wanted the incident over.

George trotted back to his post clapping his hands and calling out fresh encouragement to Ally. The kids had been watching wide-eyed throughout the incident and needed calming. The inane ritual chatter that accompanies slack times in a baseball game are quite helpful in this respect however and within a few seconds the rest of the team joined in as if nothing had happened.

Keathley stewed in silence and repeated the 'take' sign three more times, but he sported a fierce look of satisfaction. Both he and George knew that the tirade had been effective. The chance that this one would be a called strike was just about nil.

The pitcher shook her arm to loosen it up after all the excitement and checked the runners. One thing she was sure of was that she was not going to walk the bases full with a weak sister like this at the plate.

Like her earlier offering, this one moved in a high arc, floating and growing like a balloon as it neared the plate. Alicia could not contain herself. It was only a tad higher than the first strike and just looked too good to pass up, what with her new found home run swing and everything, and she took a mighty cut at it. The hips moved out of the way, leading the shoulders and hands in a smooth copybook motion, worthy of Alicia's imaginary shot at the Braves roster. She had her eye on the gap between right field and center, which in her league was only forty feet beyond the second baseman. Unfortunately, the bat made only glancing contact with the lower third of the ball.

Now it looked like a beach ball as it popped back toward the mound, even less energetic than the pitch had been. Suliano stood to one side as the precocious blonde danced backward, stumbled, recovered just in time and gathered it in, ending the game. The St. Michael's team shrieked as only adolescent girls and dolphins can, and jumped all over their ace who held the trophy sphere aloft flaunting it for just a moment in their opponent's faces.

John Keathley exploded again from the third base box, roaring his rage and disbelief, first at the sky and then at Alicia Gordon. He kicked at the dirt repeatedly as if he were trying to bury the third base bag and stomped around before running in with short choppy steps to confront her directly. The tiny girl seemed to grow even smaller at his approach. The bill of her cap pointed perpendicularly at the ground and George knew it as a prelude to a sobbing jag.

But before he could move in his daughter's direction, Pete Suliano stepped right in his way as if the earlier confrontation had been with George instead. He swore again, more softly this time and stuck his finger in George's chest assuring him that this was the last straw and the Men's Club at the church would have to deal with the situation.

"He's a goddam menace, George. I'm starting to really worry about the guy. It's more than just temper. I'm not kidding, he's certifiable!"

"Calm down, Pete," said George, holding his palms facing the part-time softball official.

"Calm down, hell! I'm telling you, he's losing it. One of these days we're all going to be in the paper like innocent postal workers at a slaughter."

"Okay, maybe not that bad," Suliano allowed when George didn't say anything. "But how long can we put up with displays like this in front of the kids? It's not right!"

"I know what you're saying, Pete. I don't know exactly what we ought to do, but I understand. You make a proposal at the meeting Tuesday night and I'll support you a hundred percent."

"I mean it, George," Suliano blustered one more time as he backed away. "I'm not putting up with this crap one more day."

George agreed with him again and patted his shoulder half-heartedly as he looked for Ally.

The opposing teams were forming their lines to shake hands and demonstrate their good sportsmanship, but Keathley and Alicia were missing. The only possible place out of sight was that behind the ancient, weathered Sno-Cone stand. It was adjacent to the left field line and opposite the field's only parking so everyone else was moving generally in the other direction. Keathley had a massive hand on either of her tiny upper arms at the bicep and her feet were off the ground. The scene looked like a grizzly bear holding a squirrel.

George ran toward them, overhearing a few words in a sharp hiss when he got close enough. The only one he could make out was 'bitch'. Ally was so frightened that she had forgotten for the moment even to cry. White was showing all the way around her irises.

George put a hand on Keathley's forearm and pressed down until he had released Allie. Then he pushed his way between the two of them, pulling his daughter behind him with one hand. Keathley was a really frightening man. Aside from the complaints from parents, there were stories within the company about his violent nature at work and in his private life. Without taking his eyes off Keathley, George quietly prodded his daughter backward.

"Go to your mother", he said to the quivering girl, and waited for her to collect herself, pick up her mitt from the ground and disappear back around the corner of the little structure.

George said evenly, "Get hold of yourself, John. Calm down. It's just a game and the game is over."

"I'm sorry, but it was the *take* sign, God damn it! The *take* sign! All the hell she had to do was *nothing*! NOTHING! The little . . . . !"

George put a palm flat on his chest when he seemed to be trying to push past him. He had come to the end of his own tether and his nostrils flared and his eyes widened, even though the other man was far larger.

"You weren't going to say the word 'bitch' again were you, John?"

Keathley's gaze shifted to his assistant coach. His eyes were glazed and unfocused. The two men stared at each other in this way for several seconds. George was so close to him that he could faintly detect Aqua Velva under the acrid musk. Keathley looked around quickly and saw that they were still hidden from view behind the flimsy building. George Gordon had a sudden insight of what might have happened if they had been truly alone and in that moment he knew what had to be done.

The furious mask of the head coach's face flickered in and out as he struggled for mastery.

He uttered one more expletive as he pushed George out of the way with some force and stalked away.

George stumbled, began to pursue the man and then thought better of it. Loudly he said to the big man's back, "I'll talk to you later about this, John."

Keathley made a noise which might or might not have been words and left George to try and compose himself.

George's thoughts were jumbled as he made his own way to the parking lot and his family. He looked over at Keathley's big SUV. The coach seemed unaffected, loading the bats and catcher's equipment in the back.

Even as he pasted a half grin on his face for the benefit of his family, George pondered the salacious stories about the man and the new incidents with Pete Suliano and his little girl. He thought about the father's club meeting Tuesday night. Jesus! All this drama just for a girl's softball game? Obviously something had to be done.

Reunited with Alicia and Valerie, George didn't let on. He was all comfort for Ally, calming her about the experience with the junior girl's softball coach. Emotions can run high and sometimes unpleasant things happen. No big deal really. Keathley's been under a lot of strain lately. Shake it off. Let it go. That was what he was *saying*.

Katherine was even more upset about the temper display and the sobbing child than Val. She was chattering venomously about John

Keathley in a diatribe that would have been completely out of character except where her niece and nephew were concerned. Divorced for over ten years and having only the barest suggestion of a social life outside her work, Kate had channeled all her maternal instincts into her sister's children. Her emotion made George smile. Ordinarily, she would have considered such an outburst a betrayal of her training and education as a psychotherapist.

Val was imperturbable as always, Kate having shown more than enough condemnation to meet the family obligation. Val's quiet smile often made her an island of tranquility. She interpreted her role as the one responsible for maintaining the proper balance for her beloved circle and she generally achieved it.

She closed her eyes and held her little girl close, cradling the button on Ally's cap under her chin and suggesting that they should go on to dinner. Switching gears with enviable deftness, she praised Ally's handling of a routine ground ball in the third inning, which had 'saved' an extra base hit. Ally rather sullenly denied this interpretation but the atmosphere had nevertheless become noticeably less gloomy and then almost bright as Val solicited and received enthusiastic agreement from George and her sister. Following up with a favorable comparison to the Braves shortstop got a tearful giggle from Ally and by the time she gave her only daughter a last squeeze and a kiss right on that cap button, calm if not good spirits prevailed. A quick swipe with a crumpled tissue and they were ready to go.

The drive to the restaurant was composed mostly of skillfully light conversation designed to cheer her Ally up and for the most part it succeeded. She was heading to her favorite dinner spot, her brother Matt was staying with friends and she knew there were pastries of some kind in her future. By the time they got back in the car she was laughing musically, if rather unkindly, at the stories of her brother's failures at her age, the peculiar nastiness with Mr. Keathley almost forgotten.

Though charmed as always by the unsinkable spirits of the women in his life, George's mind was already working on the issue at hand. Because he and Keathley worked for the same freight company, George knew he would be out of the office the following day. In fact, George knew a good deal about his travel schedule and he had already calculated that the best place might be away from the office and maybe even away from their homes.

Shortly he would be traveling to Mississippi. He would be driving there and staying over, because Meridian was too close to fly to and too distant to drive to a morning meeting.

George did not know what he would do exactly, only that the intervention would begin by observing the man from a distance and, when the time seemed right, creating the confrontation. There was a sort of odd premonition that made him shaky and nauseous. The Keathley situation simply had to be dealt with.

When his wife came in, George began to gather up his travel things. Without explaining, he knew she could never approve and he could never share any of this with her.

He told Val a story about a new account needing attention and a meeting set up for early in the morning without consulting him.

Valerie Gordon expressed her displeasure, but George pointed out that in these days of wholesale layoffs, it didn't do to antagonize anyone at the home office. With an ease that comes from thousands of repetitions, he packed an overnight bag in less than two minutes. On his way down the hall George's progress was interrupted by the sight of school books on his son's bed.

He stopped suddenly and made a guttural noise in his throat. "We had this discussion just yesterday, didn't we?" he asked.

Hearing the tone of his voice Val followed his gaze to the stack of books.

"Matt's homework you mean?"

Snapping the phone out of his pocket, George called for the boy but after four rings he just snapped it shut again without leaving a message. Matt was obviously too busy to answer the cell phone purchased for just this sort of occasion.

"I want him home. Right now. Grounded. Two weeks. He has got to learn some responsibility. You should have known he wasn't going to Terry's to study."

Val looked hurt but the furrow on his brow just deepened more.

"Oh, George, he's only just begun to make any friends. You know how sensitive he is . . ."

George cut her off. "The next infraction was to be a two week grounding. Did we or did we not just agree to this yesterday?"

"Yes, but . . ."

"There is no 'but' dammit. You sound just like the boy."

"His name is Matthew."

"I know what the damn boy's name is."

Her lips compressed into a thin line. "I'll take his books over there."

"I'm not going to discuss it any more," George said. "The boy is grounded. If you want to go get him and bring him home that's fine but

I expect him home—alone—studying, within the hour. I need to go or I would do it myself."

"Then it won't get done because I'm not going to do it."

"What?" Now George was really steaming.

"I know his grades could be better but he's doing all right and his social development is important as well and I won't have him embarrassed in front of his new friends."

There was a silence of twenty seconds or so broken only by the heavy breathing that accompanied George's rising anger.

Then there was a shaking of his head that grew briefly but fiercely in frequency and then stopped as he turned.

"Home. Now. Grounded," He seemed to say to the floor and the stalked down the hall, turned at the staircase and continued down the stairs and out the door, leaving Val standing at the railing.

He slipped out the back door, threw his bag in the back and took off as fast as his sedan would allow. Originally he had planned to wait on a side street where he could wait unobserved for John Keathley's car and follow it to its destination. It would have been easier that way, but he knew the town where the man was headed and it was not that large. George was confident that he could pick him up at any point along the route and certain of his ability to find him again if they separated. He took off out of the neighborhood and didn't stop until a gas station at the entrance to the highway they would take. He filled up the tank, got a cup of coffee and then he waited.

In the darkness between streetlights almost directly across the road from George's house, a faded yellow and black truck belonging to Memphis Light Gas and Water pulled to the curb. The two men inside registered the fact that all the lights in the neighborhood appeared to be in working order. They too waited, unaware that the object of their visit had other plans that evening and had in fact, already gone.

The sign on the four-lane declared that they were on the way to the Birthplace of Elvis Presley, but that was not their destination. In a fairly direct route they traveled past a series of small towns, convenience store/ gas stations and a long stretch of farmland. From memory George knew they grew mostly cotton and soybeans but it was a cloudy night and his vision ended at the edge of the twin cones of brightness created by his headlights.

John Keathley's blue Mercedes made a good companion on the road. He maintained a steady speed, just over the limit but not fast enough to be stopped even if local cops were about at this hour. Highway 45 made a few twists and changed to two-lane and back several times. Both drivers managed it smoothly.

In less than four hours the two cars pulled into a Hampton Inn parking lot in Meridian Mississippi. George watched Keathley extract his overnight bag and go in the front door. For a large man he had an astonishingly fluid grace to his stride that George had noticed before. He waited a minute or two and walked around back by the pool where he could see the front desk through the windows. As luck would have it, John was assigned a room on the ground floor, not far from where George loitered. Gordon counted windows and made a quick note about the location and went back to his car to wait a while. He didn't want to take a room here, but it was a good place for their chat after he gave John Keathley a minute to relax and settle in. This time while he waited, George fell asleep.

Chapter 4

The killer moved about the motel while the rest of the town slept. First he went to the room next door to scout the exercise equipment. What he needed was there.

His target was sleeping on the other side of one wall and a storage area was beyond the other. Yes, this was adequate; convenient even. He had left weapons of several varieties in his innocent looking car, because they would not be needed. Before that foreign guy in the freight yard had stumbled on his 'special' car it had been a long time but his hands had served this purpose many times before and they had not forgotten.

Many times? One part of his mind puzzled over the certainty of this judgment. When? How? The man they called The Mechanic was a child of the sixties and had long ago accepted and exceeded the principle of living for the moment. With neither past nor future, he thought of himself not as a man at all, but an instrument, like an arrow which could be pointed at a target—a missile whose simple nature was to fly straight and true and destroy without thought or selection.

Holding a device whose edge resembled the card key used by the motel, he quickly defeated the lock on room 109. The chain restraint had not been employed. Outside, the night was hot and humid but when the door opened, the air was uncomfortably cold. The latch clicked softly shut. Inside, it was very dark and loud with the roar of the air conditioner. The Mechanic savored the experience for a few seconds before feeling along the wall to his right and switching on the bathroom light.

In the folded mirror door of the closet a strange reflection glared back at him. It was a dark figure wearing black canvas chinos and a black T-shirt that said *St. Anne—Bartlett* with a kind of coat of arms in faded and cracked orange. It seemed perfectly normal to the Mechanic that he didn't recognize the man in the mirror.

Still the room's occupant had not awakened. The dark man moved into the bedroom and switched on another wall-mounted lamp.

This time the sleeping figure stirred. He had been deeply in REM sleep and was slow to comprehend the situation. He sputtered and mumbled for a few seconds and finally recognized the intruder.

"What the hell are *you* doing here? Christ, you're a lunatic. What do you want?"

"I think you know."

The larger man had gained the edge of the bed and squinted in the light as he attempted to massage and scratch himself into wakefulness.

"Goddam it George, what are you talking about?"

The unwanted visitor blinked twice.

"No George," he said. "It's just me and you."

John Keathley shook his head, still trying to clear it. "And just who the hell do you think *you* are?"

"Nobody," the man said softly. "Nobody at all."

"Great," the larger man growled, rising to his feet. "Then you won't mind being tossed out on your ass."

The Mechanic was sitting at the edge of the dresser. Keathley got to him and gripped him by the upper arms with the idea of picking him up and flinging him across the room, not unlike the way he had handled Alicia Gordon. It should not have been difficult.

As the two large hands closed on his arms just below the deltoids, The Mechanic shot out his right fist with a single index finger extended. He did not seem to exert himself but John Keathley folded instantly back on the bed. Two more light blows on either side of his neck toward the back of his head followed quickly and the air in his lungs exploded in a gasp of instantaneous and widely distributed pain. It was several seconds before he could breathe again and look up at the face of his tormentor, who spoke just above the din of the room's fan. Keathley was shocked to discover that both arms were now tingling and almost useless.

"Now, I know what you did to George Gordon's youngster today," he said almost casually. "That was very bad. You could have hurt her permanently . . . inside. And it makes me wonder about your own family?"

The Mechanic pushed the big man over so he could sit at the edge of the other bed.

"Jonie, for instance. What have you done to her?"

"How the hell did you do that? What are you talking about, you crazy old bastard?" He gasped.

"There were some marks on Jonie's legs and arms, marks that she couldn't explain. George remembered several times that happened. He didn't believe it because he didn't want to believe it."

Even without the events of the last few minutes, Keathley had strong opinions about people who spoke of themselves in the third person.

"You're nuts."

The comment was ignored.

"There have been marks on Joanna's face too. Haven't noticed anything on little Jennifer. How about her?"

The Mechanic, who had long since lost track of the number of lives he had taken in violent, even grisly fashion, wrinkled his face as if he smelled something distasteful.

"It's just not right, John."

"Gordon, for Christ's sake! What the hell do you want from me? Look I'm sorry about today. I flew off the handle—it happens sometimes. Look it won't happen again. And I don't beat my family! Jesus!"

Keathley's eyes darted around the room as if trying to decide what to break over the Mechanic's head.

"That's not what Jonie told Ally Gordon. They're good friends, you know. She let her read her diary and she knows for sure that at least one time you even drew blood. That time she had a mysterious 'infection' that caused her face to swell up and turn blue."

Keathley's still-deadened hand moved toward the bedside phone. Like lightning the Mechanic chopped at his wrist, eliciting a soft howl. When the larger man tried to roll toward him he was met by another strike, a single extended thumb that found its mark and returned in a blur. There was only a faint little wheezing sound because most of Keathley's breath had been expelled again in a rush.

"There's nobody on either side of this room you know, and I don't think they can hear you across the hall. Come on, let's go where we can stretch out. A big tough guy like you would like another shot at me wouldn't you? Sure you would."

He went into the bathroom and emerged with one of the large body towels. Then he dragged Keathley out of the bed. He was still in too much pain to straighten up but he staggered at the Mechanic's lead because by now he was utterly cowed and unable to do anything else. They left the room and went up the hall to the workout room next door, which was flanked by glass partitions. They entered and the bent man was pulled to the edge of a sunken hot tub.

"Take off those pretty shorts before you get in, John."

He was dressed only in boxers, which were light blue and covered with tiny anchors. Keathley grumbled in a whiny voice but was afraid not to comply. He half crouched there before his assailant naked and defenseless. The throbbing from some of the Mechanic's ministrations was still very much with him.

The man he had known as George Gordon put a hand in the Jacuzzi they were standing next to. Then his mouth formed a shape that might have been a smile but wasn't.

"Get in the tub. It'll make you feel better."

"Leave me alone," he all but whimpered, but he started to lower himself in the water anyway. The Mechanic had only turned it on minutes before, so it was still lukewarm from being shut off for several hours. Keathley was too frightened and angry to feel anything more. He was shoved out to the edge of the underwater seat so he was sitting more or less in the middle of the tub.

There was glass on two sides of the room and they were no more than ninety feet from the front desk where there was surely at least one other person awake. But The Mechanic was unconcerned. It was after two A.M. in a small Mississippi town and he knew the percentages. He strolled across the room for a moment to look out into the pool and parking lot area. Keathley's eyes followed him. He scanned the area several times.

"It's okay," Keathley heard the man who looked like George Gordon say. "I just came down here so we could be alone . . . so there would be no misunderstanding. I wanted to make sure that anything you were doing to little Jonie stops now and never happens again."

"Absolutely! Yeah sure," Keathley croaked. "Never again."

Sauntering back he bent over to place his hand in the water. It was just beginning to really heat up.

"That Ally is pretty smart," the Mechanic said. He let his hand linger in the water savoring the warmth from the jet after the cold room next door.

"She told her daddy about a time she was reading about where the pages had been torn out of the diary and Jonie wouldn't answer questions about it. Ally said Jonie got so angry when asked about the missing part that she quit asking, but she knew. She knew.

"Her daddy didn't pay much attention to his sensitive, smart little girl. Even after he was told, it was a long time before he stopped to think how touchy Jonie is. Sometimes when one of the other girls would put a hand on her shoulder unexpectedly she would let out this little yelp and they would make fun of her. Did you know that, John? George never really put it together even with the help of his beautiful little angel. You know her as the *little bitch*, of course."

The water was quite warm now, but Keathley was shivering. He was gradually curling into himself, quaking and shaking his head back and forth as if to negate the reality. He knew the truth. If Gordon had gone this far already, he wasn't going to stop with a stern talk.

"George, I didn't . . . something's wrong with you, man. Let me out of here and we'll get a cup of coffee or something. I won't call the cops. You don't want to hurt me. I got a family . . . I . . ."

The Mechanic smiled. A real, if ironic smile this time. Keathley had no way of knowing, but it was a rare occurrence.

"That's pretty rich, John. Protecting the family is a pretty interesting argument coming from somebody that bullies and abuses them."

Keathley began to feel a desperation mixed with the pain and fear. He changed strategies.

"They need me. They need the money. Joanna hasn't worked in fifteen years. They . . ."

"No, not true John. In fact, materially, monetarily may be the only way you were a decent family man."

"I got no money in the bank! I . . ."

"No, John but you're well insured—George checked."

He had strolled back to the edge of the water and bent over in a crouch so his face was as close as possible to Keathley's. The toe of one rubber-soled shoe was over the lip of the tub and braced by the safety bar at the steps.

"Two hundred grand plus the policy for travel on company business."

The big man's eyes grew larger, looking around hoping for someone or something. The shivering got worse.

The Mechanic had always relished those occasions when he was using his skills for personal retribution, but he knew he was taking longer than he should because he had wanted to taunt this particular victim. It was time to get on with it. As he spoke, he curled the ends of Keathley's room towel around his fingers.

"Plus I know how to double the benefit. Can you guess?" He smiled again.

In a single explosive motion like the striking of a snake, the Mechanic caught the face of John Keathley on the towel now wrapped around his hands and shoved it backward and down. The big man was forced off his seat and fell diagonally, with all the force that the killer and gravity could manage, concentrated at a single point. The base of his skull landed against the edge of the porcelain-coated iron, making a sound like a dropped refrigerator. What remained of John Keathley slid quietly off the seat and below the foaming water.

"Accidental death," said The Mechanic, straightening up and using the towel to brush off water he had splashed on himself. "Double indemnity."

The eyes which had revealed such anger and evil a few hours earlier stared with a vagueness that was almost benign from under the warm, eddying liquid, now growing redder by the second. The towel was dropped by the steps, next to the card key for room 109.

The body would not be found until almost 7 o'clock when a young office supply salesman came in to do her minutes on the Stairmaster.

Just about the time that the Meridian police arrived to investigate, George Gordon woke up from an abbreviated rest 85 miles away in a room in north Jackson, Mississippi. He shaved and put on a suit, skipping breakfast in favor of a leisurely drive and an early lunch in Memphis. He was aware that something had happened overnight, but simply chose not to think about it. Whenever an unpleasant memory broke through, he would think of Matt and Valerie and Alicia at the end of his journey. One thing he did take away from the experience was that there would be no need to call a special meeting Tuesday to deal with the John Keathley situation. He would remember to be surprised.

Ninety minutes later he was in a very different state of mind. He had made the first call shortly after leaving Jackson.

'There's been some kind of accident' the voice had said to him. *Bullshit.*

George's Thunderbird was flying north on Interstate 55 at nearly a hundred miles an hour. In his mood, an encounter with a Highway Patrolman could be deadly for either or both of them, but in this small thing at least, luck was with him.

What was it he had said exactly? Let's see, first he spoke with his secretary and he could tell instantly that she was upset.

"Hi, Jill. What's going on? Any calls?"

After a moment's pause, a husky contralto said, "Oh, Mister Gordon. Please hold for Mister Walsh. Oh, Jesus!"

"What? What is it, Jill?"

Her voice began to quaver noticeably and she stammered in reply.

"I—uh. I can't. I'm so sorry. There's been . . . some kind of accident."

And then after a pause, "Mister Gordon, uh, please hold on. Just a minute."

The Coastal Freight sales manager, Bob Walsh came on the line almost immediately.

"Damn, I wish you weren't on the road, George. I really don't want to talk over the phone, but I guess you need to hear right away . . ."

Gordon held onto the little cellular phone as if it were a threat to his life. The plastic of the case bowed outward with the pressure. On the other end of the line, silence persisted. They couldn't have heard about Keathley already.

"What is it Bob?"

"Your house, George. Haven't you seen the paper this morning?"

"Only USA Today. Would you just tell me what's going on?" His hand shook uncontrollably.

"There was an accident of some kind, an explosion. They found Val and Ally. They thought you were in there also. God, I'm so sorry, George, they're both gone."

Now Bob Walsh waited on a prolonged silence. There was a minute where George thought about the event clinically, before the reality of it struck him fully.

"Are you there, George?"

The possibility that it might really be an accident never crossed his mind. He knew immediately that it had something to do with the Russian he had found prowling about near his trailer. There must have been more of them, although he still had no clue what, if any, their relationship could be to The Mechanic. And why use enough explosive to destroy his whole house when it was him they wanted?

Of course. His bedroom. With him gone and after her harrowing experience of the day, Ally would have been allowed to sleep in her mother's bed. If he had been there, she would have been in her own room at the other end of the house.

"An explosion? Gone? You mean they are dead?"

"Yes George, I'm afraid they are. It was instantaneous, as I understand it. There was no . . . ."

"And Matt . . . . is he all right?" Now the voice was deeper and void of all modulation.

"Yes, Matt is fine, thank God. He was with friends. Jill told me that Val's sister picked him up there an hour ago. Are you going to be okay? Can we send somebody for you?"

He grimaced at the blurred white lines of the highway streaming past. Valerie . . . *gone?*

"George, are you there?"

But George wasn't really there any more. Walsh was speaking to the master assassin known as The Mechanic.

"Yes. I need some time. I will call you soon. Thank you," he said into the tiny mouthpiece and in the unaccented monotone that Bob had never heard before.

He pressed the END key and held the phone in his lap for a moment. After a second or two he flipped the phone into the passenger seat.

For George there occurred an odd discontinuity of time. When he looked away from the spot where the phone had landed he saw the exit sign for a town that had been eighty miles away when his conversation with Bob Walsh had begun. He looked at his watch and almost an hour had passed.

"Valerie is dead." George said it out loud, took a breath and said it again.

He pulled over to the side of the road and stopped the engine. When he glanced in the rear view mirror he saw Ally's cap on the shelf behind the back seat and he began to cry. It had been many years since he had done this and it took most of another hour to spend the decades of tears, regret and anguish that he felt—and decide what he had to do.

Eventually he started the car back on the road to Memphis and made another phone call.

Chapter 5

Enclosed in his office on the third floor, the nervous man re-opened a double-locked drawer and extracted an old-fashioned black telephone, leaving in the drawer a connected answering machine of similarly advanced age. He put it on his desk and dialed a number scribbled on the back of a card. After passing through two subordinates and supplying adequate reasons, he reached his party.

"I need to know why you wanted Parker," Clark Mooney said into the secure phone line."

"Who?"

"Robert Parker. George Gordon. Whatever. You know who I mean. The individual we spoke of in Tennessee. Parker is the oldest name I know for him."

"I believe you asked such a question the first time we spoke."

"You wouldn't be specific."

"This, I fear is still our position. You have been paid well for your information and there is the end to it."

"Hardly! Your employees have missed again."

There was silence for a moment.

"What do you mean?"

"I mean he called me five minutes ago. It's the first time he's done that in nearly ten years. Apparently your boys blew up everything *but* him."

"I . . . Is there any way to confirm . . . ?"

"I already looked up a copy of the Memphis paper and the story is there just as he said. His wife and daughter are dead but he wasn't in the house at the time. Now you've lost the element of surprise and he's pissed! He's coming after me and anybody else he can think of."

"He said that?"

"Of course he didn't say that! He's not going to tip his hand and naturally I denied everything, but I could tell he wasn't buying any of my bullshit. He knows that if you found him after twenty-five years of being invisible, the information almost had to come from me."

"You really must calm down."

"Easy for you to say, you bastard, you didn't hear him. He called his daughter 'the little girl'. Like she was nobody! '*The little girl*'! Yesterday he would have taken a bullet in the head for her and today he can't even use her name. The son of a bitch is crazy, man! I mean *way* the hell out there! Or maybe he's not human. Either way he's bad news for me and for you if he gets close enough."

"Yes. Yes he is. When he spoke to you, what did he say about the deaths? Did he know where the order came from? Any hint of me or the *Matrosskaya*?"

"No, he just hinted about how he was found out. He didn't seem too concerned about why somebody wanted to kill him. I guess he figures there are so many reasons that he would never be able to guess which of his contracts prompted this one, but he is pretty damn certain after all these years that nobody could track him down without help?"

"What will you do?"

"There's one other who could have turned him over. And he knows a lot more about the guy than I ever did. He's in the Federal Pen at Leavenworth. If I go immediately to see him, Parker might think it was him instead of me."

"Then you might be able to find out something helpful to us while you are there."

"Maybe. He used to work for Webster in the old days in Vietnam before he went independent, but he doesn't trust anybody. Besides, I'm telling you he's nuts. Trust has nothing to do with it. He may not even remember Webster or Air America or his Mama for all I know. All I know for sure is that he remembers me . . . and you, although he doesn't know your name . . . yet."

"That sounds dangerously like a threat, Agent Mooney."

"Not from me, Ivan Ivan'yevich, but you know his track record as well as I do. I need protection and so do you."

"I am more than adequately protected here."

"You mean more of the Chechen meatheads that just botched this job? You must be kidding."

There was a pause on the line.

"As insurance I have been in contact with an associate in New York. He will lend me one of his men with a similar reputation."

Mooney paused to wipe perspiration from his brow though the room was quite cool.

"Bruno is going to let Lucchesi do this for you? Well that's good. You need all the help you can get, believe me."

"That is why I have a suggestion for you."

"Yeah?"

"I would think your choice is clear. I can offer you a place with me here. If necessary, we will take steps to draw him to me here. With the staff I have assembled here we can create a killing box which will protect us and from which he will be unable to escape. This must happen quickly but first I am suggesting that you proceed with your contact of this man Webster and find out what information he can provide to help us. It is obvious that The Mechanic must be neutralized or neither of us will be completely safe."

"I see your point," the agent rasped. "Okay, yeah."

"I will have some duties for you, otherwise you will be my guest until this matter is handled."

"Yaponets is never coming back is he? You are number one with the *Matrosskaya Organizatsia*, aren't you?"

There was a short silence on the other end of the line. It was Ivan Balakova's turn to clear his throat.

"You have my numbers. You will inform me when you know which way he is coming and you will tell me any helpful items you learn from the other. Are you certain he will not seek out his old employer first?"

"I told you where Webster is. An outfit with your connections could bribe somebody to get to him, but The Mechanic is alone. He's always made it a point to know as few people as possible."

The pitch of Mooney's voice rose an octave. "Besides, *screw* Webster! He's safe from the bastard and you've got your castle full of guards. I'm the one in trouble!"

By the time he had hung up, Agent Mooney began to think about his future and what he could do to prolong it.

Chapter 6

Gaby Bernard was working at her word processor when she heard a tapping on the doorframe behind her. It was Tony Metcalf again.

"Bernard, are you in the middle of anything?"

This confused her. Metcalf's tone seemed jovial and he had pronounced her name almost correctly.

"Just explaining the more subtle principles of probable cause to field offices for the thousandth time," she replied. "Nothing that won't wait. What can I do for you?"

"Be in my office in five minutes? It won't take long."

"Of course. What's it about?"

"We'll talk about it," he said, and disappeared.

She said "Oh, shit" out loud to the empty room and scowled at her video screen.

Gaby reread the last paragraph of impossibly dry and boring legal jargon and hit the 'save' icon with her mouse pointer. The bottom right corner of the screen told her that it was 11:44.

She picked up the gray jacket to her suit and put it on. It felt like dressing for a firing squad. But Metcalf didn't seem to be bent out of shape. *Oh, the hell with it*, she thought.

Gaby certainly cared whether her plan had worked—that was after all the point of taking this kind of risk. And as much as it would irritate and embarrass her, she was prepared for the personal consequences. What was really causing her stomach to churn was the prospect of trouble for her accomplice.

Riding up in the elevator, Gaby thought about how casually she had risked the job of someone who was not only her closest friend in DC but maybe the nicest person she had ever met. Unlike Gaby, Karen's daddy wasn't rich, the general consensus was that her momma wasn't good looking and certainly her job wasn't just an exercise in personal redemption and fulfillment. Karen Elias needed that job. It became utterly clear in hindsight to Gaby that she had never really considered the impact this defiance might have on that marvelous woman's family. By the time the door opened on the fourth floor and she shouldered her way through the workday crowd, the queasy feeling in the pit of her stomach had become a knot of anticipation. The second person she saw was Karen. She was standing a few yards away at the fax machine watching pages fall into the 'sent' tray until she heard Gaby.

"Karen, I . . . uh . . ." she called out. Should she warn her? No point in it.

"I may be a little late for lunch. Can you wait for me?"

Karen glanced up too briefly to see the worried expression on her friend's face and turned back to the machine to will the stack of papers to feed properly. She waved backward at Gaby.

"Sure, the calories will still be there when we're ready."

Agent Bernard ducked into the nearby Ladies' room. She had halfway hoped that Karen would cancel. If this meeting was what she suspected, the two of them were in for a long and unpleasant lunchtime conversation. Gaby took a moment to wash her hands though there was no real need and splash a bit of water on her eyes. Long dark lashes and generously arched eyebrows inherited from some distant Spanish ancestor made most eye makeup unnecessary so she was able to accomplish this with a minimum of repair. What she saw in the mirror when she was done was a look of determination.

No regrets, it was a chance she was forced to take. Whatever happened she would protect Karen. She would act completely ignorant of the whole affair—just stonewall it. *I'm sorry, sir, but what folder are you talking about?* They wouldn't believe it but they wouldn't be able to prove anything either. Sure. They're only the *FBI! Anyway, don't let them see you sweat,* she said to herself and thought immediately of Mrs. Dupree`, who had taught the students of Loyola Preparatory Academy for Girls that *ladies* do not sweat, they glow. That made Gaby chuckle softly and she forced the smile to last all the way down the hall and into Metcalf's office.

The door was open. Gaby paused just a second and squared her shoulders before she rounded the corner, prepared for a confrontation. But when she started in there was someone already seated in one of the chairs in front of his desk. It was Deputy Director Gerry Fallon, the second in command in the entire agency. The man had now survived four bosses and become something of a Bureau legend.

"Sorry," she said, a little startled. "I'll come back."

"No, no," Fallon said, rising. "Come right in. I'm Gerry Fallon."

Gaby shook his hand.

"Yes, sir, I know who you are, of course."

He indicated the other chair and they both sat down. My God, thought Gaby, did he bring in the Deputy Director just to fire me?

"I was just telling Tony what a good opportunity this could be," Fallon began.

She looked back and forth between them, her breath coming a little easier.

"Opportunity?"

"Gabrielle—I'm sorry, may I call you Gabrielle?"

"Gaby, please, sir."

This set off new alarms. The Bureau is very 'old school' and at his pay grade, FBI managers just don't use first names for the rank and file. Something was obviously up.

"Gaby, do you know anything about somebody called The Mechanic?"

She shook her head.

"No, sir I'm sorry but I really don't."

"That's all right because a lot of people even in this building never heard of him either. A number of assassinations over the years have been attributed to this man by hearsay alone. He has never made the Most Wanted list simply because we have never had enough information to publish and make a credible effort at apprehending him. Frankly a lot of professionals in this organization and others have been skeptical that he exists at all. One opinion that has been expressed is that The Mechanic is a composite of several killers that has been used as the prime suspect any time a high profile murder occurred without any substantive clues, but he exists all right."

Fallon passed her a folder with a foreign name on it.

"This man, Yevgeny Malenkov, was killed last week in Memphis Tennessee and the circumstances surrounding his death were placed in our unsolved crime database which I'm sure you know is used as a resource by international enforcement agencies as well. Tony tells me you had some ideas about it."

Gaby glanced across the desk. There was absolutely nothing to be read in Metcalf's face.

"I gave a few opinions to Tony," she said, "but I didn't know any of the details. I wasn't sure if it was a hypothetical."

Fallon grunted. "The MO was one unique, as far as we know, to this Mechanic. This prompted a call I received from a highly placed official at Interpol who thinks that this could represent a break in two unsolved murders they are concerned with—a man named Ishii in Tokyo and another, Valenciaga in Bogotá. There are many others associated with this guy but those are the ones that made him famous. Neither was killed the same way, but The Mechanic was implicated. Both of them were associated with organized crime."

Fallon looked at his watch.

"Anyway, to make a long story shorter, Interpol is sending an investigator to Washington to pursue the matter and we would like you to act as his liaison with the Bureau while he is here. You are familiar with our computer facilities and procedures and I think you would be an excellent choice. Are you interested?"

"Yes, sir. Of course I'm interested. I've been trying to get an enforcement assignment for some time."

"Yes. Well, it would be only a temporary assignment, naturally. After that you can talk to Tony about finding something more permanent."

"Great! I look forward to it, sir."

Fallon got out of his chair, mission accomplished; buttoned two of the three on his jacket.

"I'm sure you will do well, Gaby. The Bureau appreciates your contributions. Tony has more of the particulars and I'll just leave it with you."

He shook her hand again, glanced over and nodded to Metcalf and exited.

"This is wonderful!" she said to her boss. "I thought I was in some kind of trouble. Thanks for getting me this chance, Tony."

A slow grin that was more of a grimace emerged on Metcalf's face. He let the silence gather while he looked her up, down and sideways like a supermarket scanner but Gaby was determined not to show her nervousness and certainly not to be the first one to speak. This was one of the first lessons her father had taught her about playing in the 'boys club' and how she played her hand right now might make the difference for Karen.

Finally Metcalf shifted in his seat and said, "Can you give me any conceivable reason why you shouldn't be fired?"

Gaby wrinkled her pretty forehead and struck a quizzical pose. "Fired for what?" she asked.

"How did you do it, Bernard?"

"How did I do what, Mister Metcalf?"

He sighed deeply. He clearly knew she was responsible for her folder being sent to Fallon with the ones he had selected but it was equally obvious that he hadn't figured out how she had done it, certainly not how to prove it. At the moment, Gaby was glad that Fallon stayed so aloof from the troops that he had no idea who her friends in the bureau were or Karen's name would already be at the top of a suspect list. The truth was that now that Fallon had actually pulled her name it would make pursuing the matter potentially embarrassing for him either way but he wasn't the type to just let it drop.

Gaby was looking particularly angelic.

"You know we have rules about access to personnel files and such", said Metcalf. "It's grounds for immediate dismissal and possibly indictment."

"Oh, yes sir. I believe I even know which statute you might use to prosecute such an act although I suppose it would be awfully embarrassing to management. Why do you ask?"

He was staring into her eyes now. She hadn't even blinked.

"Somebody moved your file in with the ones I gave to Fallon. You don't know anything about that I guess?"

"Absolutely not."

"You didn't do it?"

She decided to take a chance.

"I'm just one of the legal staff, Mister Metcalf. I would think a thing like that would take . . . brass balls, wouldn't you?"

Metcalf rocked back in his chair. After a few seconds the beginnings of a smile flickered and disappeared. He was still angry but there was something else mixed in as well.

"Well, I don't know why Fallon picked your name from that group. It caught me off guard and you've obviously guessed that I haven't told him what you did. But your little plan backfired anyway. It turns out this assignment is not what you think it is."

"What do you mean, it's not what I think it is? It's an investigation isn't it?"

"Sort of."

Metcalf gave her the tired, patronizing look she had grown accustomed to.

"Okay, as long as it's your assignment anyway, I'm going to tell you straight out what's really happening here.

"The DD is in a sensitive phase of negotiating some new informal agreements with foreign agencies regarding the sharing of information on possible terrorist cells. Interpol is the most sensitive because the organization is headquartered in France and they are the least cooperative country in the EU.

"The guy who called is a Russian who says he will grease the skids for us there but he has this little pet project and wouldn't we like to help him out with that first."

"I see," Gaby said, her enthusiasm waning.

"He is sending his personal representative to make a big show of pursuing high profile crimes that have remained unsolved through the incompetence or complicity of his predecessors—that's his opinion anyway. Both the murders he mentioned are over ten years old and they had no leads when they were active investigations. It's all Euro-bullshit. This Russian Bozo is not going to solve them at a computer terminal whether he has Nancy Drew at his side or not."

Gaby made an effort not to show what she was feeling.

"I uh . . . appreciate your candor," she said.

"It's more of a social assignment. You'll be kind of the spokesmodel for the Bureau. You just lead this guy around and point at things. Right up your alley. Are you still interested? You can refuse it, I suppose."

Gaby had a momentary pang of regret that she had not just been fired outright.

"When you interrupted me a little while ago I was writing an opinion for the Counsel General's office about why using the new revision of the Carnivore program as a general eavesdropper on Yahoo's mail server would be a bad idea. You know I'm not going to refuse."

"Fine. Here is the background on your guest. He's arriving tomorrow.

"I hope you haven't made a serious mistake," he added with his smirking condescension fully restored.

Gaby wanted to use the term 'brass balls' again conversationally but figured she had pushed her luck just about as far as it would stretch. Instead she just thanked him again politely and marched out.

Karen had befriended Gaby almost immediately from the time they met in the Bureau cafeteria and sat at the same table they occupied today.

They would always have seemed an unlikely pair. Karen had been the lowly ranked but highly regarded veteran and Gaby the latest hot shot Academy graduate with high scores, high expectations and no real experience at all. Karen was plain, overweight and relentlessly ebullient while Gaby was a heartbreaking beauty with a generally quiet personality. Somehow Karen had made Gaby's brief marriage and rather nasty divorce seem like a shared experience in spite of the fact that she remained married to her high school sweetheart. Her South Philly background offered no real insight into the life of a wealthy New Orleans family but she had managed to make that difference seem trivial. And of course when it was learned over that first lunch of a shared love for trashy novels and Antonio Banderas the friendship was sealed.

It had taken a bit longer for Gaby to decide that she had met a truly unique individual, but it became more and more obvious with the passage of time. Karen's faith in the rightness of what she had done for a friend, the risk she had knowingly taken without the tiniest hesitation was astonishing. Gaby had asked herself in turn what she would have done if their positions were reversed and was embarrassed by her answer. It made her a little self conscious when they got together about an hour later than usual.

"You're kidding! You actually said that to his face? That's fabulous!" Karen enthused when Gaby recounted the conversation with Metcalf over their salads and Diet Pepsis.

"Oh, my victory didn't last long," Gaby replied. "Metcalf managed to pour yellow rain all over my little parade."

"What did he say? He doesn't suspect that I slipped that folder in for you does he?"

Gaby shook her head vigorously as she took a sip from her straw.

"Oh, no. I'm sure he knows I managed it somehow and that's all he cares about. I think now he's irritated all over again that it doesn't seem to be something that he'll be able to hang me over when I mess it up. It looks like a 'nothing' job.

"He more or less told me the assignment was a babysitting job unworthy of a real agent but given that there were no real performance requirements to it that I might be able to handle it without embarrassing the Bureau."

"He is such an asshole!"

"It's not just that. He has a prejudice against anyone who went to an Ivy League school, women in law enforcement and people from the South. Since I fall into all three categories I never really had a chance with Metcalf."

"You did take the job though?"

"Of course I took the job. Anything that gets me away from a video screen for a few hours can't be all bad."

"Good for you. You know, Gaby, I work for a bunch of those guys from time to time and you're smarter than all of them put together."

"Thank you, Karen. That's sweet of you to say."

"I'm not being sweet. It's just true. This place really is a showcase for testosterone, isn't it?"

Karen grabbed her shoulder in both hands and shook her enthusiastically as she spoke. It was exactly the kind of physical emphasis she had used on her nine year old at the breakfast table.

"Lord, yes," Gaby agreed, laughing. "But what are you going to do? They wrote the rules."

"Yeah, but this time I think you've got them. I think you are going to solve these murders and be a big hero and Metcalf will have to explain why he hasn't given you a chance before."

Gaby chuckled again as Karen beamed at her like a proud parent.

"I can't get over it," said Karen. "My little New Orleans debutante pal breaking all the rules and rolling the dice with the big boys."

Karen sometimes talked about her as if she were some kind of hero. Under the circumstances it brought back the feelings of guilt. They had dodged the bullet but there was still the matter of the disproportionate risk her friend had taken. Maybe Gaby would buy her something nice.

"I've been breaking the rules since I joined the Bureau really."

"You mean your parents' rules," Karen said."

Gaby nodded.

"I suppose expectations would be more accurate than rules. I disappointed them; that's for certain."

"You know I have never understood that. Working for the FBI is a fine thing, a great thing really. I don't see why just because your family has money . . . Do they think this sort of thing is beneath you or something?"

Gaby said "Yes!", then thought for a second and took it back. "No! Oh heck, I don't know, maybe. It was all a part of my serial disappointments. The divorce had already fouled up my Mother's plans and then the FBI fouled up my Dad's plans. My mother barely speaks to me. My Dad's not so bad, but it was obvious that he was hurt. I guess I can sort of understand."

"It's not disgraceful work you know."

"No, but it's work. Mother never spent a single minute at a real job and she never thought I would do anything but give her grandchildren and attend Mardi Gras fundraisers with her. I didn't mean it that way but from her point of view it was a rejection of her whole life. And my Dad—he had pulled a lot of strings to get me into Tulane after my marriage broke up. He assumed that I would pass the Louisiana Bar and join him in the firm. He never made a thing about it but it was obviously a fantasy of his from the time I was little."

Gaby sighed.

"It was a little tacky on my part, I guess. I'm sure I wouldn't have been accepted into Law School in the first place without his help. I had been out of college for three years and my grades at Princeton weren't that hot anyway."

"You should be ashamed, wasting a chance that most people would kill for. And as smart as you are?"

"Oh, I know. It didn't seem important. I was in love in those days."

"Are you sure you can use the past tense?"

Gaby gave her a corrosive look and Karen cringed.

"Sorry. Sorry. I know you don't like to talk about it, but I'm telling you, you give off a funny vibe about it for someone who has been divorced for almost five years."

"You're wrong. That's all I can tell you," said Gaby.

"You have to admit that your lack of a social life is a little strange for a beautiful girl like you. You've had like, what? Ten or fifteen dates in the last year with like six or seven different guys? You could lighten up a little. I admire your ambition and all, honey, but sometimes you seem to be trying to prove something that doesn't need proving."

"It's not the job. It does keep me busy and all but I just haven't found anybody that interests me. I'm on the lookout all the time."

"Oh *puhleez*! What about Andrew? When are you going to go out with him again?"

"Good example. Andrew is exactly the problem."

"Are you kidding me? Andrew is gorgeous!"

"Yes," Gaby agreed. "Yes he is. But He's an overgrown fraternity boy. I was married to one of those. I don't need another one."

"All right. All right, I give up. How about this Russian visitor you're going to have? Do you know anything about him?"

"I glanced at his dossier. He was in their militia for a number of years before Interpol. Successful, decorated, blah, blah, blah. When I was reading, all I could think of was Leonid Brezhnev."

"Oh, God," said Karen, "I hope not."

"Hey," Gaby replied, "if he can make something productive out of this junk project he can look like Brezhnev's uglier brother and I'll kiss him right in the mouth."

Karen slurped the last of her soda into the straw and made a gurgling sound. She looked sideways at Gaby under arched eyebrows.

"That's progress. At least you'd be kissing *somebody*."

"Karen!"

"I'm sorry," she whined unconvincingly.

"Look, I'll get back out there when the time is right."

"Just trying to help. Forgive me!"

Karen was a clerical GS-5 with two little ones in day care who half the time was also supporting the seasonal work of her blue-collar husband and here she was trying to work out the problems of someone who was born to a social stratum that required almost nothing from a girl who looked as Gaby did and gave a life of unremitting decadence and ease in return. Gaby felt a new wave of guilt.

"I know that. It's just that . . . . Come on," she said, getting out of her chair. "Let's get back to the office. If I can find out something significant about this Mechanic guy, that'll make me happy. Somehow I need to read enough files to find out what goes on in his head."

To herself she added, *And I need to buy Karen Elias something very, very nice.*

Chapter 7

At its very best, Memory is an imperfect lens through which to view any life. For any man, and particularly one as comprehensively flawed as the man who had been known as George Gordon, it can be fickle, even cruel. Sitting in the church pew at the funeral services, with only more sorrow to distract him, reminiscences of his life with Valerie—the only pleasant time he had ever known—became vague and distant while the pains and transgressions of his earlier existence returned with holographic clarity.

It was the rural Georgia of the early seventies and the boy becoming a man stood in a similar pew alone. He was wearing a brand new US Army Class A uniform, holding a leather-bound missal opened to the Requiem Mass and trying to comply with the demands of propriety by grieving.

In truth, base personnel and townspeople also had universally unpleasant memories of the dead man, but they thought the son was callous and maybe a little bit 'off' when he showed so little concern at the death of his own father.

The small to moderate size of the turnout for the services allowed plenty of room to avoid close contact with Michael Hogan and indeed, whether deliberately or not, no one was nearer than the senior Hogan's old company clerk two rows back. On that occasion too the young man's thoughts wandered, viewing through that pitiless lens the time he had spent with the man in the coffin, Master Sergeant Eugene "Buck" Hogan.

Michael had been nearly a head shorter than some of his classmates for most of grade school and the disparity was further exaggerated by comparison to his parent, who at six-five and 235 pounds was far and away the largest DI on the base. The crude meaning of the oft-used phrase that he 'must have pulled out too soon' when he was 'making' Michael escaped the boy but not its accusatory tone.

When Peewee football began, his father put the boy's name at the top of the signup list. Buck had made All-State in his junior and senior years as a tackle for his high school and he had similar ambitions for his only son.

One day Michael arrived home from school to find his father in the back yard. What little that could be seen of his buzz-cut hair was mostly gray now, but there was only a hint of fat around his middle and he could still double-time ten miles in full field gear without showing the slightest fatigue. In one fist was a hammer. A massive thumb and forefinger of his other hand delicately held a can of Pabst Blue Ribbon. By the steps were the remains of the first five in the six-pack. There was an indecipherable webwork of boards before him.

"What is it, Daddy?" the boy asked.

"It's for you, boy." His voice was gruff; its tone peremptory, as if he was embarrassed by even this feeble attempt at parenting and comradeship with his only son.

"Go get that box off your bed."

Delighted, the boy took the blue-painted concrete steps two at a time and disappeared into the house, allowing the spring restraint to slam the white screen door with a percussive wooden clatter behind him. Seconds later he emerged grinning broadly from under a shiny blue helmet and carrying a box filled with pads and a jersey.

"Go ahead," said his father, "put 'em on."

While the elder Hogan continued his clumsy carpentry, the boy struggled into the whole football outfit, meticulously snapping and lacing everything tighter until it was secure if not stable on his undersized frame.

When he was ready, Michael walked around to get in his father's line of sight and stood excitedly waiting for his expression of approval.

"Look, Daddy, look," he said when he couldn't stand it any more.

The outfit looked as though it were wearing Michael instead of the other way around, but Buck bellowed "Yeah!" and gave him a kind of half-mast thumbs-up.

Hogan made an effort at an encouraging smile and patted his son on the head.

"Now you're looking like a player. Now stand right over there and be quiet, I'm almost finished."

"Can I help, Daddy?"

"No."

"Pleeaase?" the boy whined.

"I said I'm almost *finished*," Buck Hogan snapped. "If you stand right there and don't bother me, I won't be but a minute. If you piss me off I'll just see if the store would like all that football shit back."

Chastened, the boy stood silent for nearly a half-hour, sweating. An early morning rain had soaked the yard and his new outfit steamed under Georgia's afternoon sun. It was taking longer because Buck Hogan's carpentry left a great deal to be desired and his understanding of the simple task was as superficial as his manual skills. He was a lot more comfortable tearing things down than building them up.

At the five-minute mark, the boy had started into the house before Buck ordered him back to his place, telling him that it would only be another minute. He hopped from one stepping-stone to the next until he reached the "T" of the clothesline pole, turned back and straightened in his father's direction, leaning only slightly on the silver painted steel. The heat was terrible. Instead of its usual refreshing scent, the stand of honeysuckle along the wire fence behind him began to nauseate Michael with its cloying sweetness.

At the fifteen-minute mark, the boy slid surreptitiously into the shade of the little peach tree by the back fence, never losing his makeshift 'parade rest' posture. His wait was seasoned by occasional recitals of the most creative profanity from his father.

Finally the man stepped back from the lopsided tangle of badly braced two-by-fours. It was almost five feet on the higher end and wrapped with foam rubber and old G.I. blankets secured with duct tape.

"Want to throw the football around, now, Daddy?" the boy asked as he moved off the spot he had been occupying and approached his father.

Buck Hogan put his arm around his son and hammered casually on his shoulder pad, buckling his knees. They grinned at each other.

Michael would remember that as the last truly pleasant moment he would ever share with his father. Buck took the ball from his son's hand and tossed it casually into the box the pads had come in.

"Throwing the football is for pansies. This will make a *real* man out of you. Don't you know what this is?" the big man asked in return.

It looked like seven dollars worth of two-by-four 'seconds' had been reduced to out-and-out scrap lumber and then hammered together in a random fashion. Saucer sized eyes and a shrug almost invisible under the pads was the boy's reply.

Buck Hogan cleared his throat in preparation. This told Michael that what was coming was not just important, as was everything his father chose to share with him, but urgent. He stooped down to improve eye contact as he revealed his insights. His speech, never far from an aggressive bark, quickly assumed drill instructor cadence.

"The game of football is a war. Territory is gained or lost by the application of force and the key is right here." He drove a rock hard index finger into the boy's chest under the jersey'ed pads. "You want to learn about football don't you, boy?"

His son nodded wide eyed and enthusiastically.

"I'm giving you the whole secret to the game right up front so you can learn it right. It's about team coordination, sure, but it gets down to individual toughness. Each team member is assigned a territory to capture or defend and the most important territory is the one around the ball. My old coach called it the trench, the line of scrimmage. When you dig in opposite a man at the line you have to decide in your head and in your gut that he is your enemy. He needs and deserves to be knocked flat on his ass. That's your job. He may be bigger. You've got to be tougher. No matter what he does to attack, you will never, *ever* give up your position. You will defend your own territory and if you are attacking, you will do whatever it takes to conquer his. You see? It's combat, pure and simple! Developing the power to take down your enemy with force. *This* is the real definition of a man."

It was the longest speech the boy had ever heard from Buck Hogan. Buck stood back up and pointed at his project. Clearly intending this statement as a continuation of his previous thought, he said, "This is a blocking sled."

Vaguely explaining its purpose as a training aid and pushing the boy aside for his demonstration, he lowered himself into a three-point stance and charged the sled in a kinetic explosion. Its weight was no match for his and he hit it as low as he could, holding on to the bottom edge of the beam to keep it from rolling. The skids cut two four-inch furrows twelve feet long in the rain-softened yard as he pumped his powerful legs eight or ten times in choppy succession.

Michael Hogan's jaw dropped in awe and admiration. His father was like a force of nature.

"The balance is a little off," his father said, and jogged into the nearby storage shed off the narrow carport. In a moment he returned carrying a fifty-pound sack of Portland cement under one arm. Shortly it was placed on the sled in the open area he had left for weighting.

"There," he said.

"Well, go ahead. What are you waiting for, boy?" he added after Michael hesitated.

"Go ahead and what?" the boy asked.

"Hit the sled, of course. Just like I did. Shove it from here over to there," he gestured.

Michael approached it in exactly the same way he would have asked a girl to dance at the sock-hop. It was a hesitant saunter between unlikely glory and certain humiliation. Cautiously he put his head between the duct-taped pads on the wooden monstrosity and dug his US Keds into the ground as well as he could. Then he looked backward for a judgment from his father.

"That's it. Now move it!" Buck Hogan called.

Braced as well as he could be, the boy heaved and promptly slid his shoulder pads sideways though the opening and landed on his face in the middle of the sled. He landed on the cement bag with a hard grunt and some of the powder from it sprayed out and into his face. The boy coughed and had begun to push back when he heard the expulsion of breath behind him that meant impatience from his father. Embarrassed, he struggled to extricate himself quickly as if speed would erase the fact that his father had witnessed it. Twice more he slipped before a huge hand grasped the back of the pads and pulled him abruptly out. On the way back, the boy's helmet banged hard on one of the boards and his arm was scraped by an angled ten-penny nail protruding from the upper bar support. It was a deep cut and he cried out a little as he began to bleed.

Buck Hogan mumbled an oath and quickly tore a strip from the undershirt he was wearing. He used a continuous stream of derogatory adjectives as he made a pass at tying off the wound. When he was done, blood rolled down the boy's arm at a slightly reduced pace.

"Center, boy, *center*!" the deep voice said. "You got to hit the damn thing balanced. Jesus Palomino!"

Michael held out a hand with blood on it, more pleading than anything else.

"Well, shit!" said Buck. "I flattened all the nails on the outside. I didn't know you'd fall on your ass inside the goddam thing.

"Come on and try it again. This drill is important. If you don't get it you'll never understand trench football and if you don't understand trench football, you'll never understand combat. And if you don't understand combat, you'll never be a man."

It never occurred to Michael to question this leap of logic.

He hesitated but finally dug in and ran full tilt at the sled this time, reasoning that he would need the extra momentum to make up for his lack of size. The sled moved not at all and he contacted it at an angle that stretched his shoulder joint underneath the pads. His shoulder separated painfully as he bounced off. The sight would have been either funny or pathetic to anyone else but Buck Hogan was furious. His only son looked instantly, comprehensively, ridiculous. Oaths mixed with Michael's howl as he curled up on the ground.

"God *damn*, boy!"

"Ow, my shoulder, Daddy! It hurts."

"I've told you a thousand times, boy. Pain is all in your mind. Now get your skinny, worthless ass up and move that sled!"

The senior Hogan's voice boomed off the asbestos shingles of the house and the narrow wall of the storage shed. It was a sound that could be *experienced* as well as heard. More sweat ran down his cheek and glistened on one particular vein in his forehead. There wasn't a recruit at Fort Benning that wouldn't have tried to run through a granite wall rather than face that look.

The boy struggled to his feet. Now his left arm hung close at his side while he held it firmly with his right. The broad pads and his narrow frame made him look like a wobbly letter 'T'. As he wavered, a steady drip of crimson fell on his new padded football pants. Swimming eyes moved from his father to the sled and back again. He tried to control the whimpering which he knew from experience tended to enrage his father.

"Come on! Hit that sled!" the man's voice boomed.

"But, Daddy," he began.

"Daddy nothing. Hit . . . the god . . . damn . . . sled."

A sob escaped Michael's throat.

"Jesus Palomino Christ! Be a man! I come home on my one day off and build something for you in the back yard and you won't even use it 'cause you're just a little crybaby candy-ass. Is that it?"

"No, Daddy."

"Candy-ass!"

"But, Daddy . . ."

"You sound just like a little baby girl. Did the hospital get it wrong? Drop them pants, boy. I want to know did I get a doe instead of a buck?"

"No, Daddy," he murmured.

"Drop them pants! You can't be no son of mine!"

"D-d-daddy," he warbled.

"It must be Michelle, not Michael, right? I had a Michelle in my house all along. Maybe I should take back your football and pads and get you a dress, somethin' lacy and nice. Would you like that better? Mee-shell?"

The boy said nothing, his lip quivering and tears falling from his face to blend with the fresh trickle of blood on his arm. The warm breeze had freshened from that direction and the honeysuckle smell was stifling.

"Well? Answer me when I talk to you, Cutie Pie? Are you a man or a little girl?"

When he still didn't answer, his father pumped a fist the size of a canned ham into his chest pads. It was a gentle shove by the man's standards but the boy left his feet and landed, sliding in the mud on the seat of his new canvas pants.

"Man or little girl, dammit?"

"Man", he said.

Seldom has a statement's tone more belied its meaning. It was a squeak almost beyond the range of human hearing, but he climbed back to his feet.

"Then move the sled, God damn it! Be a man!" He thundered in his obvious disgust.

"I'll tell you what. I'll lift up on the sled and get it out on a downhill slope where even a candy-ass crybaby can move it. If you can't be a man about it, see if you can sashay your ass over here and just move the sled a foot, Candy Boy—just a foot. 'Cause I'll tell you one thing, by God—boy, girl or green Martian, you're not gonna leave this yard until you do it!"

Michael's face was hot with humiliation and he was becoming a little dizzy from the pain and nausea and from holding his breath against the sobs.

"It's too damn big," he blurted. "You move it!"

The infraction this time was not a marginal failure of abilities; it was an out and out breach of discipline. It was . . . *backtalk*.

In a sudden roundhouse motion that would have split one of the sled's wooden braces he struck the side of his ten-year-old son's shiny new helmet right at the ear hole. As the boy went down again, the strap on his chin came loose and the helmet flew against the carport wall and bounced off the bumper of the ancient Ford F-50. For an instant, Buck Hogan must have thought his son's head was still in it. The boy was such a pitiful, frail little thing.

When the ringing in the boy's head abated, his father was standing over him with a savage expression, brandishing the helmet by its face guard.

"Just who do you think you're talking to, boy?"

Teetering once more to his feet like a newborn fawn, Michael Hogan had an unfocused and feral look in his eyes. Buck Hogan was prepared with another round of helpful instruction but Michael paused only until the shaking lessened, then, without the protective headgear, dug the edge of his sneaker into the soft earth and hurled himself full speed at the blocking sled. He cried out with the impact and pain as the recoil threw him backward on his tailbone. He rolled first onto his back and then flipped all the way over. It was like throwing a bb at a baseball.

The sled had moved—an inch.

Without waiting this time he jumped to his feet and charged again, grabbing onto the frame to avoid the backward bounce. It held firm. He backed up farther and did it again, rocking the sled off the ground before it settled. The pain had become an abstract concept to the boy. A grunt would occasionally escape his lips as he struck and recovered. It was perhaps an expression of human suffering, but in form it was a purely animal sound. The boy was not in a position to see it but the look on Buck Hogan's face altered slightly. He folded his arms and stepped back to observe in the same pose he often used on the obstacle course.

Fourteen more times the tiny figure plunged at the rough wooden frame. When the boy finally collapsed, the sled was moved more than double the required twelve inches. In truth, it was more sideways than forward but even Master Sergeant Hogan could see no point in further criticism. He hesitated a moment, looking back and forth from the makeshift wooden structure to the glazed expression on the boy's face.

Michael's breath came in ragged gasps and his irises were pinpricks of black, each surrounded by a disc of blue and a saucer-like expanse of white. For just a moment the Sergeant was at a loss. Buck Hogan was a very experienced judge of what he thought of as the 'manly' emotions but the scorching rage that had moved the sled was almost frightening even in one so small.

Recovering quickly, he said to his son, "There. I told you you could do it. Maybe next time you'll pay better attention."

The boy wobbled briefly and collapsed in place. He sat unmoving on the ground, unfocused eyes and legs pointed straight out ahead of him, one arm at his side. The other shoulder jutted at an odd angle from his body. His left leg twitched as if it were getting leftover commands from a now-disconnected brain. Leaning down, Hogan tore another strip from his dirty undershirt and wrapped it around the boy's arm without removing the first one.

"It's for your own good. It's good for you," Sergeant Hogan said. The dazed boy said nothing. Hogan looked briefly into Michael's glassy eyes, and swore again. After a few more seconds of no response he picked up the empty beer cans, deposited them in the nearby galvanized garbage can with a clatter and then climbed the steps to the house, shaking his head all the while.

When Michael's mother walked up the driveway after a bus ride from the diner where she worked, she found him curled fetally by the screen door, a fresh deposit of vomit on the hexagonal concrete stepping-stone nearest the back steps. He still wore the bloodstained uniform and the helmet lay in the grass nearby. Without going in the house or calling out, she carefully pulled off the uniform pads, leaving Michael in shorts and a t-shirt. First opening the door of the family pickup truck, she wrestled her son off the ground, dragged him across the grass and placed him gently on the bench seat for the trip to the base hospital.

Michael did not awake until he had been put on an examination table by an orderly. As they awaited the doctor's arrival, their conversation was not the one most mothers and sons would have had in similar circumstances. Rather it was confined to the moment—where the pain was and what the doctors were going to do to make it go away—how she could get the blood stains out of his new pants. She did not have to ask what had happened and as of that afternoon they each shed their last tear on the subject. The woman had simply expended the last of her supply while the boy determined in the future to be a *real man*, now that it had been made clear to him what that entailed.

Buck Hogan died some nine years after the incident of the blocking sled and Corporal Michael Hogan returned to participate as an unaffected bystander at the service. Michael still hadn't attained a size that would have impressed the old man but he was far from the cowering runt that his father made him out to be. Now broad, stocky and hard-muscled, the boy had become an athlete and a fierce competitor. Army boot camp and Special Forces training completed his transformation into a warrior.

He had been on his way to Vietnam when the word came of the sudden heart attack and there was no one else to make the few decisions required at a military service. Noreen Day Hogan had not been heard from since three weeks after the building of the blocking sled. She had gathered enough courage to try to save herself but was too cowardly to bring along the son. Even though he had no real affection for the boy, she knew that he would never allow this visible evidence of his manhood to be removed without pursuit and a struggle that she knew she would lose.

Corporal Hogan, acknowledging but not understanding the cultural sensibilities of his surroundings, had expected tears at the service. Almost, he had tried to squeeze out a few at several times during the vaguely worded eulogy but it was useless. He could dredge up not one kindly feeling toward his departed parent. It was as if he had weathered a decade-long storm that had finally passed. Besides, if he were to cry even a little he suspected that it might be enough to raise Buck Hogan from the coffin for one last contemptuous sneer.

Somewhere, he thought, there must be a sad-eyed husk of a woman, maybe just getting home from the night shift or beginning to relax from the breakfast rush who breathed a sigh of relief without knowing why. He wished that she had left some way for him to contact her, though of course that was impractical. Corporal Hogan wanted to tell her that even though her desertion had increased his daily exposure to this hard, unfeeling man, she was, for his part, forgiven. After all, his only good memories of childhood were entirely framed by the smell of her fresh starched uniform, the nasal commiseration in the tone of her voice and whatever dregs of sympathy Buck Hogan had left in her tired blue eyes. Michael loved his mother and did not begrudge the high cost of her salvation.

After the funeral service, when the bugle's last mournful note had drifted away with the report of the honor guard's rifles, Corporal Hogan received the consolations of the military men who had been his father's friends along with the flag that had draped the coffin. Most of them he recognized as members of the inner circle of similarly disposed non-coms who had drunk with him, hunted with him or whored with him in the off hours from his life as an army drill instructor. One man who seemed more reverent or subdued than the others wore the twin eagles that identified him as a full colonel. He clamped a big paw on the boy's shoulder and inquired solicitously about Michael's future and his immediate orders. The Colonel gathered that the boy was about to land in the middle of Quang

Tri province in Vietnam and he had disquieting memories of Khe Sanh that did not allow him to pursue that line of thought very far. The will to fight the war might be winding down but the fighting certainly wasn't.

Looking down into the open grave he said, "We were lucky to have known him, you know that don't you?"

You would have had to know him very well indeed to see the spark of irony in Michael's eye as he answered, "Yes sir, we were that."

"I'll tell you son, there was a good man to have beside you in a fight, one of the best that ever lived. He saved a many a life in Korea, mine among them. He was a great, great soldier." He intended to be disarming and humorous when he added, "And when he wanted to be, he was absolutely the toughest and meanest S.O.B. I ever knew."

"That's all he ever wanted to be, sir," Michael answered, staring unblinking into the Colonel's eyes.

When the officer finished searching for any evidence of answering irony from the young man, he folded his face into a smile that was more confusion than anything else, patted the boy's shoulder—more tentatively this time—and shook hands, quickly excusing himself and moving away.

Families on the base and the few townsfolk who cared, talked of the curious reaction of Sergeant Hogan's son for several days, but in less time than that the boy was landing at Tan Son Nhut air base and far beyond their homely criticism.

Michael rejoiced in the certainty that he was done forever with Master Sergeant Hogan, yet every single day of the next six hundred and ten that he spent 'in country' he thought of the man at least once.

More than three decades later and, as the crow flies, some 350 miles away from the Georgia churchyard where he had tearlessly buried his father, the stoic son had become a man called George Gordon. Even broader and heavier now, the corded muscle had been layered by time with thirty extra pounds that made him look far more harmless than he really was. Underneath, habitual workouts kept his conditioning excellent.

George was widely known in the parish as a doting family man—involved in parish life, committed to his duties as Christian, as citizen, as father, as husband. Yet mysteriously he showed no real emotion at the funeral of his loving wife and daughter.

And even for the services of a young child and parent, it was an unusually moving scene. Twin caskets of pure white crouched at the foot of the altar's gray marble steps next to two fair-sized portraits draped in black cloth. Nearby, large sprays of flowers had banners with the names of church and school organizations stamped in gold on the dark ribbons or touching phrases like *Heaven Sent, Heaven Bound* and *We'll Miss You*. Alicia's remains would rest forever in the Hyperion Youth model number 12, heart wrenchingly smaller than the one next to it. Both had blankets of red roses, providing contrast with the coffins' hardware colored with tasteful antiqued silver. Monsignor Berryman had come back from his new job in Nashville just for the Mass. He spoke of the transitory nature of their loss and the promise of eternal renewal that would inevitably follow. One of Alicia's teachers delivered a eulogy that left no dry eye in the house—save one pair.

The looks on the faces of their friends told George that they were more puzzled than appalled by his seeming lack of reaction because no one could have seen them together and doubted the depth of his feeling. But by then he had wrested back control of his memories and George Gordon had no part of them. The Mechanic was far better prepared to deal with the emotional situation and more importantly, with the tactical situation that he was certain would reveal itself presently.

Two more caskets. Two more dead among so many—what was that? 'George' couldn't be allowed to think about any of this. The Mechanic had immediate duties. He knew how to interpret things in a manner that didn't get in the way. Violence, like death, was an immutable fact of life and this loss confirmed his original suspicion that women would always desert him.

Even when he stunned the congregation further by abruptly bolting the service in the middle of the proceedings, it was not because of an emotional desire to revenge himself on the killers of Valerie and Alicia Gordon. Emotion clouded the perceptions. He would seek out the killers rather as a duty he had accepted on behalf of the equally departed George Gordon—because that is what Gordon would do—if he could.

The killers, likewise, would come to the church because that would be the last place they could reliably hope to find him. He knew this because that is what he would have done in their place.

When the man everyone thought was George Gordon saw what he had been looking for, distorted by the primitive partially stained glass of the church window, he crossed in front of the surprised parish priest to the sacristy exit at the opposite side of the church and left without looking back and leaving his sobbing son alone in the front pew until his aunt Katherine moved forward to take him in her arms. Most observers thought the boy's father was finally overcome with the paralyzing grief they knew he must possess.

Chapter 8

"I met Maskhadov, you know," Shamil said in Russian as he examined the Kalashnikov's curved clip for the third time and snapped its breech closed.

The two men sweltered in a rented brown Lincoln Town Car on a side street leading to the little church where services for half of the Gordon family were being held. The open windows did little to relieve the heat. Though they were countrymen, Shamil, in the passenger seat, had a much darker, almost Mediterranean look.

"Liar," replied Vlad. "You never even met your father."

"I swear! Really. In 1994 the FSB took me to a ministry building for questioning. When I was coming out of the room, there he was—like Stalin's ghost!"

"And then what? He put his arms around your filthy shoulder and offered you a dacha on the Black Sea if you would join him?"

"No!" he said with a hurt expression. "That pig! I wouldn't take a Mercedes-Benz from him if I had to walk the road on my knees. I told him that he was destroying our country. Right to his face! I called him a puppet from Moscow and I spat on the floor at his feet."

"You, my friend, are more full of lies and cow flop than Maskhadov and Stalin and Bill Clinton put together. You were never even in Groznyy until 1995. I was with you the first time you met with the Federal Counter-Intelligence Service and even after we wiggled our way out of their charges, you shook for hours like my little dog Putin passing a stone."

"Your brain is as poor as your patriotism," answered Shamil. "That is why you abandoned the Mujihadin."

"It was not I who lost Gordon."

"In what way was it not you? I was busy finishing the device while you were to watch the house. You told me he was in the house, did you not?"

Suddenly, a voice at his ear said in English, "He probably told you I was in the church also."

Both men jumped at the first sound but quickly saw the old Smith and Wesson with the oversized silencer on it and shut their eyes in disbelief.

"Idiot!" said Shamil.

"What do you mean? He is on your side of the car," answered Vlad.

"The church is on your side. You were supposed to be watching him."

"Listen to me," Vlad began, looking at the gun and directing his comments at it's owner. "*Vy govorite po-russkii?* We can make deal."

"Some. Enough to keep you honest, but we'll talk English from now on. And don't either of you bother to pretend you were sent here without knowing the language. The next Russian or Chechen or whatever—the next words I hear that I don't understand will be followed by something you won't like at all." He gestured with the pistol.

"Yes, a deal. We have plenty money." This time Shamil spoke in accented English.

"Open this door and slide those rifles into the back seat, butt first," the Mechanic said. When they had done that, he got in the car and collected their sidearms. He had them kneel on the front seat, briefly checking them for other weapons that really didn't concern him much. Then he produced a large plastic tie-wrap with which he secured Shamil's hands behind his back.

"Now drive," he said to Vlad. "South. I'll tell you where to turn. Don't make any kind of a problem. I don't have to kill you yet."

The Chechens pled their case of innocence, of only following orders for most of the thirty-minute drive. They alternated between this argument and the promise of great wealth if he made a financial arrangement with them. If he would let them go back to Florida, they would see to it that he had a lot of money and their boss was made to believe he was dead. After all, that was in their best interests as well.

The Mechanic listened closely to everything they said but did not utter a syllable other than directions until the car pulled through a gap in a tall chain-link fence and parked in an intermodal railroad container yard. The space was completely obscured by acres of truck trailers and boxes but there did not seem to be any people around.

The American assassin got the car keys and lined the prisoners up next to a freight container on wheels, a twenty-footer ready to be taken over the road or by rail. It was an ocean going container like the Molotov box but this one had a white rectangle with a stylized eagle logo in red and blue on its side. It said American President Lines and the number 25128 just above Vlad's eye level. He tied Vlad's hands just like his partner and forced him over until he was at a sixty-degree angle and supported only by his head against the steel wall. Shamil he led back to the car.

The Mechanic opened the trunk and told him to get in and lie down. When he turned his back, the killer put the pistol in his belt to free his hands. Just as Shamil got into position but before he could turn around he felt stone hard fingers at his neck and tried to call out but it was over almost instantly. The second man never even turned his head back to see what was happening. The only sound Vlad heard from behind him was the click of the trunk catch followed by the whine of a little servo as it pulled the lid tight, but Shamil was already dead.

Out of the corner of his eye, Vlad could see his captor performing some arcane operation on the steel plates beside him and the next thing he knew, the wall had opened and a ladder hung from the passage. The door to the container that had been designed by its manufacturer remained sealed at the far end. Vlad was directed to climb the ladder and seat himself against the opposite wall inside while the Mechanic followed. In a moment the hidden door was shut and he could hear the sound of strong latches being slid home. It was totally dark until the American hit a switch.

The light revealed a single bed, several large cabinets, a chair and a table. All of them were framed out of steel and welded to the deck. On the largest cabinet, which was ten feet long and about waist high, was a small refrigerator. Another held a microwave oven, a laptop computer, and a small television. They were all attached firmly. There were even a few posters on the walls from art expositions and movie openings. The killer hit a second switch and much needed air began to flow from a grate.

Vlad understood immediately where he was and made an expression of appreciation. "A man staying inside could become invisible, yet travel," he said.

"I'm glad you approve," said the man who had been his intended victim. "I haven't used it much in a long time but it has served me well from time to time."

"Is brilliant." His captor was pleased to be showing off an idea that few had ever seen. If Vlad had known that none of those visitors had survived the experience he might have reacted differently.

"Yes," The Mechanic agreed.

He picked Vlad up by his shirt and shoved him in the chair, using three more heavy tie-wraps to secure him to it. Then he produced a stool from the cabinet and sat facing the Chechnyan.

"What about deal?" the prisoner asked.

"What's your name, comrade?"

"I tell you. Vladimir Ilyich Digaev. We just hired not knowing who and what. I am Chechnya. I have no loyalty for Russians. I am like you. I make deal for you." The Mechanic congratulated himself on his choice. Vlad was already wavering. Shamil seemed to have had a bit of the *jihad* in his personality that could have postponed the inevitable.

"We can make a deal," said The Mechanic. "I'll make you an even better one than you offered me." He leaned forward.

"You know I have to know who sent you. You know I have to know that. You tell me, and I'll give you enough money to live like the Romanovs at home and produce a cover, a story to protect both you and your partner." Vlad's eyes went upward and to his right. He bit gently on his lip.

This was really unexpected good fortune. He was going to take the deal already.

"I . . . do not know," he said.

"Fifty thousand dollars American and a new life versus a lot of pain and a bullet in the head," answered The Mechanic.

"Honestly," there was a thin semblance of a smile, "I don't know what you're thinking about. You said yourself you have no loyalty to the Russians but what they pay you."

Sweat ran down over Vlad's lips and he licked them nervously.

"You are right. You are right. I agree. Cut my ropes."

"Who sent you?"

"They are *Matrosskaya*. We job—contract for them. Cut my rope."

"Who are the *Matrosskaya?*"

"*Organizatsia* in USA. Very big. Very powerful. Many KGB. Many connections. Cut rope."

"In a minute," the American said. "About three weeks ago, I killed a man, a Russian, because he saw me come out of the hatch to this container we're in. It happened about forty yards from where you're sitting. I know that's why you were sent after me but I don't understand it. Who was he?"

"I think Yevgeny Malenkov."

"What do you mean? You're not sure? Who was Malenkov?"

"Bookkeeper."

The Mechanic used an expression that indicated a lack of belief. "Why would a bookkeeper be sniffing around me?"

"Have told you all. Malenkov was bookkeeper for *Matrosskaya* in US."

"I found out later that he was inspecting a damaged container stored in this yard. The next day, after the investigation was called off, it was on a flatbed on its way out of town. I remember it was one of those odd named containers. Molotov was the company. There is another one still in the yard at the moment. What was so special about that particular one?"

"Don't know. Loaded, maybe?"

"There was almost nothing in it. I looked inside it myself, yet they transported a damaged 'empty' down there like it was a Faberge` Egg. How come?"

Digaev looked mystified.

"So you were sent to kill me just because I offed the *Matrosskaya* family accountant?"

"*Da.* But business only. Let me go now."

"He just ran into me out of coincidence?"

"Da. Cut rope."

"Bullshit! Who sent him? The same guy that sent you, I suppose. What was his name and what does he do?"

"Balakova. Now he is *Vor v Zakonye.* Pretends to work for *Yaponets* in Miami Florida but since he is arrested, Balakova is *Vor.* You know *Yaponets* And Balakova?"

"I've never crossed paths with them, but I know who you mean. And Balakova is the Godfather now. Right?"

"*Da. Vor v Zakonye.* Cut ropes and go before someone comes."

The Mechanic got off the stool and began to walk back and forth in the confined space.

"You knew who I was."

"*Da.* After Malenkov, *Vor* was told of bruises, tech . . . uh, method that are like other murders. Know Mechanic is killer."

"Yes, but you also knew I was Gordon. How?"

"Balakova."

"Yes, but who was it that told him?"

"Do not know. Really! Let me go, please."

Something about the pacing or the inflection in his voice had begun to disturb Vlad anew. The man did not appear to be someone who had just found a friend.

"I still need to know where the information about George Gordon came from. Do you know anything at all about the one Balakova talked to? Where was he? A city? A state?"

"Do not know. Have told you everything! Let us go now, please."

The Mechanic paused in his walk and began to rummage around in the large steel cabinet again.

"Were there any other instructions? Something before you were to return to—where, Miami?"

"*Da*. We are to check truck."

"Truck? What truck? Where?" The mechanic paused his redecoration of the inside of his storage cabinet to give Vlad a hard look.

"Here."

"What here, goddammit? Where exactly is the truck you were supposed to check?"

"Other Molotov truck," he gestured with his head.

"What were you supposed to do with it?"

"Nothing. Just check. Shamil says *Vor* owns all trucks—containers. Don't know."

"What's supposed to be in those Molotov boxes?"

"Do not know. I swear!"

A minute passed whose silence was broken only by the clatter of objects moved within the cabinet and increasingly urgent entreaties by the Chechnyan. The American's hands were full and he stopped for a moment.

"I think I believe you," he said. The Mechanic then placed several objects on the floor in front of him and straightened back up. He squinted at the prisoner.

"What were you thinking when you wired the house?" he asked. "It was a shaped charge on the east wall of the house, wasn't it? Did it occur to you that there were others in the house?"

Vlad's mouth was becoming cottony as his intended victim continued.

"What were you thinking?" he asked again. "You must have been observing. You were in the utility truck I saw when I left weren't you? You knew that there was a woman and a child. Did you think that nothing would come from that?"

Vlad had seen and even felt many hard looks in his life yet something about this 'Gordon' and his soft brown eyes made his blood cold.

"Did not mean to harm them," he rasped.

The man stood quietly and regarded the objects at his feet. There were two lengths of rubber tubing, brass attachments and two small tanks. His expression was unchanged and the movement of his face toward the frightened captive was slow, almost languid.

"A woman of beauty—" he was very still for a long second before he continued. "Great beauty and intelligence and loyalty and strength. One who would never have left Gordon on her own. And then there was the girl. A little girl of just over ten years, barely out of diapers it seems like. There was not a blemish on this child, body or soul. She was an angel of God."

The Mechanic leaned into the face of his prisoner with a hand on each of the chair's armrests. Briefly and for the first time the eyes of the girl's father showed real emotion. It was not even anger at first, only consternation and unutterable pain.

"Did you see her, Vladimir? She was an angel. Did you bother to look at her? Did you not think that even if Gordon didn't make you pay, that God Himself would be offended by the murder of such a . . . a . . . ?"

The Mechanic blinked several times and tensed the muscles of his forearms as if he were about to explode into action. If the chair had not been made of steel, its arms might have snapped under the pressure. Vlad squirmed in his seat.

But instead of violence, The Mechanic relaxed his grip and asked, "Do you believe in God, Vladimir?"

Knowing it was pointless, but unable to stop himself, Vlad threw himself against the slender restraints in a panic and when he had failed, he tried to rock against the back of the chair which was bolted to the deck and then welded with a half inch bead of metal.

"I just hired," he said in a high-pitched voice. "I not decider. Matrosskaya makes decisions. We are weapons in hand of Matrosskaya. We are like you. Hired worker. You are like us!"

Vlad's glance alternated between his captor and the little door that was the only way out of the box he was in. His whimpering was almost out of control but finally he gave up the hopeless assault on the metal chair.

"That's true," The Mechanic answered eventually, his bland expression restored. "I have done these things."

A tiny flicker of hope was in the Chechnyan's expression. "And we help you. Can lead you to Balakova. He has many guards, but with our help you can do it."

He wanted so very much to believe. The Mechanic leaned down to his level again and held Vlad's eyes with his own.

"You give me your word that if I let you go you will help me long enough to take my revenge?"

"Da! Yes, yes! We help absolutely!"

"And you've told me everything you know about who sent you and why?"

"Da! Yes!"

The Mechanic picked up the small tanks and lengths of hose from the clutter at his captive's feet and put them away.

"That's good. An acetylene torch is an ugly way to make an agreement," he said. "If Gordon had been here, he would have used it—whether you talked or not."

Vlad gulped hard. His relief blunted for a second, he stared away from The Mechanic, assuming a submissive posture and trying to make himself very small.

The moment passed and Alicia Gordon's father produced a knife and quickly cut the four plastic restraints, freeing her murderer who breathed a sigh of relief.

"Gordon?" the Chechen said, adding puzzlement to his terror. "But you are Gordon."

Turning his back on Digaev, The Mechanic opened the steel plates of the makeshift 'door'.

"Come on." He gestured at the steps. The Chechen climbed laboriously to his feet and crabbed his way around the Mechanic hugging the wall until he encountered the opening he so craved. He backed down the ladder, stumbled and fell in the dirt of the freight yard. Vlad got to his feet and waited. He was too cowed to run. He looked around. There was no point to it. Then he saw a small tire emerge from the door.

"Here, grab this for me, will you?" asked The Mechanic.

Vlad helped him lower the Honda Mo-ped to the ground.

"What for?" Vlad asked while he watched The Mechanic secure all the door's hidden catches.

"For later," was the reply.

"You better get your partner out of the trunk."

When Digaev was almost to the rear of the car, the trunk sighed open. Before he could call out to his partner or notice his state he felt a hammer blow behind his right knee. He spun on his good leg to see The Mechanic holding the remote control to the Continental in one hand and the old Smith and Wesson in the other. Swiftly there were two more quiet shots, a burning in his stomach and a shove, which toppled him backward into the cavernous trunk on top of Shamil's body as the lid closed.

Vladimir banged on the inside of the trunk and called out to his tormentor. He was too restricted to generate much force and too short of breath in the baking air to scream for very long. The Mechanic moved the car onto the carrier he had picked out. The engine labored up the steep incline and he attached it with chains.

The killer walked to the back of the car carrier with its load of seven cars increased by one. He put his mouth down by the red and chrome Lincoln logo on the trunk.

"Be glad I didn't have time, Vladimir," he whispered, knowing Vlad would be unable to hear even if were still conscious.

It was a struggle just to pick up one end of the massive wheel ramp and slide it back under the trailer carrier. Cars would be removed onto a truck, the carrier would be re-coupled and some of the cars would continue on a journey all the way to Seattle—he had seen to that by checking the rail schedules with the network in Chicago.

Idly the killer wondered how far Vlad would make it. Certainly not across Arkansas, probably not across the river, but he hoped it would be hours yet. It was really too bad he couldn't take the time to make the men who exploded George Gordon's life pay properly, but Vlad had a point. Balakova was the real culprit—Balakova and the traitor who led them to the Gordon' family. The Mechanic realized that it was this identity that he had come to think of as his 'real' one and these people had ended his life just as surely as they had ended the lives of his women.

The little engine on the Honda kicked over immediately and the man who used to be George Gordon made his way back.

Chapter 9

The tall figure stood in the Hoover Building's lobby directly in the center of the marble inlaid FBI logo. He was wearing a big smile and a much less attractive gray suit with ugly black buttons.

"Like the poet, right?" the young woman said, voicing her second thought and shaking his outstretched hand.

Special Agent Gabrielle Bernard had just been introduced to Lieutenant Aleksandr Pushkin, the investigator from Russia via Interpol whom she was to escort on his assignment.

Almost as soon as she had spoken, Gaby's face flushed a bit. *Like the poet? Really!* The comment sounded so girlish and banal. But her first thought, which had been '*he looks way too good to be Russian*' would certainly have been far worse—accurate as far as the stereotype she had in mind, but far worse. A third, and even less worthy thought, was that he must be gay, given that she had read in his dossier that he was single. Russian women could not be so different in their judgment.

Pushkin, in fact, had more of a Scandinavian look than the usual Slavic types common to his home. He was tall, blond and athletic and the suit notwithstanding, he looked more like a movie star than a cop, much less a cop from Russia. His skin had the reddish glow that happens when a fair person spends a lot of time outdoors and it made his teeth look even whiter. There was an engaging spark of humor in his gray-blue eyes and smile wrinkles at the corners that Gaby liked. She guessed he must be almost six-two because when she got close enough for the handshake she had to tilt her head back quite a bit to look him in the eye. The hand was large and warm.

"The poet, yes!" the man said, brightening further at her comment. He shook her hand enthusiastically. "You know Pushkin?"

"Barely more than an acquaintance, I'm afraid, but what I know, I like. Not as well as you seem to know English. I'm so pleased that language will not be a problem. I have no Russian, my Spanish is terrible and my French is barely passable."

Pushkin seemed captivated by her. A young woman who looked as good as Gaby was accustomed to stares but those smiling eyes played with hers in a way that made her uncomfortable.

Pushkin continued to stare at her longer than would be customary for a professional meeting and held onto her hand a second too long as well. If he is gay, she thought, he is certainly covering well.

"I am honored to use your language to the extent that I am able, Special Agent Bernard. And I am pleased that you recognize Pushkin the Greater and accept Pushkin the Lesser. I am acceptable?"

"Of course, very much so," said Bernard, hoping that the awkwardness of the response would go unnoticed.

"Please, come with me. And call me Gabrielle—or Gaby if you like."

"Gabrielle," he said as if he had just sampled a new flavor. "It is a beautiful name."

"This way," said Gaby, and she led Lieutenant Pushkin through the security checkpoint and onto the elevator.

With nothing scheduled for an hour, Gabrielle conducted a quick tour, familiarizing him with the general layout of the huge building where she understood they were to spend his visit in research. She was pleased that at least her technical and legal experience allowed her to speak knowledgably about the areas of the Lab most likely to impress: the vast computer room and some of the specialized workstations that supported FBI efforts with state-of-the-art electronic tools. Gaby had never taken the public tour that was available before the Trade Center attack but she had the statistics ready for him too—600,000 pieces of evidence processed per year, 5,000 firearms in the FBI collection and so forth.

Pushkin made all the appropriate noises of approval as they made the rounds but the young FBI agent found herself impressed in return as she watched the visitor meet various people in both official and casual situations. He had, she decided, an abundance of what was called in the old movies Gaby loved, *Charm*.

The abbreviated tour ended in the area of Gaby's office and of course Karen was there, growing very noticeably wide-eyed at the sight of the Russian. She was wearing the new silk blouse Gaby had given her and taking no chances on missing the subject of the new assignment.

"Lieutenant Aleksandr Pushkin, this is my friend Karen Elias," Gaby said.

"Very pleased to meet you, Lieutenant Pushkin," Karen said as she stepped forward to shake his hand.

"I am honored to meet you, Karen. Please call me Alex." Pushkin smiled at her and Gaby thought it was almost comical to see the reaction on her face and the body language she used.

"Great! Alex, then. Is Gaby taking care of you all right, Alex?"

"Splendidly," said Pushkin. "Agent Bernard has been most helpful and kind enough to show me some of the workings of your fine organization."

"Your English is just wonderful. How ever did you learn to speak so well?"

"Thank you. I studied throughout what you would call High School and later as a member of our Border Police I was selected to attend a language school in England."

"It's just great. I would never have guessed that you were Russian." She caught herself in a perceived faux pas and added quickly, "Not that there's anything wrong with being Russian. I just meant . . ."

"I know exactly what you meant, Karen and I am pleased that you think as you do," Pushkin said.

"Can I get you anything? A soda or a cup of coffee—or tea? Don't Russians like tea?"

"As a matter of fact many Russians drink tea. I prefer coffee, but nothing for me at the moment, thank you."

"Karen," Gaby said, "we have a meeting in a few minutes."

"Yes, of course. I'll just leave you to it then, but first I need to see you for just a moment. Will you excuse us Alex?"

Still smiling, Pushkin watched Karen lead Gaby by the elbow inside her office and shut the door. When it was closed, Karen leaned back against it and pantomimed fanning herself with her hand.

"Oh, honey!" Karen said, shaking her head. "Are you kidding me?"

Gaby had to laugh. "Jesus, Karen!"

"That is the best looking man I have ever seen! This is Leonid Brezhnev?"

"Keep your voice down," Gaby said softly. Then she added, "Doesn't look much like him does he?"

"Brezhnev? Honey, he looks like Brad Pitt's better-looking brother! I'm leaving Ben and moving to Moscow tomorrow. Girl, did you ever hit the jackpot!"

"Karen, I was serious, we have a meeting to go to. Maybe you can drool on him some more later this afternoon."

"Oh, I wasn't *that* obvious."

"Obvious? You looked like a starving dog in front of a pound of ground Porterhouse. Now we have to go!"

Gaby shouldered by her and started to open the door but Karen was still fanning herself and rolling her eyes. "Talk about 'From Russia with Love'!" she said.

Gaby cracked up again.

"Stop that! I can't go out there giggling. He'd want to know why. Get hold of yourself, girl."

Karen turned that into a much more lascivious remark but eventually she was able to stifle her enthusiasm for the moment and they went back to the open office area.

"We're wanted on the fifth floor," Gaby told Pushkin.

"It was a pleasure to meet you, Karen," he told her.

"It's mutual," she said, still glowing. "I hope we'll see you again."

On the way up in the elevator, Aleksandr made a comment about how friendly everyone seemed. Gaby couldn't tell for sure if he was having fun with them, so she took the statement seriously and simply agreed with him.

The first meeting with Deputy Director Gerry Fallon was as casual as she had expected. Fallon sat behind the imposing acreage of his desk and the accompanying litter of papers, memorabilia and awards, sipping coffee from a ceramic mug the size of a beer stein with a four-color Bureau logo on it. After the introductions, even Fallon's first question was the standard conversational opener.

"How was your flight?"

"Very smooth," Pushkin said, "but a bit longer than I am accustomed to."

"I have spoken to Mister Dashenko several times in the course of arranging your trip, and I hope, our new cooperative agreements. I must say he is very complimentary of your abilities, Aleksandr."

"The Colonel is too kind. Any ability I may have is a direct result of his guidance, I assure you."

"Colonel? I didn't know such rank existed within Interpol."

"Sorry. No, you are quite right. Mister Dashenko was my superior several years ago in the Militia and at Interpol only recently. To me I think he will always be the Colonel."

"He seems a very capable man."

"Sir, you could not have encountered any better. He is a brilliant tactician and an inspired leader. If he has committed to a new agreement you may consider it accomplished."

"I see the admiration runs in both directions. Excellent."

Fallon took another sip of coffee and belatedly asked Aleksandr and Gaby if they would like some. They both declined.

"Why don't you take a minute to tell me about your mission as you understand it," Fallon asked.

Pushkin leaned forward, fixing Fallon directly with his gaze.

"I am sure with all the superb people and facilities at your disposal and no results over the years of chasing this Mechanic person it must seem a remote possibility—almost frivolous. I think you would call it a long bet."

"A long shot?" Gaby offered.

"Yes, thank you—a long shot. It may seem pointless to pursue this man who has left behind so little information. And certainly the passage of time has made the assembly of any new facts more difficult. Some of the assassinations attributed to him may well be the work of someone else and it is logical to assume that there are some of which he is not even suspected that he in fact performed. All these things make progress even more unlikely."

Fallon smiled. For the moment he was completely disarmed by the unexpected degree of the Russian's candor.

"So far we are in complete agreement, Aleksandr."

"Internationally you may be familiar with the most famous crimes attributable to him, those in Columbia and Japan. Less known is an incident in France that Colonel Dashenko believes involved The Mechanic. And there are other international occurrences that may be subtly related. I won't bore you with the details here but coupled with what you have learned we believe that there is a realistic possibility of solving all these crimes at once with perseverance and luck."

"Yes," Fallon said, "I suspect a little luck will be required in this case."

"Additionally, the Colonel is convinced that more will be revealed by the Mechanic himself in the next few days."

Fallon's eyes widened.

"That's an extraordinary statement."

"Sir, the Colonel was at one time the finest analyst and investigator in the Soviet Union and you may believe me when I say that he has lost none of his skills. In addition to his intelligence, he is also remarkably intuitive. I am a poor substitute for him, but I will continue to communicate by way of extending his reach beyond the executive offices and into the field. I understand that he has . . . political reasons for wanting a resolution to this matter."

"So I gathered."

"Yes, sir. For that reason he has committed fully to this pursuit and when he does that . . . well, let us just say that his failures have been very rare."

Fallon put his cup down and leaned forward in the big leather chair.

"Aleksandr, you make me believe that you have a chance to accomplish this thing. And you make me certain that I should be even more careful and respectful in my dealings with Mister Dashenko. I think he has sent the right man for the job."

He got up and swept his arm in the direction of the door.

"Let's move down and see the Director. He should be ready for us now."

Fallon ushered Gaby and Aleksandr down the hall to the bureaucrat's holy-of-holies, The Director's conference room. Standing when they entered were Phillip Barrett, the US Attorney General's Chief of Staff; William J. Perdue, the newly appointed Director of the FBI; Tony Metcalf and two staff people seated along one wall who were apparently considered part of the office furniture since they were never acknowledged. Gaby didn't notice at first because she was preoccupied with all the A-list names but one of the staff people was Phil Cannon, Metcalf's protégé and pet bulldog.

The obligatory pleasantries were exchanged again. Pushkin was welcomed to Washington and he was grateful for the kind reception. So far it was less than a babysitting job for Gaby. She felt like she should join the two staffers along the wall.

Perdue was asking Tony Metcalf to summarize the facts when he was interrupted by Gerry Fallon.

"Excuse me, Bill. I've got a feel for the expectations involved here and I think we can take it that the project is in good hands. It only remains to talk about facilities and personnel issues. I know we have some manpower limitations at the moment."

Pushkin spoke up. Even in the company of these high-ranking officials he seemed perfectly at ease.

"Mister Director, gentlemen, if you please, I am very aware that I am here as a favor to Interpol and that you have made no elaborate promises of assistance, nor do we expect any. We in the Federation and at Interpol recognize that terrorism quite understandably consumes much of your energies at this time and I have no wish to divert attention from these important matters. The man I have come to investigate and the crimes he has committed over the last decades, heinous though they are, are as nothing by comparison."

Perdue seemed a little puzzled by this opener.

"Not at all," he said. "As a matter of fact, I was speaking to my counterpart at Interpol just last night and I assured him that we would bend every effort to assist in the capture and conviction of this man—what is he called?"

"The Mechanic," Metcalf volunteered. "We have resources available within the Center for the Analysis of Violent Crime that should be very helpful without any great expenditure of manpower."

Pushkin looked first at Tony Metcalf and then allowed his gaze to wander to each of the other men.

"Exactly. Excellent organization. Marvelous technical abilities. We completely agree and have, I'm sure you are aware, already been corresponding with your agency and find its facilities second to none. What I mean to say is that we have come to the conclusion that since this mystery has survived many years of the most advanced technological analysis, perhaps plain police work is called for. That is why my superiors have sent me, a plain policeman."

The men at the table answered another of those Pushkin smiles that Gaby was becoming familiar with. Looking briefly around the other faces, Perdue responded.

"We are all great believers in diligent police work, Lieutenant. So what is it we can do for you?"

"As I say, we have no wish to waste your efforts. My superior has directed me to use minimal assistance at your headquarters and in the field if required. We believe that this might be a pivotal moment that would allow us to solve this mystery in very short order, but if we are wrong we wouldn't want to place extra burdens at such a time as this. If you can allow me nominal access and the same level of cooperation I have enjoyed so far, I believe that in a week, I will be on my way back to France to report to my directors and in the mean time your organization can concentrate on its more important work."

"Again," said Perdue, "I likewise wouldn't want you to think that we do not highly value the work you will be doing. However if that is all you ask, please consider it done. Whatever you need."

"Agent Bernard has been so helpful with my orientation so far that if you will allow her to continue in that capacity I will be more than pleased. Other than that, I think we will require only a little, ah, latitude to pursue this matter. As my superior put it, I am for the most part looking for your support in the form of—permission to use my judgment and discretion. The rest of your resources and the FBI can continue its other important work."

Perdue looked once more at the bland expressions around the table.

"I see absolutely no problem with that. Tony? Are we done here?"

Metcalf nodded with a slight shrug, Perdue stood up and after more handshakes, the meeting was over.

As they filed out, Tony pulled Gabrielle to one side for a moment away from the others.

"You watch this guy, Bernard," he said. "He is pretty smooth. This meeting was supposed to dazzle Pushkin with all the titles in the room, tell him that our resources were a little stretched at the moment and send him home in a day or two. The way he made a point of asking for nothing put the Director in the position of almost trying to force resources on him to save face. Obviously Fallon didn't brief Perdue properly. I told the kid we didn't have resources to spare, he tells the old man he doesn't need any and then he basically got *carte blanche* to do whatever he wants with whatever he needs. 'I'm just a plain old country policeman.' 'All I want is a little latitude.' What the hell does that mean? Shit! Did he tell you what he was going to say?"

Gaby shook her head. "I was as surprised as anybody."

Metcalf had a sinister grin on his face as he added, "Well I hope you liked his little speech because you're his now for the duration, I guess you realize that."

"I work for him now?" she asked.

"No, I suppose in a purely titular way . . ." he put a nasty emphasis on the word that may or may not have been accidental this time. " . . . you would be lead agent because of the jurisdictional issues involved but you heard what the Director said—'Whatever we can do'. Just keep an eye on him, lead him around, show him the database cross-references and try not to screw it up. And let me tell you something, little girl, if this is another one of your antics or if you try to use his role to make something more out of this, I'll have you back in the deepest records dungeon in this building—and I know where all of them are."

Gaby nodded impatiently.

"Of course. I get it. I'm in charge, only—not. It's a real assignment, only—not. And Cannon—what was he doing in there?"

"I wanted him briefed because he'll be your backup in case you get in over your head."

This statement required more time for response than she had at the moment.

In the evening Gaby's babysitting duties had expanded to include chauffeuring. The ten-year-old Mercedes she had insisted on paying her mother blue book value for when she started law school objected several times before finally starting. When she glanced over at Pushkin in embarrassment he seemed content to sit in the passenger seat the rest of the night watching her turn the key. Gaby made two mental notes to herself: first, to maintain a professional distance with her colleagues and second, not to refuse an offer of a new car the next time her father tried to force one on her.

When she tried to drop the Russian off at his hotel he insisted that she share dinner with him and she could think of no good reason to exclude an after-hours meal. If the Russian on this assignment had been a stocky Ukrainian woman, Gaby reasoned, she would certainly have expected to socialize a bit just to lubricate the wheels of investigative rapport. Armed with this potent and in fact, accurate rationalization, she accepted and shortly they were seated in the hotel's best restaurant.

Her reservations notwithstanding, Pushkin quickly had Gaby laughing out loud at the absurdities of dealing with the remnants of Soviet bureaucracy and she delighted him by listing the similarities in the paramilitary system that is the FBI.

"One of the cases we studied kept mentioning an IED but I knew from the narrative that it was a pipe bomb. Our system inhales jargon and exhales acronyms. Well, I assumed that this IED thing must be some radical new advance in explosives or maybe an advanced trigger of some kind and naturally in my position I didn't want anyone to know that I wasn't familiar with the latest thing. I went through two more studies that referred to the same thing before I figured out that IED just stands for Improvised Explosive Device, basically anything that blows up that wasn't made in a factory. There were hundreds of them! OCG, NCAVC, CALEA, NCIC, CODIS, IED. My God! If you haven't memorized hundreds of these absurd letter scrambles they act as if you have had a defective education. It makes me long for the overuse of Latin legal terminology. At least the Latin has intrinsic meaning."

After Pushkin stopped chuckling, he said, "You truly have a degree in the law, yet you choose to be a policeman? This indicates a great dedication or some private motive does it not?"

They had finished their salads and were sipping a cabernet waiting for the main course. Gaby looked hard at him when he said 'private motive' but his expression revealed nothing but an intense focus.

"Not really," she replied. "The Bureau in America is much more than a police force."

"Many agents are similarly educated?"

"Actually, yes. It's quite common."

"And you have always wished to do this?"

Gaby shook her head.

"Not in my wildest dreams. The truth is that until my last semester I had never considered it. It was a combination of things."

"What things?" he asked.

Gaby hesitated. The conversation was going beyond the limits she would have expected already.

"My father is a lawyer in New Orleans. Do you know the city?"

"Of course," he said. "French Quarter, Superdome, Katrina, Mardi Gras, Happy New Year."

"Yes, anyway that's why my French is so bad—too much Cajun influence.

"My father is a lawyer and that was what drew me to the law. His specialty is corporate rather than criminal. Anyway, I didn't enter Law School until several years after my undergraduate degree. When I finally returned, I was doing okay in my studies, but when the time came, I just couldn't see myself practicing it. It began to look as if it would be just as dull as what I had been doing. Unsatisfying. I have always enjoyed puzzles and to some extent that's what investigation is all about. The legal puzzles of corporate and tax law are just too convoluted and you never have the satisfaction of getting the right answer. It's just less wrong than some of the others, or in some cases, completely wrong but defensible."

Gaby was again conscious of how much she was talking and afraid that a continued personal conversation might turn to what she was doing in those years between Princeton and Tulane Law.

She paused, took another sip of wine and waved a conversational shift with her free hand. "Look, we've been talking about me all afternoon and all night. Tell me about Moscow, about yourself."

"There is nothing to tell. I joined the Militia twelve years ago. I have never had another job. I was fortunate enough to catch the attention of a great man. It was he who has helped me to any success I may have had, created my position within Interpol and influenced my assignment to this case. I can summarize: Moscow is cold. Pushkin is boring. Please continue with your story."

"Oh, pooh!" she said.

"Pooh? What is 'pooh'?"

Gaby reddened. It was a word she had not used in some time. The salty language that she had adopted as part of her personal rebellion might have made her look less professional in this situation, but at that moment it seemed better than sounding like a debutante who cracked a nail.

"It's an expression meaning 'I don't believe that last part'."

"Oh no! Is true, I promise you."

"Well I believe Moscow can be cold . . ."

Gaby realized what she had just implied and blushed more deeply this time. She got the impression that Pushkin noticed and enjoyed it. She became aware that she had been leaning closer and closer to Alex Pushkin as she spoke and pulled back very deliberately hoping it wouldn't be obvious.

Pushkin covered the silence smoothly.

"Please continue to use such expressions. My English is good—is okay, but I have little experience with expressions; American idiom. The first Aleksandr created entire branches of Russian literature using idiom to break free of restrictive traditions. Now it is my tradition to learn."

"I'll try to help," Gaby said. "But I've been on my best behavior tonight. I've been told that I can be overly competitive. In the course of an investigation, you may find some of my idiom crude and . . . quite unusable in all but the lowest level of society. One of my study partners in Law School passed on some bad habits, I'm afraid."

"Unusable?" He was confused for a second before he deciphered the mischievous twinkle in her eye and smiled. "Oh, I see. No, please, I am not a delicate tropical blossom."

"Anyway, please tell me more about Aleksandr Pushkin," she said. "What is your family like? What do you like to do when you aren't chasing people for the State?"

"Sailing, when I can. My father has always been a sailor at heart and I like boats also. Someday I will have one of my own."

"That has to be unusual. Except for little fishing boats, only millionaires have their own even in America. Was he a commissar or something?"

Pushkin seemed put off by the question for a moment.

"My father gained a love for the sea serving in the Navy or I suppose we would never have been exposed to it. I had my first experiences with them only when he could borrow a small sailboat on the Black sea for one or two days at a time. But . . . May I tell you something that I have never shared with anyone before?"

Gaby managed to say, "Of course," without changing expression too much.

"It is a dream of mine," he said, "that some day I would like to sail the world from one port to the next, in my own boat with someone I cared for—when I find the right person."

This time it was Pushkin who was leaning closer as he spoke. The low light cast a soft glow over his handsome features. The temperature was suddenly making Gaby uncomfortable and she resumed what she hoped was a more businesslike tone.

"That's wonderful, Alex. I hope someday you can make it come true."

She took a sip of ice water and smiled in gratitude at the waiter for the interruption as their entree was delivered. Maintaining a professional distance was going to be harder than she had thought. The forced silence allowed her to change the subject when the waiters withdrew.

"Aleksandr, you did tell me that we could discuss the case when you suggested I join you for dinner. I assume that the pile of papers in that chair contains some pertinent notes."

"Agent Gabrielle, you spoil my fantasy, but yes, I do have some things here which could be helpful. But now that we have talked a bit, I think it might be better if we left these things for the morning. The details are quite complicated."

She considered the alternative to an immediate business discussion and found a change advisable.

"No, I'm anxious to continue, but I don't understand what details you could have brought with you. I was told that Interpol had absolutely no specifics on the deaths of Ishii or Valenciaga that were not in the media."

Pushkin pulled a folder from under the table.

"True, but I speak of a different murder, one which is a closer relative to the one in Tennessee. Also two other deaths that are said to be accidental."

"You've lost me."

"Then I must find you again. That was idiom was it not? Excellent!"

"The incident I speak of took place in Moscow at the Molot Metallurgical Works nine years ago. This is a concern that supplies lorries—trucks—and auto parts. Two men died for need of oxygen while working on part of a lor . . . truck. At least that was how it is described officially. They were supposed to have closed the doors and simply exhausted the breathable air. Ridiculous!"

He pulled two photos out of the folder and leaned them against Gaby's water tumbler. While she examined them, he continued.

"My supervisor in Moscow is a great mind. The greatest!"

"Yes, Aleksandr, I got that impression from your description earlier. You made him sound like a superman."

"Before the Soviet Union was cut up, he was a senior official with the KGB, but his earlier positions opposed to perestroika left him in disfavor. He joined the Militia, lucky for me and for the Militia. He was also one of the highest-ranking chess Grandmasters in the former Soviet Union.

"These murders—he has been unable to prove anything because there were no details, but he knows there was something wrong—something smelling bad. While he could not come personally because of his position, he used what is remaining of his influence in the government and at Interpol to get it assigned to me. That way he could collaborate with me without letting it become known that he is involved. When we uncover the truth, it will bring him back to power and me to a new position."

"Wow! Wait a minute," said Gaby. "You're making my head spin. What has all that, and two deaths by suffocation, got to do with the assassinations of Ishii and Valenciaga?"

"Spin?" he said. "More idiom! Very good! But the answer to your question may be 'nothing'. The murder that those two have been connected with however was the latest one, that of Yevgeny Malenkov in Memphis, Tennessee. He was the brother of the third dead man in Moscow. He was killed by a single bullet on the property of Molot Works a week after the suffocation. That is the connection that excited Colonel Dashenko."

He added a third picture. It was the stare of a man holding papers in a literal death grip.

"And you think the Mechanic killed the other Malenkov as well?"

Pushkin made an odd expression and said, "No. We do not know who did that."

"On second thought, maybe we should wait until tomorrow," Bernard offered. "Maybe you have to be a Grandmaster to understand this story. Tomorrow afternoon I can get my boss involved. I don't think he understood that this situation was so visible in your country."

"No, no! But it is decidedly not. No one but you and myself has heard this line of theory. It is not purely supportable by facts, but as I told the Deputy Director, Colonel Dashenko has also great intuition. He is certain that this is the true connection, not the murders of Ishii and Valenciaga. If he is certain then I am also."

Pushkin paused, sat straighter in his chair and dabbed at an imaginary drop of wine with his napkin.

"I hope that you will support my desire to go immediately to Memphis Tennessee."

"I'm sorry, what was that?" she asked, although she had heard every syllable.

He repeated himself, aiming his gray-blue eyes directly into hers.

"Aleksandr, to be honest, this visit was described to me as more—uh, ceremonial in nature. We are expected to meet daily with various field Directors and sift any information that may come in, but clearly this was not intended as a real field assignment—not on this side anyway. They had no intention of letting you leave Washington until it's time for you to go home."

"Sift information," he said from under a wrinkled brow, then brightened. "Yes, as in adjusting the texture of flour. A good one.

"You are quite correct of course about the expectations of our government officials and yours. That is why I was allowed to come. It is considered unimportant. Likewise that is why a twenty-six year old agent with little field experience is permitted to accompany me. You can see why I am so pleased that they have unexpectedly sent me someone who is also bright, well educated and not completely without ambitions of her own that might be served. They would certainly not permit me to launch a field investigation on my own. I would of course have to be accompanied."

He smiled as he had all evening and Gabrielle Bernard said nothing for a moment. Slowly she handed the three photographs back to Pushkin. His expression softened and then fell abruptly.

"You are angry," he said.

"Lawyers don't get angry," she answered, "they get even. It's just that I begin to see why you have seemed so attentive to me all day—schmoozing and laughing at my little stories. You want something. I suppose that's what you meant when you told the Director you needed 'a little latitude'."

Still holding her forgotten glass aloft and staring at him she added, "And I can't say that I'm pleased at the prospect of being used as part of a little international plot, regardless of how good its intentions are or how well it is mounted."

"We have misinterpreted something. Perhaps I have stated badly. My English is not as good . . ."

"Your English is fine, as you damn well know. And no, I can't fault your interpretation. It has already occurred to me that this assignment would always fall to an agent that they considered . . . well, to a less senior agent. I guess it annoys me that I am that agent and it really annoys me that I was starting to like you."

Pushkin laughed softly and covered his mouth by dabbing again with his napkin. This irritated her further.

"Forgive me," he said when it seemed that his laughter had annoyed even more, "but your anger makes the candlelight dance in your eyes."

Gaby's eyes widened and her jaw dropped for a second involuntarily. The man was shameless. Pushkin surely must realize how ancient and transparent was the cliché he was trying.

"And your liking for me," he continued. "This great honor for me is now an annoyance for you?"

"Well, yes. You've been trying to manipulate me ever since you got here. All these compliments and attention to my dreary little life-as-a-bureaucrat story. The whole time you were just angling for my cooperation in this wild goose chase."

"Ah, that one I know. That is Chekhov. And if this turns out to be as you say 'a goose chase' then the consequences should be small since the expectations are likewise. Also, I was unaware that my attentions to you personally have been so obvious but if you conclude that I have been motivated by something more than the equally obvious, then you wrong both of us."

He was still staring fixedly at her and Gaby was having trouble concentrating on her negative reaction. Besides, she was excited at the prospect of a real agent's assignment.

"M-maybe I spoke out of turn about the manipulation thing, but you just admitted that this has been your goal all along and yet you said nothing of it in our meetings today. You are trying to manipulate me into doing it for you, are you not?" Gaby asked.

"Special Agent Gabrielle, I would never ask that you participate in something which would not benefit you and your fine organization. Although it seems a remote possibility now, if Colonel Dashenko is correct and we can bring our enterprise to a successful conclusion there will be many positive results for you as well. Surely you will concede that. I did feel that it would be premature until we had discussed . . ."

"Maybe as you say you are being manipulated in turn by your Colonel. That hardly makes me feel better because I am only the pawn of a pawn."

"If I have made you feel badly about my trip to your country it is not my intentions but my clumsiness which is the cause. And however poorly you may estimate me, I assure you that Colonel Dashenko has never participated in a pointless enterprise. I am sure he is not doing so now."

"Clumsy you are most certainly not, Mister Pushkin. But I notice that the Colonel is not the one who will be left with the smell of goose shit from this particular chase, it will be you and me."

Aleksandr smiled again broadly and Gaby was powerless to avoid a similar response.

"I am familiar with that one also," he said. "Agent Bernard, if I have offended you in any way, I swear to you that it was very far from my intention. And in the event that an undesirable odor results that I would do my best to guarantee that there is none clinging to your agency, or more particularly to your lovely person."

The agent shifted uneasily and began to scratch absently on the linen covered table with her bread knife. A corner of her mouth twitched upward.

"I see. Well, I think it's safe to say that we have taken this particular fowl metaphor as far as I care to."

She was staring at a point on the tablecloth. The Russian cocked his head to one side to try to see her face more clearly.

"You do understand the situation, then? The opportunity I lay at your feet?"

"No. Eat your dinner. By now it is as cold as your plan."

Satisfied, Pushkin picked up his fork and they ate in silence for a minute. Like a good salesman, he knew when to wait quietly for an answer.

Gaby chewed one bite for an extraordinarily long time, swallowed and said, "You want to turn a ceremonial visit into a major field investigation.

You know how unlikely it is that you will get approval for this secret mission of yours, even if I were to choose to support it?"

Pushkin almost suppressed his expression of victory and waited politely until he could swallow a mouthful of poached salmon.

"Considerably better than without your help," he said. "If I understood the statement of your Director today, it is all but given. In fact when you join me in the request to expand our learning experience and assist the investigation we will be assured of approval."

"And what makes you think that?"

"Colonel Dashenko. It is a certainty."

"I have a feeling I am going to grow weary of the former Comrade Colonel."

"Special Agent Gabrielle Bernard, what would you be doing this week if not given the duty of shepherdess to his wayward Russian sheep?"

She gave him the same look she tried to give to street vendors of designer handbags, but finally admitted, "Paperwork, I suppose. I'll grant you that almost anything is an improvement."

"You may thank the Colonel. When Deputy Director Fallon described available personnel, you were chosen from a list for this deceivingly important mission."

"So it was him. I don't think I like that either," she said, thinking that now she understood why she was chosen. "And I am past my twenty-ninth birthday. I guess he is also the one who told you to call me twenty-six?"

Pushkin turned up the wattage on his smile.

"I told you he is a genius."

Chapter 10

At one point in his life Conrad Webster was known in San Francisco's finest restaurants as a frequent, but very difficult customer. Once in early 1985, he was confronted by the chef at *Gary Danko's* after sending back a lobster. Webster had called it a 'rubber chicken', loudly proclaimed the man a 'fry cook' and asked for management. He was quietly banned of course, wealthy customers being easier to come by in the Bay Area than five star chefs, and he enjoyed the stigma and accompanying reputation for years.

Webster had lived life large and openly as a banker and businessman until it became known that he handled the West Coast operations for a New York Crime Family. Now he tried to live just as large but, temporarily at least, on a much smaller stage—the minimum security Federal Prison Camp at Leavenworth Kansas. His stay was originally scheduled at the much larger and more draconian Federal Penitentiary, but the venue was mysteriously changed. Every day he could look up at the rotunda, which was its most prominent feature, and appreciate the perquisites and influence, even diminished, of money and political power. Though he had earned an involuntary stay in the shadow of 'The Big Top', his experience of incarceration was not the same as most of his colleagues—even the other 'country club' inmates. He had semi-private accommodations, a personal cook and the protection that came from being a 'righteous', and high-ranking, wise guy on the inside.

On this day he was outdoors seated in the bleachers of the athletic field, reading a week old copy of *Barron's*. He was wearing a wheat-colored straw hat that shaded his face and most of his shoulders from the Kansas sun.

A wrinkled, slightly built black man named James Booker Pettaway, who could have been sixty or a hundred and sixty, weaved expertly through the midday crowd of white-collar criminals in Polo warm-ups. No one knew that name, of course. To most he was Skokie Jim or just Skokie. He was of an age when men in his social circles frequently went by the same name as the towns in which they were born. It had helped to identify faces in the anonymous army of homeless hoboes who had struggled through the fourth decade of the last century. No one knew his whole story, at least no one still alive, but what was known was that he had killed a railroad cop over sixty-five years ago on a federal reservation. His youth had saved him from the electric chair but he was never going to be released—nor did he wish it after all that time. After a half century of good behavior he was allowed a substitute—a new life term in 'The Club'. He would have seemed profoundly out of place if it had not been for the fact that he had been there twice as long as anyone else—inmate or official. Also he was on Webster's payroll as 'provider' and general factotum.

"Hey Mistuh Connie!" his voice called out from behind the field's steel mesh enclosure. "You been greasin' people again? You got two different visitors waitin' at the same time."

With a nod of the head, he acknowledged the old trustee. It was hard to hide his eagerness, but the bulky figure forced himself to fold the paper slowly and rise with as much grace as his fifty extra pounds would allow. The *Barron's* went under one arm as he used the other to smooth his impressive mane of silver hair. Handing Skokie the straw hat, Webster ambled casually around the backstop, and the pair made their way back in the direction of the administration building.

"Naturally, my good Skokie," he said loudly to the partially deaf trustee when he was close enough. "Probably some Wall Street hacks seeking my guidance again."

"Not this time, Boss. You got some legal talent on your hands."

"Really?" Webster said, thinking he knew the identity of one of them. "And who would that be?"

"Your lawyer for one, but I ain't never seen this one before."

"Yes, I was expecting him," came the answer. "They've been promising to put somebody new on my appeal. What about the other one?"

"Didn't say, but I seen a badge. FBI. Maybe you under arrest, man."

"Right. Perhaps I'll give you to them and get myself in the witness protection program."

Skokie turned up an incredibly leathery, wrinkled nose in a sneer.

"You let somebody hear you say that up yonder and you liable to not think that so funny."

Skokie Jim had a kind of horrid nostalgia for the Federal Pen and it was always referred to as 'up yonder'. The Camp was 'down here' and he regarded its temporary denizens as mildly effeminate by comparison. Webster laughed and slapped the old man on the back.

They were clomping down a bare hallway in their oversized Government Issue shoes. It led to the visitor area. It was about half the size of the cafeteria and had the same sets of tables and chairs. Between gray panels, the walls had alternating pastel pink and mint green tones that the industrial psychologists had assured the Bureau of Prisons would be most soothing. At the door they stopped and the trustee pointed to the far end of the hall.

"They told me to tell you you didn't have to talk to this ol' boy. He ain't spoke to the warden or nothin'", Skokie said. The volume of his voice was deliberately loud enough to carry to where the visitor waited but he could see that Conrad Webster had begun to smile faintly.

"Thanks anyway, pal, I think I'll hear what this guy has to say."

When he reached the table, Webster looked around him before he sat to see if anyone would be able to hear them. The nearest conversation was at least twenty feet away.

"What's the gag?" he said to the visitor. "You find a badge in a box of Crackerjacks?"

"Duly issued by the federal government," said Clark Mooney.

"Yeah," said Conrad Webster returning part of his grin with the irony intact. "Some phony ID geek at CIA. What the hell are you doing here, anyway? I haven't seen you in ten years and you should have been retired five years before that."

Mooney ignored the comment and slid the steel chair around to the corner closest to Webster so he would be able to speak softly. Then he waited a few seconds examining the craggy face. At one time this man had controlled a flow of illegal narcotics through Vietnam, Laos, Cambodia and Thailand amounting to nearly a billion street dollars annually—and he had been shrewd enough to be decorated by the Nixon White House for his patriotic war efforts. Mooney had been one of the many inside and outside the government who assisted him. Conrad Webster was once his mentor and still his model for criminal activity.

"The Mechanic," said Mooney. "What do you really know about him?"

"I know he hates that name. I wouldn't use it to his face if I were you. Other than that, not as much as you do. I haven't had any contact since that last time. You should remember. I still had to go through you."

"And he didn't tell you where he lived or how you could get in touch with him directly?" Mooney asked.

"You know better than that. Bob never talks about anything personal."

"Bob? Why did you call him Bob?"

"I don't know. That's the name he used to go by between jobs, I guess."

"You mean Bob Parker?" said Mooney.

"Yeah, Bob Parker. Actually Robert Leroy Parker."

"But that's not his real name?"

"No, it was Butch Cassidy's real name, you nimrod. What are you getting at anyway? You're his bloody 'Control' or dispatcher or whatever for the last thirty some years. Now you need an introduction all of a sudden?"

"Yeah but in all that time I never really found out anything that wasn't a part of one of his 'roles'. I had to know how to get in touch with him in Memphis but that was just another name to him. In Vietnam I never learned his real one, the name he was born with. Do you know what it was?"

Webster leaned back in his chair. "What's the matter with you, Mooney? You tell me right now or this interview is over. If you're here to offer me something, then get to it. If not then you can just go back to polishing that chair with your ass. I have my attorney waiting."

"We need to stop him. The Mechanic has gone completely off the wire and you have known him longer than anyone."

"What does that have to do with me?"

Mooney tapped on the table and looked away for a moment to formulate a reply.

"Somebody found him and killed his family, that is George Gordon's family, and he's certain they couldn't have done that without help from somebody who knows him. As far as I know you're the only other one who ever knew more than one of his names and lived."

The color had drained from Webster's face at this revelation.

"Killed his family! Christ, I didn't have anything to do with it! I did my best to know as little as possible about him. That son of a bitch is scary."

"Spider, Spider," Mooney intoned with a hint of a smirk. "Spare me. I was his dispatcher, remember? You used him more and spent more time with him than anyone else by far, professionally that is. Besides, you know as well as I do that the normal response for him would be to kill everyone who it *might* have been. I thought you should know."

"You'll pardon me for seeming ungrateful for your concern, but it occurs to me that if I'm the only other possibility, you could be trying to lead him here and away from yourself," Webster said.

"You wouldn't want to have this conversation over the phone, would you?"

"No, but you could have got word to me."

A crafty look came over his features.

"It was you, wasn't it?" said Webster. "You dropped a dime on him after all these years."

Mooney tried to look hurt. "I don't know how they found him."

"Bullshit!"

Mooney waved that point away. "Okay, none of that matters anyway. The fact is that he will be after both of us, regardless. He won't stop to ask questions and he wouldn't believe you if he did. We need to pool our knowledge and resources to stop him."

Webster gestured around the pale toned walls of the room, depressing in spite of the sunshine flooding through its chain-linked windows.

"I'm a little short on resources these days," he said.

"But I'm not. Interpol has implicated the international criminal known as *The Mechanic* in several recent assassinations and called in the Bureau. If we can just lay low and maybe give them a little help, they'll take care of the problem for us."

"Idiot!" Webster said. "He's too tough to break in the conventional sense, but he's also crazy. The last goddam thing you want is for the Bureau to pick this guy up and start questioning him."

Mooney shook his head impatiently.

"They'll never see him. They're just going to bird dog for us. They don't know about 'Gordon', just about the Mechanic operating around Memphis. They've thrown a net over it and made it easier for us to catch him with what we know. There's a specialist from New York working on it. We'll just have to see that the questioning never happens."

"A 'net'? For that guy? What a laugh."

Webster pulled out a pack of Kools and indulged a habit he had resurrected since moving into his new home. The blue cloud from his first puff had begun to dissipate before he spoke again.

"Why don't I just sell you out like you did him? You have offered me no inducement. I could tell the Bureau—or even better—I could tell *him*."

"Don't think it would work, Spider old boy," he replied, again using the Vietnam code name Webster had used there. The man had never been lanky enough to deserve the nickname, but now the old man's girth made it comically inappropriate.

"Seriously, I don't think he would believe you unless you had proof and I can't believe he would allow you the time to prove it even if you did. You know what he's like. It's not as if leaving you dead or alive would make a big difference to him. Your best chance is to get under cover with me and wait. I can help you, if you'll help me."

"*With* you? Can you get me out of here?"

"Not right away. But if you cooperate I can get the ball rolling. For the time being, I can get you transferred to a solitary situation."

"Screw solitary. I'm not that worried about population around here. I just want to get out of stir completely. I don't want to spend the next few weeks looking at the same four gray walls," Webster said.

"I don't mean that. I just mean we can fix it so that the only people you see are the ones we know—the ones who we know are loyal because we're already paying for it—just until we can come up with some way to get you out."

"Okay," Webster answered with a slow nod. "That's not bad. That would be okay. As long as you understand that I expect to be out of here in a month."

"Now," Mooney said leaning forward, "is there anything, anything at all that might help us find the guy when he goes underground? Some insight, however small?"

"Not much consistent. He's a hell of an actor for someone with no background for it—a chameleon, but you already know that. Besides, I'm not sure he's really acting. I know he never went to college but he can speak four languages that I know of and carry on a conversation about any subject you can come up with. I can tell you his real name. It was Michael Hogan when we recruited him, but I'm certain he hasn't used it in thirty years. No reason to. I don't think he has anybody from his real family. And he is from the Deep South somewhere originally, but you wouldn't know it by listening to him now, that is unless he *wants* to sound Southern."

"No women? A mistress?"

"I have no way of knowing, but he was playing the part of faithful family man, and I think he *lived* it—the way he lived all his roles. I'd bet against it."

"He was in the Army. No buddies from an old outfit he might contact? Nobody special?"

Webster seemed almost to shudder as he put out his cigarette in the flimsy aluminum ashtray provided.

"When he left the Army, deserted really, although officially he was listed as MIA—that was when he really went round the bend. No, I think you can be sure that he isn't talking to anyone from his Vietnam hitch or anyone from his life before that for that matter. When you say his family was killed, do you mean everyone? How about his wife's family? There were attachments there."

"So you did know about his life in Memphis."

"When I called on him for those last jobs, just before I got sent up, I took the trouble to find out a little, just in case. Have you checked on the family angle?"

"Actually his son was away the night it happened, so the boy's still alive but when I spoke to the man he acted as though he never met any of them, wife or kids. It was cold, scary cold and really weird."

"They didn't get his son. Okay. It doesn't matter how he reacted that day, he was dealing with the emotion and he's not real good at that. Eventually he'll remember the boy. That's how you get him. Get hold of the boy and he'll come to you. Can you do that?"

For a moment, it was the Spider of old, making snap judgments and giving orders. He lit another Kool with a flourish as Mooney shot him a skeptical look.

"Not exactly, no. The Bureau isn't going to put an innocent teenage boy in custody unless I get a hell of a lot more specific about the reason than I can be. I can get him watched though, I think. And then if he shows . . ."

"You can't be that stupid. The last thing you want is a long conversation between him and a Federal Prosecutor. Besides, you know as well as I do that if he's coming after us, he'll have to be stopped permanently. There are no halfway measures with him and you can't very well count on the Bureau to shoot first and do your work for you. You'll have to snatch the kid."

"Do you know what you're asking me to do? I'm a government agent, with a real life, a pension and all that stuff."

"Of course I understand," answered Webster. "And I understand something else too. I understand that you've cranked up about the most efficient killing machine on this planet, put it in gear and aimed it right here." He pointed at his own brow between the eyes. "It's time to put up or shut up, *Agent* Mooney."

"Okay, okay. There are bulletins out for him now. Wherever he is, he's stuck there. We managed to fake an eyewitness report so we could explain the existence of a composite drawing of him. The airports are being watched. They've got his picture and his description is everywhere now that the Bureau is involved. It's just a matter of time till we get a call telling us where to pick him up."

"Yeah, right."

"Okay," said Mooney, "I know we're in a little trouble or I wouldn't be here, would I? Like I said, we need to work together on this thing."

Webster was idly scratching his jaw line and wrinkling his face in thought.

"Yeah, you have to get that boy and he'll have to come to you wherever it is. He won't be able to stop himself. But look, when you get the kid, you need someplace secure enough to hold him, but not visible to the Law—a real fortress. It would have to be a damned tight layout or it won't work. He gets in just about anywhere he needs to. Can you do that?"

Mooney was thinking hard.

"Yes. I think there is such a place," he said.

"You'll need help. You want me to make some calls?"

The faux FBI agent shifted uneasily in the hard chair.

"No, this place has its own protection."

Webster rubbed his hand over the stubble he was just scratching. "So this was an Organization thing all along. Your friends put the word on Parker?"

Mooney nodded. When he was asked if they had also made the original contract on The Mechanic, he nodded again but could only shrug when asked why.

"I got no idea. I was hoping you might have some clue."

"Kind of hard to keep up in here," the older man said.

Mooney stood up to go.

"Wait a minute. You can't leave until you get my transfer going. If you cross me on this, I can still make it very uncomfortable for you, you know—or better still I'll make sure Parker . . ."

"Calm down, Spider," he answered putting a reassuring hand on Conrad Webster's shoulder. "I understand the situation, believe me. You and I are best buddies from now until Parker, or Hogan or whatever, is history. I'm on my way to see the warden right now. Don't sweat it. Anything else?" Now the man spoke as he backed away from the meeting table.

"No. You just get me moved out of population—as long as I can take my people with me. I can't imagine how the bastard would get to anyone inside Leavenworth, but he's done such things before. I'm not going to be the one to underestimate him. Get me out right now. He might be here any time, for all I know."

Mooney waved backward at the aging convict.

"And tell them to send my lawyer in here."

Webster had been at the table unattended for nearly ten minutes, fidgeting and lighting two more cigarettes in a smoldering chain when a suited figure lurched toward the table.

"Mister Webster," said the man, "my name is William Burr of Gelman, Calder, Bellow and Stein."

Burr was an older man, quite rumpled-looking, not the young lion Webster had expected. The lawyer had a thick manila folder under one arm with a briefcase in that hand and a box of Kleenex under the other arm. Before he could even use his free hand to greet his client he had to hastily manipulate the box to grab a tissue and sneeze into it. His eyes looked swollen behind his thick glasses and his voice was thick with the congestion.

"I really apologize, Mister Webster," he said thickly. "It's these darn allergies. When I travel . . . you know."

The prisoner peremptorily waved off the handshake when it was offered. He gave the lawyer time to put down his burdens, coughing and sniffing.

"Ah! So sorry," he said again finally.

"I quite understand," said the client in a tone that indicated otherwise.

"I know you want to get right into your appeal," Burr began. "There are definitely holes in both the capture and legal proceedings. With review I'm sure we can prepare a more effective brief. We can improve our chances with a short background session, if you'll agree. I know the main points of course, from the file, but when the officers entered your home on the day of your arrest, were they specific about . . ."

"Hold it right there!" Webster said. "Do I understand that you are just *researching* the appeal?"

"Mr. Webster, my specialty ordinarily is tax law, but I've handled a great many criminal cases as well and yours is very promising. I just need a little more background before . . ."

Webster slammed his hand on the table in front of his new attorney. He turned his head to one side and rolled his eyes slightly.

"Background! You can't be serious! Didn't you even *talk* to Bailey? I've been in this place for two years and now my attorneys—who have been getting my retainer for almost forty years, by the way—send me another *retread* who wants me to read the files to him? No. No way! We have been all over this material and all I'm interested in now is results! You can just go back and tell Sid to kiss my . . . to handle it—that's all just handle the damn thing!"

"I apologize again, Mister Webster. I have read the files of course, but I thought we could benefit from a fresh beginning, a face to face before . . ."

"Listen, what was it? Burr? I don't give a shit what you thought. I'm telling you I've pored over this stuff chapter and verse with everybody from Sid Gelman to your bloody paralegal staff. I'm not about to rehash it one more time for you. Hell, I was expecting to get sprung this week, or some news at least—a new trial date, not a 'fresh beginning'. Christ!"

The lawyer looked exhausted, and a bit as if he were about to cry. Coughing loudly, he pulled out a roll of mints, LifeSavers candy, and offered Webster one, which he refused.

"Please, Mister Webster, I don't know what to say. I . . . I . . ." The man sneezed again, covering his mouth with the hand holding the LifeSavers roll. A slight patina of mist from it covered Webster's left arm.

"God *damn*, man!" Webster blurted, rubbing the moisture off pointedly and jumping to his feet. The lawyer reached for the tissues again, sputtering apologies.

"Look mister, you better go back there and pack up your desk, because you and whoever sent you here are history." He began to back away toward the doorway still rubbing his hands on his pants.

"I am *so* sorry and I really apologize for the misunderstanding, Mister Webster," the attorney said as he gathered up the items he had only just set down. "I'm sure we can straighten this out."

Skokie was waiting at the hallway for Conrad Webster, shaking his head.

"Really sir," they heard the strained voice from across the room, "terribly sorry. The whole point of my mission was to 'take good care of Spider', that's what my boss told me."

When the two inmates rounded the first corner the sound of the lawyer's posturing faded.

"I reckon you ain't goin' home today, huh, boss?" Skokie asked.

Webster paused to brace himself against the steel lattice over a window before continuing. "Give me just a moment, Skoke, I'm afraid I let that display of incompetence get away with me a bit. My first visitor was bad and I was expecting better news from my lawyers."

"That was the 'new guy' you was talkin' 'bout. Damn! He didn't look like nothin' about him was new exceptin' maybe his leather case."

"I quite agree. Get me up to the top of the telephone privileges list. I need to call them right away, while the whole thing is fresh in my mind. It makes me so . . ."

Webster took two steps down the hall, but suddenly stopped again, not breathing, eyes wide, his face as gray as the wall he leaned against. A half-burned cigarette fell from his fingers and rolled across the linoleum tiles. He held his bare arm up to his face and looked at the spot his lawyer had just *sneezed* on.

"Skokie Jim," he said, "did he just call me 'Spider'?"

Clark Mooney was still waiting in the warden's outer office when a cadaverous man with dull eyes and a less-than-eager handshake approached him. He introduced himself as Warden Sprague."

Mooney wanted to cut the meeting short, so he jumped right into an introduction of his position and the key prisoner that he was concerned about before they even moved, but the warden made it even shorter.

"Agent Mooney, I know why you're here, my aide briefed me, but there's no point in continuing."

"I don't understand."

"I just received a call saying that Conrad Webster died in the corridor downstairs, just ten minutes ago."

A jolt of adrenaline flashed through Mooney's system.

"He's dead? Now?"

"He was just pronounced DOA at the infirmary. Apparently a heart attack or a massive stroke. There will be an autopsy, of course."

Mooney's pulse was racing. With Webster and the Chechens dead, he now knew of only two obvious targets for the Mechanic, himself and his new boss in Miami.

"Could it have been foul play? Who . . . who was with him when he died?"

"One of our oldest trustees, a man named Skokie Jim Pettaway was escorting him back to population, but he had just come from a meeting with one of his lawyers."

After a few seconds, Mooney shrugged and sighed deeply. "Well, Warden, I guess our business is concluded. Thanks anyway."

The men shook hands and moved in opposite directions.

Just as Warden Sprague's hand touched the brass knob of his office door, the agent remembered an item he had provided once from his sources in central Europe. It was a vegetable alkaloid called ricin that in sufficient concentration could be absorbed through the skin in less than three minutes causing a death very like a heart attack and leaving almost no trace. He asked another question.

"Warden, do you happen to know the name of his lawyer?"

"As a matter of fact, yes, I've got his papers right here. He hasn't been here before, but he's from Webster's San Francisco firm." He consulted the forms.

"William S. Burr," he answered and gave Mooney a quizzical look. For some reason, Mooney seemed more than a little rattled by the prisoner's death.

"Is he still here?"

"No," the warden replied. "We tried to notify him but he had just cleared outer security."

"Burr," Mooney repeated. "B-U-R-R, Burr?"

"Yes, why?"

"Perry Mason."

"Huh?"

"Perry Mason, the old TV series. I was just wondering what Raymond Burr's real name was."

Sprague was puzzled by the exchange, but the door closed before he could ask about it. Agent Mooney was in a hurry.

Chapter 11

The dust and steamy sunshine smothered the truck and rail yard under a blanket of heat. A revolving electronic sign they had passed on the way indicated that the temperature was 103 degrees. It could be felt almost as a living thing, its hot, moist breath nearly void of oxygen. Though the area was in the midst of a month long drought, the accompanying humidity rarely dipped below the 80 percent mark and the mercury stayed likewise in the nineties until well into the night.

The metal building where the terminal's general manager and foreman had their offices was on an elevated platform that was reached by three flights of metal stairs. Gaby and Alex Pushkin accompanied an overweight Memphis policeman to the top.

The cop's name was Detective Lieutenant Frank Gallagher. Because the case had only recently become of interest to Washington and beyond, it was thought that a police representative would be more helpful than local FBI. He was a bulky man of medium height with hair colored more salt than pepper, wearing a poorly fitting tan suit improved not at all by the amount of moisture it currently held. Even on the ground he had moved with an implied fatigue. On the stairs he looked like a coronary in the making. Once inside the door and the blessed relief of the air conditioning, he let out a deep sigh and wiped his brow with a wrinkled white handkerchief.

"The heat is unusual?" asked Lieutenant Pushkin.

"Not really," the detective answered with a rueful glance. "This is just in the high normal range."

"I did not know Memphis Tennessee is so far to the South," said Pushkin.

"Son," the cop drawled without a trace of humor, "this time of year you got to go north to burn in hell."

Dave Wilson, the general manager, was expecting them and waved to them when they arrived and signaled that he would be finishing his phone call momentarily. Behind his desk, a large picture window overlooked a series of switched railroad tracks and two of the huge machines that lifted the metal containers from the roadway to the flatcars and vice versa. From another window hundreds of the metal boxes used for bulk shipments could be seen singly and in geometrically arranged rows, some of them stacked two and three layers high.

Wilson hung up the phone and shook hands with Gallagher. Meeting the other two, he reserved his biggest smile for Agent Bernard.

Turning back to Gallagher he said, "As I told you, I have no problem cooperating, but the container you came to see is not here any more—hasn't been for five days."

"I understand that," said Gallagher, "but Lieutenant Pushkin here wants to see the murder scene for himself."

As he spoke he shrugged slightly and rolled his eyes as if Gaby and Alex couldn't see. He wanted it made clear that he was not the cause of disrupting the manager's day.

Wilson looked at his watch.

"Okay, okay. But it's way the hell at the far end in the holding area. You'll have to take your car. I can't get everybody in my cart."

Gallagher agreed and listened carefully to the directions. Then all four descended the stairs again with Wilson going ahead in his modified golf car.

On the way back to the unmarked police car, the Memphis policeman and his two visitors hugged the shade provided by the metal building. Waves of heat assaulted them from all sides.

The Russian was wearing the same dark gray suit that Gaby had seen on his arrival. It was thick and almost painful to look at in the natural sauna of the yard. Sweat ran down his face and through the open coat she could see the plain white shirt clinging wetly to him.

"You should have worn something else," Gaby said to him.

He looked hurt. "At home I must wear uniforms. This is my only suit. You are wearing a suit. Are you not hot?"

She looked down as if noticing her clothing for the first time and shrugged.

"I told you I'm from New Orleans," she said.

Pushkin opened his mouth to ask how that served to selectively lower the temperature for her, but Agent Bernard had already retreated to the air-conditioned car.

Gallagher followed the route he had been given, leaving the acres of paved area bustling with trucks and heavy equipment. In a twisting path they navigated the broad steel canyons formed by rows of oblong boxes of uniform height but ranging in length from 20 to 48 feet. It was several minutes before the big Crown Victoria pulled up and parked next to a shortened truck trailer. It was dirty white with the logo of a blue eagle on the side. They sat for a moment with the engine running and the cool air blowing, unwilling to confront the heat again until they saw Wilson arrive by some other path. Shortly he appeared in his open golf cart with a clipboard in his hands.

The smells of hot machinery, diesel fuel and thousands of cargoes assaulted them on the gravel path. Wilson had parked at an intersection of the makeshift road and when they walked there, they could see that they were in the right place. Pushkin had insisted on touring the crime site where the Russian Malenkov was killed. As they had been told, the actual container in which he had been found was gone, but there was another identical rectangular shape nearby with the identifier of the Molotov Corporation. The four of them gathered in its shadow. This time coats were left in the car.

Gaby noted that a chain link fence marking the edge of the yard property was only a few steps beyond the last container.

Wilson seemed to be leering a bit at Agent Bernard. Pushkin interrupted whatever unseemly thoughts he might be having with a question.

"Where was the victim's body, exactly? I mean where was the truck and the position of the body?"

Wilson didn't have to walk far. After fifteen steps he looked back and forth a few times to be sure of his bearings and turned back to the Russian.

"Right here," he said, holding both his arms out away from his body in a straight line. "The box was in this position, parallel with that one there and only one layer. The body was in the far corner away from the door. There was nothing stacked on top because of the accident."

"What accident?" Gaby asked.

He consulted his paperwork.

"Last Tuesday, it was, one of the equipment operators was working with a lift truck in the south yard and it was a minute or two after five. No big deal really. That ol' boy was in such a big damn hurry to get off that he clipped the corner of this box here on the way around it—bent the corner bracket and ripped a big gash in it. We covered the opening with a tarp, but they sent the guy right away. Never saw anybody get to an accident scene so fast and they had to come from Atlanta or somewhere, too—must have flown him in here on the next flight!"

Pushkin wandered off into the glare, shuffling slowly around the spot indicated by Wilson, staring at the ground.

Gaby felt obligated to fill in with some questions of her own.

"By 'the guy' they sent, I assume you mean the victim."

"Yeah, the Russki."

Gaby flinched at the way he said it, making it sound like 'Roozkey', but if Pushkin was annoyed he didn't show it.

"I've got the jacket right here," said Lieutenant Gallagher. He was reading from a manila folder. "It says he was killed outside and shoved partway through the hole made by Mr. Wilson's employee."

"Strangled, wasn't he?" Gaby asked.

"No, actually his neck was broken but that was withheld from the press."

"Was there a sign of a fall of some kind?"

"The paperwork says no," Gallagher answered, "but I wasn't on the initial investigation."

Pushkin spoke loudly as he toured the spot where the body was found, "Mister Wilson, how long after the murder was the truck, the container, moved?"

"Almost immediately. The cargo owner has paid us to store a lot of these containers—until recently we had a bunch of them. So when they showed up with wheels and a driver we released it right after the police did, which was the day after the murder, I think. Strictly speaking it wasn't the murder site so they didn't make them keep it around once they vacuumed and dusted it."

Gaby asked, "What was the victim doing here, exactly, Mr. Wilson? Do you know? Am I missing something?"

"He was an internal adjuster as I understand it. We thought at first that he worked for the insurance company that the freight owners used, but I called the company of record and they never heard of him. He worked for the owner, I guess."

"You mean Molotov?" Gaby asked.

"No, the cargo owner. Vista Imports. I know it's them because they also have freight in that other one." He gestured at the end unit of a double-stacked row of steel boxes.

"And what was the cargo, please?" Pushkin asked from across the way.

"On that one the original manifest out of Korea said machine tools," he replied. "It was mislabeled."

"Oh? You checked because of the accident?" The question came from Gaby again. She was beginning to become interested in what she had first interpreted as an eccentric waste of time to further international relations.

"No, I would never have noticed except that at the time of the accident a box fell out of there. I remember I was surprised because these Molotov boxes had been sitting here so long I assumed before looking at the papers that they were all stranded empties waiting for a load to be shipped home. When we saw what was in that box we looked in and found more lampshades. Korean lampshades."

"Lampshades? You're sure?"

"Hell, yeah! I'm not supposed to be responsible for unsealed freight around here but I didn't want anybody thinking that I couldn't tell the difference between $300,000 worth of machinery and some cheap Korean shades. I still can't believe someone else hadn't already caught it."

"Did Malenkov say anything about a substitution?"

"I think the security guard was the only one he talked to at all—pretty thick accent he says and the guy didn't say more than a dozen words to him. Not only that, but the claim hasn't been filed yet because I spoke to the underwriter this morning."

"Maybe they're embarrassed to put in a claim for lamps when they insured machines," said Gaby.

"Yeah, maybe," Gallagher sighed with sweaty impatience. "Listen, are y'all about done here? No offense, Agent Bernard but they told you there was nothing to see here."

Pushkin leaned up against the shady side of one of the aluminum walls wiping his brow and the back of his neck with a large white handkerchief. He murmured something softly, confident that he could curse in his own language with impunity.

"Officer, you cannot be more miserable than I. Until now I have never encountered conditions that made me pine for the winter in Siberia," he said to Gallagher and then turned toward Wilson.

"Can we open the other car?"

Wilson gave him a look of incredulity.

"With a federal warrant and an ICC inspector present. I'd be surprised if they recognized the need for that, though. And, I'm with the lieutenant. If y'all are through with me, I'd like to get back to the office, too."

"Yes", said Gallagher with an envious look as the man walked back to the cart, "I think we can find our way out from here." Wilson waved quickly at him and was gone in the cloud spun up by his electric Club Car. Before the dust could reach him, Gallagher turned down the row where they had parked.

"I'll be in the car if y'all need anything," he called out. Shortly after the sound of the door closing they heard the engine start and then idle down as the air conditioner kicked in.

Gaby still leaned against the shady side of the other Molotov container and watched silently as Pushkin continued to scour the ground with his eyes, stooping occasionally to pick up some item invisible to her. Invariably he had discarded the nit after a moment of scrutiny. At those times his attention was striking in its intensity. It was the same focus she felt so strongly when it was directed at her. His voice and those ice-floe-colored eyes. There was a near-hypnotic quality in the combination. Facing away from her in a crouch, ever more of his cheap muslin shirt clung to his skin revealing the contours of the muscular back underneath. *Damn!* Gaby was getting that feeling again and she didn't like it—or more accurately, she resisted it.

"Hey, Rasputin!" she called out. "Aren't we done here?"

Even though he was turned away, she could see his cheek widen into a grin, but at that moment he held up one finger in her direction for silence and stooped once again to the ground. After a second he stood again and began walking toward Gaby, producing his handkerchief again, which he used to wipe off more of the newly accumulated perspiration.

"I am pleased you have begun to see me in a personal way. Thank you."

"What do you mean? I was just observing that you had a kind of 'Mad Monk' look crawling around on the ground like that."

"Ah! But that was not the true name of the great lover of the Romanovs. Jealous people called him that to criticize Alexandra and ridicule Nicholous. In my language the word means—ah, 'debauched one'. He was a charismatic man who believed in redemption through sin."

She noted that he was staring again—a detestable little look from under arched eyebrows clearly meant to indicate irony.

"It was my hope that you were making an offer," he said.

Gaby raised a hand to move her hair away from her face, forgetting for the moment that it was pulled back with combs and secured with an elastic band. It was a characteristic mannerism of embarrassment or self-consciousness for her to twist the hair at her temples between a thumb and forefinger. When she realized there was no lock to twist, she covered the gesture by changing it into a casual tug at the tiny golden sphere in her earlobe.

"We should get back inside, Mister Pushkin. The heat is having unforeseen effects on your mind. Did you find something or are you in the midst of a stroke?"

He laughed his big baritone laugh. It was a hearty, musical rumble delivered all the way from his diaphragm.

"Rasputin should have met you first", he said. "First he would have forsaken the gold of the Czars to pursue you and then he would have gained wisdom and humility from the encounter."

Gaby played with the collar of her blouse as another surrogate before forcing the hand to remain at her side and adopting what she hoped was a completely indifferent expression.

"Yes", he said finally in answer to her question. "I did find something, or I may have. I don't know for sure."

He flattened out the damp handkerchief in one hand and placed a shiny sliver about three inches long in the middle of it for Gaby to inspect.

"What is it?" she asked.

"I am unsure. Can you have it tested?"

"Of course, but what do you think it is?"

"It may be a piece of the damaged container in which the body was found. You can see on this side what appears to be the color of paint used for the other one."

"What kind of test would you want for it?"

"Metallurgy. I should like to know what is its exact composition."

She hefted it. The piece made almost no impression on the palm of her hand.

"It's got to be aluminum, doesn't it? It feels too light to be anything else."

"Could be," Aleksandr said.

"And what would that prove about the murder?"

"Perhaps nothing," he admitted. "Certainly nothing if the murder happening in this place was coincidence and nothing more."

Gaby frowned. "I'm afraid if you want me to send a piece of a truck off to the lab you're going to have to give me a little more in the way of reasons. It's obvious to me that you know something about this, or think you do. If I understand the situation properly, this chunk was already on the ground—off the container before the murder of Malenkov ever took place, so it's really not obvious to me why we should care."

"Please," he said, "in time. For now we have only speculation. It is better if I, as the guest of your government, am the only one doing the speculating. If the investigation goes the way I think—the way Colonel Dashenko predicts, you and I will both benefit. We will share in the credit. Believe me, in many ways I am as much at night as you are, but I have learned to trust what he tells me."

Pushkin seemed once again to make Agent Bernard the concentrated focus of his universe for a moment. He wrapped the metal piece in his damp handkerchief, folded it into an unwieldy ball and pressed it into her hand with theatrical solemnity.

"Your patience—please?" he begged again at her doubting expression.

"In the dark," she said after a moment.

"I beg your pardon."

"You said 'at night'. It's 'in the dark'. It means I don't know what the heck is going on. You're keeping me in the dark."

Pushkin nodded.

"You think the container itself," she consulted the side of the neighboring panel, "that particular Molotov box, had something to do with the murder?"

"I am very sorry to seem so secretive, but truly it will all be explained to you as soon as I can. One truth is the one to which you already refer. The metal you are holding may be nothing to us. In fact, it very likely is just what you would expect. But if it is not, we will be on our way to a discovery for both of us—the kind of large scale investigation that could—I believe the phrase is 'make' a career."

She considered a few possibilities.

"Okay, I'll send this in now, but you have to make a deal. Regardless of what they find, no matter if this case is a big international story or the ramblings of a chess-playing alcoholic, you will tell me everything you know or suspect about it when the results come back. I mean it. Everything! I'm a professional too and I don't care for the idea of holding your coat for you while you fight the bad guys. Is it a deal?"

"Holding my coat?" His serious expression departed. He took her elbow and began to retrace their path. "I agree, of course. Now, let us return to the air conditioning where you can send your package to the laboratory and I may breathe again."

Chapter 12

Gaby finished her report quickly and sent it to Metcalf by e-mail. Nothing in her expensive liberal arts education had taught her to embellish enough of the details of their efforts to make them sound like progress. The metallurgy lab request in particular was impossible to explain since Pushkin hadn't even given her a suspicion to cite. What were they doing anyway but trailing behind local detectives with more experience at crime scene investigation than either she or Alex Pushkin had. The only advantage they could possibly enjoy was one of perspective—the ability to put these factual pieces into a larger puzzle.

Perspective. That was something she did not intend to lose with Alex either. She was being forced by circumstance to spend several days with a very attractive man who had been almost relentless in his attentions toward her. For his part he seemed able to shift flawlessly between his chosen roles. When there was something that might be substantive to do, there he was crawling around in the dirt for clues. But as soon as he was done with that he was asking personal things about her or—or dammit, just being funny and charming. Gaby was not certain that she could make that kind of abrupt transition and more to the point, she was fairly sure that it would be dangerous to try. She told herself that she was glad she had refused when he wanted to have dinner together again.

At that moment there was a knock at the door. When she opened it, there was Aleksandr Pushkin wearing khaki shorts and a black t-shirt with a big Elvis picture on the front. He had a big smile, a brown paper bag in his hand and some papers under one arm.

"When you told me you were too tired to go out to eat, I thought I would bring food in and we could go over some more of the Malenkov depositions from the first murder."

Gaby rubbed her eyes with one hand to cover the smile that was building on her own face. Relentless.

"Come in Alex," she said. "What have you got there?"

"Hamburgers. It is very American food, yes?"

"No. When we sent *McDonald's* to Moscow it was only a propaganda ploy to corrupt your system. Now I can tell you the truth. Only Americans too lazy to feed themselves real food eat hamburgers. I'm not going to pretend that I never eat them, but not tonight."

He looked contrite. "But you are tired."

She looked down at the paper sack and saw grease already soaking through.

"Not *that* tired."

"You don't get out in the sun much do you?" she added, looking pointedly at his muscular but pale legs. If she had hoped to embarrass him, the effort failed.

"I ski when I can," he replied with a grin, "but this is rarely done in short pants."

"Anyway, those papers you brought are in Russian?" she asked.

"Yes."

"So you would have to read every word to me and I would have nothing to contribute even if you hadn't already read them a dozen times."

"I could get your reaction to some of the testimony?" Even he sounded dubious now that he had heard it stated out loud.

"That's your story?" she asked, with what she assumed was a coy smile.

"Yes. What do you mean?"

For a moment Gaby had become the incisive, cross-examining attorney that her father had envisioned.

"Let's be honest for a moment, Alex."

"Good."

"You brought these things to my room not because you thought I would go hungry and not because we could make progress in the case but because you wanted to spend time with me. Correct?"

He chuckled softly.

"I must admit that I find it difficult to disagree with your conclusions."

Gaby paused to weigh what she wanted to do against what was the proper thing to do, even though she had already made up her mind.

"All right, we'll spend the evening together, but not here. Take those papers and put them away. Then for God's sake, take that sack and throw it out. Then wait for me in the lobby. I have some shorts in my bag too. You want a little bit of America, I'm going to show you some."

Ten minutes later Gaby and Alex were walking down a rather unpresentable alley less than a block away. The temperature was still high but almost pleasant compared to their experience of the day. Also they were now dressed more appropriately for it.

"Where are we going?" he asked.

"First we're going to eat some real Memphis food in a real Memphis place. This is The Rendezvous. I came to town as a kid and this is the first place we went to eat."

It was growing late but the sun was still relatively high in the sky, throwing bright patches across buildings they could see in the distance. Alex had walked right by the restaurant entrance without noticing it as he looked around and Gaby had to call him back. She liked the way he moved as he turned and the way the big muscles of his calves worked under the too-fair skin when he walked, although the fact that she noticed these things continued to irritate her a little.

They descended a flight of foot-worn steps to the basement where the hostess station was and asked for a table. Like the steps themselves the surroundings gave the appearance of many years of enthusiastic use. To be kind, the restaurant is rustic, even considering its location, consisting of a series of atmospheric rooms on multiple levels all of which have walls of exposed brick. Decoration consists largely of celebrities' pictures and an eclectic mix of memorabilia from local events, sports teams and advertisements dating back to long before Gaby was born.

It was mid week and still early so they were soon seated past the bar in a room on the basement level. Their table was nestled under an 8 by 10 black and white photo of Elvis on a motorcycle and a poster with the 1954 season schedule of the old Memphis Chicks minor league baseball team.

Though there was a lot of room elsewhere, the room they were in was filling up quickly and was very noisy already. Alex was pleased.

"Thank you for bringing me here," he said.

"Oh, we're just getting started," Gaby replied.

"What do you recommend to eat?"

"When you come in the door, you have already made your selection," Gaby replied.

Alex shrugged, smiling and Gaby looked around for their waiter. After a full minute, she caught the eye of a black man wearing a short white coat and a bored expression.

"We'll have a slab for two and a pitcher of Miller," she said to the waiter when he sauntered over. He mumbled another question. Gaby thought she heard 'cheese plate' and something else, but she refused whatever it was and the waiter gave her a disdainful look and yelled out twice to somebody called 'Larry' who was apparently across the room somewhere, then he wandered off.

"Have you ever had ribs, Alex?" she asked when the man was gone.

"I am not certain that I know what you mean."

"Never mind. It's not a lot less greasy than a burger, but it's a lot better, I promise."

It had become a bit noisy for quiet talk, so Pushkin occupied himself with gazing around at the decorations and the people and giving Gaby a look that made her uncomfortable. She didn't find it all that unpleasant, but was relieved when the waiter returned with a long slab of dry pork ribs and two paper plates with baked beans and slaw. Alex looked questioningly from Gaby to the plates as she arranged their dinner for them.

"Like this," she said and tore one of the ribs off with her fingers. When she took a bite she made a little yummy sound. The taste was just as she remembered from fifteen years before. Often they can be too dry and chewy but these had come out perfectly.

Alex did likewise and nodded eagerly. Memphis food was a hit with Russian officialdom. At first he was hesitant to lick his fingers between servings, but Gaby assured him that it was de rigueur among rib fanciers. As much as she was enjoying the food, she was enjoying his reaction even more. The astonishing thing was that the Russian officer from Interpol with the cheesy Elvis T-shirt on looked absolutely at home in a rib joint in Memphis Tennessee.

When they finished, Gaby refused the offer of dessert for both of them, enduring another dubious look from the waiter and picking up the check. She insisted on paying for the whole thing and answered Pushkin's objections by explaining the use of the wet wipes in foil packages that were brought. He finally acknowledged that the check was gone with a sigh and joined Gaby in the lane between tables that led to the door.

"Excellent!" he said, meaning the whole experience.

In a few minutes they emerged into the now-dark alley and the sounds of Beale Street were filtering over from three blocks away.

"Perhaps we could go to a club?" Alex suggested, but Gaby had other plans that did not include a Blues bar and sexy music until all hours.

"No, the hotel had a notice about a game in town tonight. Have you ever seen a baseball game, Alex?"

He shook his head, as she expected.

"Well you can't get more American than that."

The Memphis triple A farm team was playing Albuquerque and tickets were available at the stadium only a short walk away. Gaby bought programs and Alex bought a beer for himself and a Coke for her and found that they had pretty good seats down the third base line.

Redbird Stadium in Memphis may be the best ballpark in the minor leagues. It reminded Gaby of Camden Yard in Baltimore where she had seen two Oriole games last year.

She explained all you can tell about baseball in a paragraph to Alex and laughed good-naturedly at some of his increasingly complex questions as the game wore on.

They adopted Memphis as their team, naturally, and cheered enthusiastically for the Redbirds at every opportunity. Between every inning there were silly entertainments or giveaways of one kind or another sponsored by local radio stations. One involved a footrace to first base between a four-year-old girl and the team mascot in a ridiculous bird outfit who mysteriously stumbled and fell two steps from the bag, awarding the girl's family a dinner for four. At the seventh inning stretch they sang 'Take Me Out to the Ballgame' in a loud voice, a laughing Alex always one lyric behind as he watched her lips to divine the next word. In the end the home team won 5-4 on a run scoring double in the eighth.

On the walk back to the hotel Alex casually put his arm around her as he leaned down to tell her again what a wonderful time he had. Just as casually Gaby walked out of the light embrace.

"Me too, Alex," she said. "But let's not forget why we are here."

"You said you would not talk of business tonight."

"And I didn't. But the night is over now."

"It need not be," he said.

"Alex . . ." she began and then couldn't decide where to take her statement. She decided to redirect instead.

"Look, we have covered all the evidence in the Malenkov murder and we're no closer to The Mechanic than we were in Washington. Do you have any idea where we go from here except back to headquarters?"

Alex sighed his reluctance at this return to the businesslike Gaby instead of the playful companion he had enjoyed for the last several hours.

"I propose to go back to the murder scene once more."

"For goodness' sake why?"

"I would like to examine the other Molotov container in that yard more closely."

"No. Absolutely not. We need something of substance to show them in Washington and you've already been told that you just can't break the seal on trucks like that and search them just as a fishing expedition."

Alex smiled.

"You are a treasury of American idiom—among other things," he said. "I would hope that the report from your lab will be available by the time we could examine the other."

Gaby shook her head in exasperation but she really didn't feel it. They talked about smaller subjects on the way back to the hotel and Pushkin waited patiently.

The elevator door had already opened on their floor when gaby turned back to the case at hand.

"Why are you so fixated on the other box anyway? The first one was the crime scene."

"The coincidence of the names 'Molot' and 'Molotov' is too great," he said. "There must be more than appears on the surface. The word means 'hammer' in Russian."

"As in hammer and sickle, like the Soviet emblem?"

"Yes. Two brothers, both accountants, both killed and associated with Molot in some form."

Gaby wrinkled her brow and pursed her lips for a second.

"But you already said that you don't believe that The Mechanic killed the other Malenkov?"

"No, in fact I am certain that he did not. The commission of the crime is more closely associated in a practical way with the two deaths by suffocation that I told you about. However the reason behind the Malenkov deaths is that Molotov box. I am equally certain of that."

"All right. We'll do as you say, but I'm telling you if we make no progress tomorrow there's nothing we can do but go back. Believe me, I don't want to do that. My career as a field agent and investigator will be over after three days and it'll be back to the salt mines for me."

Alex laughed again.

"Gaby, you are wonderful," he said. "And this is all going to work out. Trust me."

They had reached their rooms by this point. She put her key card in the slot and the door opened.

"I hope you're right, Alex. Tomorrow you can show me."

Gaby stood at the threshold for a second. Alex seemed to be hesitating.

"Thank you again for coming with me tonight. I had a marvelous time. Good night."

Alex said good night and she shut the door almost in his face. Gaby flipped on the entrance light by her hand and stood there until she heard him move away from the door. When she knew he was gone she leaned against the door.

'Trust me' he had said. Could she really do that? There was no choice but to follow his lead on the investigation. Metcalf must be delighted that his predictions of futility were proving true so far. She knew that the only reason he hadn't sent Cannon down here was that he didn't want his protégé associated with a useless excursion. How could she avoid another negative report if Alex didn't know where the investigation was going either?

And how about personal trust? Gaby remained defensive toward him though she wasn't sure why. Perhaps she couldn't discount the notion that she was still being manipulated. He was such a good listener. Most of the men Gaby had known—even the ones she liked—hell, even the few she had slept with—were far more interested in talking about themselves while Alex had charmed most of her life story out in rapt attention. On the other hand, he was going to be gone in a matter of days regardless of what kind of relationship they had developed.

It would be better, Gaby decided, if they had sent that portly, female, Ukrainian investigator after all or maybe just someone more like Leonid Brezhnev.

Chapter 13

"It's only a precaution, Doctor Wallace, but we feel strongly that Matthew should be in protective custody until the criminal or criminals responsible for the deaths of his mother and sister are caught."

Matt Gordon fidgeted, shifting his weight and casting flickering glances back and forth between his Aunt Katherine and her unexpected visitors. They were in the front room of her midtown Memphis home, confronted by three men in dark suits, one of whom was explaining why they had to take her nephew away. The woman's bright emerald eyes were edged in red and her normally excellent posture was rounded.

Katherine Wallace had married far too young, she now admitted, at age eighteen and divorced at twenty-three when she was still in graduate school. In the intervening ten years she had had exactly two relationships involving physical intimacy and they had both ended badly. Though she proclaimed a lack of interest at achieving another, her assertions that she was devoid of any physical vanity and would never consider coloring her hair were weakening now that she was experiencing the first encroachment of gray in what had always been dark red tresses. Twice a month, with almost clocklike regularity she maintained a passionless relationship with a divorced orthodontist who shared space in her office suites. The only real emotional exchanges in her recent life had taken place with either her older sister or her own psychoanalyst, both of whom had offered the observation that she really didn't seem to like men very much in general. Each member of Valerie's family had become vitally important to her and Matt was her favorite. Without thinking about it Kate adopted a protective stance with her nephew. In speaking with the visitors, she held the boy nearly behind her.

The spurious 'agent' Mooney was using the same FBI identification he had produced at Leavenworth. It said his name was Turner. His associates were two of the more presentable members of his benefactor's organization in Florida but were a lot less believable.

"Your Dad, Matt, did he say anything to you about . . . anything? Did he tell you anything unusual after your Mom died?"

The boy's eyes darted from the silent men accompanying the agent to his aunt. Then he looked at the carpet and shrugged.

"I don't understand," Katherine said. "I don't understand who could possibly have wanted to hurt Val and Alicia and I certainly don't see why they should want Matt."

Mooney made a show of his reticence.

"I can explain some of it to you," he said finally. "But Matt, how about you and Agent Smith going back to your room to pack up a toothbrush and a few things for a little trip while we talk?"

The boy didn't move until he got a hesitant nod from his Aunt. When Matt and the 'agent' were gone, Mooney closed the room's paneled sliding doors behind them. The heavy curtains were drawn and the room was rather dim with one table lamp and the afternoon sun through the front door's lacy sheers providing the only light. The furnishings were antiques with ornate fabric designs from roughly the same period as the house itself. Delicately formed figurines and bric-a-brac dotted the bookcase and dark cherry claw-foot tables. Mooney strolled slowly back to the sofa and took Katherine Wallace's elbow, pulling her gently backward. He was charming, if a little patronizing, and had a commanding grandfatherly manner.

"Please, let's sit for a moment," he said. "This is going to be a little hard."

She was seated very formally, smoothing the front of her outfit and now making her spine even straighter than normal in preparation for whatever unpleasantness might follow. Mooney joined her on the sofa, leaving the third agent standing unmoving at the door.

There was a pause and a fresh sigh suggesting again how reluctant he was to share the information.

"We are positive that the assassin who placed the bomb at your sister's home will now try to harm Matt."

"So you do know who did it?"

"Yes. I'm sorry to have to tell you this way, but it was the man you knew as George Gordon, Matt's father."

She moved backward abruptly and blinked twice as if she had been struck.

"What? You can't mean that. George? My brother-in-law? You're crazy."

"No ma'am, I'm not, but he apparently is, crazy I mean. I know this is really more your field, but he did disappear suddenly at the funeral leaving you with no explanation and custody of Matt, did he not?"

Katherine stared stupidly at the man as if he had suddenly begun to speak an alien tongue. Without conscious volition, her head was moving in back and forth. No way.

"I, uh—he left a note, sort of. I admit a few times in the past, he exhibited some bipolar personality traits, but certainly nothing as severe as the kind of psychosis you suggest. I'm sure it was just the stress of the moment."

"No ma'am. You don't understand what I mean—not entirely. He just went back to his normal work. Two more bodies were found in the trunk of a car out of state that we're sure are the work of Matt's father."

A variety of facial expressions ranging from angry to dumbfounded fought for ascendancy. Katherine tried to laugh but it didn't come off.

"Bodies in a trunk? George Gordon went from little league coach to maniacal bomber and serial murderer in the space of a day? Absurd!"

"There was nothing sudden about it, I'm afraid. He has murdered at least twenty high profile individuals over the years—more than half of those since his marriage to Valerie. There are dossiers open in his pseudonym all over the world. He is known as The Mechanic, probably the most successful murderer for hire in the experience of law enforcement. After the murder of his family I would add 'most ruthless' to that assessment."

"Absurd," she said again.

Katherine Wallace's eyes widened progressively as Mooney continued with the story of his assassin. Since he had dispatched the Mechanic on most of those jobs and collected most of the money afterwards, he was in a position to provide an impressive level of detail to the Gothic horror tale. He was succeeding in making it very real to Katherine Wallace. The fist in her lap repetitively clenched and released the material of her skirt. Beginning with the murder of a mob boss and ending with an explosion aboard a bus, the man wove a convincing tapestry of deceit. Like all who are similarly gifted, Mooney understood that the very best lies are mostly true and his knowledge of the Mechanic gave him a great deal of latitude. At the end he placed his hand over the top of hers.

"I'm very sorry to have to tell you all this, ma'am," he added with bowed head.

Doctor Wallace pulled her hand from underneath his and rose abruptly, withdrawing to the far side of the room.

"He's too old for all this," she countered. It was a weak argument, but she said it anyway. "George is no spring chicken you know—for wandering the world and doing all this kind of . . . stuff."

Agent Mooney reached for something on the coffee table. Once Spider had pointed him in the right direction it was easy to build an impressive file using Agency resources. The man who had existed as a phantom for over thirty years suddenly had some much more factual entries in his record thanks to Mooney's personal experience.

"He was born Michael Edward Hogan in Columbus Georgia. Here is his high school graduation picture and here is a picture of him in Da Nang, Vietnam. Do you recognize him?"

Curiosity drew her back to Mooney's side.

As she looked at the photos she said, "George was never in the army. We talked several times about his time in Canada waiting for the amnesty. He was very specific about his job in Mississauga and his apartment. It looks a little like him, but . . ."

"Naturally his story would be good. He's been doing this all his adult life. We've checked his fingerprints. Believe me it's the same guy."

"And this Michael Hogan was the assassin you spoke of?" Katherine asked softly.

Mooney looked at his Russian assistant stationed by the door before he continued. Even for Mooney, condemning an innocent woman to death was not something to be done lightly and this knowledge would most certainly be fatal.

"Yes," he replied. "Even in the Army, yes. He was one of the finest in Special Forces but he was lost shortly after that picture was taken. His whole platoon was wiped out on a classified mission of assassination. Hogan was assumed dead but we now know that he deserted through Cambodia and Thailand. He just continued his profession in civilian life under a lot of names. In police and intelligence circles he became famous, or infamous, years ago. Now he is more of a legend. Everyone knows him simply as The Mechanic."

"This is just too crazy. Even if you're not as wrong as I think you are, none of that explains killing his own family—and with a bomb, yet!"

"As I said, this is really more in your line, but there is some anecdotal evidence to suggest that he is schizoid in the extreme—a likely Multiple Personality Disorder. Police records suggest that he suffered a good deal of physical abuse as a child. He may not even be aware of what he is doing. You already said you noticed things about him which were out of the ordinary."

"No. Well, yes, but nothing like this. I know such things happen all the time on television, but do you know how rare MPD really is? A lot of professionals don't believe it exists at all."

Katherine opened her mouth to add something but just then there was a tap at the door. When it slid open, Matt stood holding a weathered red nylon backpack with a Poke`mon logo and looking about half of his nearly twelve years.

"Aunt Kate, do I gotta go?" Matt asked in a tiny voice. The fresh tragedy looked at her out of those green eyes just too similar to his mother's—in fact even more like his grandfather's, Kate thought. The Wallace eyes had always been the family's most consistent genetic marker. Nearly breaking down, she smoothed his hair and softly bit her lip. She transformed a sob into a cough and straightened his collar.

"'Have to go', Sweetie. Don't say it like that. And yes, I suppose it would be best if you went with these gentlemen. I don't think they're right, but it won't hurt anything to be on the safe side. Have you got my work number?"

Matt nodded. Mooney took a half step toward Katherine.

"Actually, Doctor Wallace I was going to leave Agents Smith and Johnson here to protect you, since this is the first place he will look for the boy."

"Excuse me?" she said. "That's a little too much. He wouldn't . . . nobody is after *me*."

"We can't be sure, Doctor. Please. I can't force you, of course," he added, with every intention of forcing her cooperation if necessary. His eyes darted back and forth between the boy and his aunt. "But remember," he said, "if it's about *his* family, we have no way of knowing how far the hostility will extend."

Trembling, Katherine refused to look at him. She adjusted little Hummel figurines on the mantel and listened to the resonant ticking of the old Seth Thomas clock until she felt Matt's eyes on her. She returned his pitiable stare as long as she could bear it.

Turning away again, she asked Agent Mooney, "How long?"

"One, two days at the most. We'll have caught him by then and even if we haven't, he will have moved on to, uh, another target."

A period of strained silence indicated her acquiescence.

"Come here, Matt. Give your Aunt Kate a big hug."

He dragged himself toward her, submitting blankly to whatever affection she chose to administer. She held him close for several seconds, tears welling in the corners of both eyes, then one more quick kiss and she was nudging him out the security door.

"Wait on the porch for just a minute, honey. I need just a second with Mister Turner."

Again he slouched along, neither resisting nor fully embracing the idea of movement. The white wrought iron door hissed shut behind him. The boy went over to stand by the old-fashioned porch swing, running his fingers over the many layers of paint on the ancient supporting chain. Katherine was standing at the opening and hurried the latch closed.

As it clicked, Katherine spun almost violently on Agent Turner/Mooney. Her voice was quavering but she backed him up a half-step with a finger in his chest.

"You listen to me," she said. "This boy—he's been through too much. You protect this poor boy—and I'm not just talking about bombs. Two days ago he lost his mother and sister. Yesterday, he was deserted by his father and now you want to tell him that the last member of his family is trying to hurt him physically. He has been acting very strangely. Do you hear me? Near to a breakdown! I mean it! When you get him in custody you get him a counselor—I know you people have them—and get him some help. He really didn't need any more stress right now."

"I completely agree," Mooney said when he recovered. "There will be plenty of help for him where he's going."

"Where will that be? How can I contact him?"

"I'm sorry Doctor, there won't be any contact in either direction. It's like Witness Protection. We'll be incommunicado. Even the local office will not acknowledge that he's there."

The woman lost her aggressive front to fear. "Just a quick phone call?"

"No ma'am. Sorry. It's only for a day or two."

Mooney gently moved her out of the way, squeezing her shoulder and smiling encouragement at her. He thanked her again, patting her hand in a gesture of counterfeit admiration, and exited.

Katherine stood at the door and watched the tall agent and her nephew of the beautiful, soulful eyes negotiate the concrete walkway, which had been cracked and almost perilously tilted for decades by the roots of a huge sycamore tree in her yard. They crossed the narrow strip of carefully trimmed Bermuda grass between the sidewalk and the curb, got in the first of two tan Buicks and drove off.

Unbidden, the image came into her head of the night almost a dozen years before when Matt had been born and how she had reacted. The teenaged version of herself had cried pitying tears for poor Valerie, who had endured nine months of ever-increasing torture and bloated humiliation only to deliver seven pounds of what Kate characterized as a red, hideously malformed, hairless entity resembling a capuchin monkey. Now she wanted to cry again. She excused herself from the company of the two bodyguards, went into her room and indulged the impulse.

Chapter 14

The Mechanic barely missed them. Less than an hour after Matthew Gordon was taken, the aged silver Thunderbird drove slowly by the intersection closest to Katherine Wallace's house.

Only the size of the trees had changed in this neighborhood since the homes were built in the twenties. Lots were narrow and deep. Houses invariably had large covered porches—some wrapped all the way down one side. A few had side portico 'carriage' entrances and even narrow garages built to resemble the carriage houses that preceded them by several decades. The picture of tranquil gentility was completed by the canopy of assorted deciduous trees whose branches stretched across the roadway to touch some thirty or more feet from its surface. Many of them had already been mature when the homes were built. The attendant shade and cooling breeze must have brought fifteen degrees of relief to the man slouched in the tan sedan that was now parked three doors down from the Wallace house.

The Mechanic saw just what he expected and turned into the service alley after a few more yards. Visitors to the area would not know that there was a narrow path leading the length of the block, which had allowed sanitation and other service personnel to do their jobs without bringing unnecessary disturbance into the ordered lives of the Jazz-Age gentry.

He parked behind the home opposite the tan car. When he had looked the rear of the house over carefully, he got out and strolled through the back yard and down the steeply sloped driveway. A navy blue canvas windbreaker was slung over his left arm, though he was naturally right-handed, and held forward almost over his belt buckle. The man in the car had just begun to turn his head to see who was walking in the street on the driver's side.

An observer would have noticed something, but it is unlikely that anyone would interpret the cues properly. The man in the street covered his mouth and appeared to cough. There was some vaporous movement around him—perhaps he was smoking. In the car, the head of the other man disappeared from sight. He seemed to have leaned over to look for something.

The Mechanic never broke stride, only glancing at the car before climbing the next driveway to get back to the alley and his own car. Some residents still used the alley for a rear exit and he didn't want to block anyone in and create a memory. Quickly he restarted the Thunderbird and pulled around to the street, in full view of the now unoccupied Buick.

By his usual standards, the Mechanic was in a confused and dangerous state. He had worked hard to assure himself that the events of the last few days had no effect on him personally, emotionally. After all, they were just people that George Gordon knew. That he had failed was something he had not yet conceded to himself, but was about to prove beyond doubt. Under normal circumstances he would never have made the mistake of assuming that Katherine was alone after he had dispatched the watcher in the tan car. He simply climbed the steps and knocked on the door. While he waited, he wrapped the windbreaker around something and tossed it onto the wide bench seat of the porch swing. The impact made it creak minutely as the ancient chains moved a few inches in either direction.

Katherine answered the door, her face an amalgam of so many emotions that at first her former brother-in-law saw none, her body motionless and stiff. Her brow was lined with stress and worry that made her appear older—made her look even more like her older sister.

"What is it?"

She said it as if he was a stranger, and of course he was. Katherine looked past his shoulder toward the tan car parked across the street.

"I came for Matt," said her visitor, puzzled by the question.

"He's gone. He's in protective custody. You . . . you missed them."

Katherine Wallace made no move to invite him into her home. Neither did she begin to close the door when the conversation would seem to have been at an end. At first they both just stared; he, trying to decipher her mood. It was the expression his wife had displayed whenever he was very late getting home. Angry? No. Jealous? No. *Betrayed.* Not quite, but that was closer to the mark. He wrinkled his face in a scowl. Something else was wrong. For some reason the sonorous ticking of the clock through the open door seemed unusually loud and distracting to George.

"Was it Mooney?" he asked. "Did he call himself Mooney?"

His sister-in-law said nothing and now chose to turn away from him and toward the fireplace. She tilted her head as she did so. Everyone does that, but something about the exact angle was very *Valerie*—Valerie when she thought she had done something wrong.

Tick-tock. Tick-tock. The hundred-year-old Waterbury gears clicked four more times while he arrived at two conclusions. First, Kate Wallace had been told something of George Gordon's secret life. Second, she had undoubtedly known of the armed man watching her house who could only have been there to take his life. Even so, he was still unaware of the second man as he pushed the door open a bit more and began to enter. He was simply seeking better information about Matt Gordon.

Tick-tock. Her back was still toward the front door. She was looking at the roman-numeraled white face on the mantel as if it were about to do something extraordinary.

Tick-tock. The Russian behind the heavy door cradled his antique Soviet automatic more firmly, positioning it at eye level. Softly he placed a fingertip of his other hand on the oak surface as it swung slightly more open. Nothing about his presence could have been transmitted to the newcomer, yet as his foot crossed the threshold the American reacted.

Tick. The Mechanic had an instant and painful flash that revealed his folly. His thought processes had been slow, his level of awareness far below what was normal for him, but his instincts were honed by years of violent self-interest.

Now less than an arm's length away, he shoved Katherine Wallace completely, brutally across the room and out of the way. Using her hands to soften the impact, she hit the brick façade of the fireplace and overturned the brass bucket with its cast iron poker and shovel. As The Mechanic dropped to the floor, a shot rang out, filling the space recently occupied by his head with fire and smoke. Rather than pushing the door backward against the wall as the Russian expected, he hooked a leg around its edge and pulled. At the same time he strained upwards for a handhold, capturing the sleeve of the man's gun arm with one hand. The explosion sounded again, its missile showering German ceramic couture over the hearth and its mistress.

When The Mechanic achieved a firm grip near the pistol, he was able to go to work on pressure points at the elbow. Quickly the weapon fell out of the man's limp fingers. With his free hand, the Russian had been clubbing his intended victim ineffectually for several seconds before he received the killer's full attention. Instead of the contact he anticipated, he was released and shoved forcefully into a dark corner by the bookcase. Slowly both combatants rose again to their full height. The Russian looked longingly at his gun, which was now within easy reach of the other man, who ignored it.

The Mechanic placed his feet at nearly right angles, left one forward, and bent his knees and arms slightly.

"What's your name?" he asked.

The man didn't answer. His eyes swept the room, searching.

After a few seconds The Mechanic raised an eyebrow and said, "Ah, Russki. I should be bored with killing you guys by now."

The Russian feinted with his left shoulder and launched two quick kicks at the smaller and older man, who dodged the first without moving his lower body at all and blocked the second with a flick of his left wrist.

There was a stirring at the fireplace. Katherine Wallace had been stunned by the collision but was coming around. For just an instant, the Mechanic turned his head microscopically toward her and his opponent charged. This time there was no chance of evasion. The Russian closed instantly and managed to get his hands around The Mechanic's throat and both men staggered almost to their knees. At first the Russian didn't know what to think because the shorter man was so passive, but the corded neck, which fit so well within his powerful fingers, seemed to be knit of steel cable. Then the Russian felt his own neck similarly held. His breath came in gasps. The assassin turned assassin's target was overmatched and he knew it.

"Get gun," croaked the Russian to the woman, too involved in the moment to attempt his rehearsed Midwestern accent. "He will kill us both."

Katherine Wallace shook her head, unsteady from the collision with the fireplace and terrified of the macabre dance she was watching. Locked in this deadly embrace the two men staggered slowly back and forth, upending antiques. Soft guttural noises like the breathless moans of lovers misrepresented the struggle. Katherine saw the Tokarev. She had never held a weapon of any kind, but she crawled toward this one and picked it up.

"Shoot him", hissed the man she thought to be an FBI agent. When she held the gun in an awkward grip and hesitated, his eyes screamed at her. "Now!" he spat out, and she pulled the trigger in their direction.

Neither her wrist nor arm was lined up in aiming and the recoil almost threw it out of her hand. From point blank range she had scored a clean miss.

Knowing he was near unconsciousness and almost ready to surrender to it, the Russian was completely surprised when, abruptly, he was released. The Mechanic dropped to one knee and out of his opponent's grip, but giving him a chance for a deep gasping breath. Then he spun the man around and got a new grip, his whole arm this time, around his neck.

Katherine fired again from six feet away. Her technique was no better but her luck improved a little. The Mechanic flinched, but instead of relinquishing his hold, he adjusted it minutely, stood, and lifted the Russian over his shoulder and off the ground by his neck. When the right position was reached, he jerked violently and there was a sickening crack, the suddenly limp body crashing to the floor. For a second Katherine was paralyzed with the horror of what she had seen; the grisly sound of a life's ending she had heard.

When her ex brother-in-law turned toward her again, she could see a spreading stain of bright red on his light blue shirt. She began to pull the trigger again but by then he was within reach and easily twisted the automatic away from her.

"God damn, Kate!" he said in an offended tone.

For a brief moment the two held each other's eyes. Katherine appeared dazed more than terrified as she tried to read his expression. He backed her up two steps until she fell into one of the wingback chairs. Shock froze her in place while The Mechanic went into her nearest bathroom.

The face of Turner's 'agent' was pointed in her direction, its unfocused stare seeming to follow her movement as she shifted in the chair. The only sound to disguise the monotonous cadence of the clock was the faint racket of unscientific search coming from the other room. Like a hollow wooden heartbeat it droned on. Katherine felt physically held by the lifeless gaze and tortured by the sound. Not squeamish by nature, seconds passed as she stared and felt a wail rising in her throat.

Abruptly the head that held the mesmerizing, vacant eyes was kicked out of position as George Gordon returned and saw where she was looking. He was stripped to the waist and held a green bath towel to the wound on his side. His chest and shoulders had already purpling bruises that showed the effects of the Russian's blows.

"You got a shirt around here that would fit me?" he asked.

In slow motion she lifted her gaze and shook her head from side to side but managed to look at the towel rather than directly into his eyes. He moved the terrycloth and revealed a square gauze pad already secured to his side. It had a horizontally elongated oval of red in the middle. He seemed to consider for a moment, casting his gaze briefly at the doors to the rest of the house. He dropped the towel in a chair and began to undress the body of the Russian. In a moment he had separated a white shirt from the cooling corpse and began to put it on. It was a size too big, but by the time he tucked it in his trousers and rolled up the sleeves it looked entirely acceptable.

When he was dealing with his shirttail he winced and cursed loudly. Katherine's sensibilities and fear for herself began to return.

"What are you going to do now?" she asked quietly.

He ignored the question.

"I'm not the bad guy here, Kate—at least not by comparison."

She said nothing.

"So I guess when you said he was in protective custody, you meant that some friends of this guy had taken Matt? That it?"

Katherine had known the man for over a decade as George Gordon. They had laughed and cried together—watched movies together—shared holiday meals and a love for Valerie Wallace. As from a great distance, she could even recall a vague attraction to the older man's short but powerful-looking body and what she believed was his quiet strength of character. That seemed so grotesque now. She thought longingly of escape but was unable to move from the spot. Her glance fell first on the front door and then on the overturned claw foot lamp table Valerie had helped her pick out on a trip to North Carolina. George set it back upright and replaced the miraculously unharmed lamp, straightening its shade. Then he picked up the business card from the floor.

George Gordon's face half smiled as he flipped the card back on the table. He sat down on the forward edge of the cushion on the other big brocaded wingback chair and put an elbow on his knee with his chin on his fist. His pose was a fair approximation of the Rodin sculpture.

"Doesn't matter what it says on there. It was Mooney all right. Can't really blame you for believing the guy," he said. "He's a professional liar."

"What are you going to do now?" she asked again. There was a trembling in her voice.

"What've you got to eat?"

"You're going to eat? Now?" She asked.

"I don't know, what've you got?"

Katherine shook her head. "I don't . . . Wait here and I'll see."

She made a move as if to rise toward the kitchen but George rose more quickly and took her by the elbow, guiding in that direction.

"That's okay, let's look together." When he noticed her expectant glance out the curtained glass of the front door, he added, "There won't be a third for lunch. The guy across the street can't make it."

"My God, uh . . ."

He said, "Kate, they were not from the government. They were here to kill me and would certainly have killed you when it was done. You can believe that or not. We're still going in the kitchen to find a bite to eat."

"G . . ." She began. "D-d-do I call you George?"

For a second he seemed confused by the question.

"You gotta call me something," he replied with a shrug.

Doctor Wallace kept a meticulous house in her spare time and had the capability but was not deeply committed to cooking or provisioning without a special occasion. In a few minutes she had provided the murderer with the same lunch she had made for his son—a peanut butter and jelly sandwich with a glass of milk.

George sat down and waited quietly at the plain table, idly toying with the salt and pepper shakers and a pencil with paper where Kate had been making out her shopping list.

When she was done, he made her sit next to him. She said nothing while he calmly ate the food. For her part Katherine Wallace could not look at him directly, risking only an occasional sideward peek. He seemed completely at ease while her trembling was getting worse. She hugged herself tightly with her arms under her breasts but couldn't stop the shaking.

When she could stand it no longer she blurted the same question again, rather louder than she intended.

"What will you do now?"

He licked his lips for a bit, sucking the peanut butter between his teeth before replying. He looked quizzical as if he didn't understand why she would ask such a question.

"I've got to go get the boy."

"You're planning to attack the FBI?"

"I told you, those guys were no more FBI than you are, not even the guy with the card."

"I saw their identification, G-George. I wouldn't let just anyone into the house. They were real."

"Yeah, I'm sure their ID was real good. Go in there and look at the label in that suit—if there is one. He's Russian. Unless I miss my guess, so was the guy in the car outside."

"And how about agent Turner?"

"He's an agent all right."

"I told you they showed me credentials."

"Kate, Kate. Has it occurred to you that the guy lying out there tried to put a hole in my head without so much as a 'Freeze!', 'Stop! Police!', 'Kiss my ass' or anything else? I'm pretty sure that's a civil rights violation."

That was a hard one to argue with.

"And Turner's real name is Mooney, but he's not FBI. He's been flying a desk at the CIA for almost thirty years. Never made a serious error in all that time that I know of—until now."

"You mean taking Matt?"

"No, given that he had already decided that he had to take me on, that was a pretty good move, really. I might have done it that way myself. He was in Kansas at the same time I was and he knows that I knew. He's the one that betrayed me and he knows that I know that too. He also knew how much George cared about the kids and now he figures to draw me into a trap he and his friends have made somewhere. No, his mistake was betraying me in the first place without making sure that I was dead."

"What do you mean, 'George cared'? You're telling me you're not George?"

His brow furrowed as he continued to move his tongue over the remains of the lunch between his teeth.

"Not entirely. George was a better man than I am."

Briefly a wistful look spoiled his stoic façade but it hardened again.

"Mooney did make one other mistake though," he added.

"What was that?"

"He hasn't realized yet that for me this is a 'scorched earth' scenario no matter what happens to the boy. He doesn't want the real authorities to find me because of what I might tell them about him and his friends, but there's no reason why I shouldn't complicate his life now. If they knew what I know the FBI would be looking for him just as hard as they are me."

Kate frowned. The momentary appearance of the familiar George Gordon made her braver.

"I must admit you really had me fooled. I had no idea. I actually liked you."

"I liked George too."

"Oh come on! I'm not buying it. You expect me to believe that you are the highest functioning schizophrenic in history who . . ."

He said, "Kate, I don't give a shit what you believe," but he wasn't very convincing.

"What about Mike Hogan? Was that a lie too?"

He looked confused.

"Hogan?"

"Yes. He said you were really named Mike Hogan, a deserter from the army before you became this—whatever you are. He said you're a murderer and that's obviously true whether you killed Valerie or not."

The killer rose, slamming the milk glass loudly on the table and grabbed her by the hair on the back of her head.

Katherine tried briefly to pull away but couldn't, her pose of boldness destroyed. A little abbreviated shriek escaped her throat.

He pulled her face to within inches of his own.

"Hogan has been dead for over thirty years, Kate," he said. "And nobody, nobody I've ever been would have killed Val. Killing those two was a crime far worse than anything Hogan . . . worse than anything I've ever done."

Katherine Wallace swallowed hard. "So . . . so you're not Hogan?" she said.

He looked intensely down for another moment before releasing her and moving back a little. "Not any more."

"But you're not really George Gordon anymore either?"

"I can't be George Gordon. Matthew can't afford for me to be George Gordon."

"So who are you now?"

The time had come for the Mechanic to seriously consider. The boy's kidnapping had compromised both his plans and his safety. He turned his back on Kate and stood for a moment looking out the back window at the two mammoth Pecan trees. It was late in the day now and the air conditioner was getting a rare break. In the quiet, the ticking of the old clock could be heard again from three rooms away.

"Where are your car keys?" he asked when he turned back around. "We've got to go."

"I don't care what you say, If you think I'm going anywhere with you, you really are crazy."

He just looked at her. After a few seconds she pointed at a carved wooden four-leaf clover hanging on the wall by the back door and he pulled the key ring from the hook in its center.

"You go right ahead. I won't call the police for ten minutes."

"Stand up," he ordered.

She sat farther back in the kitchen chair.

"Stand up, I said."

Katherine's lips became a straight line and she hugged herself even tighter.

"I don't have time for this, Kate. Stand up!"

When she still refused, George grabbed the back of her collar and yanked her violently to her feet. Startled, Kate was going to bluster some further indignation but only got as far as "What . . ." when George Gordon hit her in the side of the neck, just below her ear. She folded instantly. He caught her as she began to fall.

"Christ, you were always a stubborn bitch!" he said softly, placing her limp figure over his shoulder. He walked out the back door toward the garage in full view of neighbors if there had been any to see.

The Mechanic returned briefly to the house. He gathered Katherine's purse from the dining room table where she always left it along with a few of her things, his pistol and jacket from the front porch swing. On the way out he took the last bite of his sandwich. With Doctor Katherine Wallace under a sheet in the back seat, he drove her car south out of the neighborhood.

Chapter 15

Agent Bernard had been in line at the *Corky's Barbecue* in the B Concourse for over ten minutes when she heard a public address page over the crowd noise. Unaccountably she had not exhausted her craving for ribs, the wet variety this time, after enjoying the other kind the evening before. God, she was going to have to double up on her workouts, but at the moment she needed comfort food. She motioned to Aleksandr Pushkin who was leaning against a post, his tie pulled down a few inches, looking at a small notebook.

"Please get that for me, Alex, and tell them I'll return the call right away. If I have to go to the end of this line again, I think I'll starve to death. Pick up one of those phones over there and explain it for me, will you?"

Pushkin nodded and wove his way through the crush of angry travelers toward the courtesy phones. Besides the usual airport traffic, four Northwest flights had either been canceled or delayed and the crowd was double its normal size. One of the flights was theirs, the non-stop to Washington National. Like several others it was over two and a half hours behind schedule and a lot of people who had planned to make it home that evening were swelling the ranks of the Memphis airport diners.

Gaby was tired and more than a little irritable. They had spent another day trying to make good a theory whose details she didn't even know, by an equally unknown Russian Grandmaster whom she had begun to actively resent. Memphis police had cooperated well enough but there was no reason to give it extraordinary attention. They wanted to close, or at least shelve the Malenkov case as an unsolved professional assassination—probably, but not positively, committed by the one known as 'The Mechanic'. There were plenty of those cases open on the books worldwide and it was certainly no disgrace.

This useless trip to Memphis had been a waste of money and was going to make her look stupid no matter how cleverly she worded the report. The Russian had doggedly scrutinized every piece of evidence in the murder and endeared himself further to the Memphis PD by insisting on a second trip to the same sweltering intermodal freight yard, for a similarly fruitless survey. To compound matters, Gaby had been unable to get the simple metallurgy tests expedited at the lab in Washington. Except for the Rendezvous and the baseball game nothing had gone right since they hit this overheated town and now she overheard from just ahead in the line that they were out of pork ribs. A Memphis restaurant, even at the airport, out of ribs? Impossible!

Pushkin nudged her from the other side of the chrome railing.

"Did you get the number?" she asked.

"We will not need one. It was the Memphis police advising us not to board our airplane and that Lieutenant Gallagher is on his way back to pick us up."

"What happened?"

"They think they know the identity of the Mechanic."

There were no sirens and only one late-arriving cruiser still had a flasher turning. The garish colored lights joined with the occasional streetlight and every front porch fixture for a block in every direction, burning the street's usual tranquility with their harshness. Three other cruisers and two unmarked cars were already at the scene when Gallagher arrived with his dubious VIP's. The yellow plastic of the police cordon was everywhere, surrounding two cars parked at the curb and limiting access to one of the houses. There were a few onlookers craning for a glimpse of the corpses or the crazed killer of the rumors they had heard.

Gallagher showed an ID but there was simply no place to park near the house so they pulled to the side street and the trio walked the rest of the way.

"You say this—what was he? Salesman?—killed his family and these two here?" Gaby asked Gallagher as they walked.

He shrugged.

"I'm not saying anything, Ms. Bernard. I'm repeating what I was told. One of the two victims here was almost certainly killed by the same man who killed Malenkov at the freight yard, almost certainly The Mechanic. It's not my theory so anything beyond that—I don't know, but I'm taking you to the man who does."

When they got to the front yard of Katherine Wallace's house Gallagher displayed his badge to the officers and they all slid under the barrier tape. Ordinarily the badge would have been unnecessary, but for this crime scene some units from the North and East Precincts were called in whom Frank Gallagher didn't recognize.

They crossed the wide front porch with its rose trellises and old-fashioned swing into the front room where they saw the white taped outline on the floor. A uniformed officer emerged from the interior.

"Is this the broken neck?" Gallagher asked him.

"Yep. Just like the Malenkov guy," he said. "I don't think I'd like to meet the sumbitch that did it."

"Yeah?"

"Yeah. That guy," he said, pointing at the outline, "was the one with the gun. Looks like the perp took away his cannon, bitch slapped him across the room and then snapped his neck for good measure."

"I see what you mean," said Gallagher. "Sojourner back there?"

"Yeah. He's in the kitchen through there."

The visitors found Inspector Paul Sojourner two rooms away seated at a faux antique cherry dinette suite. They were expected, mostly.

At the sight of Agent Bernard, Sojourner had a lopsided smile on his face. Plain, mannish clothes, no makeup and a lack of sleep were unable to completely conceal her charms. When they were introduced, he made some attempt at cleverness.

"I told Frank we're about ready to pack up now, so there was no need to bring you here, but now I'm glad he did," said Sojourner. "What can I do for you?"

For most men his age, the expression on his face had died with disco. Gaby shot him a chilly look.

"So how's the wife, Paul?" Gallagher asked. Sojourner sneered a vulgarity in return.

"Besides," Gallagher added, "it ain't her you got to worry about. It's Lieutenant Pushkin here that has strong ideas about crime scene investigation," Gallagher said, raising his eyebrows.

Sojourner smiled. "Oh yeah, the freight yard. I heard about that. What's the matter, Frank? He making you work for a living?"

Gallagher responded with an obscene hand gesture of his own and hopped with surprising ease considering his bulk up on the counter top, indicating the kitchen chairs for the out-of-town visitors.

"I take it Forensics is done in here?" he said.

"You're a little late in asking but yes, they left a little after the meat wagon," Sojourner replied.

"By the way," he said to Gaby, "I got a call from your Evidence Response Team and I told them where to stick it. They wanted me to leave the scene untouched for four hours while they flew in some of your Washington eggheads."

"Then I've got bad news for you, Inspector. That was before some of the facts came out. What I've heard already sounds like one or two counts of kidnapping and that makes it just as Federal a case as we want to make it. Would you like me to call the local Bureau office for you?"

Sojourner gave her a poisonous look. Casual lust had been replaced by something else.

Aleksandr Pushkin chose the seat nearer to Sojourner and pulled out the farthest one for Gaby. He leaned forward in the chair with forearms on his thighs as he spoke.

"We are not here to hinder your investigation, Inspector, and we would not want to use very much of your time. We wish only to learn the essentials of what you have discovered and wanted to take advantage of your expertise while you are here. After all, you are the one who made the connection with the other homicide. One might say you have made more progress in this Mechanic matter in a few days time than the international community in many years."

While she was sensitive about not being seen as subordinate in the process, Gaby was interested to watch from the sideline. Pushkin had deflected Sojourner's attention and inserted himself as a pupil and admirer and yet dominant member of the visiting trio. The kind of intense concentration Gaby had received in her own seduction, ideological only of course, was now being directed at someone else, with somewhat similar result. Alex Pushkin was really quite an operator.

The Inspector tried in a slow Southern drawl to be self-deprecating with limited success.

"Well to be fair, it would appear that most of this is just happenstance—luck, if you will. The Mechanic chose to settle down in Memphis for quite a while and when he decided to leave, he wanted to sever all ties—in a real final way. We have our share of murders here. Hot-blooded fights, brawls, gang violence, but this kind of calculated execution is pretty unusual. With these killings I think he all but filled in the details for us. We know who he is, now. We just have to catch him before he gets out of town."

"And what are the details, Inspector?" Pushkin asked, pulling out a notebook.

Sojourner opened the folder in front of him.

"Okay, to begin with, his name is Gordon, George Gordon. He lives, or lived about twenty minutes northeast of here with his wife of fourteen years and two children, Alicia, eleven and Matthew, thirteen—a real solid citizen. He told everyone he was a salesman for Coastal Freight Consolidators, but their general manager told me he worked there quite a bit but was never full time. He said he assumed the man had another source of income but he was a pretty good contributor. I guess now we know what he was doing on the side.

"We still have nothing on the Malenkov murder, but aside from the method, the fact that it took place in an intermodal freight yard seems indicative.

"Then early last week there was an explosion in his home. His wife and daughter were killed instantly, but he had been called away mysteriously just in time to avoid it. At the time it looked suspicious to the investigators because of the explosive but nothing really indicated him. They interviewed several associates who claimed that there was absolutely no sign of trouble in the marriage. He did travel quite a bit legitimately and he had a receipt from a hotel in Jackson.

"Two days later he disappeared right in the middle of the funeral services and these two guys turned up dead at a Little Rock car dealership—one of them had his neck broken just like two other guys we know."

Sojourner flipped two crime scene photos on the kitchen table for Pushkin to examine and leaned back in his chair to take a breath from his long explanation.

"You said 'wife and daughter', Inspector," Gaby interjected. "What about the son?"

"Yeah, it looks like that's what brought him here. The boy was staying with his aunt, Katherine Wallace. This is her house."

"So that outline in the front room is actually hers?" Gaby asked. "The officer out front said . . ."

"No, that's right. I mean no, it was this guy here," he said, tossing another pair of pictures toward her and pointing at them in turn. "He's the one whose neck was broken. This one was shot in the temple as he sat in one of those cars at the curb."

Gaby looked confused. "What did they have to do with anything? Who were they? And who were the men in Little Rock for that matter."

"The whole thing's pretty weird. They had only fake paper on them—excellent fake paper. We don't have positive id yet, or even a good guess for that matter, which makes us think mob or intelligence service. All we know for sure is that they made the wrong guy angry at them. I think we're going to find the papers on the two stiffs here will be just as phony."

Alex placed one of the first pictures In front of Sojourner.

"This man's name is Digaev," he said. "This one looks familiar but I cannot place him. It is a certainty that he was a former Soviet citizen."

The Inspector raised his eyebrows.

"Are you sure?"

"Yes. We had this one in custody during the first Chechen Rebellion years ago but let him go through a bureaucratic error. He left the country and has since been a killer for hire but we lost traces of him. He was without conscience and very deadly. Bypass your domestic data sources and go right to Interpol. They will no doubt have impressive packets on both of these men."

Sojourner nodded appreciatively.

"Thanks, Lieutenant. That will help a lot. How about the others?"

Pushkin shook his head and Gaby asked, "Do you know what they were doing in Little Rock and can you place The Mechanic over there?"

"No. They just went there to be discovered in the trunk of their rental car when the car carrier started to unload," the inspector replied.

"And it had come from Memphis?"

"Yes, the day of the Gordon funeral. First Malenkov, then the guys in the trunk and now these two here. I'd have to bet they are going to turn out to be Russian too."

"I am sure of it," said Pushkin.

"What did The Mechanic do to piss off the whole Russian Federation?" Gaby asked her partner.

The Russian frowned.

"My country is not really involved, of course, only our expatriate trash. Yet your question is a good one. Why? Even for an assassin of mythic proportion this is a great deal of attention and expense. Once again I say the Molotov box is somehow the key to understanding all of this."

"Yes, but why?" Gaby asked. "What have Korean lampshades to do with anything?"

"I do not understand. I have admitted it," replied Pushkin. "But when we do understand, we will know how to find The Mechanic and the people who seem to be trying to kill him."

"So where is the sister-in-law?" Gaby asked again. " . . . And the son? Any ideas?"

Sojourner looked at his notes again.

"As near as we can place everything, this is the way it happened," he said. "This afternoon there was a second car out front just like the light colored Buick sedan. Three Caucasian males were initially in the cars. A little later there was only one car and two Caucasian males. Then a short time after that, it was joined by the silver T-bird. That's the Mechanic's car—registered to George Gordon."

"Inside the house, we know that Doctor Wallace and her nephew were here at lunch time, before any of the cars."

"Doctor?"

"Clinical psychologist for the University of Tennessee. Anyway, she and the boy were here before the first car pulled out. We don't know who stayed and who left.

"Four shots were fired from this gun." Sojourner said, holding up the Tokarev in a plastic bag. "Our shooter must be the sentimental type because it's almost older than you are, Gallagher. It's Russian. They used to be standard issue for the KGB."

He looked over at Pushkin who identified it down to a probable year of manufacture some thirty years before his birth.

"We don't know who it was fired at," continued Sojourner, "but we found the right number of holes in the woodwork and a fair amount of blood that doesn't belong to the guy that was popped out there and neither does the shirt we found in the bathroom. Apparently the killer put on his victim's shirt after patching himself up with four butterfly clips from Ms. Wallace's medicine cabinet. Other than that, we have to wait for the lab. The guy outside in the car had a gun just like this one. What else? Oh yeah, somebody, probably the killer sat at this table, right where you are, and ate a peanut butter sandwich with milk, our lab guy claims *after* breaking the guy's neck."

"You're joking," said Gaby.

"Nope. Pugh claims to be able to tell within a half hour how long a smear of Jif Extra Creamy has been hardening on a counter. He says the guy took his time and sipped his glass of milk. Naturally I can't prove any of that, but Pugh is uncanny. If he said it, you can write it down. Also, it would fit in with what little we know about The Mechanic. He's supposed to be about the coolest customer around anywhere."

"That's true," she admitted.

"He also said Katherine Wallace. Actually he wasn't that specific. He said a woman, had made the sandwich. That would make the three of them leaving together, or the two of them. The boy *could* have gone with this Turner guy. Anyway, the sister-in-law and the son are gone, we don't know where, or who forced them, if anybody. I would guess that they're still alive for the time being simply because this would be a fine place to dispose of bodies in bulk if you were going to kill them anyway."

"Quite logical. It remains to ask who was in the first sedan," said Pushkin. "You said Turner? Who was that?"

Sojourner reached into the pile of plastic bags. "Yeah, that would have been the Turner guy. He left his card. This was next to the body on the floor."

"FBI!" Gaby exclaimed, and reached for her cell phone.

The inspector held up a hand.

"Easy, Honey. It wasn't the Bureau. Whoever this Turner guy really is, the Bureau never heard of him. He seems to have been the one who drove off in tan sedan number one about a half hour after arrival."

Gaby was rubbing the rectangle of linen textured pasteboard lightly between her fingers and ignoring Sojourner's familiar reference to her.

"I swear this does look just like my cards. On the other hand, he must have had better ID than this or surely Doctor Wallace wouldn't have let him in."

"Maybe," said the Inspector, "but everything is speculation from here on in. Oh, except that Wallace's Ford Explorer is gone from the garage."

She said "Okay, so Wallace and her nephew are still alive. Where do we think they are? Escaped somehow?"

"Don't know but they're not around here. Both of them either left in the Buick or the Explorer."

"Or one in each," said Pushkin.

"Quite right, Lieutenant," agreed Sojourner.

A uniformed patrolman appeared at the kitchen door. He motioned to Gaby.

"Agent Bernard?" he asked. "There's a courier outside that needs your signature."

Gaby left the room to surreptitious glances from the assembled law enforcement males.

"Nice," said Sojourner to no one in particular when she was out of earshot. "Special Agent Bernard could put me in custody anytime."

Pushkin feigned interest in a wooden napkin holder while Gallagher laughed out loud. The cop looked from the Russian to the Inspector and back again. He had spent enough time on this FBI wrangling assignment to see what was happening between Gaby and the Russian and he thought it was pretty funny.

With the same surprising grace for a man of his girth he hopped down from the tiled counter after he had appropriated some Ritz crackers from the shelf behind him and begun to munch.

"You better watch what you say about our lovely visitor from DC, Paulie or you might have to fight a duel with Comrade Pushkin. He's been workin' on this babe like a Vegas gigolo, but it looks to me like he ain't gettin' anywhere. I think maybe he's trying too hard. Don't they have no beautiful investigators where you come from Alex?"

Pushkin shot him a venomous look.

"Very rarely," said the Russian. "But sarcastic investigators are commonplace."

"Interesting," said Gallagher. "We got to get some of those."

Pushkin rose from the table and stepped over to the counter where Gallagher stood. For a moment the two locked eyes wordlessly. Pushkin towered over the broader but smaller detective, even as he sat on the counter. Gallagher met the perceived challenge by widening his smile. Without moving his gaze, the Russian leaned in even closer, almost nose to nose, and reached around Gallagher to the shelf behind him, coming away with a handful of crackers.

"Thieving investigators are not rare in my country either", he said, biting into one of them.

"Don't get me wrong, Comrade. I don't blame you a bit." The smaller and older policeman was still looking directly into his eyes. "Every man's got his appetites and it seems like you and I obviously agree on ours."

Pushkin flinched at that last part and Gallagher added, "Ritz Crackers, son. We both got a yen for Ritz Crackers."

Sojourner guffawed and the other two had to smile. The moment passed just in time for Gaby to reappear in the doorway. She was reading from a single sheet of paper on top of an open manila envelope. She did not seem to notice the laughter.

"It's your lab report," Gaby said handing the page to Alex Pushkin. "Is this what you expected to find?"

He brushed the crumbs from his hands and took the paper, scrutinizing the numbers on it for a minute. The two Memphis cops looked at each other and shrugged.

"Yes," Pushkin said finally. "Exactly. We must go immediately."

"Now? We wait three days for a lab report and now it's an emergency. Where is it you want to go at 11:30 at night?"

Hesitantly he looked sideward at Frank Gallagher.

"South Central Rail Yard," he said.

Sojourner looked at the lieutenant and began to laugh again.

"You have *got* to be shittin' me," Gallagher murmured.

Using nothing more than a wrinkled brow, Pushkin appealed to Special Agent Bernard.

"Kidding, joking," she answered the unspoken question. "'You must be kidding,' he says, or just plain nuts. And I must say I agree."

Chapter 16

"Six percent aluminum and four percent vanadium."

Gaby was half turned in the passenger seat of Gallagher's unmarked car as it sped southward once again. She was holding the report under the dome light and speaking to Alex Pushkin, who as always rode exactly in the center of the wide back seat.

"Correct," replied Pushkin. "And the rest is titanium."

"Right," she said. "So now that we know that, what do we know?"

"Do you know what truck trailers and freight containers are made of in your country?"

"I don't know—steel?"

"Yes, steel and aluminum mostly," Pushkin agreed,

"But in your country they are made of titanium?"

"No way!" interrupted Gallagher. "Even raw titanium costs four times as much as the best steel. The damn truck would be worth more than the cargo."

"Not only that," added Pushkin, "but it is far more difficult to work with. It has special requirements whenever it is melted—even welded. This would add to the expense of producing such a thing also."

"Let me understand what you're saying. You found a little piece of very thin, bent metal with white paint on one side in a freight yard where twenty thousand tons of varied freight cycles through every few days. And your hypothesis is that not only did this particular piece fall off that particular truck where Malenkov was found, but also that the whole thing was made of it. Is that it?"

"Correct."

Gallagher interrupted again. "That's nuts. Nobody could afford to throw that much money away on a box to haul something. And why would they think they needed it anyway?"

"Weight. That is the only possible reason, weight and the accompanying strength characteristics. This particular alloy, called Ti-64 is even used in aircraft engines. Among other places it is manufactured at the Molot Metallurgical Works in Moscow."

Gaby said, "That's where . . ."

"Yes, it is where the two men were found asphyxiated. After the autopsy I requested a second examination. Only then did they discover traces of argon gas in their lungs. It did not change the view of the pathologist but it certainly changed mine. This 'accident' came days after the murder of the Molot Steel Fabricating Plant's accountant. His name was Malenkov, your victim's brother. I believe the two workers saw something that was important enough to risk drawing attention to the operation."

"And what's the significance of the argon?" Gaby asked.

"Whenever you weld titanium the whole atmosphere around it has to be inert gas or else stuff gets into the weld and makes it unstable, brittle," Gallagher said.

"Quite right, Lieutenant," said Alex. "You surprise me."

"We got libraries here," he said with a sneer.

Pushkin continued. "The two workers built truck frames for Molot, but only in steel. This gas not only convinced me of foul play but also made me think of the other side of the plant that works in Titanium. It is very specialized. Not so long ago there were only four locations in the US qualified to deal with the simplest Titanium construction. This was one area where the Soviet Union was far ahead. We were building nuclear submarines out of it."

Gallagher said, "Okay, I get the titanium—Soviet connection and I understand that there were two Malenkov brothers killed. But we're supposed to be investigating The Mechanic. If you're not saying that he killed all of them, then what in the flaming hell does any of this have to do with our investigation."

"He means . . ." Gaby began.

"There is no need, Gaby," Alex grimaced as they passed under a streetlight. "I think I understand his meaning. The truth is that I do not know. The only things we are sure of after today's events are that the Mechanic killed the second Malenkov brother and that his—that is, Malenkov's—employers seem to be trying to retaliate. Why the Mechanic would be engaged to murder an obscure accountant, I admit I cannot see, other than to say that I believe it is all intimately related to the Molot murder and the Titanium smugglers vessel."

"And do you know who Malenkov's employers really are?" Gaby asked. "You promised to come clean when the test results came back."

"Clean?" he said.

"You know exactly what I mean this time, Alex. You were supposed to tell me everything you know about this."

"And I will," he assured her, looking sideways at Gallagher's profile. "In time you will know everything. For now, I will answer your questions as well as I can. The Malenkov brothers were in the employ of the *Matrosskaya*."

"Who is *Matrosskaya*?"

Aleksandr looked at the Memphis detective and Gaby could see why he was hesitating.

"You've talked me into this, Alex but I'm a big girl and I came along of my own free will. Officer Gallagher here was more or less Shanghaied. If you want to include him—at least while we're in his jurisdiction—that's your call."

Pushkin looked as if he were considering that. In the rear view mirror he gave his local driver a speculative look. Gallagher chuckled when he noticed it.

"If you can think of a way to get me out of this, or if you can get me reassigned, by all means do it," he said, exaggerating his drawl. "Otherwise y'all are gonna look pretty silly goin' behind every tree and bush so you can whisper secrets."

Pushkin hesitated for another few seconds but finally continued.

"In America you would call them a syndicate or a crime family. They have been smugglers since long before the end of the Soviet era. We believe only a small number of this particular branch remain in Russia. They are now headquartered in Florida. The *Vor v Zakonye* lives in Miami Beach."

"The *Vor* viz-whatever is the head of their organization, I take it?" asked Gaby.

"Yes. The translation is something like 'Thief Within the Code'. You would call him the Godfather."

Gallagher blurted "So what the hell did The Mechanic want with their bookkeeper? And why was he so important that they are now willing to risk exposing themselves this way?"

"I have already said that I do not know," answered Alex. "I am simply investigating the smuggling to give us an idea of how to proceed further. We do not know what they are concealing but we are certain that it is very valuable. A great deal of time and effort has been put into this operation. The Colonel believes that there is no connection between The Mechanic and the smuggling operation. He said that the likelihood is that he is being pursued not because he murdered Malenkov. He does not seem to have been very important to anyone. In short, the random circumstance that brought them together may have been fatal to both the accountant and his killer. The location more than anything else may have indicated some knowledge of the smuggling that they did not wish the killer to have. That is why we must go back again."

Gallagher already knew from overheard conversations who 'The Colonel' was but they had another discussion about the various merits of his apparent remote-controlled operation before they arrived at the now familiar freight yard entrance. They were fortunate enough to find the watchman at his post. Gallagher flashed his badge and informed him that it was a crime scene investigation follow-up that would not take long. In saying this he made it obvious that it would be okay with him if the night watchman objected and forced them to call it a night but he gave them a bored wave and they drove in.

"Damn," said Gaby, drawing her own conclusions from Pushkin's explanation. "You never really intended to catch this Mechanic. You came over here to investigate the smuggling."

"Partially true," answered Pushkin. "But I think you can see that both solutions lie in the same direction."

"More wisdom from Colonel Dashenko I suppose."

The service road they followed had several turns, but by now it was almost familiar. The Memphis detective switched off the engine at the same spot they had parked in the first time, next to the trailer with the eagle on it. There was complete silence and no one moved for a moment. Gabrielle was feeling superseded again and was sulking a bit.

"This is why I'm divorced, you know," said Gallagher, "stupid midnight excursions like this and the 'winding down' afterward. By the way, why the hell aren't you married, Ms. Bernard? Same answer?"

Gaby was distracted by her resentful thoughts and answered without thinking.

"I was married. It was a long time ago."

"What happened?" Gallagher asked.

Damn! She had managed to avoid this subject with Pushkin and wasn't about to talk about it now.

"Stuff happens. That's about it. Now can we get back to the subject at hand please?"

"A little touchy ain't ya? 'Scuse me! I'm just saying that if it hasn't been a problem before, it will be somewhere down the road. Both y'all are still young. I advise you to find another line of work while you can. Get yourself a personal life and forget this kind of shit. It just ain't worth it."

Gallagher looked at his passengers and he could see that between the excitement of the hunt and the evident sexual tension it was a bad time for such a message. He swore softly.

"Oh well," he said. "Here endeth the lesson."

"So what do you plan to do now that I've delivered you to a deserted yard that has been scraped over for almost two weeks for anything that looks like it might be third cousin to a clue?"

"First we will check the other box to see if it is made of the same material", Alex replied. "If it is, we will open it and see what is inside," said Alex.

"We've been all over that. You can't just go around breaking seals and opening transportation containers. Besides it was lampshades. As I recall, the first one had lampshades," Gaby chided.

"Yes, but we cannot count on that. The cargo may have been discovered and switched, or maybe there was something else in with the lampshades that was missed. In any case we need to open them now. There may be material evidence to a kidnapping."

Gaby made a sharp intake of breath. "Lieutenant Pushkin! You aren't even investigating the kidnapping. You just admitted as much. How can we claim . . . ?"

"But I also said that the solution to one problem may be the solution to all."

Gallagher rubbed his eyes with fatigue and impatience.

"You still want to check that other white container? The company couldn't be making all of them out of titanium. The boxes alone would be worth millions before you put anything inside. Or at least they would have cost millions. That's crazy."

Pushkin was unmoved.

"Perhaps, but only if they paid for the metal. I believe the plant built containers for this organization during a supposed work stoppage out of materials paid for by the Soviet Union. No one but a plant boss and maybe a few workers knew—and of course an accountant named Malenkov. And after what happened to him and the workers, I think it would be a secret worth keeping, don't you?"

Gallagher, who was acting paternal in spite of being only a dozen or so years older than Pushkin, looked back toward the front seat and the downcast eyes of his other passenger. "Are you going along with this?" he asked. "You seem like a smart . . . person." He almost said the unthinkable—'girl'. "You must have better sense. However you slice it, Lieutenant Pushkin is going after things way outside the scope of our investigation—maybe even outside of your jurisdiction."

"This is pointless," said Alex. "We are here now and I will not leave until I have had a look into the other Molotov box, or at least get a sample of the material. You need not come along. I will take responsibility."

He extracted a Gerber Multi-tool from his pocket that had a sturdy set of pliers as part of it and the big flashlight from the glove box, got out of the car and had Gallagher open the trunk, where, after some rummaging, he extracted the tire iron. Then he started down the gravel path alone. Gaby and Frank Gallagher looked at each other for a moment. Gallagher shrugged and shortly they were following him.

Gaby pointed her own penlight at the Russian's profile when she caught up with him. She was almost pleading. "At least let me call the terminal manager. If we tell him a kidnapping is . . . well, *may be* involved he might . . ."

They had rounded the corner leading to where they knew the Molotov boxes had been. Pushkin took five steps, each one slower than the last until he came to a halt. The other two looked down the powerful beam of the flashlight. Augmented as it was by the clear night and a full moon, they could see very well. Where two days before there had been three hundred and fifty tons of freight in containers, Gaby looked down the row and saw a gaping empty space. The entire column of containers where the remaining Molotov box had been was missing. Alex began to walk in that direction again but slowly. He said something unintelligible in his own language the other two assumed was swearing.

"Gone?" Gaby asked no one in particular. "All of them? Could we be in the wrong place?"

Chapter 17

"Could we be in the wrong place?"

Those were the first words Doctor Katherine Wallace heard when she began to return to consciousness. The question was close; muffled but quite intelligible because of the utter silence surrounding it. She opened her eyes, blinking several times in confusion. She remembered being struck almost casually but quite accurately by the murderer she had thought that she knew and now she noted with clinical detachment that her unconsciousness had been prolonged by some kind of tranquilizer. Katherine could see absolutely nothing. Panicked, she began to stir, feeling of the rough fabric on which she lay and a wall adjacent to her left hand. Before she could try to bring herself upright or make much of a sound, she was pinned to the surface like a captive moth. Already restricted to the cot by what felt like leather or canvas straps, a powerful arm wrapped around her upper body and held her mouth and jaw like a vise.

"Quiet," said a voice an inch from her ear, but she continued to struggle. It was George Gordon. The depth of darkness was the most complete that she had ever known. Her first reaction was that she had somehow been blinded. Her eyes were wide open and she could feel nothing covering them. The struggling continued and she made a frantic mewling sound around the muffling hand.

"If you don't stop that, I'll pop you again," he whispered. Then he added so softly that it could almost have been in her head. "After that, I'll have to kill you."

It was George Gordon's voice—or nearly George's voice. Katherine went limp except for a slight trembling. The pressure lessened but the thumb under her chin and the hand over her mouth felt like iron still warm from the forge. Absently she noted that the finger under her nose smelled of cigarettes. George had never smoked.

She could now hear the sound of people nearby. They were walking on gravel. If they were speaking, it was for the moment too faint to make out. She was inside some kind of structure and these people were outside. The tiny echo from the nearby wall of her frenzied breathing was dull and hollow. Frightened and disoriented, Katherine waited.

"Wrong place? You gotta be jokin'," said a gruff voice with a thick Southern accent. "After all the time we spent here? No, this is it all right. The sumbitches are just gone."

A woman's voice swore. It had a strident tone, but sounded more like amazement than anger.

"What could have happened to them that fast?" the same woman asked.

The sound of their shoes and the rattle of small stones that had been receding now began to get slightly louder. The man and woman were approaching Katherine's place of imprisonment.

"This is just a holding yard, not a destination. They're here to ship and they shipped," the Southerner said.

The wall next to Katherine's cot felt almost like wood on her fingertip but it was softer. From the sound the people she was listening to were now directly opposite her on the other side. The sound of shoes on gravel had stopped for the moment. If she could move her foot far enough to kick the wall a bit, it might be enough of a noise to let them know that someone was inside this—whatever it was. It might be just loud enough for the people outside to hear. Then it occurred to her that even if they investigated it would probably cost them their lives. After what she had seen George do that afternoon she hesitated to test him again. Kate strained her senses to determine exactly where George's face was, but it was dark as the inside of a collapsed star and her former brother-in-law made not so much as a vibration. She could pick up nothing louder than the faint voices outside or the pounding of her own heart as she lay soaked in the sweltering blackness.

"Quite a coincidence," the woman said.

"I must know where the second Molotov box was sent," said a third voice. This one had some different accent. The foreigner said, "Please call the yard manager."

The woman's voice answered him. "Don't be stupid. It's after eleven and even if you disturb the man at home there is no reason to believe he could answer you without the papers that are about four hundred yards over that way locked up."

More steps sounded in the gravel.

"Don't even think about it," she said, and the steps slowed to a stop.

"The trailers'll still be gone in the morning," said the southerner. "C'mon I'll take y'all to a hotel and maybe we can all get a little sleep."

Another exchange took place between the woman and the foreigner, but Katherine couldn't make it out. The southerner laughed and urged them to leave again and the sound of their shuffling got a little louder again and then faded. After a few seconds more, three car doors opened, there was another inaudible exchange, then the doors closed and an engine started. With a spray of small stones from its tires, whatever chance of help Katherine had imagined was gone.

Even so, it was more than a minute before her captor released his grasp. He waited with animal patience to be sure that all of the unwanted visitors had been in the vehicle when it departed.

When the hand came away from her mouth, she gulped in the first few breaths. The air was thick with heat and moisture.

"Where are we? I can't breathe," Katherine said.

Out of the dark she heard a shuffling sound, a click, and the salvation of a faint draft of fresh air. The fans that produced it were extremely well made and nearly silent. Nevertheless, the Mechanic had shut them down while the intruders were present and the temperature in the enclosed space was almost intolerable.

"Who were those people?" Kate asked.

"The woman was an FBI agent who came here looking for me. I'm sure the other two are cops."

"How could you know that?"

"This is their second visit here. I saw them yesterday just before I left town."

"Tell me where 'here' is," she gasped "and what you are going to do with me."

Kate repeated the question several times to utter silence. She tried to guess from instinct and the reflection of ambient sounds where George Gordon was. Suddenly there was a loud flutter right over the cot and she let out a startled scream. It was a sheet that settled over her. The smell of detergent came off of it with the movement. It was the brand favored by her lost sister.

"Don't hurt me," she said. "Don't let it hurt. Please just get it over with."

An abbreviated chuckle erupted and Kate turned her head the thirty degrees or so it took to aim her view uselessly in that direction.

"Do you think I brought you here to kill you?" asked the point of darkness in a monotone.

"Why wouldn't I?" she replied. Katherine was proud of how steady she was able to make her voice. "After what I heard; after what I saw? They told me you set the explosive at your house."

"And you believed that?" he asked.

"I saw what you did to that man in my living room. His boss said you were somebody I don't even know. Somebody he called The Mechanic. Is that true or not?"

"I've been called that. I've been called a lot of things."

"If . . . if any of this is true, it's obvious that I never really knew you. What am I supposed to think? Besides, you did just knock me unconscious and kidnap me for god's sake."

"I'm . . . sorry about that," said the voice. And for a moment some undertone made it sound true. Then he added, "Well *shit*, Kate! You didn't give me any choice!"

He swore again and there was more noise from across the way. A zipper pulled up or down followed a deeper fabric scraping noise. A small steel cupboard door slammed and the fabric slid across the floor next to her. Sleeping bag? With another click of a switch further cool air began to circulate. She could hear his ligaments protest as he bent to the ground; then only the hiss of her own fevered breathing.

The voice spoke from the floor at her side.

"Look, I don't really care what you think but if it'll help you to get to sleep, I'm not going to kill you."

"You said you would if I made any noise."

"I . . . exaggerated. I brought you along so there would be someone to take the boy back. That's all—you just take the boy. But god damn it! You have to do what I say!" He paused and then in a quieter voice he added, "just for a little while."

"Where are we?"

"We're going to follow a train south from here. Then I think we're on our way to Florida from there but I have to make sure."

"What do you mean?"

"A truck will pick us up in the morning. A whole trainload of containers is on the way to New Orleans. One of them is special to the men I'm after. That's all I know for sure, except that where that one goes, that's where the boy will be. I think the tracing on those containers is going to get confused on the way and that one is going to get re-routed to Miami."

"And you . . . really don't plan to hurt me?"

"I would never really kill you. Until you shot me, I never even thought of it. I just told you I want you to take care of the boy. Besides, you're too much like . . . her."

Everyone used to say that the sisters were similar but Kate had never really seen the resemblance. To her, Valerie was this dark, delicate beauty and even with the decade of age advantage, Katherine had always seen herself as just a chunky, plain, woman with some pretty nice auburn hair—and even that was beginning to show some gray.

Kate started to say something but he quickly added, "I'd much rather have your cooperation but don't get the idea that I won't put your lights out if you try to get in the way. Tomorrow we'll talk and you'll see that this is the only way to save Matt. And in a day or two you and Matt can go back home. You'll never have to worry about money. I've taken care of that."

"Don't you mean 'George' has taken care of that?"

"Don't make fun of me, Kate. I don't like it."

Doctor Wallace said, "Sorry. I'm not, really, it's just that I don't believe this line you're feeding me, or maybe feeding yourself. I have experience with multiple personalities, you know and I don't think you're one of them."

"I never said that. That was what your fake FBI agent with all the dead Russian Pals said."

"So are you really what that man said you are? You really killed people for money?"

"I said we'd talk tomorrow. Go to sleep now."

"Valerie couldn't have known."

"Of course not. Don't be stupid."

"But you were married for all those years. How could you share so much and withhold something like that?"

"Go to sleep."

"I know how much you loved the kids. Val knew it. Anyone could see it. How could you live in such different worlds?"

"I never think about it."

"You selfish bastard! How could you have done this to Val?"

A sound somewhere between a grunt and a mirthless laugh came out of the darkness.

"You don't have to tell me that I was never worthy of somebody like Val. Christ, don't you think I know that? In a way I guess it's the worst thing I ever did—keeping her from somebody that deserved her. But she loved me. She gave that to me and I took it because . . . well hell, I couldn't *not* take it. Val was fine beyond anything or anybody I ever knew, beyond anything I could imagine and that's the God's truth."

After a bit of silence, he said, "You're right, of course. It was a selfish thing, but . . . I always tried to make her happy and I think I did, mostly. You know, that's all I ever worried about. I never worried about death, mine or anyone else's, not even Val's really, because I couldn't think about that. The only thing that ever kept me awake at night was worrying that she would somehow find out about me and I would have to look into her eyes.

"Now I'm tired and I want to sleep. Please just shut up about it."

"If you didn't kill Val and Alicia, who did?"

The voice swore in irritation.

"Two other Russians. The two at your house were just part of the team. Your Agent Turner and all of the others work for the same man. He lives in Miami and that's where they will be taking the boy."

"How do you know?"

"Because they sent five people up here, not counting 'Turner' and I killed them all. Just as god damned dead as I could make 'em. If I could dig 'em up and bring 'em back to life, I'd kill 'em again. How's that?"

Kate was too shocked to respond.

"They want me dead and they can't risk any more failures. They know they can do it easily if they control the location. I'm sure that's why they snatched the boy. By now they've made a killing box around him to trap me."

"A k-killing box?"

"That's a term we used to use for an ambush that had no line of retreat. It's like a roach motel for assholes like me."

"If you're this heartless, crazy killer, what makes them think you'll come?"

Out of the dark Kate heard a sigh.

"Mooney. I saw him in Kansas but it was too late to do anything about it there. Too bad. It sure would have saved a lot of trouble. I guess Mooney figured out before I did that Matt is the important thing—the only important thing left. And now that I've admitted that I have to try to forget it."

Kate frowned into the utter darkness.

"What are you talking about?" she asked.

"All those years before Val I went into every mission and every job like I was already dead. I didn't really care and that's why I'm still alive. Passion was the enemy's problem. Passion for life, passion for money, passion for a woman; all these things make them weak and predictable.

"I was driving back from . . . I was driving back this morning when it hit me that this was my real life. You and Matt are all that's left of the only life I had that counted—all that's left of Val. I don't intend to let anything happen to either one of you.

"I have to live long enough to get Matt out. Then you can take him home and finish raising him like Val would. If I can make this outfit dead, you can bet I'm going to do that, but I know Matt is more important than that. That's why you're here."

Katherine felt some germ of self-control returning, so she felt a need to understand all this.

"Okay, you said Matt's just a lure to draw you in, right? He should be okay if you just go on your way and say nothing to the authorities. They have nothing to gain by harming him."

"No, and nothing to lose by killing him. At the moment he has value alive and when that value is used up they'll kill him just the same. He's all right for now, but if I don't get him out, he's dead. Believe this if you don't believe anything else. It's a certainty."

"What will you do?"

"I need to know more about the setup, but basically it's pretty simple. First I have to make sure about those containers. That's the way to be certain to find the boy. Then I'll kill them all and get the boy out, or get the boy out and kill them all. The order is not important. I'm going to start with the head man, the one who set all this in motion so I'm sure about him. As long as I'm breathing, everybody who had anything to do with killing Ally and Valerie or taking Matt is going to die."

The absence of emotion in his voice gave Katherine more of a shudder than raw hatred would have, but she understood it either way. Although half of her was repelled by the promise of violence, the other half had to agree that the murderer of her sister and sweet little Alicia surely must die horribly or the balance of the universe could never recover.

Still, the profoundly disorienting feeling associated with all this casual talk of murder and kidnapping persisted. Several minutes went by before Kate spoke again.

"George?"

"For Christ's sake, go to sleep," came the slurred reply.

"These straps are too tight. Could you loosen them just a little?"

Kate was aware that her tone had grown submissive, but she was unable to master it, and under the circumstances, was unsure that she wanted to.

"Not tonight. Go to sleep."

"No matter who you are, if you're really out to save Matt, you know I'll help."

"Yes."

The word was a soft and fading hiss. The Mechanic was asleep, and although she had thought it extremely unlikely, Kate likewise succumbed to her exhaustion.

When Kate awoke, the darkness had given way to a faint glow. Though parts of it were covered in fiber insulation, there was enough of the steel door exposed that she could tell that she was being held inside some kind of truck. There were still no lights on, but sunrise revealed a few cracks along the roofline where the corrugation hadn't been completely sealed and a row of bullet-sized holes leaked the morning light in.

For the first time she could see that she was in a barren oblong enclosure furnished only by the cot she lay on, a steel chair and a long metal cabinet that made a shelf or workspace on one wall. Just where she had guessed in the dark, her former brother-in-law, George Gordon was curled on an open sleeping bag.

Thinking it must have come from outside, Kate was searching for the noise that awakened her, staring at the wall next to her as if sight would aid her in listening when she heard it again. It came instead from George.

In the gloom it was difficult to be sure of anything but she believed she could see him moving minutely. Then she identified the faint high-pitched sound. It was a childlike, almost infantile sob coming from her captor, the killer to whom she had only recently been introduced. George was in a classic fetal position facing away from her with his arms wrapped around his knees.

Instinctively Kate tried to get up but the straps still held her tightly to the metal frame. She almost called out to George, but remembering the circumstances, changed her mind. She lay quietly in the semi-dark while the forlorn figure alternately shook and was still.

After a few minutes of this, George uncoiled and lay on his back. He let out a long breath and rubbed his eyes. As he did, a tiny continuous beep began to sound, George touched his left wrist and it stopped. He turned his head, looking straight into Katherine's eyes.

"Have you been doing that long?" she asked.

He sniffed and rubbed his nose, casually dragging a finger across the corner of his eye.

"Doing what?" he replied.

Kate didn't answer.

George hoisted himself from the floor rather faster than he needed to, switched on a light and folded up the sleeping bag in one swirl of motion. He shoved the new bundle in a cabinet under the counter on the opposite wall, returning to stand over Kate. He reached down and popped the clamp on her restraints. The belts hadn't really been all that tight but she felt better anyway. Going back to the long cabinet on the opposite wall, he opened another clamp, releasing a section that could only have been a chemical toilet. As Katherine looked on, he turned his back to her and began to use it.

Kate wanted to express her indignation but there was no one to show it to. When he was done, she said, "Do you expect me to use that thing?"

"Yes," he replied.

She opened her mouth to protest further, but it was just too pointless. Eventually she would be compelled to humiliate herself but she was determined to postpone the moment as long as possible.

"Where are we? What is this place?" she asked.

"From the outside it looks like an ordinary freight container on a trailer. I've done some modifications. I've used it from time to time when I couldn't take a chance that my movements would be known and it makes pretty handy storage," George replied.

"How long are we going to be locked up in here?"

Kate sat on the edge of the cot. George pulled a folding stool out of the cabinet and pulled it up next to her so he could look directly into her eyes.

"Just today, Kate." He replied. "But that brings up the broader subject. There will be a trucker here in about an hour who will run this trailer into Mississippi. I don't want to keep you strapped down and gagged while that happens and afterward it will become completely impractical."

"Yes?" she said, waiting.

"I need your word that you won't try to call out or send a message or any other means of getting me captured. I need you to swear on Matt's life, because that's exactly what you will be doing."

Looking at the pain and burning need in George's face made her question again the reality of the crazy situation. She looked deep and just couldn't come up with 'murderer' even though she knew it was true.

"I've told you that as long as I believe it's for Matt I will help," She answered.

"Well I'm asking for you to take it as an article of faith that whatever I do, by definition, is the best thing I can think of to secure Matt's future. Can you do that?"

Kate broke eye contact. This was a big step.

"You're right to hesitate," said George. "Even if the plan goes perfectly, you're going to see some ugly things in the next day or two. Yesterday was just a hint. The people who have Matt wouldn't think twice about killing him or you. I'm not going to lie to you; you'll be in danger every minute you're with me.

"But for whatever it's worth, I'll give you my word on this: I won't let anything harm Matt or you if I can help it and I won't lie to you any more. What's more, I'll do whatever I can to protect you legally as well as physically from whatever happens. You're just an innocent kidnap victim under duress. Now, can you do it Kate? I need you to swear it—for Matt."

If she needed any more proof that this had become the strangest person she had ever encountered, Kate got it when she looked back at him. There were more tears welling in George's eyes. In ten years of counseling neurotics and psychotics, there had been the prize of them all right there beside her at Thanksgiving dinner. She chose to believe him and make a promise she could live with—she hoped.

"I swear to you on Matt's life that as long as I believe we are working to save him, I'll help you."

He looked so deeply into her eyes that for a second Kate thought she had misunderstood something. Finally he nodded and she could see some of the tension leave him.

"Good," he said and began to prepare for the next stage of their journey.

Chapter 18

The sights, sounds and, God help them, the scents of her youth were all around Special Agent Gabrielle Bernard and her companion. From down the street they could hear the pulsing refrain of a tinny bump-and-grind instrumental coming out of a disreputable looking place that had vaguely woman-shaped legs wearing red stiletto pumps alternately appearing and disappearing through a second story window. On the other side was the plaintive wail of a B-flat cornet taking its turn at interpreting a song whose notes were never played the same way twice. Over all this hung the fragrance of flowers, Cajun spices and some very stale and very fresh biological smells best left unexamined.

Gaby and Aleksandr Pushkin were turning the corner of St. Peter and Bourbon Street in the French Quarter. From routine toil in the sterile confines of FBI headquarters, she had become completely caught up in the romantic foreigner's enthusiasm and *joie de vivre*.

There was guilt of course. FBI agents are not supposed to have fun at their job. Without actually saying so, her training had made that clear. And the irony of her first real field assignment meandering through a baseball game in Memphis and pausing in the entertainment hub of her famous hometown was not lost on her. But at the moment the pangs of conscience had been completely subsumed by an excellent meal and the company of what she continued to think was the most interesting man in her experience.

That she was staying at the Fairmont Hotel had been justified by the fact that she had arranged a meeting there with a prominent local attorney who could help cut some corners with the Port Authority. The fact that it was her father need not really appear in her report, as it was an irrelevant fact. Likewise the choice of her favorite restaurant in the world was simply happenstance. Arnaud's was just a place to get a good solid meal. Yeah, that was it. Besides, Pushkin was a guest of the Federal Government and he had insisted. Okay, she was going to catch hell when she got back but once you jump off the cliff you might as well enjoy the scenery on the way down.

It was not a particularly busy night in the Quarter. Foot traffic was mostly confined to the sidewalks—nothing like the human menagerie that occurs every Fat Tuesday. Yet without turning her head, Gaby could see a couple in formal dress, a not very subtle panhandler, a black kid that looked to be nine or so dancing on the curb, a group of four frat boys arm in arm singing at the top of their lungs and a guy in a Hawaiian shirt sauntering along playing a soprano saxophone. Inured to the patent strangeness of the place by long exposure Gaby was able to experience a first-timer's view vicariously through the eyes of Alex Pushkin and it was as intoxicating as quart of 'Hurricanes'.

She looked at him and his face was alight.

"Some place, huh?" she asked.

It was actually noisy enough that it was hard to carry on a conversation so when Alex put his arm around her shoulder and put his mouth up close to her ear, she allowed it.

"Gaby," he said, "I have not lived my whole life in Moscow or the small town where I was born. I went to school for a bit in London and after becoming attached to Interpol, I lived for a while in Paris. I have visited Copenhagen and some of the other capitols in Europe, but I have never seen anything quite like this."

She smiled and they walked east, the opposite direction from Canal and their Hotel. It was still some time before the meeting she had scheduled and they were enjoying the stroll. He did not remove his arm. With gentle pressure, Alex maneuvered her against the façade of the Royal Sonesta just past the entrance. When he turned her to face him she looked up, and without any prelude, he kissed her.

His lips were warmer than the sultry night and much softer than she had imagined. Imagined? Wait a minute, here! She had imagined no such thing! Had she?

It was tender rather than passionate and lasted only a moment. She moved him back just a few inches and stared briefly at the ground between their feet.

"I think we should get back," she said. "It's almost time for our meeting."

She walked stiffly away a few steps before Alex moved. He called to her and she kept walking.

"Gaby," he said again. He caught up to her.

"Look," he said. "Please, if I . . ."

She made a gesture of dismissal and they walked the three blocks with a near-military cadence, immersed in the mélange of sad, energetic music and the sights of colorful street characters, saying nothing more. Alex tried again while they waited for the light at Canal but it changed too quickly. When they reached the lobby, he began again.

"Gaby, please let me . . ."

"He is to meet us in the bar," she interrupted. "I think we should wait for him there."

Gaby still had not looked at his face since Bourbon Street. She quickened her pace up the ramp past the closed shops in the lobby concourse. Alex didn't move for a second or two and she was all the way to the bar entrance when he caught her again. He was determined to make her listen this time and took her arm, spinning her around. This time she had to look into his eyes.

Yet again, he began, "Gaby . . ." and at almost the same moment a rich familiar voice called her name from the darkness inside.

"Dad, hi," she answered and the Russian's hand fell away from the fabric over her upper arm.

Charles Antoine Bernard was a large man, taller even than Pushkin's six-one yet the last few of his seventy-three years had made him smaller than Gaby remembered. His hair was silver and full over bristling brows with much of the black color intact and the eyes under the brows were the same color as Gaby's—a piercing, almost golden shade of brown. Though it was nearly ten in the evening, his dark suit and white shirt looked freshly pressed. His mouth was full like his daughter's too, but where hers curved playfully upwards at the corners, his turned down. When relaxed it made him look dour or cruel. He was a man accustomed to deference who was certain that his assumption of superiority was simple accuracy rather than arrogance. He spoke with the thick New Orleans accent common to the people who run the city and are not concerned with whether some out-of-towner thinks it parochial. He was 'old money' in a very old town with a lot of it and among other things he was on the board of the Port of New Orleans Authority, whose logo adorned the cover of the folder he was carrying.

"Hello, Gaby," he said, but he pronounced it Gay-bee. "I made it a little early. Are you all right, Sweet?"

As good as her posture was normally, Gaby managed to stand even straighter as he approached.

"Of course, Dad, I'm fine," she said and kissed him on the cheek. The senior Bernard barely tilted his head forward, forcing Gaby to stretch tiptoe just for the glancing contact.

"Charles Bernard, I'd like you to meet Lieutenant Aleksandr Pushkin. He is the Interpol officer assigned to this case.

They shook hands and Charles' glance wandered from Pushkin's face to the spot on Gaby's arm he had just released. For a moment he seemed to be waiting for an explanation but when none was forthcoming he gestured toward the darker interior and they moved that way.

When they neared the table a man sitting there got up and Gaby's heart stopped for a beat.

"Hello, Gab," the man said in a deep, musical voice and it was like an icy knife in her ribs. "You look marvelous."

"Hello Gran, you too," Gabrielle replied.

To her knowledge she was the only one other than his maternal grandmother who had ever called him Gran—the grandmother because it was a reference to Granville, her mother's maiden name. He was born with the unlikely moniker of Granville Mouton Boudreaux Galvez. Among his friends, he was called by his initials, G.G. or Gigi. In his fraternity he had been called by a corruption of his middle name, Mutton or just Mutt. Born into the lofty level of society that she was, it didn't occur to Gaby until very late in adolescence that many of the given names and nicknames hung on her family and friends were utterly absurd as was their acceptance of them. 'Mutt' for example with its implication of questionable breeding would, one would think, have insulted and scandalized families with far less pretentious lineage but she couldn't remember ever hearing anyone remark on it beyond a casual clucking of the tongue by his mother.

He was wearing an embroidered white linen shirt open at the collar. Missing was the mounted twenty dollar gold piece on a heavy chain that he had worn the last time they met, but the Rolex Presidential was still there in all its diamond encrusted glory. On his fingers there was only the Princeton ring. He smiled but didn't show any teeth in the process, which was his habit, though when he chose to turn it on it was engaging, dimpled and a brilliant shade of enamel white.

Granville Galvez's hair was longer, still almost black and his eyes hadn't begun to age and get the dark sub orbital lines one associated with his olive complexion even before the middle years. He did still look great.

Gaby introduced Aleksandr again and they sat down so that her father and Galvez were on either side.

Without asking preferences, The older man held up two fingers to the barman who quickly brought over two more of the drinks whose names came from the Sazerac Bar where they sat to join the two that had already been served. Charles Bernard had been frequenting the spot since he discovered that his father had shared the same table with Governor Huey P. Long so many years before. He knew that it was proper in this place, particularly after an absence, to drink Sazerac.

"I didn't know you would be here," said Gaby to Galvez.

Her father spoke up as he moved Gaby's drink by the stem and tossed the folder across the small table in front of her.

"I told you I would get these reports since you thought it so important that they couldn't wait until morning. Gigi is on the board too now and he knows all the operations people."

"I see."

"So how are you doing, Gab," Galvez asked. "Still playing policeman are we?"

Gaby took a deep breath.

"Yes, I'm afraid the Federal Government insists," she replied.

"Well the regimen seems to agree with you, darlin'. You look as delicious as ever."

Granville Galvez appeared earnest and interested but Gaby had long ago admitted that she was really never able to read him that accurately. She looked down and didn't respond so he continued in a more sarcastic tone.

"Will the folks at Tulane still take your calls? Civil Service is not a very common goal for their Law graduates I should think."

"Only for honors grads, Mister Galvez. We thank you for your help. I hope it wasn't too much trouble."

"As a matter of fact I'll owe a favor for this one, *Cher*. The IT Director interrupted his dinner to come back in and run the queries himself," Galvez said. "Unfortunately it seems to have gone for naught. He told me that there was no incoming cargo that even partially matched the kind of shipments you are looking for, either river or ocean-going."

"They must have missed them somehow," said Gaby. "They have to be there."

Galvez shook his head.

"Your information must be bad. They had record of some recent Molotov equipment moves and they are listed there, but nothing in the last two days. If the Port Authority doesn't know about it, it simply is not here."

"Do you know if it could have been diverted upriver?"

"I anticipated that question and I asked some of the traffic people before I came over here to confirm what I already knew. The answer is of course it could."

"Where?"

"*Cher*, there are a hundred ports on the river between here and Memphis. Dozens of them have rail connections. Some of them are carrier sidings and there are quite a few spur lines owned and operated by corporations—Chemical companies, Forestry products and so forth. You may be able to discover something from the rail carrier."

Gabrielle looked crestfallen and Pushkin still sat in uncomfortable silence.

"What is it, Sweet?" her father asked.

Gaby had opened, examined and set aside the papers they had provided. Now she was twisting a lock of her hair at the temple between her thumb and forefinger and seemed disinclined to answer.

"Sir," said Aleksandr after another pause, "since New Orleans was the original destination we had hoped to be able to find the shipment here. It was our only lead."

"Then the railroad will be able to tell you where it is."

This time Gaby spoke up.

"The CN Railway reported twelve hours ago that the load was coming here to the Nashville Avenue wharf. As of three hours ago, they have no record that the shipment was ever made."

"I'm sorry, Sweet. I don't know what to tell you," Charles Bernard said. "That's just not possible. Can you think of any other avenues, Gigi?"

Galvez shook his head toward Charles Bernard and then looked over at the other two.

"Anything further would indeed have to wait for the morning. I could call some friends tomorrow, but offhand I can't think of a thing that seems likely. Isn't that pretty much what you people do?"

"We'll be pursuing other avenues," Gaby said sourly.

"How about Interpol?" He directed the question at Alex. "*Êtes vous postés á Lyon?*"

"*Seulement brievement, monsieur.* I have lived there less than two months and I don't expect the assignment to be extended for long."

"Too bad," Galvez said. "I have always found Lyon to be one of the underrated cities on the continent. Marvelous cuisine, superb location and a short ride from Geneva and Milan. Do you remember, *Cher*? We passed through on the trip from Biarritz."

Gaby smiled thinly.

"No, not really."

Galvez chuckled as at a private joke.

"That's a shame, Darlin'. I remember it very well indeed and it's well worth remembering."

She wanted so badly to pull out her service pistol and whack him over the head with it. He consulted his Rolex and stood up. Gaby's father and Alex Pushkin followed suit.

"Regrettably, I must take my leave for now," Galvez said

Gabrielle remembered how much he liked to use that kind of flowery phrase, particularly in front of her father. She thought she had a pretty good idea where he had to go. The scent of expensive after-shave freshly applied brought back unpleasant memories of the end of their marriage. She wondered if there was someone waiting for him at this moment who had questioned his need to freshen up for his late night business meeting—someone who would still be waiting for him several hours from now when he returned with a completely different scent.

"Oh, you don't have to begin the investigation this late at night," she said, shooting him irony in a sideward look.

"Not just yet," he said. "I had a previous social engagement which I postponed so that I could perform this little service for Charles. And Gaby, darlin' I must say I'm a little surprised that the International police and the FBI could have misplaced an entire train. That must be a record of some kind, *n'est ce pas?* One would think that you would have better sources than a little old Louisiana businessman?"

"Not at the moment, it seems," said Gaby.

"Then I shall pursue the matter forthwith. Can I reach you here?"

She reached into her purse and searched for a moment by touch, handing him her business card when she was done.

"My cell phone is on there."

"Very good," he said. "Thank you for the drink, Charles, I'll see you at the Thursday meeting if we don't meet at the club first. It was a pleasure to make your acquaintance Lieutenant and Gaby you may expect my call before noon. Au revoir, all."

Galvez smiled and actually made a half bow as he exited. The others resumed their seats. Gaby emptied her lungs in an exhausted sigh. She used to think that bowing crap was continental or gallant or admirable somehow.

"Daddy, you should have told me you were going to involve him," she said when he turned the corner.

"Nonsense. He was the logical one to call. Not many people could have produced that report, whether you find it helpful or not, in just a few hours. You might have been a little more gracious."

"Yes. As I recall, both of you always felt that lack of grace was my major shortcoming."

"Gabrielle . . ."

His use of her full name was always a prelude to some homily or other and she was in no mood. Besides, she always lost the argument. Somewhere down deep where she had no logical control, she too believed that between her rejection of her traditional wifely role and the barrenness of her womb she really had been at fault.

"Sorry, Daddy, I don't want to get something started. How is Mother?"

"She is fine. She wanted me to tell you that you could at least visit your home while you are here. Trey and Binnie are both doing well and your godson just graduated eighth grade without so much as a card from you I understand."

"Sorry, Dad I have just been so busy."

"It is so good to see you, Sweet. I wish you would come on home now."

"I'll try to stop in on the way to the airport and say hello."

"That's not what I meant."

"I know, Daddy."

Gaby looked into his eyes and actually saw pain there. It was true what Trey had said when they last spoke, that age had finally softened her father. It had made him sentimental without altering the hardness underneath. He did want her to be happy and it made him confused and a little angry that he was unable to make it so by demanding it. She knew it mystified him that almost seven years after he had thought her life to be ordered and complete, his beautiful daughter was still searching for . . . what? Happiness? Redemption? Validation? Even Gaby wasn't certain.

The elder Bernard drained the last of his drink and stood up slowly, looking as old as he was for the first time.

"It's getting late and I need to be getting home. You will let me know if you need anything else?"

Barring extraordinary circumstances, Charles Bernard was in bed every night at precisely 10:30 and read, usually periodicals, for precisely 30 minutes. He slept seven hours every night almost without exception and opened the door to his office every morning at exactly ten minutes after eight. It occurred to Gaby that if it was this predictability she had objected to, her rebellion had failed comprehensively—she was more or less the same way.

This time Gaby reached up and pulled on the old man's shoulder until he either had to lean over and meet her kiss or pick her up off the ground. He met her half way and she whispered, "I love you, Dad," in his ear.

"It was a pleasure to meet you, sir," Pushkin said when he shook his hand.

Charles Bernard again looked hard at the Russian as if he wanted to say something more, but didn't. Instead, he nodded and walked away, again ramrod straight, and out of the Sazerac Bar. They stood quietly for a moment and watched him disappear.

"Would you like another drink?" Pushkin asked Gaby.

"No," she replied and threw the rest of her first one back like a rustler at the Long Branch Saloon before leaving at a pace that made it hard for Pushkin to keep up.

In the elevator the Russian punched the button for the fifth floor and said, "Your father seems like a fine man."

She thanked him with one word. Her preoccupation was apparent.

"And Mister Galvez seemed . . . formidable," he added.

"Yes. Formidable is one interpretation," she answered.

"You seem to know him well."

"Yes, I do. Often one doesn't get to know a person just by marrying him, but after a divorce, everyone knows everyone very well."

"This is the man who was your husband?"

"Almost three years."

"You had no children, then?" he asked.

She winced at the question and said "No" just as the fifth floor door opened.

For once Aleksandr Pushkin was not as glib. As they walked to their rooms he said, "Shall we meet at 7:30 as usual?"

"Yes, 7:30," she replied softly as if she were answering a voice in her head.

Gaby stopped in front of the door to her room with a card key in her hand and Alex continued to his. He put a card in the slot in the door and the tiny green light came on. The hinges creaked slightly and he heard or felt movement behind him. When he turned, there was Gaby with outstretched arms and needy, luminous eyes. Aleksandr Pushkin was enveloped in the sudden heat of her kiss and they half fell backward into the darkness of his room.

Chapter 19

Another mistake?

Yes, Gaby decided, but not one she would have to live with for very long. In a few days or a week, Aleksandr Pushkin would be on a plane back to France where he was no doubt allowing other women to forget for a moment the insecurities and the wrong turns they had taken in life. These thoughts took less than a second to be born at an advanced age, die and be buried in her subconscious. That distasteful exhumation would certainly take place and soon, but for the moment she was enjoying the basic and profound experience of being a woman again.

Alex could be heard padding about in the bathroom and the little coffee maker there was just beginning its noisy cycle. Gaby lay diagonally across the bed with her head on his pillow. One leg up to the hip was unprotected by the single sheet, which came only as high as her bottom rib. The rough linen had the faint pungency of cleaning chemicals but when she moved about, the scent of the fluids left behind by their couplings covered it. She breathed it in and moaned softly with the memory.

The first time, her need had been too urgent to enjoy the details fully. Afterward, they lounged for a while. Gaby explored the smooth, hard curves of his body as they talked of harmless things—warmth, softness and pleasant discoveries. The glowing clock by the bed had said 11:35 when Gaby said that she should be getting to her own room. Aleksandr objected gently and without words. This time with more subtlety and grace, he took her beyond the delight she had just experienced and into a pounding, repetitive ecstasy she had rarely achieved. Afterward, lacking the energy or the desire to move further, she fell into exhausted sleep filled with dreams she enjoyed but couldn't remember.

When she awoke perversely at first light she draped one long leg over his sleeping form and pressed her breasts into his broad back. It was not a great surprise when he groaned pleasurably, rolled over and made love to her again. Their effort lacked the nuance of the night before but the substance of it was a wonderful punctuation at the end of their night together. After a short time Alex kissed her once more, rolled out from under the sheet and went into the lavatory, leaving her to bask for another few minutes in the cooling embers of the fire they had made together.

Alex's head appeared around the corner.

"Can I bring you a cup?" he asked.

She said yes with some enthusiasm and he brought a white ceramic mug over while she wrapped the disheveled remains of the bedclothes around her and sat up. Under other circumstances she would have pointed out that the coffee was bitter and a little too weak, but at the moment it seemed beyond praise. Alex was dressed in his slacks and undershirt. He sat in a chair facing the bed with his feet propped up.

"You are quite wonderful, you know," he said.

Gaby gave him a feline smile.

"Yes, you told me," she replied. "Repeatedly."

"I mean it," he said, rubbing her exposed leg with the edge of his foot.

"Well, you are quite an experience yourself."

"No, Gaby. It is more than that. I mean that you are the most marvelous lover, the most marvelous person that I have ever known."

"Alex, you know that what we had, as wonderful as it was cannot become . . ."

"Yes, yes, I know we said that this was a thing of the moment and that our involvement cannot develop . . ."

"So don't talk about it, Alex."

He sighed and made a gesture of submission with the cup he held in his hand. The morning light was streaming in the window full on his face and his eyes were glowing softly with it, looking almost a pastel shade of blue.

"Alex, how is it that you never married?"

"So you read my *zapiska* as well, Special Agent Bernard?"

"Just procedure. But it did make me curious. I know your record with Berkut was exemplary and there was no fault to find with your investigative history, but . . ."

"What? What were you thinking?"

Gaby laughed. "Under the circumstances it seems quite absurd now but when I read it and then saw you, I thought you must be gay—you know, homosexual."

Alex smiled. "You mean because I have not married?"

"No, because you are gorgeous and have not married. Women must have been chasing you since you were fifteen years old."

"My social life is not as you imagine."

"Everything is relative, as Comrade Sakharov would have said. You are the one who had protection last night, ready for action as it were, not me."

"Protection?"

"Condoms, Alex."

"Ah. Protection."

"Yes. That could have been very embarrassing, frustrating or both."

"They were merely artifacts of national pride, Agent Bernard. Mother Russia invented the condom you know."

Gaby kicked his foot playfully.

"It is true that I have never been married but I was engaged once for more than a year," he said.

"Oh? What happened? I'm sorry, that's a little personal, I guess."

"We have been a little personal with each other, have we not?"

"I have to agree there," Gaby said. "Then tell me."

"I was advised against it by Colonel Dashenko."

"You know, I am beginning to absolutely loathe this man. Didn't you think that was a little presumptuous on his part?"

"No. The Colonel has been very helpful to me. I think you would call me a protégé of his. He simply advised me that at that point in life it would hinder my career—that there would be a proper time for a family after I had achieved a bit more."

"Alex, that's just terrible!"

"Not at all. Everything has happened exactly as he foretold. I was promoted as an officer in the Berkut and received the Interpol assignment. When I return, I will be . . . I will be more financially secure. Perhaps then I can think about marriage and children."

"How romantic!" Gaby said.

"It must be very hard, perhaps impossible for you living in all this plenty to understand conditions in my country. The collapse of the Soviet rule has meant freedom, yes, but poverty and chaos also. We can now go anywhere we want and do whatever we want to do but very few have the means to do that. We were unprepared for democracy. Government agencies have reestablished themselves in the large cities, but in some areas what you call the Mafia is still in complete control because its model, harsh as it is, is closer to a free market than the socialist system."

"I have read a little, but you're probably right. No one can really understand another culture without living in it."

"Freedom is wonderful, but it implies an opportunity to fail as well. This is one freedom I do not choose to embrace."

"So how about your ex-fiancée?" she asked. "When you get back this time, will you have achieved enough?"

"That was some time ago. Things are . . . different now."

Alex seemed lost in thought for a moment. Gaby put her cup on the nightstand and swung her legs over the edge of the bed.

"Which reminds me that it is time to face the music," she said.

"Yet another idiom?"

"Yes. It means that the time has come for me to report my total failure in my first and only field assignment. I have lost two kidnap victims and an interstate trainload of supposedly smuggled goods and have no idea of where to look for any of them."

Gaby set about putting on just enough clothing for the forty foot trip to her own room.

"Tell you what," she said, looking at her watch. "Let's take an hour to get cleaned up and make reports. Then what say we stroll down to the French Market for coffee and beignets? That will allow me to extend my good mood a little while longer before I have to go back to Washington and fall on my sword."

"Another expression, I hope?" Alex said.

Gaby kissed him on the cheek and touched him briefly.

"An hour then?" she asked and he nodded.

It was only after she had traveled the forty feet, shut the door to her room and looked around that the awkwardness of the situation began to sink in. Then she saw the little red light flashing on the bedside phone. Gaby groaned and dialed the front desk. Please, she thought, let it be a message from Dad last night reminding me to meet in the bar at ten o'clock. Wrong. It was a voice mail stamped at nine forty-five from Tony Metcalf wondering in so many words where she was. He pointed out that she had been cleared for a visit to the Memphis crime scene but nothing further. He mentioned Cannon's name again. Shit!

She looked at the clock again and added an hour for Eastern Time. Thanks to the fact that her day had begun delightfully at dawn, it was still too early for him to be in the office. Shower. Focus on the shower. That always made her feel better.

But it always made her think too. Some of her best ideas happened in the shower. This time it was hard to get beyond dread and recrimination. What must they be thinking back at headquarters? Gran was just being nasty last night but his judgment of her job performance couldn't be far from theirs. Let's see. You first went on this cross-country tour with promises of solving several murders. Then more people were killed practically under your nose. Then an innocent woman and child were kidnapped and you announced that you were going to track them based on the location of a freight train. Then you lost the train! Oh yeah, this would be easy to explain.

Then there was the matter of sleeping with a visiting international official. What if they found out about that? No way! And yet . . . Oh Gaby, you are going to go far, girl.

What about Alex? What if he didn't want to let go? What if he assumed something more from their liaison? Again, unlikely. It would interfere with his career and the godlike Colonel wouldn't allow that. And what if he didn't assume anything at all from their liaison? How would that make her feel? In spite of her impulsiveness of last evening, she was not one to sleep around. She had formed genuine feelings for Aleksandr Andreyevich Pushkin—or had she? How genuine were they?

Gaby shut off the water and grabbed one of the big body towels. As always it was coarse from a thousand washings and the accompanying chemicals. She looked at her dripping body in the mirror and posed for a moment in profile. It was a good one she knew, in spite of that unfortunate little reproductive defect. Except for those little extra deposits over the hip joints. No matter how much you worked out you could never get rid of those. Saddlebags? Yecch, what a term. And the full breasts she had been so proud of in her youth were beginning to show signs of gravity's effects already. What did Alex think about it, really? He didn't seem to object to any flaws last night but he must have had hundreds of girls. Come to think of it, just why *had* he brought condoms on this trip, anyway?

Oh well. She wrapped the towel around her and blew the remaining water from her hair with the hotel dryer. First things first. She would call the office and admit that things weren't going so well and suggest that they should call on some of the likely rail ports up river before giving up.

She was brushing her hair and wondering about her resignation and what the FBI could assign her to that was more boring than what she had already been doing, when there came a knock on the door. When she opened it a crack there was Alex with his rumpled suit, a fresh white shirt and a mischievous smile on his face.

Suddenly she was embarrassed about her nakedness and didn't want to let him in.

"Alex, I said an hour. I'm not ready yet."

He handed her a piece of paper through the opening. It looked like an e-mail but printed mostly in a Cyrillic typeface with three lines in English. It was an address in Miami.

"What's this?" she asked.

"That is the address of a warehouse where the first freight container, the one that was damaged, is located.

She opened the door a little wider but still hadn't let him inside.

"How in the world did you get this?"

"From my laptop computer a few minutes ago. It was sent by Colonel Dashenko."

"Colonel Dashenko! How the hell could he possibly know . . . ?"

"I told you he is a genius."

Gaby called him and his boss names and told him to give her ten more minutes. Then she shut the door and started to dress, excited about the new development.

Less than a minute more had passed when there was another knock on the door.

She pulled the towel back around her and pulled the door open a few inches again as she said impatiently, "I told you to give me a minute, Alex."

But when she looked into the hall there was Phil Cannon, looking deadly as usual in his dark blue suit.

Chapter 20

By the time the trucker hauling the American President Lines container number 25128 pulled in for a stop at Grenada Mississippi, Katherine Wallace was almost completely convinced that she would not be killed. She was convinced as well that the George Gordon she had known was well and truly gone—almost as dead as he claimed to be. Not that the man she was traveling with seemed like her notions of a murderer, just that he seemed to be someone else. She tried to be clinical about it—more precise anyway, but beyond the glimpse of the man's violent capabilities it just came down to that. He was just different.

Before, George had seemed open, occasionally talkative. Now he spoke only when it was necessary or to avoid being openly rude. And when he did, his speech patterns were very different. He chose words, profanity for instance, that George would never have used. His accent and pronunciations weren't the same either. She couldn't place it but from what Turner/Mooney had told her she assumed it was South Georgia. At first she thought he was putting it on, or exaggerating with her to make a point but once established, it didn't vary.

At Grenada, Kate wanted to sneak out to go to a real rest room. George said no emphatically.

"It won't be that long," he added. "We'll be getting out of here at Jackson."

George was sitting in front of a laptop computer. It was connected to a cell phone and he was surfing like a born geek. The George she knew was computer illiterate.

"I thought you were following some freight shipment to New Orleans," Kate said, looking over his shoulder.

"It got diverted. I expected that."

"Where?"

"A facility south of Vicksburg. But that's just where they're switching it and there won't be any more recognizable tracing on it. We'll probably have to go there to see where it's really going."

Kate was further reassured that he had used the plural.

"Can you . . . ?"

"Can I what?"

"I still need to use the bathroom."

"So use it."

"Can't you at least turn on a radio or something and look the other way?"

He listened. The truck stop was fairly noisy. George got up and pulled a radio from the cabinet—from her experience already it appeared that George had one or more of everything in there. He switched it on, turned the laptop about twenty degrees and adjusted the stool he was sitting on.

Kate sighed and pulled down the little toilet. The radio was playing classical music. George didn't like classical music. When she was done, she came back to look down at his screen. The mouse pointer was flying over screens from the Canadian National Railway and Kleinschmidt, which he explained was something called a VAN, in this case a tracing company.

"Nope," he announced. "I know where they sent them first but not where they went from there. You better belt in. He'll be starting up again in a few minutes."

"If you know where we are going," she asked, "why do we have to ship ourselves there?"

"We're not. This box is just going to Jackson," he replied. "They're looking for me in Memphis now, not in Jackson. I've got a clean car and . . . some stuff ready down there."

They could hear the thrum of the diesel and shortly they were on their way again. George rode strapped in the padded chair that was welded to the floor and Kate was forced to take the bed. The floor made a pretty rough ride. After a few attempts at conversation it became obvious that George was all talked out for the moment. He had the faraway stare of a yogi in a trance state.

Kate knew that he had been a voracious reader on a broad mix of topics. She asked if he had any books to help pass the time. He surprised her by offering a choice of four: an issue of Popular Science, an electronics textbook, a leather-bound bible and a paperback issue of The Lord of the Rings. Kate shook her head and took the Tolkien book. The bizarre was becoming commonplace. Ninety minutes later the tractor had delivered them to a yard and they heard it drive away.

George spent a minute looking out of several slots and an improvised periscope to be sure they would not be observed. He commented to Kate that if he had been more diligent at this the day he had to kill the first Russian, then none of this need have occurred. She wasn't sure what he meant by that but she let it drop.

When George was certain that no one was there, he opened the trick hatch and unhooked the little Honda. In another minute they were on the road to a self-storage facility that George had obviously prepared for this sort of purpose. Riding double on the belching little two-stroke powered thing they must have looked quite ridiculous but it was less than a mile to the storage facility.

George entered a digital code into a keypad by the entrance and in another minute they had pulled up in front of a unit with a fairly conventional garage door. When opened it revealed a Ford Taurus that was at least seven years old. It looked to be a horrid shade of green but it was difficult for Kate to tell through the layers of dust. There were four cabinets mounted in the space at about eye level.

George immediately opened door and got in. Shortly a clicking sound emanated from somewhere under the hood area and he got out and began looking through one of the cabinets on the driver's side. He came out with a heavy bright yellow gadget she recognized as a portable battery charger and while she watched, he put it to work. Kate didn't offer to participate and he didn't ask for her help. With the clips in place the engine turned over immediately and he put the charger back in its place, still ignoring his interested spectator.

George backed the car out, put the moped inside the storage unit, locked up and pulled a ragged bath towel from the back seat whereupon he proceeded to whack, scrape and pummel enough dust off of the windows to make the car drivable.

It was a nondescript color of green and one of the commonest cars in the America of its vintage. It was an old, boring, American car with dings down the passenger side. It occurred to Kate that if she were trying to select a car for its blandness and forgettability, this one would be a heck of a choice. George still hadn't spoken to her, but when he had sat idling and adjusting his mirrors for a few seconds he looked over at her and waited until she got in the passenger side.

As they drove off the lot, Kate settled in and opened a canvas bag she had appropriated from the trailer. Inside were two bars of granola, her borrowed book and a few things George had stolen from her house along with her. After a few miles she continued her reading. Frodo was almost to Rivendell by the time the car stopped again.

They had driven a long way on ever decreasingly traveled roads and Kate resisted the urge to ask questions, but she began to get anxious again.

"I've got to see a guy," George announced when he turned off the ignition. "Come with me for just a minute, but I'm warning you, don't say anything. It wouldn't do you any good anyway; this guy wouldn't be calling the police whatever you told him."

With a little sigh of relief Kate replied, "Don't worry, I promised I wouldn't get in the way. But why do you want me to come?"

"If he's looking for me he'll be looking for a man alone. It'll give me a little extra time if somebody else is around."

Reluctantly, she got out and walked up the gravel path toward the only building in sight. It was a small white clapboard with a window air conditioner hanging out of one of the two windows they could see.

On one side of the structure was a set of railroad tracks with a lot of grass and weeds growing all around. On the other was a flat area with some heavy equipment, five truck trailers like the one they had just left and two stacked containers.

When they got to the office, George greeted the man inside like a lost cousin. Kate was already growing more nervous and her eyes widened at the change in her companion. He sounded newly emerged from the cotton fields of the Mississippi delta.

"Hey, man," he said, making 'man' sound like it had two syllables. "They got you workin' by yerself today?"

Sure enough, the man behind the battered desk smiled back at him.

"You got it! What can I do for you?"

George had his arm around Kate as if it belonged there.

"Ahm lookin' fer Luther Peavey," he drawled.

"I'm Luther," the man said.

"Mah name's Billy Pratt and this is mah Wife, Thelma."

They shook hands.

"You know Bobby Whalen up in Memphis? He said you could prob'ly hep me."

The man nodded eagerly.

"There was one shitload o' twenty-footers come down this way in the last week or so. I'm lookin' for one in particular."

The smile left Luther Peavey's face like it had been slapped. Under his leathery tan, the blood drained from it. He recovered about half of both.

"Naw, man. You tell Bobby to get his shit together. Ain't no dry vans any kind been down here in a week. Sure not no international shit."

"Aw, come on Luther. You couldn'ta missed all that shit. Even if you was off yestiddy you'da heard."

"Nope. Coupla reefers is all."

George looked at Kate.

"Say Honey, ahm tryin' to do some bidness here. Why don't you get on back to the car and wait. Luther's jist givin' me a hard time."

Fascinated as she was by the quality of George's performance, Kate was eager to leave. She knew something bad was about to happen.

As she excused herself and walked out she could hear more protestations from Peavey and repetitions from George. She was thirty yards away before she heard the first crash. Two more happened before she could get inside the car. She reached over, started the engine and turned on the air conditioner. She didn't hear any more.

Ten minutes later George walked briskly back to the Taurus. He showed her a scrap of paper with an address on it and handed it to her.

"Miami," he said. Then he put the car in gear and spun back down the two-lane blacktop that led to the highway.

"That Luther is one stubborn sumbitch," he said. "I need to get off this damn road before his relief comes on duty and here he is givin' me a buncha shit."

He was still 'in character' and that worried Kate a little.

"Who is Billy Pratt?"

She was curious about the name he had given.

"You mean besides me?" he replied with a strange look. "Boris Karloff. When he was born, they called him William Pratt."

He was still 'on', but the thick drawl began to fade. Kate didn't say anything until they were back on US 61.

"Did you get what you wanted?"

"Yeah, mostly. There were two recent shipments. The first box was damaged and it passed through old Luther's hands last week. He sent it on to Miami. That confirms what I thought so we're on our way there. That's where Matt will be. The rest were loaded from that same dock onto a boat a few hours ago. They'll probably end up in the same place, but the first one would surely have gone to the head man, and the head man lives down there."

"What . . . what did you do to that Luther man?"

"He shouldn't have lied to Billy Pratt."

George heard Kate's sharp intake of breath.

"These men are bad, Kate, real bad. I didn't actually kill him though. I want the folks in Miami to know I'm coming."

Kate was relieved at that but curious.

"Why would you want to warn them?"

"Because if they thought I wasn't, they would have no reason to keep Matt alive."

She wanted to ask another question but was afraid of the answer so she just settled in and let the long drive calm her down.

They stopped for gas twice and Kate was allowed to visit the rest room and get whatever food and drink she wanted. They even visited a Wal-Mart store near the highway so that she could get some things for herself that George had overlooked. Kate continued to read and George just drove like an automaton with his eyes straight ahead and his hands at 10 and 2 o'clock on the wheel.

George wasn't driving very fast and it had become late by the time they pulled into Tallahassee Florida on Interstate 10 where he had announced that they would stop for the night.

"I'm just going to get one room," he said as they slowed for the exit. "But you know it's not . . . I mean I wouldn't . . . It's just because it will be less conspicuous that way. It'll be one with two beds."

My God, Kate thought, *he's actually embarrassed to have to talk about that.*

"And so you can keep an eye on me, is that it?"

"No, not . . . I mean not the way you mean. I'm pretty sure that nobody could be following us but if they were I wouldn't want anything to happen to you."

Twenty minutes later they were safely checked into a La Quinta Inn a hundred yards or so from the entrance to the expressway. George asked repeatedly her preferences about showering schedules, the bed she would choose and several other matters of astonishingly trivial importance under the circumstances.

He was so solicitous of her comfort that she almost began to feel like a guest instead of a prisoner but Kate's experience with the new George had already demonstrated that she could never allow herself to relax. Every time she thought she had taken the measure of the situation at last, he would do something or say something that didn't fit with her new interpretation and she would have to begin again.

After they had cleaned up and settled in, Kate drank a little soda while they watched a few minutes of the news. The volume was turned low enough for conversation and the lights were off in anticipation of sleep. Kate was tired but still keyed up and her curiosity, personal and professional, was unsatisfied.

"What was your childhood like, George? Tell me about your father."

"You're still trying to analyze me aren't you? I don't care; knock yourself out."

Then he grunted out a laugh that had no humor in it.

"You mean was he abusive and like that?

"Yeah, I think you could say that. The truth is that he was only a little worse than the average lifer in the military. I knew a lot of Army brats and their stories weren't that different. I just disappointed him, that's all. He wanted a big bruising linebacker and he got an undersized safety. By the time I had my big growth spurt, which as you can see wasn't all that big, and gained a little coordination, he was beyond caring."

"Do you think . . ." Kate hesitated. "Do you think that's why you . . . you know, got this way?"

George chuckled and she tried to apologize.

"That's okay. No, it wasn't my old man. I did it, I guess, to myself . . . in Vietnam."

A loud commercial came on the TV. Kate reached for the remote and turned it off. Now she could see his features only as highlights in the shadows from the window's glow.

"Tell me about it."

"You don't want to know, Kate. You really don't."

"Yes I do. It might be good for you George."

She was thinking of reasons why he might open up to her.

"Someday, Matt might want to know his father better and right now I wouldn't know how to begin. If you understand it, please tell me."

Very softly, his voice barely above a whisper, he said, "All right.

"Mike Hogan was a Special Forces grunt for twenty-one months and twelve days late in the war—just before the bug-out. I had sailed through the training because I had already dealt with the meanest son of a bitch Drill Instructor in the Army.

"Vietnam was bad, but what they say is right. You can get used to anything and I mean absolutely *anything*. I did my job, but I couldn't shut off the thinking, at least not without the dope. I got to where I didn't want to meet any FNG's because I'd just have to meet their replacements in a week or a month."

Kate asked, "What?"

"Fuckin' New Guys," he replied.

"Trouble was that those poor bastards weren't dyin' for anything but that fuckin' body count in Saigon. What it really was was a fuckin' pinball game that if you win, you just get to play again and that bothered me.

"But let me tell you somethin', honey, Mike Hogan was a goddam pinball wizard. I was pilin' up dead rice eaters faster than the Stones were sellin' records."

Instead of relaxing with his reminiscences, his breath had begun to come in ragged spurts, and Kate was never more sorry to have asked a question. In the dim rays from the window she couldn't see George's face clearly but the covers on the other bed were moving spasmodically as if he were far more deeply into the story than she had anticipated. His speech had changed again. He didn't sound like George or even like Billy Pratt.

"George," she said, "I'm sorry. It's obvious that this is upsetting you. You don't need to tell me . . ."

"I'm not tellin' you all this like it's some bullshit excuse. You asked. I'm just tellin' you.

"So, I got this reputation as a badass and this bunch of Special Ops assholes recruited me and my buddy into doing wetworks jobs for the CIA. Something called Project Phoenix. That fuckin' Mooney you met yesterday was in there with them somewhere but I hadn't met him yet. He was a paper-shuffling pimp even then, I guess. I know he was too big a pussy to be doing any of the stuff we were doing, even long range sniping or demolition.

"So those guys were hooked up with an outfit inside of this fake Company Op called Air America that was hauling drugs and making quiet money that they could then turn around and spend on these 'special' jobs without asking the government. They were selling a lot of it to the mob back here. Ain't that some shit? I actually ended up working for a fuckin' mob boss who Saigon thought was working for them."

Kate Wallace knew from her clinical experience that there was a point in any therapy, particularly conscious regression, where the therapist became superfluous. The mere fact of verbalizing a traumatic experience was either doing the job by itself or it wasn't. She could tell from his invariant monotone that George wasn't really talking to her but to himself and the ghosts he carried around with him.

"All that would have been bad enough but I got into the product—real heavy into the product. Smack, crank, blow, reds, green dragons—anything available, and absolutely everything was available. My new buddies were real accommodating about that. At first, I didn't do too many jobs while I was using. It never interfered anyway. But by the end, if I wasn't up to my ass in a rice paddy, I was on another planet. In some ways I might even have been better at it when I was high.

"So anyway, after a while the regular Special Forces, the part that still lived more or less in the real world, hears that there's somebody out there along the Mekong running drugs and guns and they ask the Company to go out there and take him down. I remember we thought it was pretty funny at the time. They wanted us to go out into the jungle and shoot ourselves.

"So we mount this Op as a simple assassination. We take out the leader and let the rest of the organization fall apart on its own. It was supposed to be just me and my partner, Tommy his name was. He was okay, but for these purposes way too much of a fuckin' Boy Scout. He blew a little dope like everybody but he refused any of the real shit that I was using, and he wasn't in on a lot of the 'special' stuff I did for Phoenix. He sure as hell didn't know that he was sharin' a hooch with one of the fuckers we were supposed to be hunting. But that was okay because all I had to do was lose him for an hour on recon, then come back and report the mission accomplished. The Air America dinks would switch to another staging area, we could go back to shootin' gooks and heroin and everybody would be happy.

"The trouble was that at the last minute, Saigon sent a whole platoon in with us for support. That complicated things so the Company boys gave me coordinates near where this evil drug boss supposedly was and told me to lead the platoon there, get my ass out of the way and they would take care of it. Well, I knew that a real soldier, a real man fuckin' takes his orders and that's it.

"I told myself that I didn't know what they were going to do . . ."

There was a long pause before he added, "that was bullshit. I knew damn well they'd have to sterilize to protect the op.

"Some of these fuckers they sent with us were right off the boat, man. I could have told them anything. So I led them to the coordinates and called it in to my contact, we called him Spider, and told him I was buggin' out.

He says fine. *Roger, Mechanic. Out.* I used to like to work on cars back then and that was my call sign.

"So anyway, I take off. I just left them there but I didn't get very far before the firefight started. It must have been the best fuckin' ambush in history considering that they had two days to prepare for it. About that time I changed my mind. It was the God damnedest thing! I had been doing a ton of greenies and some Thai Stick that would knock you on your ass. Then all of a sudden I heard that first shot and I felt like death takin' a shit but I was by-God sober as Billy Graham. I double-timed it back, but of course by the time I got there it was over. There were probably half of the twenty left and they had led two full companies of NVA there to wait on us. I came up from behind and probably wasted a dozen of them but there was no real point to it. All of the friendlies were dead by then except my buddy Tommy. He lucked out but he was sure I was caught with the rest of them. I just took off again. This time I didn't stop."

George paused and his breathing slowed a little. Kate wanted to say something. She couldn't even decide what *kind* of thing to say.

"There was a long time after that that I don't remember much. After they smuggled me back to the States I started doing jobs for Spider and Mooney until a little after I met Val—all those years.

"Tommy was the only one that came home. I killed all of the rest including Mike Hogan. That bastard is buried over there with them."

Kate didn't agree. Clinically she still didn't see George as a Multiple Personality Disorder case but emotionally she was convinced that she had just met Michael Hogan for the first time. She was short of breath from holding it while she listened. Her muscles under the covers were so tense that she began to be aware of painful cramps in her arms and legs. Her professional instinct was to preach self-awareness and self-forgiveness but regardless of his love for her sister and protective attitude toward her, how could she tell this man to forgive himself for what she had just heard?

"I don't know what to say, George. It was a long time ago but that's just a terrible, terrible story. You've never told it to anyone have you?"

"Just Tommy. I finally told him a couple years ago but he'll never tell anybody."

She wasn't sure what that meant.

"Why did you tell it to me?"

"You asked. I told you I'm not making excuses. I fucked up. But that's the way it happened."

"Yes, but . . ."

"I guess I just wanted you to know why I can't take the chance of raising Matt without Val, that I'm not just deserting the boy. Before Val I had never done anything . . . right. I've got this one talent—one thing that I'm probably as good at as anybody—and now I might be able to use it to save Matt's life. Then I'm going to let him go. If someday you think he needs to hear it you can tell the story to him."

Again, a part of Katherine Wallace wanted to disagree with his assessment, to reassure him of his own humanity at least. The George she had known was a decent, caring man, but it was simply impossible to reconcile that with his past.

"Jesus, George," she said in a breathy whisper.

"You can't let Matt find out about any of this any time soon. It's not because of me. Knowing would be bad for him."

"Yes, I can see that," Kate agreed. "And after this is over, what will you do?"

"Honestly, Kate, I really don't think that's going to be a problem. But if I was to make it, I guess I'd end up just like I was before Valerie. Without her, I'm the same man I was before."

Kate was now both horrified and surprised.

"You'd go back to doing . . . all those things?"

"Hemingway said something I've thought about a time or two. I can't remember exactly but he basically said that there's no hunting like the hunting of man and that those who have hunted armed men long enough and liked it, never really care much for anything else after that. Granted, Hemingway never met Val. She was a miracle, she really was an exception to all the rules, but he had it about right. Sometimes it was . . . satisfying."

Kate had literally no more to say. She heard the other bed shift and in five minutes or so he began to snore softly.

Kate was not as lucky this time. She slept only intermittently that night in spite of her fatigue. The sound of gunfire and men's cries disturbed her dreams.

Chapter 21

"Subject structure was part of a crime scene, Your Honor."

"And what crime was that, Mister Bell?"

The deep suntanned and perfectly coifed FBI agent consulted his notes and glanced at Gabrielle Bernard.

"The murder of one Yevgeny Malenkov," he replied.

"Mister Bell, I'm looking right at your brief and I believe it says that Mister Malenkov was dispatched in Memphis, Tennessee by person or persons unknown, does it not?"

"Uh, yes sir."

Judge Harry Cruz sat at his desk in the Dade County Court House, with no jacket and his sleeves rolled up. He looked sardonically over his half-glasses at both agents.

"Are you sure you are in the right court? I don't think I have the right to issue a search warrant in Tennessee."

Gaby knew then that she had been lucky in the assignment of one of the local staff from the Miami FBI office. Agent Bell was young and bright and the two of them had hit it off quickly in their brief conversation before the trip to the courthouse. Now it was obvious that Judge Cruz liked him also from previous encounters. He was just playing with him.

"No, sir, I . . ."

"Your Honor," Gaby interrupted, "we need to inspect a freight container that was in Memphis at the time. The body of Mister Malenkov was discovered partially inside. We have reason to believe that it is now in a warehouse at the 54th Street address."

"Well that's just fine," said the judge, "but that's not what it says here. If it was material evidence, why did the Memphis PD allow it to be shipped out in the first place?"

Gaby got as far as "Sir, there were aspects to the slaying that they . . ." when Cruz stopped her and picked up his pen. He adopted a magisterial tone common to judges and college professors when they wish to assert their position, still peering over his glasses.

"Never mind," he said. "I can see where you were going and I'm going to sign your order, but this request is sloppy. I trust the quality will improve the next time we meet, Mister Bell?"

While he spoke the judge was striking through some of the text and making initials and notations in the margin.

"Yes, Your Honor," said Bell. Gaby rather enjoyed the experience of being the senior agent for the moment.

Cruz signed the second set of papers stapled with the blue backing and held them up for one of the pair to take. They stood up and Gaby took the document, thanked him and they left.

Walking down the courthouse steps Bell asked what else he could do to help. In the course of making her original request at the local office she had dropped some heavy names from headquarters and Bell was eager to be involved in what seemed to be such a visible case.

"How much backup would you like?" he asked. "Should we get the lab people over there?"

"I don't think so," Gaby replied. "At least not yet. This may be a closed warehouse rather than an active freight operation and the container could easily have been moved again in any case. Would it be possible to have a locksmith meet us in case we can't find the owner?"

He nodded and shook her hand. "Yes, I can take care of that for you. And anything else I can do for you while you're here, please call me, Gaby. Good luck."

Phil Cannon was waiting at the curb with Alex and the rental car. Gaby didn't like the man but he was no one to take lightly. Even now, in the wilting Florida heat, he stood very erect and unmoving like a granite statue. Almost as tall as Alex, he was broader and heavier. To Gaby he always looked on the edge of some violence or at least sudden action, like a steel spring coiled to its limit. Perhaps that was one reason she resented him so. He was such an archetype of the macho law enforcement image she was always fighting against.

Agent Bell nodded to the other two and went toward his own car farther down the block.

Cannon had announced that he was sent to help and not to interfere. Gaby didn't believe this of course but so far they had been civil to each other and so far he had allowed her to keep the investigative control due the lead agent. It emerged that Metcalf had been copying Cannon on all her reports as her 'backup' so at least she didn't have to brief him in any great detail.

"Tell me again," Alex asked, "why we had to ask so elaborately for permission just to search for evidence?"

"It's not enough for the FBI to be convinced that there is contraband on the premises. A judge must be convinced also," Gaby replied.

"I suppose it's different where you come from, Aleksandr?" Cannon asked.

"Oh, yes," he said.

"The Cossacks live," said Gaby, opening the car door. "Come on, Rasputin."

Alex just smiled.

The address was only twenty minutes away. Cannon's presence had put a serious damper on conversation so only silence was interrupted a few minutes later when Gaby's phone chirped two bars of The Minute Waltz. It was Bell.

"We found the owner's representative," he said. "The owner of record is Vista Imports but the contact number was their lawyer. He may be there ahead of you."

"Oh, shit," Gaby said without thinking.

"What is it?" Alex asked but she waved him off and listened for another few seconds before she tapped the 'end' key.

"There's no need for the locksmith," she told them. "The owner's attorney is waiting there for us with a key."

"Is that bad?"

"No, not necessarily, but I'd rather not have some litigious toady looking over my shoulder while we search." Unconsciously she looked at Cannon, who had taken the front seat next to her.

It occurred to her that Alex might not get the negative reference and Cannon might be offended, but it didn't seem to bother either of them.

The building was an older structure, small and run-down by comparison with its neighbors. What paint still clung to it looked to have been a dark rust color originally and the many-paned windows were painted white on the inside and covered with black steel mesh on the outside. The man standing at the curb when they arrived was wearing an aquamarine golf shirt with ivory colored slacks and carried a briefcase. He didn't look happy.

"Are you the ones responsible for this?" he asked without any preamble when they emerged from the rental car.

Gaby responded quickly before Cannon could get a word out, although the lawyer was looking at him.

"I'm Special Agent Bernard with the FBI, this is Agent Cannon, and this is Lieutenant Pushkin on assignment from Interpol. We are indeed the ones who requested the inspection. And you are . . . ?"

The man leered rather than smiled at her.

"My name is Ira Levin with the Bearman Levin and Stern firm and I'm the attorney for Vista Imports. Look, what's this all about? This property has been inactive for many years. It was purchased by my client out of condemnation proceedings in 1999. It has remained completely unused by them and is scheduled for demolition in the next couple of months."

"Good," said Gaby. "Then it shouldn't take long to search and anything we tear up wouldn't upset anyone."

"I can't allow anyone inside," Levin said.

"I'm afraid you will," she said, again before Cannon could respond. He really did have a great deal more experience but Gaby was eager to share her foul mood.

"Would you like to see the Search Warrant?"

"Yes I would," he said. "But it won't matter. It was sealed by the state as part of the Florida Urban Reclamation Act of 1998. The City can't order the seal to be broken without a writ of mandamus from the state."

"Swell. This is a Federal Warrant. Are you familiar with the statutes regarding obstruction of justice and hindering a federal official in the performance of duty?"

"Look, honey. I'm sure this plays well downtown. But if you think you can intimidate me you are out of your depth. You may roll into Cruz's chambers and show a little leg and wiggle your ass and get what you want but it doesn't change the law. We can get that rescinded within the hour. Also this building has been declared unsafe so unless you already have the Waiver of Responsibility drawn up, we'd have to wait for that anyway."

Gaby raised one eyebrow and held up a finger to pause the exchange. Now Cannon had a smug expression on his face, apparently content to let her flounder.

"Just one moment," she said to Levin before turning toward Alex. She held out a little Lanier personal recorder.

"Two things:" Gaby said. "First, go back to the car and phone the local office for the number of that locksmith. Take this with you and ask if the prosecutor's office has ever used the Freeman v. Baker, Donelson et al. of 2000 as a precedent in an obstruction or harassment case. Then have a stenographer standing by to take Mister Levin's statement when we bring him in. If it turns out that this delay in the pursuit of a kidnapper results in the victim's death he will additionally be charged with manslaughter and conspiracy. If the judge hesitates, have Agent Bell play Mister Levin's last comment about wiggling asses for him. I'll wait here."

Alex was successful in hiding his confusion. He took the recorder and turned to go as the two attorneys stared at each other.

"You're full of shit," Levin said shrilly.

Gaby's gaze never wandered as she said, "So are you, counselor, but if you're going to have a pissing contest with me, you better bring a bigger hose.

"Now do you or do you not have the keys for this rat trap?"

Levin shook his head disgustedly but produced a ring of three or four keys.

"Wait, Alex," she called out. "I think Mister Levin has had a change of heart,"

Pushkin had only taken eight or ten halting steps toward the car so he was immediately back beside her as Levin tried to open the pair of locks securing the office door of the warehouse. They resisted his efforts.

Gaby started to say something but Levin preempted her.

"Wait, wait a minute, I've got another set in the car," he said and walked across the road toward a convertible Lexus. On the way they could see him talking animatedly into his cell phone.

"Very impressive," said Alex, and for once even Cannon was smiling at her with approval.

"What?" Gaby asked.

"What you just did. It was not as violent as a forced entry by Cossacks but just as effective. You told him a case, a legal precedent that changed his mind?"

"It did sound like that, didn't it?"

"Why, what was it?"

"I don't know. I made it up."

"What?"

She broke into a grin but hid it quickly.

"I made it up. Nobody reads the case law, certainly not a reptile like Mister Levin. Don't worry, I'm fairly certain he made up all that crap he was selling too."

Cannon nodded appreciatively.

"And the tape recording?"

"I use that for my notes. Right now I think it may still have my grocery list on it from last week."

Alex covered his mouth with one hand as if to stifle a laugh as he returned her electronic grocery list.

"Agent Bernard, you continue to amaze me."

The trio was still smiling, but in a more subdued and dignified manner when Levin returned and produced the right key. The lawyer opened the door and stepped aside sporting a look that would surely have killed if he had his way.

The office itself was not so bad, but when they went through the inner door, the warehouse was very dark. The paint on the windowpanes was nearly opaque. Gaby searched the gloom until she found a large bank of switches. She flipped a group of them upward and half the overhead lights came on. When she had finished, every one of the forty bulbs burned from the suspension fixtures.

It was about the size of the gymnasium at a large high school. Except for a cluttered area in one corner by the loading dock, it was completely empty and clear of obstruction other than the steel I-beams every thirty feet or so supporting the roof. They walked in the direction of the pile of debris at the big overhead door.

"How long did you say since this facility had been used, Mister Levin?" Cannon asked.

"I'm not sure exactly. It has been many years I understand."

"Damned clean for a condemned warehouse, wouldn't you say? And amazing that all those light bulbs are burning, both because the electricity is still on and because someone must have been replacing the lights."

Levin didn't reply.

When they got closer to the corner pile the first thing they saw was a stacked wall of boxes. The writing said they were from a Korean company and contained lampshades. Next to them were two acetylene torches with the tanks of gas. On the valve of each of them hung a pair of protective goggles by the elastic strap. The interesting thing was the debris itself. It was obviously the remains of the freight container but if they hadn't known what it used to be it would have been impossible to identify. Every single bar, rivet and panel in the structure had been cut, melted or ripped out. It looked as if it had been through a giant shredder.

"My God," said Alex. "It is the Molotov box. It is still here."

Gaby didn't understand his amazement. She pulled out her phone and dialed the local office.

"Of course it's still here. Why did you think we came?"

Agent Bell was away from his desk but she left a short message. He had been prepared so little detail was needed.

"Come on," she urged Alex, who hadn't moved, "let's check it out."

Gaby opened one box and it indeed had a dozen lampshades inside. Alex kicked a few more stacks down the row and the all moved in the same insubstantial way. They agreed that they were safe in assuming that all the cartons contained just what the labels indicated.

When they reached the pile, Alex picked up the metal piece nearest him. It was painted white on one side and was of extremely light metal.

"We could have this tested also," said Alex, "but I think there is very little reason to do that. It is possible that this is not the same container, but not likely."

Gaby addressed the Miami lawyer.

"You still contend that this is an unused facility? Two weeks ago this was a cargo box in Memphis Tennessee."

"My client would naturally have no knowledge of unauthorized access to this property."

"Okay, counselor—bullshit—but okay. Please stand over there out of the way, or better still, you can go. We'll lock up."

"I . . . I can't."

"Can't what?"

"My client has instructed me not to leave the premises while you are here. We are within our rights to be . . ."

"Yeah, yeah," Gaby interrupted. "Then stand over there by that supporting beam and try to keep this condemned building from falling down on us."

Alex was pulling at random on the larger pieces and looking underneath.

When Gaby bent over, he said, "Careful. These edges are all jagged and some are very sharp."

"Yes they are," Cannon agreed and looked around him. When he checked behind the big rolling tanks he found two pairs of dirty leather workman's gloves and threw one of them to Alex. Before they began in earnest, each of them removed their jackets and draped them over the tank dollies since they were slightly less dusty than the floor. Gaby walked around the periphery looking for a likely area of the heap to check.

The men pulled on the pile actively for several minutes accomplishing nothing but making it broader and shallower.

"What are we looking for?" Alex asked her. "It is clear to me that if there was some contraband transported inside this shell it has been extracted and moved."

"I agree," she said, "but I'd like to see the part that was originally damaged by that machine in the yard. I'm not really sure we would be able to tell."

Alex nodded.

"It would have been one of the four corner braces. The yard manager said the vehicle was turning a corner when the collision occurred."

It had been a long time since Gaby had worked a jigsaw puzzle. She struggled to hold up a long strip carefully in her bare hand.

"Would this be one of them?" she asked.

"Yes, I would say so. It has the right angle turn and is painted white on the outside radius. But the one you are holding was cut with the torch. You can see the melted edges."

It took ten more minutes of searching. Both of them were winded from the effort and Alex had torn his shirt on one of the shards of a side panel when he held up a curved four-foot strip like the first one Gaby had found only shorter.

Cannon and Gaby joined him and they looked it over. It was no different at all except that it had been crushed and ripped off instead of dismantled.

Alex shook his head.

"I do not know," he said.

"I don't either," Gaby agreed.

"See that flange right in the curve?" volunteered Cannon. "That doesn't look like standard construction. It could have been designed to hold something in the hollow there, but there's nothing there now."

She sniffed it. Nothing.

"Doesn't matter," she said. "We'll get it to the lab. Maybe they can find some kind of residue. There has to be more to this than lampshades."

They threw the gloves down and picked up their coats. Gaby looked at the tangled jumble of metal and shook her head.

"What the hell do you think is going on here, Phil? It makes no sense to build a vehicle for smuggling that has to be destroyed down to its component elements in order to recover your goods. What could they possibly have been moving? And what does it have to do with The Mechanic?"

Cannon shrugged.

"Could be anything, but if we're talking the tiny space inside the braces, and considering we're standing in one of the premier narcotics conduits in the world, you'd have to think along those lines."

Levin was waiting by the door. They walked out together.

"Mister Levin," Gaby said when they emerged back into the sunshine, "you may as well leave the keys or take up residence in there because I'm calling the Evidence Response Team to go over this place with a microscope."

"As a matter of fact," announced Cannon, "I believe I'll just wait here for them."

"Here," Levin said, and handed him the keys. "My clients will be happy to cooperate under the circumstances."

"The circumstance being that they cannot avoid it?" asked Gaby.

"Thank you, Mister Levin. Somehow, I think we'll meet again."

He gave them another sour look, strolled back to his car and burned some rubber off his tires leaving the warehouse district.

"How long for the lab people?" Cannon asked.

"Curt Bell had them prepared. He said no more than thirty or forty minutes," Gaby replied. She had mixed feelings about leaving him on his own. "You've got my number if anything turns up."

He agreed, waved a quick farewell and went back inside, presumably to snoop around a bit before the reinforcements showed up leaving Gaby and Alex alone.

"Okay, Lieutenant, your theory about smuggling still looks good and the lab will probably be able to tell us if anything was in there, but what do we do now?" she asked.

"I should think that the best plan would be to interview the building owner's representative in the morning. And for the moment, the best idea would be to take your partner to dinner and make love to him tonight."

Gaby was a little startled by that and looked in the door to see if Cannon was still within earshot.

She said "Oh, Alex," and shook her head. But she was thinking about it.

Chapter 22

The smug expressions on the faces of Special Agents Curt Bell and Phil Cannon would have been completely insufferable except for two things.

First, Gaby liked Agent Bell. He was younger than she by a few years and extremely bright. And you could see from the enthusiastic gleam in his eyes that he enjoyed his job and took pride in his skills.

Secondly, she knew that the only thing that could give him that smirk was success at finding the information she had asked for, and that meant that her investigation was no longer at a halt.

Bell had been in the local FBI office at 6:15 and refrained from calling Gaby's room until seven. She returned his call at 7:25, explaining that she had been in the shower. In fact, she had been otherwise occupied with a visiting officer from Interpol. She returned to her room once more to find her message light flashing.

So at a few minutes after eight, Gaby and Alex walked into the main conference room to see Curt Bell looking as if he could explode if not allowed to share his news soon. He was holding papers in his hand with a kind of reverence and awe. A tired but satisfied looking Phil Cannon stood by the window. He waved them in and gestured at her to close the door.

Gaby had to comment on the obvious.

"Well gentlemen, don't we look pleased with ourselves this morning?"

"Do we?" Bell asked. "Well in a few seconds you are going to look the same way."

Actually it took more than a few seconds because Bell chose to take his time like a magician revealing his trick to a Vegas audience with flourishes and pauses for applause. He held up a single sheet of paper. He looked a bit like Johnny Carson doing the Carnac bit on the old Tonight Show.

"I have here the results of the tests on that metal frame you brought in yesterday," he said.

"Already?" Gaby said. "I'm impressed. Somebody burned the midnight oil around here. Phil must have threatened them."

He still wasn't handing the papers over to them and Gaby waited.

"Yes somebody did. In fact four lab somebodies are at this moment testing the rest of the vehicle. Metallurgy shows it to be 90% titanium and 10% Aluminum and Vanadium."

"Christ, Curt, why didn't you ask?" she said. "We already knew that. And Phil read the reports. He could have told . . ."

"*But*," he interrupted, "but, there were particles left in the interior that were tested also. There were three metals also in the second alloy. One percent was silver, two percent was palladium."

Still he dragged it out.

"Enough already!" Gaby snapped. "What?"

"It was gold," he said almost in a reverent whisper. "The sleeve inside that bracket had been filled with a bar of nearly solid gold."

Gaby sank back in the conference room chair stunned. Alex looked blank.

Bell's grin widened, satisfied with the effect he had wrought.

"Jesus!" was all Gaby could manage for the moment.

"So what they were smuggling," said Alex, "was not in the interior of the vehicle but within the structure itself."

"That's about it," Bell replied.

"Can they tell what the value would have been?" Gaby asked.

"They're in the warehouse now making more accurate measurements. But the preliminary estimate they gave was in excess of 36,000 troy ounces if the whole vehicle were set up the same way—around 29 million bucks at current prices."

"I think I understand. That's why they had a phony manifest saying the box had machine tools inside. The weight would be consistent. If they had used it for regular freight the secret would have been blown at the first truck scales they came to. So the next question is where did it come from and who has it now," said Gaby.

Cannon was nodding.

"Right. That brings us to part two. It was pretty easy to trace the warehouse back to one of Mister Pushkin's countrymen, a man named Ivan Balakova. He used to be the number two man for the Russian Mafia until we took down the number one a few years ago."

"Ivankov," said Alex.

"Right. He was the Godfather of a large organization—we can't be sure just how large. It's called *Matrosskaya*. I don't know what it means."

"The word has a nautical meaning," Alex said, "But the *Organizatsia* is named for the prison outside of Moscow where some of its founders first earned the respect of their fellow criminals."

Bell nodded.

"I get it. Anyway, since Ivankov went up, this Balakova has been running the show. Obviously we've had our eye on him for quite a while. He pretends to be the proxy for the old don while he's away, but the word is that Ivankov has been replaced permanently."

Gaby's mind was working feverishly. Her thoughts bounced all over the place, trying to make sense of the growing mystery, its importance and the tactical situation.

"Curt," she said, "we need to see this guy immediately, before . . ." She was thinking about what Metcalf would do when he got wind of this. Chances were good that he would send a third agent down to partner with Cannon and pull her ticket completely. " . . . Before anything else happens."

He smiled as if he were reading her mind. "I couldn't agree more."

"Any idea where we can get hold of Mister Balakova?"

He held up a slip of paper, resurrecting his momentarily discarded look of self-satisfaction.

"His phone number for instance?" he said.

Gaby grinned.

"I'm just sorry that I can't pin the Service Star on your lapel myself, Agent Bell."

"He lives on an estate in Coconut Grove about six miles from this chair. He has neighbors like Madonna and Sylvester Stallone and Gloria Estefan."

"Well *la*-di-*dah*," Gaby said. "Okay so call him already. Do you want me to do it?"

He picked up the receiver of the conference room phone.

"I was just waiting for a civilized hour and for you to be here when I did it."

Bell dialed the number and replaced the receiver after punching the speakerphone option. It rang twice before it was answered.

"Da," the speaker said.

Curt Bell introduced himself and asked for Balakova. In spite of the greeting he assumed that English would be spoken.

"I am Mister Balakova's assistant. My name is Smith."

This got a grin from the assembly.

"May I ask what this is in reference to?" the voice inquired.

"There has been an unfortunate incident at one of Mister Balakova's properties and we need to see him right away to discuss it."

"I'm terribly sorry, sir, but Mister Balakova's schedule is such that he couldn't possibly make time for such an interview. Perhaps if you left your number . . ."

"No, *I'm* sorry," said Bell, "you don't understand. We are *going* to see Mister Balakova this morning. Now may we find him at home or would he prefer to meet us at his downtown offices?"

"I . . . please hold the line," Mister Smith said.

There were a few flashes of Russian spoken in the background before a hand covered the mouthpiece at the other end. Gaby looked inquiringly at Alex to see if any of it was meaningful but he quickly shrugged and shook his head. Smith came back on the line.

"Mister Balakova has cleared thirty minutes from his mid-morning schedule. Would that be acceptable?"

"That would be fine."

"He will be available to you at ten o'clock at the offices of his attorney. Let me give you the address."

"Bearman, Levin and Stern?" Bell asked.

"Yes, sir."

"I know where it is. Tell Mister Balakova that we will expect to meet him there. Thank you for your help."

When the line went dead, Bell punched the speaker button.

Gaby didn't know whether it was a good idea to include Alex in the meeting. Finally she decided to bring him along but to introduce him as Alex Park, an associate. She didn't want to raise more alarms than she needed to by announcing the presence of Interpol but thought that having someone along who spoke the language might come in handy if they were unaware of it. Bell and Cannon agreed.

"I can just about guarantee that the questions will be put through an interpreter," Curt said. "These foreign wiseguys always forget how to speak the English when we are around. It's one of their favorite gags. It gives them twice as long to think up a lie and they can always claim that the interpreter misunderstood something. Now as it happens, I read up on

Mister Balakova and he is Oxford educated. I'm sure his English is better than mine, but it's a relatively harmless fiction and we may even be able to turn it to our advantage with Alex there. They know; we know, but we play the game."

They pulled up to the office building and parked on the street behind a black Chevy Suburban. There was a black Chrysler parked in front of that.

"He's already here," said Bell. "That's his car."

Gaby grunted, "That's not much of a car for one of Madonna's neighbors."

"No," he said, "not the Chrysler. That belongs to the bodyguards. The Suburban is his."

"You're joking."

"No, it's the same one the CIA uses at embassies. It's armored all around, the glass is three inches thick and the engine is shielded and oversized. The tires are non-pneumatic. Basically it's a tank with leather seats and a stereo."

There was a driver at the wheel of the Suburban. Its engine was running and three men wearing light sport jackets were loitering by the building entrance.

"Being an Importer in Miami must be a pretty dangerous life," Gaby commented.

Bearman Levin and Stern was a 40-year-old firm housed in its own building two blocks from the Dade County Courthouse. It had ten partners, twenty associates and over a hundred more in paralegals, clerical and support staff. One of the senior secretaries who had worked there for most of those years was waiting for the FBI group and escorted them to the second floor conference room closest to Ira Levin's office. She introduced the three visitors to Levin, his client and, as Curt Bell had predicted, his assistant named John Smith who would act as interpreter. The secretary asked for a refreshment preference, which was declined by all, and she departed, closing the door behind her.

"I told you I had a premonition that we would meet again, Mister Levin," Gaby said.

He smiled weakly and launched right into the same kind of preemptive denials he had used the day before. It took several minutes of fencing in this way for the actual interview to begin. When it did, Gaby allowed Cannon to do the questioning. They had discussed the questions content as a group, but she was forced to admit that he was more knowledgeable about the organization and had an aggressive style appropriate to the situation. She chose a chair at one side of the long table that would allow her to clearly see the expression on the subject's face as he answered.

The first questions involved Balakova's awareness of the shipping container and its contents. As expected, he denied through the bored voice of the interpreter that there was any connection whatsoever. As far as he was concerned some misguided burglars had broken into his warehouse and left this pile of rubbish, which had inconvenienced him. Balakova was doing a very believable job of pretending at his lack of language skills. He would look only at his assistant with a blank expression until he had heard the Russian translation and then responded directly to the agents. He made it clear through his tone, body language and frequent glances at his watch that he had better things to do.

"Have you ever heard of an individual known as The Mechanic?" Cannon asked.

At the mention of that name, a tiny facial tic affected the otherwise bland countenance of the Russian. It wasn't much but Gaby could see that Bell had noticed it too. Alex was writing something on a slip of paper, which he slid in front of Phil Cannon.

"*Nyet*," Balakova said. The interpreter didn't bother.

"Does the name Boris Malenkov or Molot Metalworks mean anything to you?"

He responded the same way, another flash of recognition quickly hidden.

"That's interesting," said Cannon. "Were you unaware that you had an employee named Yevgeny Malenkov, whose brother was named Boris, and who was murdered two weeks ago by a man we believe to be The Mechanic?"

After a longer response in Russian the interpreter said, "No, the word of that tragedy has not reached Mister Balakova. He did not personally know Mister Malenkov but then he employs a large number of people in his many enterprises."

Cannon looked over at Gaby and agent Bell. He had asked the few questions they had discussed plus the one Alex had written out.

"Mister Balakova," Gaby began, "since you have no knowledge or ownership in the metal structure we found at your warehouse, it stands to reason that you would then have no ownership of anything we found inside of it—say papers or money or a bar of something. Is that correct?"

Again there was an almost imperceptible movement, little more than a blink, exactly at the instant Gaby said the word 'bar'.

"As Mister Balakova has said, he has no knowledge or interest in anything to do with the warehouse until after its scheduled destruction. At that time it may be part of a major urban renewal project."

There was enough of a pause in the questions to give the impression that the meeting was at an end and the Russians began to gather up their belongings.

"One more thing, Mister Balakova," Bell added. "I noticed that there were three of your bodyguards in the reception area in addition to the three downstairs at the front door. Are you expecting trouble of some kind? Perhaps the local office could help."

Again through the interpreter, the Russian thanked him and replied that his business was worldwide and had many dangers but that his own security arrangements were more than adequate.

"That's all the questions we had for now, Mister Balakova. Thank you for your cooperation. We'll be sure to call if there are further developments," said Curt Bell and the four visitors picked up their notepads and departed the room ahead of the Russians and their lawyer. There were no handshakes.

When they reached the reception area, the three inside bodyguards were waiting patiently. One was flipping through a magazine; the other two sat formally upright, arms at their sides. Bell gestured toward them with a nod. Gaby had seen more lively expressions on dead men. They followed the foursome to the door with eyes as cold as the guns they carried under their coats.

Outside they got the same looks from the three curbside loiterers. The engine in the suburban was still rumbling quietly.

"Does he always travel with an army?" Gaby asked when they got in the gray FBI-issue sedan.

"No," Bell replied. "Usually two, sometimes just one guard. Something is definitely up with our friend."

"The gold shipment?"

"Maybe," said Bell.

"No," Alex disagreed, breaking a thirty-minute silence. "It is The Mechanic. I think I am beginning to understand. Mister Balakova has created a situation in which one or the other of them must die. The Matrosskaya have made multiple attempts on this killer's life and believe that he will seek out the head of the *organizatsia* for vengeance. But just to be certain that he would come to them on a schedule of their choosing, they have taken his son to draw him here."

"Makes sense," Gaby agreed. "At least we are definitely in the right place this time. We've got multiple murders, interstate flight, kidnapping and smuggling along with assorted other charges. The question now is how do we solve any of them?"

"Simple, said Cannon. "We capture The Mechanic or we find Matthew Gordon or we find the gold that came out of that container."

Gaby brightened.

"Wait a minute. If Alex is right and Balakova had the boy kidnapped to draw The Mechanic to him then they could be holding him at the estate."

"This is very likely—if he is alive at all," said Alex. "What would be the probability of getting another court order to search the estate?"

"Remote, very remote," said Bell. "You can make a hell of a circumstantial case out of it if your half-proofs aren't too rigorous, but there are all kinds of assumptions in there. We not only can't show probable cause, we can't even connect the kidnapping to the shipment—not for a judge anyway. If we got more specific information about the shipment itself, it might be worth a try though."

Just then Balakova emerged from the law office with his entourage. Four of the men got in the Chrysler and two guards boarded the Suburban with their boss and the driver who had been waiting.

When they drove off, Gaby suggested that they follow to see where he was going. Curt Bell shrugged in acquiescence and they pulled in behind the Chevy.

In just over ten minutes the two black vehicles drove through an electrically operated iron gate on South Miami Drive. Bell told the others that it was Balakova's home and they parked for a minute to observe from across the way.

It was a large property surrounded by an eight-foot stone fence with greenery running along the top surface that was obvious camouflage for some kind of protective wire. Through the double iron gates they could see several security cameras and two more men who stood by the entrance and waved at the cars as they passed. In the distance was a sprawling two-story house in the standard mediterranean style. There was a broad expanse on every side where there was no more cover for an intruder who had been fortunate enough to get that far.

"He's got better protection than the President," Gaby said.

Bell nodded

"He leaves once a day with his guards to go either to the lawyers or to his downtown Vista Imports office where he stays a couple of hours and returns. I don't like The Mechanic's chances if he's going after this guy."

"I don't know," said Cannon. "As I understand it, back in '87 Ishii was protected by his Yakuza in Tokyo and The Mechanic got to him."

Bell made a noncommittal noise and put the car back in gear. Not much was said during the return trip. They decided to debrief in Curt Bell's office. On arrival, Agent Bell picked up two sheets of paper that had been stapled together and left in the exact center of his desk blotter.

"They were way off on that estimate of how much bullion could have been in that container," he said.

"The lab is finished already?" Gaby asked. "I thought so. How much do they think it carried now?"

"They found trace amounts of gold in every rib, crossbeam and support in that whole vehicle. It was at least two metric tons. More like forty million dollars. I don't know what our chances are but we've got to try the judge again on a warrant to search the estate. We'd never get one on the kidnapping but with this much bullion we can make a case that he may be concealing it on his own premises."

Gaby, Curt Bell and Alex spent the afternoon gathering evidence for another trip to Judge Cruz's chambers. Alex, having no legal training even in his own country, made no contribution to their efforts. Gaby understood that. What she didn't understand was why this vindication of their mission had made him so quiet and withdrawn.

Chapter 23

Kate Wallace was at the Vizcaya museum, standing with twenty other people in front of a 2,000-year-old cistern. At the front of the group, a docent was droning out a carefully rehearsed speech, but far more interesting to Kate was the fact that she seemed to have become an involuntary tourist in Miami, and a loyal traveling companion to a killer in barely more than two days.

Certainly she was placing a great deal of faith in a man who had struck and kidnapped her. And the man had voluntarily confessed to atrocities beyond her experience, beyond even her imagination. It was true that the primary motive remained her nephew's safety, but it had become hard to keep sympathetic thoughts for George from intruding. Was it just the Stockholm Syndrome? No doubt that would have been the judgment she would have issued from her analyst's chair at home.

And it was truly an act of pure faith at this point. In the hours after the revelations of Michael Hogan, her former brother in law had become strangely, but randomly communicative. He continued to be completely focused on his plan for Matthew's return but confided impossibly intimate details of his life. Kate suspected that he had never shared this kind of confidence and level of detail with anyone, certainly no one that lived through the experience.

Strolling in the open breezeway of the Italian Renaissance mansion it occurred to her briefly that she could simply walk away, though she knew she would not. George had again refused the guided museum tour, leaving her alone again. He understood Kate well enough to know that her word would hold her even when he could not.

Like yesterday, he wandered the grounds while she strolled through the house for almost three hours, somewhat ruining his premise that he needed her for camouflage among the vacationers. When she was not in the group of guided tourists she certainly felt conspicuous enough.

Kate had no clue as to why it was important that they spend another day touring the same museum as the day before. Not that it was an unpleasant place to be held captive. Vizcaya was built by a turn-of-the-twentieth-century millionaire as a self-sufficient holding of 180 acres, which at the time included most of Miami, with a palatial centerpiece created by the finest artisans of Europe and America. The docent was pleased to point out that popes and presidents had visited here and that two of its current neighbors were Sylvester Stallone and Madonna. The importance of which was rather lost on Kate. It was an interesting place but it definitely didn't rate two consecutive days. When her walking tour was over this time, the patience Kate had promised was wearing thin and she wandered the grounds for most of another hour looking for George.

He finally reappeared in the garden staring out to sea past a stone dock. Kate had to look twice to be certain that it was George. He had not shaved since Val's death and with his black and gray beard and dark complexion there was already enough growth to change his appearance. Also there was something about the way he carried himself that was different as well.

Afterward, George drove her to a marina near the port of Miami, where she gathered that he had come to rent a small powerboat. He walked slowly and spoke casually and without any haste or concern to the proprietor. By now just about any situation and certainly all of the many variants of his behavior had become routine to Kate so when they had boarded the twenty foot craft and Kate asked what he was doing, she was unsurprised when he just looked at her and shrugged.

They cleared the harbor and cruised Biscayne Bay for thirty minutes or so before he stopped the boat at about three hundred yards from land. It was a pleasant enough day but the chop on the bay was almost four feet and the boat was small. George pulled a large Monocular out of his pack, went forward and sat cross-legged on the prow as he surveyed the shore for several minutes. Kate sat in the left hand seat and waited patiently until finally he called her forward also. She wobbled onto the prow, a little nauseous by this time and took the eyepiece from him, bracing herself with one hand against the swell.

George gestured shoreward and Kate could see that he was indicating a private dock some distance beyond a very distinctive stone structure built to resemble a huge Venetian gondola. Even from that distance and without optical enhancement Kate had recognized the stonework as belonging to her home away from home on this trip. It was Vizcaya. Looking through the eyepiece she could see more detail at the neighboring dock. Moored at the home a short distance from the museum was an electric blue powerboat and a small dinghy. The house to which the dock was attached was of Moorish architecture and quite large with what appeared to be a significant bit of property surrounding it, not unlike Vizcaya itself and almost half the size. She watched for a minute or so but nothing seemed to be happening.

Kate asked the significance of the stop and the house but all George said was, "Nice boat" and she lost her temper a bit.

"Damn it George!" she said, "You tell me why we are wasting time here when you and I both know you should be looking for Matt?"

"Come on," he said, "it's time to go. I've got some shopping to do."

Kate grabbed his arm with both hands and jerked at him. When this failed to move him she doubled up her fist and hit him as hard as she could in the shoulder. The impact almost made her lose her footing on the rocking deck but he barely reacted. He looked briefly from her face to his shoulder and back again

"I knew where Matthew was, but I had to be sure," he said.

Kate let out a huff of air that was almost a sob.

"He's definitely alive, then?"

"Yes."

Kate then broke into tears—an instant and total cloudburst. George had maintained throughout that the kidnappers wouldn't harm him and she had believed him, she thought. There must have been a core of doubt that his statement relieved.

George seemed a bit flustered by her lack of control.

"Stop that!" he said and she pulled out a tissue and did her best to shut it off.

"How did you find him?" she asked through the sniffling. "Where is he?"

"He's being held at that house," George replied, pointing again. "The one with the boat. He's in a second story room with your fake FBI agent. They don't have the window covered on the ocean side."

George led Kate back to the passenger seat next to him at the helm and started the engine for the return trip. Back at the Marina he completed the paper work and they drove back toward the museum in silence. He pulled into a slot at the park not far from where he said Matthew was being held and got out. He walked quickly up one of the paths to a picnic area without looking back to see if Kate was accompanying him. Kate had to use an occasional dogtrot to keep up. After a short hike George went to a vacant picnic table near the jogging track and the discreet sign that announced that the facility was named for a woman called Helen C. Wainwright.

He pulled a note pad from under his shirt, tore off the first sheet of notes and began to make a drawing on the fresh page underneath. Kate watched as the diagram developed.

"He's being kept in that house, then?" She pointed, adding, "That one down there?"

George continued with his drawing as he responded, "It's a big house on a large piece of property surrounded by a stone wall. There's probably razor wire concealed along the top—could be electrified. Iron gate at the driveway. Video and motion sensors everywhere I could see. Guards front and back. Looks like ten men and two women live there full time not counting household staff."

Kate looked again unconsciously in the direction she supposed the house to be.

"Sounds impossible," she said.

"Difficult," he agreed. "Harder than most I've had to deal with because this time they're expecting me for sure."

"How . . .", she hesitated. "How will you do it?"

George wrinkled his brow and paused a second.

"Whenever he leaves the property he drives around in an armored truck with most of his guards all around him. I'm sure he feels completely safe while he's in there."

Kate didn't understand how that answered the question. She felt many of the things he had said in the last day or so had been directed at himself rather than at her.

"Why don't we just call the police and tell them Matt is in there? Wouldn't that be better? Then you could just go off wherever you plan to go and I could take him home and this would all be over."

"The Feds were just there, parked across the road. I saw them."

"Maybe they already know he's being held in the house."

"It's possible," George admitted, "but even if they suspect it they can't just go in and get him. They enforce the rules. They don't provide justice."

"And you do?"

Kate was afraid the sarcasm had been too much but when he looked up from his drawing again, he only looked thoughtful.

"I can. In this case, yes," he said. "I'm not trying to be God, Kate, but I can make the easy calls. Matthew is innocent; the people who hold him are guilty. And I believe I can fix this when nobody else can. The way I choose to deal with this may seem . . . extreme, but no one could deny which side I am on this time."

"But the FBI . . ." she began again.

"Stop," he said. "If I thought surrendering to them would save Matt I would do it now. That's not the case. But when I do what I'm going to do, whether the plan goes perfectly or gets blown at the first step, the Feds will then have an immediate reason to search the house and get Matt out of there."

"How in the world are you going to get in there? The way you describe it, it's a fortress."

"Yes, it is. A direct assault with all of them inside would be pointless. But you see, now that I know Matt is being held in a house owned by the Russian, I've got a little edge of my own. Most of the help will go with the Russian whenever he leaves. That won't leave many guards for Matt. Also I know whatever happens, they won't kill him on the property.

"As soon as the first bullet is fired someone will be assigned to stay with Matt until they can get him out of that house. They're keeping him there because it's so defensible but the last thing they want is for the police to find a kidnap victim there. So someone will be out of play because his job will be to move Matt somewhere that his body can be hidden fast after they kill him. I'll have to move fast in case they planned to move him in that boat they've got tied up out back but I don't think they'd move him out in the open like that."

At the mention of Matt's 'body' Kate sucked in a breath of air spasmodically and her chin began to quiver.

"Kill?"

"Of course. I told you from the beginning that he would have to die as far as the Russians are concerned. This isn't a normal kidnapping. They haven't asked for any ransom or the performance of some special service. The act of taking him already accomplished what they wanted. As soon as I am accounted for—captured or killed—he's dead. They have to bury him right away."

George turned back to his notes for another few seconds and then folded them up. He too looked in the direction of the Russian's house even though there was no way at all that he could have seen any of it.

"Are you hungry?" he asked Kate.

This time it was Kate's turn to shrug but first she shook her head at him in general disbelief at his callousness.

He rose, unconcerned and put away the paper he had been working on. Again without looking back to see if she were following or whether she could hear him he began back toward the car and said, "I got some errands to run first."

He continued back to the car with kate trotting again in his wake and, true to his word, led her on a lengthy, if baffling, shopping spree.

First stop was a Target store. Kate watched him buy a boy's bicycle and backpack. When she asked why, he talked about the nice weather and how the constant breeze made the high temperatures bearable. From there they went to a Home Depot where he purchased a length of the heaviest chain they had and a case hardened steel padlock. There was a Radio Shack across the way where he picked up a stopwatch and some electronic gear whose purpose was even more obscure. Kate was farther than ever from understanding the plan but she did learn that the fringes of a tropical depression might cause showers in the early evening. The last stop was a scrap yard. George bought a three quarter inch thick steel plate, which he had cut to his specifications in their machine shop and smoothed around the edges.

By that time it was after seven, though the sun was still high in the sky, and George suggested that they have dinner out. The level of his trust had seemed to be rising anyway so Kate wasn't too surprised. He chose a hotel restaurant across the bay from where they had been staying and the food was excellent Cuban American cuisine. He was in a cheerful mood for some reason and they talked about old times. They reminisced about shared experiences and affections with Val and Ally the way people do when they celebrate the life of a loved one and forget their grief for a moment. For a few minutes it was as if none of the nightmarish events had happened. It was easily the most pleasant time Kate had had since her sister's death.

After dessert, George ordered coffee and became very solemn. Kate knew somehow that he was saying goodbye. He pulled two items out of his pocket and pushed them in front of her. One was a plain white envelope. The other was her wallet.

"You had that all the time?" she asked.

He didn't say that he kept it so that it would be harder for her to run away, only that she hadn't needed it, which was true as far as it went.

"There's money in that envelope," he said. "Use it to stay over a while if you like and give Matt a chance to heal a little or whatever.

"You have a pre-paid reservation in this hotel and there will be a rental car waiting for you in the morning at the agency in the lobby. The concierge will have the key. I'm just going to walk out of here and I want you to just sit a while and finish your coffee. I don't think you will see me again. Starting next month you'll get a thousand dollars a week every week until you die, from a bank in the Caymans. There will be no trace of it. Don't pay taxes on it. I'm not going to ask you to take care of Matt and his schooling because I know you'll do that. In a few years someone will contact you about his college fund. Make your own choice about the best place for him but the fund will take care of expenses anywhere in the country.

"Now, in the morning I want you to drive to the park where we were today, sit at that same table and wait until it's time to meet with the FBI and pick up Matt. You'll know when."

"It's important that you tell the police and FBI a consistent story. I don't think you'll have any problem considering who I am, but take no chances. Your life has been in constant jeopardy and you were too afraid to scream or run. You can tell them most of the truth. You shot me. They'll already know that. I hit you; gave you drugs to keep you quiet."

His eyes moved back and forth and he scratched at his new beard as he organized his thoughts and went down lists of things not to be forgotten. He stood up and gave Kate a kind of ghostly smile. The tenderness of remembrance was in it, if such a judgment could be made about a man like this.

"Your family gave me the greatest gift that anyone ever got," he said, and she knew what he meant.

Kate looked down at her cup and saucer for only a moment and when she looked up, the response she had formulated lay unspoken on her tongue. He was gone.

Chapter 24

Something was wrong with Alex Pushkin.

This time it was Gaby who urged the conversation on with her good mood and tried to make dinner playful and fun. He laughed weakly at her jokes and complimented the work she had done but it was an effort and she could see it.

Curt Bell had declined her offer to have the evening meal with them after a long dry afternoon of research and she hadn't pressed it. Cannon announced that he had to catch up on the sleep lost the previous night and Gaby had been happy to be alone with Alex again. Now she found herself almost wishing one of them were there to deflect some of the tension she felt and share the elation that Alex apparently couldn't.

Alex had awakened something in her that had been dormant for a long time and now their time would seem to be nearly over. Was that the problem with him? Where was Alex Pushkin, the Great Manipulator—the cheery conversationalist—the ardent suitor? She wanted to just ask that in plain English, but when she played the question in her head it sounded shallow or egotistical or maybe just awkward. They had no future together—did they?

"Please tell me what's wrong, Alex."

"Nothing at all."

"You could have fooled me," said Gaby. "Have I done something wrong? Tell me what it was and I'll make it right."

God, she hated this. Even as she spoke, the words grated on her nerves. It was the curse of her upbringing to feel responsible for every relationship. Women—no, her mother would have said ladies—are the sensitive ones. It's up to us to keep up a relationship, she had said. No, actually she had said marriage, as it was the only kind of relationship Mother recognized and she had been talking about the failed marriage of Mr. and Mrs. Granville Mouton Boudreaux Galvez.

Gaby tried not to blame her mother. The twentieth century had missed her social circles almost entirely and the twenty-first had added anger to her bewilderment. When she admonished Gaby to do something important with her life she had envisioned civic groups and charity auctions and the nurture of a proper family. That this very specific role would not appeal to someone who was so suited for it was an idea impossible for her mother to conceive.

Likewise Gran undoubtedly felt cheated when he found that he did not possess the pliant ornament he thought he had purchased with his family name. In a perverse way Gaby could almost be grateful for his bitter condescension, bullying and philandering after they found out that there would be no children. Without that persistent embarrassment to stoke the fires of her independence she might still be there at his side smiling vacantly—profoundly unhappy and guilty about being unable to produce either the family or the happy marriage it needed. The guilt always followed.

Now what had she done to Aleksandr Andreyevich Pushkin?

"Nothing. Truly, you have done nothing wrong."

"Then tell me why your jaw is dragging the ground?"

He smiled a wan smile.

"And another American idiom. You have certainly aided my education in that direction."

"Happy to be of service, Lieutenant."

"Perhaps I need a burst of energy," he said, and the smile brightened a little. "Let us go somewhere there is dancing. We should celebrate your victory in the matter of the Molotov box and I have been a poor companion."

"Hardly a victory yet, Alex. We came on this trip to find The Mechanic and if we are any closer to that at all I couldn't prove it in a court of law. Besides it won't be my victory, it will be our victory."

"Let's not think of that now. Let us go out tonight."

Gaby was pleased.

"Okay, let's."

Alex reached for his wallet but Gaby had already collared the waiter and pushed her American Express card in his hand.

"You know Alex, if you're feeling badly because Curt and I have done all the work on our new court order, you shouldn't. Your contribution has already been made, really—yours and the illustrious Colonel Dashenko."

"Yes, the Colonel," he said thoughtfully. "He has certainly contributed. But I just . . . I only wish that . . . I could do more."

"Surely your Colonel can't be disappointed with your performance."

"I have not done anything, Gaby. I have only transmitted the theories and information he provided me and taken up space at your side."

"I don't get it," she said. "When we were sitting in Washington facing a hopeless task you were all moonlight and enthusiasm. Now when we are only a step away . . ."

Gaby stopped. The cool blue eyes were so sad.

"Never mind. We weren't going to talk about that stuff for the rest of the night. Tomorrow we make trouble for the *Matrosskaya.*"

The waiter came and she signed the receipt.

"Where do you want to go?" she asked.

"I do not know. The noisiest place in Miami."

"I don't think you realize what you are asking for there. Okay, I don't know *what* the noisiest place is, but I'm betting I know *where* it is."

They went to South Miami Beach without an actual destination, parked the car and just started walking. It had many of the qualities of the walk on Bourbon Street. A space alien with three heads would barely have gotten a glance but their business attire—comprehensively rumpled in Alex Pushkin's case—got a few quizzical stares and caused a few "cigarettes" to be discarded before they were fully smoked.

Gaby selected a club that had green neon parrots over the door. She never even noticed the name. Inside they were playing Salsa. Either it was too early for the real action or it must not have been a very successful business because they were able to sit immediately at a round table the size of a jumbo pizza.

As soon as they had ordered two appropriately fruity drinks Gaby took Alex's hand and pulled him toward the dance floor. The sound was very loud, its beat a visceral experience. Alex had to shout his protests at the top of his lungs. This was not the kind of dancing he meant, but he was laughing as he said it. Gaby pulled off his jacket and tie and threw them over the back of his seat, then put hers on top. She reached up and unbuttoned his collar button and undid one more of hers, then she took his hand again and danced her way onto the floor accenting each downbeat with a pelvic thrust that would have given her mother a fainting spell.

Gaby was already lost to it. She gestured to Alex with her whole body and guided his hands where they belonged. But try as she might, she just could not get him to move on the right beat. She had never seen him make even the tiniest ungraceful movement and now he looked like a drunk trying to put on a tight pair of pants. He fell into her and she stumbled, laughing and holding onto his broad shoulders to keep her balance. He kept trying and failing until, mercifully the song came to an end. Gaby took advantage of the gap to explain some of the timing she was trying to get across and when the band started again, so did they. This number was a bit slower and easier to pick up on but the Russian never hit a single step. Gaby found his ineptitude as endearing as his considerable skills.

Back at the table she was still giggling at his efforts and sipping her drink.

"Just out of curiosity," she asked with a mischievous grin, "what kind of dancing were you thinking of when you suggested that we come here?"

"My experience is that when rock and roll music is playing *everyone* looks silly," he said, laughing. He was really taking her unkindness well.

"Also, I have learned the Waltz and the Foxtrot," he added.

"I see. It was my mistake. You wanted to go to a retirement home somewhere and check out the action."

They listened to the music until the band's next break at which point Gaby announced that they should be getting back to the hotel. They gathered their things and exited back into the cooling night breeze.

"Can we walk?" Alex asked.

"We have to," she answered, still taking the conversation lightly. "The car is six or seven blocks back that way."

Shortly Alex had made it clear that he had meant a walk on the beach and Gaby agreed that it would be nice. They crossed Collins and Ocean Drive and found the beach there relatively deserted. They took off their shoes and Alex rolled up his pants and they set off North in the general direction of the car, though they were in no hurry.

It was a very clear night. The wind off the ocean was brisk and carried an intoxicating mix of its nightly perfumes; the surf was hypnotic and just soft enough not to interfere with quiet talk.

Alex carried their coats and his shoes tied together around his neck. Gaby had the low heel slingbacks she had chosen for the day in her right hand. Her left hand held his.

They had walked about half way back to the parking lot enjoying the experience with only a comment or two interrupting the rhythm of the breakers. In spite of everything Gaby could sense the return of Alex's melancholy.

"I must tell you something, Gaby."

"As long as it's not serious. Please don't get serious, I'm having such a good time."

"But it is serious—very serious."

Gaby sighed, "What?"

"I have been happier these last days than I have ever been in my life."

"That's nice, Alex. I think it has been wonderful too."

"The moment I saw you, Gaby I wanted to hold you, to make love to you but I was thinking of you differently then. I thought you were as other beautiful women."

She was unable to resist the standard response or its lack of sincerity.

"I *am* like other women. There's nothing special about me, Alex."

He looked over at her with moonlight glittering in his eyes and laughed. It was a hearty laugh as if he could see genuine humor in what she had said. He didn't even bother to disagree as if it were so absurd that he knew she didn't believe it either.

"I set out from the beginning to seduce you. That is the right word, seduce?"

"Yes it is indeed and if this is your revelation, I'm afraid you are a little late. I knew that shortly after you did. I could tell also that you were very comfortable and experienced at it."

"There have been others, that is true, but never anyone like you. And I have never been like this before. In this case I failed," he said.

Gaby raised her eyebrows. "Failed. Failed? Then who have I been sleeping with?"

"No, I am saying it badly. I was the hunter but it was I that was trapped."

"You're not trapped, Alex."

He grimaced as if uncomfortable with the language for the first time.

"No, and I wish that I were. At least I wish that we were confined by our feelings for each other as we sailed on my boat from one sunny port to the next one. Since that first night I have thought of no one else. After the first time you let me touch you I have thought of nothing else but you and the way we could live together on my boat. Gaby, I love you."

"Alex . . ."

"No," he stopped her. "I do not require anything of you. You do not need to return my feeling and you cannot reject my feeling, it is simply there. I wanted you to know."

"Alex, I'm deeply flattered and moved by what you say. I . . ."

He dropped his shoes on the sand with their coats and picked her up in one arm, turning her toward him. He cut off her words with the urgency of his kiss.

Gaby melted into him, meeting his heat with more of her own. She hung there, feet suspended above the sand, exploring. His arms felt like steel bands, quivering not with the effort but with the restraint that allowed her to breathe. Alex maneuvered her to the ground behind a low dune with a palm tree at its peak. When she realized that he intended to take her right there on the beach, she mouthed a few half-hearted protests. There was a fiery urgency in him that spoke of desperation. What if someone saw them? Jesus, only kids did this sort of thing! But the pounding surf joined with the roar of blood in her head and rose in volume until there was nothing else.

When it was over, Gaby huddled with Alex in the lee of the mound and waited for her heart rate to slow to normal. There was sand in places where it had never been before and the discomfort made her giggle with the absurd liberation of it all. Alex had a similar experience and their laughter mingled with curses as they began to put themselves in some state of presentability so that they could return to a society not completely governed by its passions.

At length they were able to stand and smooth the wrinkles as best they could. There was an embarrassed exultation as they looked up and down the line of surf, but the nearest person was a moonlight jogger several hundred yards away moving in the opposite direction. Where had he been a few minutes ago, she wondered?

Gaby led them to one of the showerheads along the beach so that they could wash off at least the visible grit before driving back across the Macarthur Causeway to their hotel. Separate seats with a console in the middle prevented real closeness, but once in a while one of them would touch the other as if to insure that they were still together.

When they were almost in the parking garage, Alex asked, "Have you ever considered marriage again?"

"No," she answered, "not really. I mean I would like to think about it someday, sure, but no, I haven't seriously considered it."

"Would you consider marrying me?"

It wouldn't be accurate to say the question was completely unexpected after his earlier comments, but it still took her breath away.

"Alex, don't be silly. You only met me a week ago."

"Yes," he said in a tone that demanded a real reason.

"That's flattering beyond words, Alex, but just impossible."

"Why?"

"It just is."

"What if . . . I were rich? I will have that boat and I will be able to provide for you very well. What if I had more money than Granville Galvez and your father and I had that boat and we could just put all this behind us and sail away together? We could be happy, Gaby. I am sure of it."

"It's not that, Alex, please. It's just crazy."

"Crazy like making love on the beach?"

He had her there.

"A little crazy can be good. It was good—great, but for us to be married would be a lot crazy. You'll be going home soon. I've got my career. Anyway, the Colonel would never allow it."

Gaby regretted that last comment even as she said it. It was mean and hurtful and she had known that it would be, but it was too late to take it back and an apology would send the wrong signal, she thought.

Alex said nothing and he settled back into the quiet gloom he had exhibited for most of the last two days as they drove back across the causeway. For Gaby's part, she was guilty and suddenly depressed, thinking of how much she had enjoyed Alex and how much his visit had already changed her life. She took a deep breath after she had parked the car in the hotel lot and stopped the engine.

"Please, Alex," she said. "If I were thinking about marriage right now . . . I would be the luckiest bride this side of the Atlantic, but . . . Who knows? Someday . . ."

Alex nodded half-heartedly but he was still hurt and she still felt terrible. He moped his way back to their rooms with his shoulders sagging. When they arrived at her door, he took two more steps toward his own.

When she looked at him and asked if he wanted to come in, he said, "I guess we should clean up and get some sleep. Tomorrow will be a big day for you."

She had to say a lot or nothing at all.

"Okay, Alex, I guess so. Seven-thirty for breakfast?"

"Yes, breakfast," he said and continued down the hall.

Gaby opened room 610, flipped on the light and leaned back against the door as it closed. "What have I done now?" she asked the empty room. She took a shower that should have been a giddy recollection of her night of romantic adventure but became a somber exercise in self-recrimination.

Her sleep was littered with unpleasant dreams and she awoke an hour before her wake-up call, dressed and went downstairs to the coffee shop to wait. She bought two newspapers and read the headlines but found herself turning the pages without thought. Even the crossword puzzle didn't distract her from the angst of waiting for Alex.

Phil Cannon joined her at the appointed hour and when Alex hadn't appeared by 7:45 Gaby called his room and got no answer. Finally the two of them took the elevator to the sixth floor and Cannon showed his credentials to a frightened chambermaid, who opened the door to Alex Pushkin's room.

The bed was made and there was no luggage. He was gone.

Chapter 25

When Gaby arrived at the office a few minutes late and alone, a cheerful, keyed up and now curious Curt Bell was waiting for her. He asked about Alex as well as Phil Cannon, who had stayed behind to try to locate the Russian. She just covered by saying that they wouldn't be participating at the courthouse. This was no great surprise but Gaby could see that Bell noticed her preoccupation. She dismissed his concern as nothing more than a bad night's sleep. Bell tactfully allowed the subject to drop and began to prepare last minute strategy for their meeting on the short trip to the courthouse.

Judge Cruz was waiting for them in his outer office with coffee in a big mug that said Dolphins on the side and the same ironic smile on his face.

After a few sharp-edged pleasantries they went into his chambers and the mood became more serious. Curt again took the lead with the judge, stating the Bureau's desire to search the Balakova residence and citing all the favorable decisions they had researched the previous afternoon. Cruz listened patiently for five minutes, flipping occasionally through the brief they had prepared.

"Well that's just fine," said the judge. "You have just provided me with a dozen reasons to allow an enforced search of property in the presence of a clear probable cause. Now would you be kind enough to state the basis of your probable cause?"

"It's right there, Your Honor," Bell replied. "The lab report findings are clear regarding both the suspicious vehicle and the contents found on his premises."

"His premises being this condemned building which the subject states he has never operated as a business and intends to have demolished in the next sixty to ninety days?"

"Yes, sir."

"And if the police find a quantity of cocaine in Yankee Stadium it follows then that we should have George Steinbrenner's house searched for a processing plant. Is that right?"

"That's not fair, Your Honor."

"I'm not trying to be fair, I'm trying to be legal. I wouldn't sit on the bench very long if I abrogated the Bill of Rights for a connection as flimsy as this."

"But . . ."

"Look here, son. We've got a murder—several murders—none of which can be connected to this man. In fact you tell me you already know who perpetrated these murders and Mister Balakova is not even a suspect. Then we have a kidnapping for which he is a suspect, but only if you believe the murders are related to him in some way."

"The gold . . ." Bell began.

"Yes, let's look at that for a moment. He is suspected of smuggling this gold in the amount of six thousand pounds or so which you think he may have had transported—no longer in the protective camouflage of this James Bond freight box—to his twelve million dollar estate in Coconut Grove."

"It's possible."

Cruz shook his head. "Good lord, Curtis!"

"Sir, this man is the head of one of the most powerful crime organizations in the country."

"So you tell me, and I believe it. But because you can't prove it, do you think I should just skip right over those pesky little rules of evidence and let you rummage around until you can?"

Curt Bell had run out of protests. "No sir, I guess not."

Now that Cruz had sufficiently humiliated him he became conciliatory.

"Surely you can find some evidence of the transportation of three tons of goods—a witness, a waybill, something?"

"We're trying, sir. The trouble is we only inspected the warehouse day before yesterday and it could have been there as early as last week. He had ample opportunity to move it long before we knew anything was going on."

"I sympathize with you, Curtis and you too, Agent Bernard. But you should know better. You're a lawyer too, aren't you?"

Gaby had gathered from his first comment that Cruz was not going to allow their search and allowed her mind to wander around the mystery of what happened to Alexsandr Pushkin. Quickly, she refocused.

"A law graduate, Your Honor. As my father is fond of reminding me, those are two different things. But it's obvious to me that Balakova is materially involved in the smuggling, several conspiracies and murder. And every step of the way there have been Russians involved. Six victims of The Mechanic have been countrymen of Mister Balakova with a connection to his organization."

"I take it you have been chasing this box all the way from Memphis?"

"Yes, your honor. It has only been a few days but it seems like much longer. And we just can't stop now. The life of a young boy may . . .'"

He cut off her protestation.

"You remind me of my youngest, Frannie. She is at Vanderbilt Law this year and she is like a terrier with a bone when she gets something in her head. You have been from Washington to Memphis to New Orleans to Miami following this box?"

"Yes, sir," she replied.

Cruz leaned back in his big leather chair and took another pull on his coffee.

"Look, I believe you. I want to help, but you've got to help me first. Find out how the gold shipment moved from that warehouse; show me any kind of relationship between that movement and our Russian friend and I'll sign an order. As it stands, all I could do is get any solid evidence you found thrown out of court for illegal search and you two up on harassment charges."

There was more to the exchange, which made the FBI agents feel ever more like undergraduates who had turned in incomplete homework. Shortly they surrendered to the inevitable.

The FBI offices were twenty minutes away, just south of the Hialeah Race Track so the two agents had plenty of time to commiserate but when you separated what they 'knew' from what they could prove, it was hard to disagree with Judge Cruz. The Coconut Grove property was now under 24 hour surveillance and that seemed to be about all they could do.

Gaby had never been much for accepting defeat gracefully and her mood was improved not at all by concern over the unscheduled exit of her Russian partner. She wouldn't have believed that she could feel worse until she opened the front door to the Miami FBI office and saw Tony Metcalf and Cannon standing at the reception desk with their backs to them.

"Oh, shit," Gaby said under her breath.

Curt quietly asked her who the man was and she told him. He echoed not just her sentiments but her exact words.

Then he asked, "The A-team is taking over?".

"That would be my guess," she replied.

When Metcalf heard the door close and turned around, Gaby asked him what he was doing there as casually as she could manage. He ignored her, turning to Cannon and asking, "Curt Bell?"

When he got a quick affirmative, Metcalf introduced himself and said, "I'll want to talk to you in ten minutes." Then he looked back at Gaby and waved her into the small conference room where he joined her and closed the door behind them.

"Where is Aleksandr Pushkin?" was the first thing he wanted to know. He hadn't even waited to take a seat.

"I . . . I'm not sure," Gaby stammered. "He was not in his room this morning."

"Phil already told me that much. That's all you know? He just disappeared?"

"Yes. We looked his room over for a note or some sign anyway but there was nothing."

"This is quite a mess you've made, Bernard," said Metcalf. He had an expression on his face like a man cleaning up after someone else's dog.

"I know I shouldn't have to say this but I'm going to anyway. I already told Cannon. What we discuss here is beyond top secret. If I ever hear this story, at a meeting next week or a retirement party thirty years from now, I will see to it that you are *skinned*."

She nodded and Metcalf looked over his shoulder as if a spy could have come in through the closed door.

"Aleksandr Pushkin was a fake. The Director and the Deputy Director are furious. It makes us all look like idiots. I took the first plane out this morning. When Phil told me he wasn't anywhere to be found this morning I put out a bulletin on him. It was as vague as I could make it—wanted for questioning."

Gaby almost choked. She sat down hard in one of the padded chairs and Metcalf did likewise, choosing the one next to her.

"What do you mean, fake?" she said.

"I mean he was not sent on a mission to the United States by Interpol. In fact he has never worked for Interpol. Now we don't think his mission had anything to do with The Mechanic as he said. It was obviously about this shipment."

"That's impossible," she said. "What about his dossier, the service record?"

"He was a cop. That part's true. He was a decorated lieutenant in the Russian Berkut force but he resigned nine months ago. The Interpol part of his history was just fiction. Remember I told you to watch that guy—that he was a little too smooth."

"How could I . . . How?"

"The guy who arranged the visit within Interpol was another Russian named Andrey Viktor Dashenko. He has a very distinguished career behind him with the Russian Navy, the KGB, the Militia and lately, Interpol. It appears that this whole charade was a project of his."

"Why?"

"We don't know. There's no connection that we know between The Mechanic, which is the reason given for his visit, and Dashenko, except that he is Russian and the Memphis victim was Russian. Do you know anything that would help?"

Gaby had many thoughts all at once and struggled not to show how upset she was.

"There is one thing, although I don't really understand it. Alex told me that Malenkov's brother had also been killed in Moscow. He was the accountant for Molot Metal works there and that's where the special freight box was made."

Metcalf scribbled in a notebook.

"Interpol didn't mention that. I'll make sure the Russians know. What else?"

"If he wasn't legitimate, I don't get why he would help with the investigation. You saw my reports. I had run into a wall on tracing the container. The only way we found it was a tip from Colonel Dashenko."

"Colonel?"

"Yes, that's the way Alex always referred to him. Dashenko is his hero. Apparently that was his rank when he was with MVD and before that with KGB."

Metcalf leaned back in the conference room chair and then forward just a little, moving in a short and repetitive arc. Gaby couldn't tell if he was rocking or bobbing his head because either would have had the same effect.

"You and I both know you got this job through fraudulent means?" he said to her without stopping.

"I don't agree with your choice of words. According to you I was selected from a substantial list by the Deputy Director. My inclusion was questionable maybe."

"And I'm sure you know you wouldn't have been approved for this kind of field assignment if we had known where this little PR tour was going to lead?"

"Yes."

The rocking motions stopped and he pushed the seatback forward, leaning toward Gaby.

"You were selected from the list only after Fallon provided it to Dashenko. The DD wants to know why."

The hollow area in the pit of her stomach grew larger.

"You're kidding," she said, trying to control her anger. "You mean they think I am a part of whatever is going on with the Russians?"

"The idea has been considered. Is there anything you want to tell me? Why were you picked?"

"I guess the same reason you think you can intimidate me with absurd suppositions. I am junior within the Bureau, have had no field experience and I . . . I guess because I am a woman."

Metcalf snorted. His face flickered in what might have been a smile. "Actually that's more or less what I told them. Even after what you did with the files I don't think you're capable of anything as actionable as this, Bernard. But they think the sequence of events was suspicious. Now he disappears just as we discover him and you have no idea where. You've got nothing on Balakova and you've lost The Mechanic along with Pushkin. The story would play better in Washington if we had been betrayed by someone inside rather than manipulated like puppets."

There was that word again. They had all been manipulated but she was the biggest fool by far—more even than Metcalf knew.

"If you want to save what's left of your career, you're going to have to help me here. When is the last time you saw Alex Pushkin?"

"Last night."

"What Time?

"I'm not sure exactly. It was late."

"Agent Bernard, exactly how close to Pushkin did you get?"

"Are you implying something else now?"

"I'm asking a simple question!"

"As far as I am concerned, we worked well together. He seemed dedicated to the mission. I had no reason to think otherwise."

He was tapping on the edge of the conference table as if trying to figure out a better way to say something.

"Phil thinks there was something more."

"We were friendly. But I never did anything that would reflect badly on the Bureau. And Cannon should mind his own goddam business."

Now Metcalf folded his hands in front of him as if the tapping was annoying him as well. He waited a bit, thinking.

"Okay, we'll just leave it at that for now. There's a ticket waiting for you out front back to Washington on the 5:40. Tomorrow morning there will be a suspension hearing for you."

"You can't do that, Tony."

"Watch me."

"I've done a good job on this. I'm the one who found the smuggled gold."

"As I understand it you found the remains of an empty box with no provable connection to either The Mechanic or the Russians. Isn't that what the judge told you?"

"But I searched the warehouse. I've questioned Balakova. I understand the chain of evidence we'll need. You can't cut me off now. We'll find a connection. We're just getting started."

"Phil can handle it fine. You just get back there and start thinking about a defense."

Just then Curt opened the door and posed there for a moment with a stunned look on his face.

"There's somebody on the phone for you. He asked for the agent who has been following The Mechanic."

"Who is it?"

"He says he's The Mechanic."

Chapter 26

Early morning found George Gordon back in Wainwright Park finalizing his preparations. The Mechanic still thought of himself by that name.

He had noticed the car down the way with the policemen inside. He didn't know what brand of cops they might be and he didn't care. It was important they be around later but not quite that close. He had already made a subsidiary plan to get them to move until he was ready for them to be here.

With meticulous care he checked all his batteries. When one tested okay but less than perfect, he replaced it. The bicycle was ready. His weapons had been disassembled, lubricated and reassembled last night in the motel room. There were two extra clips each for the M4 and the two Beretta Parabellum 9 mm automatics. The little Ruger .762 with its one clip lashed to his left ankle and the combat dagger on the right were already in place.

Over his undershirt, George strapped the Kevlar vest that had pockets for the extra clips. Then came the shoulder holster for one of the Berettas. The other one went in the belt of the cutoff shorts he wore under the sweat pants next to his cell phone bracket. He didn't own a double shoulder holster like he had seen in the movies. He imagined briefly knocking at Sly Stallone's front door to see if he could borrow one. Only a hotdog movie star, a pimp or a drug dealer would have that kind of thing. Next he collapsed the stock on the M4 assault rifle and suspended it diagonally from a hook around his neck that he had rigged up the day before. Over everything he pulled the sweat suit top that would have been a size and a half too large except for all the hardware he was carrying. In the two side pockets he stuffed an Israeli-made hand grenade, the remote control and a small carpenter's level.

George walked around a little to get used to the extra forty pounds. He still had time on his schedule so he went to a grassy clearing on the other side of the picnic table where Kate would be in less than an hour. He stretched and performed a Tai Chi warm-up for several minutes.

All the weight and the extra clothes were very uncomfortable but the breeze was still cool. The sun bounced up into the sky giving the impression of faster movement as it always does near the ocean horizon, turning the morning from red to orange to yellow in the space of a few minutes.

George savored it all, even the sensations of pain and discomfort. He figured it was his last chance to savor anything.

He looked around one more time and ran down his checklist. The plan was a good one. It would save Matthew Gordon and mete out a swift retribution to the murderers of Val and Alicia. There was even a certain amount of ironic symmetry to the techniques he chose to employ. He regretted that he couldn't take more time and make it more painful for them but even if he had had an infinity of time for torture and the best instruments for the task he knew it could never compare to his loss.

He mounted the bicycle and checked the temporary patch over the pinhole puncture he had made in the front tire. Adjusting the muzzle of the rifle under his shirt so it wouldn't interfere with pedaling, he began to ride in the direction of Balakova's house.

The wind on his face felt good and he had plenty of time so he kept a leisurely pace. When he was passing the driveway to Vizcaya, he slowed almost to a stop so he could reach down and remove the patch. He couldn't hear the air escaping but he knew it was working because the pedaling became more difficult. By the time he was a hundred feet from the spot he picked, the tire was completely flat. He pedaled on the rim for half the distance and then walked the bike the rest of the way.

He was fairly sure that no one was watching but he went through the pantomime of annoyance anyway, swearing under his breath and staring at the bike for a few seconds as if trying to decide what to do next. He leaned the frame against the utility pole on the northbound side of the road only forty feet from Balakova's driveway. Then he pulled the heavy chain from the saddlebag and wrapped it several times through the bicycle and around the pole, wedging it tight and securing it with the padlock. Then he pulled the little bar from his pocket, placed it on top and adjusted the backpack hanging from the handlebars until the bubble showed dead level. The wires hanging from the strap were exactly eleven feet and three inches long. He walked that distance back in the direction from which he had just come and mounted the motion sensor on a tree. Standing far to one side, he pressed the button in his pocket and the LED glowed briefly before he pressed it again. The wires could be seen from ten feet or so, but only if he looked for them and they didn't have to go unnoticed for long.

George pulled the monocular case out of the other saddlebag, put the strap over his shoulder and began walking North toward his car and the Vizcaya property. At the nearest corner of the wall, he scaled it quickly, looking around to be sure he hadn't been seen. The museum had top-flight security at the building itself but nothing on the fence. He climbed a tree that he had selected the day before and settled in a nest of three big branches to wait. From there he could make out the West and North sides of Balakova's house and the gate. Using the monocular he confirmed that there was no visible activity as yet and no guard out front.

He shifted to get as comfortable as possible for a middle-aged man in a tree with all that hardware hanging from him. It should be less than an hour, but George had been in a lot more uncomfortable places for longer and he was in no particular hurry to die.

Kate would make a good mother for Matt. Her disposition was not as sweet as her sister's had been but then whose was? She loved the boy; there was no doubt of that. Could she provide the discipline to make him grow up right? Yes, he decided, for a shrink, she was pretty down to earth. Believed in personal responsibility and all that. All in all, Matt would be lucky to have her and she would be better off for having him to fill some of the hollowness in her life.

George wondered if she would ever re-marry. Matt could use the influence of a male role model but realistically he thought that unlikely if he had to depend on Katherine. Socially, she came off as a little aloof and snotty—a hazard of the PhD and her own insecurity he thought.

There was movement at the house. One of the servants was making her way down the drive to pick up the morning paper and the hood assigned to guard duty was loitering about, preparing to take his place by the gate. It wouldn't be long now.

If you could ever get past all that PhD stuff though, Kate wasn't bad looking, not at all. She was younger than Val and had kept her weight down although George was sure that it was diet rather than exercise. He had never seen her do anything more strenuous than walk from one end of the Wolfchase Galleria to the other and back. Her eyes—her eyes were great too, just like Val's. And she was obviously intelligent, probably smarter than Val and George put together but sometimes not so hot in the area of common sense. Witness that bozo she married. Jesus, what a loser.

One thing that had completely surprised George on this trip was her courage. He hadn't expected her to grasp the situation and deal with it as well as she had. It must have been hard for her. If she had given him trouble and had to be sedated through this whole excursion it would have made this a hell of a lot tougher, but she had been quite a trouper about it. The fact that she could put her fear and personal feelings aside for the boy made it that much better. Yes, Matt would be lucky and that made George feel better.

The driver had pulled the black Suburban to the top of the circular drive. The big diesel under its hood was running because he could see a wisp of its sooty exhaust curling up over the back bumper. Also the first of the early staff arrivals were beginning to make their way up the road at his back to the museum. It was almost time to begin.

The black Chrysler 300 emerged from the garage and parked at the exit of the circle. Two more Russians joined the driver of that car and got in to wait. Three in the lead car and three or four in the Suburban. They were making this easier than he had hoped.

George unhooked the cell phone from his belt and dialed the number he had looked up and programmed the night before.

"Yes, ma'am," he said when a voice answered. "I'd like to speak to the agent in charge of The Mechanic investigation. I think it's a young woman who came here from out-of-town—New Orleans, I believe."

"Yes, Ma'am, you can tell her I am the one they call The Mechanic."

It was nearly a minute before someone came back on the line. They could have been tracing the call with the wireless carrier, but that was okay with him. The new voice matched the one he had heard through the walls of his boxcar hideaway. She said her name was Bernard.

"Ma'am, I know you have been trying to get onto the Balakova property because of some shipments you followed from Memphis. If you'll meet me at the Alice C. Wainwright Park in fifteen minutes, I can promise you you'll be in before noon."

George hung up. As he expected, it was less than three minutes before the tan Ford he had seen near the Balakova place passed him going toward the park. They had to make sure he wasn't already there and the Ford was closest.

George draped an arm over one of the branches he had been sitting on and dropped to the ground. He moved to the outer wall and looked around. He discarded the monocular case, the phone and the pocket level. He wouldn't be needing them any more. Quickly he climbed over and dropped at the same spot where he had entered. Crossing the road, he began to jog back toward the bicycle and Balakova's place.

After only sixty feet or so he acted winded and bent over at the waist with his hands on his thighs. His eyes were always on the gate in the distance. He needed to be close, but not too close. He had to time it just right. He began the shuffle of a man who wanted to run but was just too tired to pull it off.

Suddenly in the distance the edge of Balakova's iron gate swung into view. Damn! They had been faster this morning and he was too far away! His pace quickened to a steady run. If he went any faster, someone might notice him. It was important that he be part of the normal background for another ten or fifteen seconds. The man who had caused the death of Valerie and Ally would be feeling quite safe in his armored car led by a Chrysler full of his hired guns. Whatever else happened, he would not be allowed to escape.

The gaping chrome mouth of the Chrysler appeared and turned in his direction on the opposite side of the road. It would be only seconds now. He pulled the remote control from his pocket and put his thumb on the button. The Suburban was already pulling out and the Chrysler was creeping along. Still too far away, his angle was bad and he couldn't be sure if the first car had cleared the motion sensor. It was important that the first car should be out of the way but the Suburban appeared to be right on its taillights from this angle. Was he even within range? He hadn't tested it at this distance. He fought the urge to sprint toward them and pressed the button.

On the tree up the shaded street the little LED decorated device glowed blood red. It came on midway through the four-second gap between the passing of the rear of the first car and the front of the second. Two seconds later, it detected the movement of a massive object. The sensor closed a 6-volt circuit in the backpack on the bicycle and three pounds of C4 ignited with a massive roar.

The first stage of his plan happened perfectly and was over in a tiny fraction of a second, but in George's mind he saw its progress in exquisitely slow motion.

Inside the pack the explosive had been distributed along the equator of a steel plate some three quarters of an inch thick. With the instantaneous heat and impact, it folded down the middle as if it had been hinged and flew off toward the middle of the window in the rear door of the Suburban, which was just over eleven feet from the leading edge of its front bumper. Given the Velocity of Detonation rating of the C4, the flattened double rectangle of metal had become a wide six-pound bullet traveling at eighteen times the speed of sound. It was propelled by the combustion of a shaped charge—just like the one that took the lives of Alicia and Valerie Gordon.

Ivan Balakova, who always rode on the passenger side rear, was the first to die, by a microsecond or two. The three inch bulletproof glass disappeared instantly along with all but the tiniest pieces of his head. As the charge and plate had been angled slightly upward at five degrees inside the backpack, the steel may have only removed the top three inches of the crown of Balakova's second in command riding next to him. The driver of the Suburban and the extra bodyguard in the front passenger seat lived less than a second longer. The impact forced the heavy truck to rotate on a longitudinal axis at the same time that the remaining force of the explosion caved in the armored side like a giant fist. The seven thousand pound vehicle leapt off the ground nine feet, flipped sideways one and a quarter times and landed on its side in a yellow ball of flame.

In his concern for whether the device would work, George had forgotten to dive to the ground after pushing the button, but he was lucky. The shock wave only knocked him off his feet; the shrapnel from it had missed. He was stunned for a second and there was a ringing in his ears.

The Chrysler had been pushed from the rear in the direction it was moving. The driver stopped almost level with George. Burning residue clung to the bumper and trunk area and the back window was shattered. One of the guards on the side opposite George got immediately out of the car with his gun drawn. When he saw George lying on his back he pointed it at him over the roof of the car and yelled something unintelligible. He was completely panicked and the other two in the car were screaming directions at the top of their lungs. George staggered to his feet remembering to look frightened and stupid. It wasn't difficult. He held his hands up, palm outward toward the gunman sputtering at the man's cries as he imagined a terrified recreational jogger would.

Just then the burning truck got hot enough to ignite the diesel fuel inside its armored tank and it went up in a second, less spectacular explosion. When the startled bodyguard turned to look in that direction, George pulled the Beretta from his waistband in one practiced motion and shot him in the head, which was the only target presented to him. Quickly he yanked the pin from his grenade and threw it under the Chrysler as he ran toward the burning Suburban and the still open gate. It detonated before the other two could get out, making a smaller but very satisfactory concussive boom as it went off and the car rocked six inches up on its springs and its interior filled very satisfactorily with fire and smoke.

George replaced the pistol in his belt and unzipped the hooded sweatshirt, discarding it beside the road. Then he unfastened the M4 and threw away the hook that had carried it. The guard at the gate showed himself to see what the third explosion had been. George quickly gave him a double tap from the rifle and that guard went down too.

It was important that he reach the gate before the cops from the surveillance car got back from the park. He didn't want two more hostiles between him and Matt and he didn't want dead officers muddying the situation when all he wanted to do was kill the Russians. The unmarked car had stopped cautiously a hundred yards from the burning truck and George was already past the searing heat, almost at the gate when he was shot.

He registered the pain before he heard the staccato report of automatic gunfire. The first bullet had hit the meaty part of his thigh and before he could react, a second went through the Kevlar in the center of his back. He twisted around and got a flash of a burly figure in a powder blue sport coat as he fell. One of the men from the Chrysler was on his knees with a MAC 10 machine pistol firing wildly. His face and the front of his clothing were covered in blood. George aimed a burst in his direction almost as a reflex and the shooting stopped.

There was no time. How bad was he hurt? The body armor had slowed but not stopped the shot to the body. There was fire in his back but his leg had no feeling at all. George pulled the dagger from its place on his good leg and sliced wide strips of the sweat pants away. He triple folded the material over the entry wound, wrapped it twice around and pulled his leather belt tight over it. There was even less he could do about the second injury. He shoved the remainder of the makeshift bandage in a ball under the armor using the tip of his knife. Then he cinched the Kevlar vest until it was hard for him to breathe.

Crawling the few feet to the entrance, he could see two more men brandishing Kalashnikov rifles standing out front in the cleared perimeter that was supposed to make the house more defensible—if you were smart enough to stay inside the house to defend it. Balakova made sure most of the firepower stayed with him at all times. These two in the bright golf shirts might be the last of them. From what George had observed, the household staff that remained was not a part of the Russian's army.

The pair radiated confusion and fear. The one in the green shirt turned his head to call out a name in the direction of the house, thereby making the second man George's primary target. He shot that man twice in the chest. The first man then turned back in a panic and began firing as he retreated to the front door. He hadn't seen the direction the shots had come from. Too late to button up now, asshole, George thought. Green shirt had just pushed the latch on the big double door when George shot him in the back, just about where he himself had been shot but this time without any interference from Dupont products.

He waited thirty seconds. Patience was even more important now that he was hurt. No one had appeared and green shirt's body still lay sprawled in the open doorway but the name he had shouted reminded George that he was not done. The accent had made it difficult to understand the rest of the message, but the man had very clearly called for Mooney.

There was nothing to do but go in after him. George struggled to his feet using the M4 as a crutch. The first thirty yards he moved slowly from one tree to the next but he had to cross that other forty yards of open ground. He opened the stock on the rifle to make it a slightly better prop and got the Beretta back in his free hand, making a painful hobble, skip, hobble across the grass and circular driveway. Even his best effort made him an easy, slow-moving target but no one challenged his approach.

He entered and stood for a moment panting in the foyer. Mooney had to be guarding Matt in his upstairs room at the side of the house. When he got to the foot of the forty curving steps that led to the second floor, he stopped again and leaned against the baluster. He was dizzy and weak and looking back he could see that he had left a wide trail of blood on the marble entryway. George took a deep breath and climbed haltingly using two of his steps for every stair. Matthew was still in danger; he couldn't die yet.

It took a few seconds to get his bearings on the landing. The room where he had seen Matt through the window should be on his left and he started to move that way. He had gone ten feet when the muzzle of a pistol appeared in the door at the end of the hall and fired at him, missing badly. George fell rather than jumped into an open door at his right. There was nobody there and he leaned against the wall for support, sliding helplessly down to a sitting position. Now he couldn't feel either leg and he was dangerously sleepy. Damn! Not yet!

George knew that he was never going to get up off that floor. He had only one card to play and he had to do it while he still could. Mooney was terrified of him—always had been.

"Mooney," he said to the hallway, "let the boy go and I'll let you live."

It was a struggle to force enough air in his lungs to sound convincing.

"No deal, Bob," Mooney yelled back. "I know you. You'd kill me anyway. I'll just wait for reinforcements. If you try to rush me, I'll kill the boy."

"Matt," he called out, "are you all right?"

"Dad!" the boy yelled before he was stifled.

"He's all right," said Mooney, "and he'll stay that way if you're smart."

George blinked, nearly nodding off. He could only buy a little time. He pressed on his wound trying to draw pain that would wake him up but the leg was dead.

"Cops are the only help you're going to get. All your Russki buddies are gone."

"I'm still not coming out."

"That's okay. You just stay there and hope they show up before I lose my patience. If I hear anything in there that sounds bad, I'll come in there and kill you slowly. If you try to make a run for it, I'll kill you fast. You know the boy isn't a big enough shield to stop me. I'm not going to say anything else, we'll just wait quietly for the cops."

Mooney swore at him and called him Bob again.

"Matt," George said as loudly as he could. "I love you, son."

With that, the little circle of light left in his vision faded to black.

Chapter 27

Gaby was sitting in the back seat with Phil Cannon and Tony Metcalf was in the front of Curt Bell's car racing toward a meeting with The Mechanic when the surveillance team called to tell them that a war had just broken out in Coconut Grove.

They were just minutes away but three police cars beat them to the scene and were already setting up a perimeter around the smoking remains of two cars. Gaby recognized them from the meeting at the lawyer's office.

"Good God!" she said, "He got Balakova. That's why he guaranteed we could get onto the property. He made it into a crime scene."

Black smoke billowed up from two sources. A steel light pole lay across the road near the largest fire. Smaller fires were burning in trees and shrubbery for fifty yards on the west side of the road and a newly arrived fire truck was attempting to deal with them. One officer was placing orange traffic cones on the roadway. One man dressed in a light blue jacket lay face down near the open door of the black Chrysler.

Bell parked his car behind one of the police cruisers when he saw Crenshaw and Yates, the agents on stakeout duty. Curt introduced Tony Metcalf and asked for status.

"We were first on the scene," said Crenshaw, "but we couldn't see much. The explosions happened while we were up the street surveying the park for your fugitive. There are at least five dead on the street that we know of. That one on the ground there, two more in the first car and at least two in the larger vehicle down there. We haven't been able to get close to that one. There was gunfire at the Balakova house but we went no farther than the driveway when we saw three more down—one at the gate and two by the front door. Local PD has been informed that we expect to assert jurisdiction here but they advised us that SWAT is on the way."

"Any recent noise up there?" asked Metcalf.

"Sounded like a single shot from inside the house but we couldn't be sure that it wasn't a small secondary explosion. That was about five minutes ago now."

"Let's go take a look," said Metcalf.

All the agents had their sidearms drawn and pulled on the blue FBI windbreakers with the big yellow letters as they walked the hundred yards to the Balakova entrance. They skirted the burning truck by forty feet but the radiant heat from it nearly took their breath away. They crouched by the big brick columns that held the hinges of the gates and its opening mechanism.

The scene was just as described. One man lay only twenty feet from them with a pistol at his side. Another sprawled at the center of a circular drive with one arm in a fountain and the other still clutching an automatic rifle. A third could be seen half in and half outside the house. None of them were moving.

"Christ!" Bell exclaimed. "Could one man have done all this?"

Gaby nodded. "This guy? Yeah, I expect he could."

Curt was eager.

"Mister Metcalf, you're senior man around here. Do we wait for SWAT or do we go in?"

"I don't know," he said. "We've got to communicate with somebody in the house. Who's got a bull horn?"

"PD already tried that, but let's try again," Crenshaw replied.

Curt called out to one of the officers for the amplifier and the man brought one over.

Metcalf aimed it at the house and called out, "Anyone in the house, this is the FBI. Throw down your weapons and walk slowly out."

There was no reply to that effort or the two that followed.

"Screw this," Metcalf said, "I'm going in. If it's okay, I'll wave you two in and the police can follow."

First he checked the gate guard for signs of life. Following almost the same path as the man he had come to arrest, Tony Metcalf moved quickly from tree to tree and then sprinted across the open area with his H&K automatic held high in a two-hand grip. At the door he bent to examine the victim at the door, feeling for a pulse that was not there. He waved at the other two and they ran a straighter route, pausing at the fountain to check the body holding the AK47.

"No signs of movement that I can see," Metcalf whispered when Gaby reached the threshold. "But it's a pretty good bet which way the killer went."

There was a trail of blood across the white marble of the entrance and up the staircase. By gestures Metcalf indicated that Curt Bell should check the room on the right, he would go left and Cannon would take the hallway. They could see partially into both big rooms that opened onto the foyer and all the way to the end of the long central hall. In a moment they each called out an all clear. Gaby kept her gun trained on the top of the stairs. Whoever had gone up, he certainly hadn't come down yet.

Curt had heard something down the hall. Moments later Cannon returned.

"Civilians," he said softly. "Two maids and a cook in the pantry pissing themselves and praising Jesus in Spanish. I sent them out the back door and told them to walk around and surrender to the officers."

Gaby was still trained on the stairs. She inclined her head in that direction and said, "Well, do we press on or wait?"

She already knew the answer. Her colleagues were high on adrenaline and testosterone.

They climbed the stairs in single file, four guns pointed at the space beyond the landing, and saw the trail of blood leading into an open door fifteen feet away.

Tony Metcalf yelled out the same warning he had offered from the gate and a voice answered, "Okay, don't shoot". But it had come from a different door.

Metcalf followed the trail to the edge of the doorway and spun quickly into the opening, sweeping the room with his gun. A figure lay collapsed against the wall in a dark pool of blood. A pistol was still in the man's hand and Metcalf kicked it away. He pulled another gun from a holster and found a third strapped to one leg. Again he checked for a pulse and couldn't find one."

He called again toward the voice they had heard.

"You get that crazy bastard out of here or I'm not coming out," the voice said.

"It's okay," Metcalf replied, "we're secure out here. Throw out your weapons and come out of there."

The door at the end of the hall opened and a gun flew out and landed on the opposite side. A little boy appeared, followed by an older man with his hands raised. The boy's face was wet with tears and his chin was quivering. While Bell was frisking the man, the boy looked into the other room and saw the crumpled figure within.

"Daddy!" he cried in a tremulous whisper and rushed to his side before they could stop him. By the time they pulled him away, he too was bloody and now crying again.

Gaby holstered her gun and put her arms around him.

"Honey, is your name Matthew?" she asked and he nodded haltingly.

"Come on, let's get out of here."

She led the boy downstairs and out of the house as fast as he would move in his dazed state.

Out front the throng had grown. Two Tactical Unit trucks had joined six squad cars, two fire engines and three ambulances. Firemen were at work on the various fires while a crowd of curious onlookers craned for a better look at what might have caused the devastation.

Gaby spoke to the police captain on the scene, telling him that the house appeared secure but that he should have his men search the house and grounds thoroughly. She gave him the number of her cell phone and he agreed to call her with an update when they had completed the search.

Out of the crowd a frantic woman's voice called out, "Matt, Matt!"

When the boy tried to run to her, Gaby held on to him but waved to the restraining policeman to let her in.

The woman saw the front of the boy's shirt covered with blood and began a frantic and shrill litany invoking the name of Jesus and several saints. Gaby told her that the boy was okay and she quickly confirmed the fact by rapid examination.

"Oh, Mattie, I'm so glad to see you," the woman said as they embraced. "Thank God."

"Ma'am, I'm guessing you are Doctor Katherine Wallace?" Gaby asked after she had given them a few seconds. The woman nodded.

Gaby introduced herself.

In a few more questions it emerged that she had been kidnapped as well, but by her former brother-in-law and brought to Miami for the expressed purpose of taking care of Matt Gordon.

"Doctor Wallace, do you know who it was that took Matt?" she asked.

Kate pointed at the group now making their way toward them.

"Yes," she said, "that man right there."

That earned a disgusted look from the prisoner Phil Cannon was leading in handcuffs.

"He told me he was from the FBI and his name was Turner."

"He's certainly not from the Bureau. Who is he really?" Gaby asked Metcalf.

"He hasn't said a thing except his lawyer's name."

"Mooney," Kate told them. "George told me his name is Mooney and he really works for the CIA."

Mooney just shook his head and sighed disgustedly.

On the way to the car, Kate asked Gaby about the man she called George Gordon and she was told that her kidnapper was dead. Gaby didn't really understand her reaction to that.

"He was always good to my sister," she explained. "He said he would save Matt and he did."

A flurry of activity erupted around one of the ambulances. The EMT's were running back with one of the folding cots. The police had detected life signs from the man on the second floor.

Chapter 28

Gaby hung up the phone in the small conference room at FBI Miami headquarters.

"He's still in critical condition," she told Kate. "When they get enough units of blood into him, they're going to perform emergency surgery at Park Plaza."

Bell, Metcalf and a stenographer were also in the room to take her statement. Cannon had been left for the moment at the crime scene to deal with local police. Metcalf allowed Gaby to conduct the interview on the theory that Doctor Wallace would respond more easily to a woman.

"What do you know about George?" Gaby asked, returning to her chair. "What did he tell you?"

Kate Wallace shifted uncomfortably and wouldn't meet her gaze.

"He killed people. That's about all I know."

"And how do you know?"

"He told me that much. And I saw him kill a man in my living room who worked with that Mooney person. It was horrible. He said that the man had come to kill him and would have killed me afterward."

"And you believed him?"

"Not at first. Actually, I shot him with that man's gun, but I barely hit him from just a few feet away, thank goodness."

"Why do you say that?"

"I . . . Because I don't think I would ever have seen Matthew again."

Gaby considered that statement for a moment.

"I understand that you are a clinical psychologist."

"Yes."

"And what is your professional assessment of George?"

The woman shook her head. "That's very difficult to say. I know some would diagnose Multiple Personality Disorder in his case."

"But you wouldn't?"

"If I believed it existed I might. The evidence is inconclusive. I believe MPD is simply a specific variety of dissociative disorder that represents an extraordinarily well-developed defense mechanism. If it were defined that way, I might agree that he has it. The way the term is abused, it covers anything from acute phobia to satanic possession."

"But you would agree that George Gordon is mentally ill?"

Kate hesitated. She was near hysterics of her own and quite irritated to be questioned at all.

"If I felt compelled to put a label on it, I suppose so. If I were consulted professionally without any personal involvement I'm sure I could define his mental state any of several ways and defend my position. Personally, I don't know that I would call him pathological. Even quite normal people have an almost limitless capacity for self-deception. And George seems to have had a number of . . . very negative experiences. Now could you just leave us alone!"

Gaby looked hard at Kate Wallace. While she was answering factual questions she had maintained steady eye contact and now her gaze was wandering. Gaby fancied herself a bit of a psychologist as well and it made her curious.

"How is it that you were there when Matt was found today? Did George bring you with him?"

"No, he released me last night and told me to go to the park this morning at nine AM and wait for something to happen. When I heard the explosions, I knew he must have had something to do with it and I walked down there."

"What do you know about the freight container?"

"Nothing," she said a little too quickly. "Oh, you mean the one that was shipped here? Just that it belonged to the same man who had sent the Russians and that it ended up in Miami."

"What container did you think I meant, Doctor?"

"Oh I don't know. I just wasn't thinking I guess. I'm a little upset. Can I take Matt and rest now?"

"Just a few more," Gaby said.

"You did come to Miami with George?"

"Yes."

"How did you get here?"

"In a car."

"What kind of car?"

"A green one. I think it was a Chevrolet. I don't know cars."

"And how did he know where Matt was. How did he even know to come to Miami?"

"I . . . I think he already knew but he got the address where some box, the one you were talking about, was shipped, from a man in Mississippi. It was here."

Gaby looked at the other two. "Are we done here, gentlemen?"

Metcalf shrugged.

"Ms. Wallace, we'd like you to stay around town for a few days. Do you need a place to stay?"

"No, I have a hotel."

"Then just leave the number of the hotel with the lady out front. The agent sitting with Matt will drive you wherever you need to go. Thank you for your cooperation."

Katherine Wallace thanked everyone and got up to leave. Curt opened the door for her and closed it behind her.

"What do you think?" Gaby asked.

"I don't know," Metcalf said. "It certainly sounds as if she is still trying to protect her brother-in-law for some reason but I don't think it matters. We wouldn't have any trouble putting him away forever just based on today's exploits even if he makes it through surgery."

"True," she admitted. "How did he do all that anyway?"

"The bomb guys said he turned some high explosive into a rocket to take out Balakova," Curt replied. "It's rare but we've seen it before. You put a shaped charge on one side of a metal plate and if it's prepared perfectly, it deforms on detonation and shoots off at the burn speed of the charge. The luxury tank never had a chance. He used a grenade on the car. That took out most of them and the rest weren't ready for that kind of all out attack. He just capped the rest of them one by one. Man, they shouldn't have taken his kid!"

"Hey look," said Metcalf to Bell and the stenographer, "Would you two excuse us for a minute? I need to speak with Agent Bernard."

Curt looked over at Gaby with some concern but didn't say anything as he and the secretary gathered up their papers and notes.

Metcalf sat facing her with his most intimidating stare, but from experience he knew it had lost its desired effect with her.

"Okay then, The Mechanic is a dead issue," he said when they had gone. "Congratulations, Agent Bernard. At least we can count part of your trip a success."

Metcalf said her name with an exaggerated French accent. He was still mocking her but she sensed that in his mind it might be some kind of positive gesture. Also it did suggest that he could be capable of saying it correctly.

"Thank you, Assistant Director. Does this mean I don't have to catch the next plane?"

Metcalf didn't react.

"You may have to make a statement to the cops," he said. "You're still suspended from duty."

"You're joking," said Gaby. "I just made the highest profile bust we've had in a year and you're suspending me?"

"As far as I'm concerned, Cannon made the bust. There are still too many questions unanswered about your involvement. Where is this alleged gold and where is Aleksandr Pushkin and what the hell was he really doing here? We still don't know enough about any of that shit. This buys us some breathing room as far as saving face for the Bureau but you're still in a heap of shit as I see it."

Gaby leaned back in her chair and closed her eyes.

"Assistant Director Metcalf, you may be a very smart man and a good cop, but may I say, off the record, that you are also a prick on a galactic scale."

Metcalf sighed and got up from his seat to leave.

"Yeah, well, I'll just have to learn to live with your negative opinion."

"Any success this mission has had we can thank The Mechanic for going down in a blaze of glory if he ever wakes up. If we get to question him, maybe he can shed some light on some of these questions and help your case.

"You left a lot of loose ends that need tying up. I know you've spent a while close to this investigation and maybe too close to Mister Pushkin, but among several things that bother me about this, I'd like to leave you with one to focus on as you ponder a defense."

Gaby raised one eyebrow and he continued.

"Why would somebody ship over two tons of contraband in secret and then leave the box with traces of it where you could find it on his own property? That was a little too convenient. And now that I know the information came from Dashenko, it's even more suspicious. If it's not some scam by you and your boyfriend, it sounds to me like Balakova might have been set up by one of his own people."

After a second to redirect her thoughts, Gaby nodded. "You're right," she said softly. "Genius or no genius, how could Dashenko have possibly known? At the time I was so glad to get a lead that I didn't even wonder about the source. Almost as if that whole thing was stage-managed also."

Metcalf picked up his things.

"Anyway, I'm going back to the scene with the lab boys. There's no telling what we may find in the Godfather's house. Good luck Agent Bernard."

Metcalf had managed to make her feel completely wretched in the midst of victory. After he left the room, Curt Bell walked in. Gaby was slumped in her chair and didn't even bother to acknowledge him. He looked at her in silence for a few seconds.

"Well?" he said.

"Agent Bell, if you get an offer of a transfer to Headquarters, shoot yourself in the leg and tell them you can't make the trip."

"I'll keep that in mind," he replied. "What did he say, or shouldn't I ask?"

"The gist of it was that I am lucky The Mechanic solved his own disappearance for me and I am suspected of . . . I don't even know what I'm suspected of in this gold shipment thing."

"Hey, Gaby, don't sweat it. Even I had heard of Metcalf. The guy's a . . ."

"Yeah, I just told him that as a matter of fact. But he's still AD and to be fair, he's still a pretty good analyst. He's right about the gold. I just don't get it."

She spoke slowly, as if she was preoccupied and Curt started to leave her with her deep thoughts.

"Hey, Curt," she said before he got to the door. "The guy who supervised the warehouse examination, is he here?"

"Yeah, he's just down the hall."

"Would you ask him to step in here for a moment, please?"

In less than a minute Curt Bell walked back in. He sat down and a burly man with a gray streaked beard stuck his head in the door.

"Hi, Dennis Todd, what can I do for you, Ms. Bernard?"

"I know you tested most of the debris you found at that warehouse."

"All of it, at least one scraping from the inside of every piece. There were over five hundred pieces."

"How about the floor? Did you check the floor for particles?"

"Of course. Luckily gold is easy to test for."

"Did you find much?"

"Now that you mention it, no, almost none."

"Why would you guess that could be?"

"Hmm, hadn't thought about it. I suppose if I were ripping something apart that had gold in it, I might want to do it on some surface I could recover any spillage from—a tarpaulin or something. It really wouldn't be worth recovering, though. You could probably get more from scraping the countertops at a dentist's office."

"What if the box had been taken apart somewhere else; the gold separated and only the pieces had been transported to that site?"

"Yeah, that could explain it too. An awful lot of trouble to go to for nothing, though. If I wasn't going to salvage the titanium, I would have deep-sixed the scrap as soon as I had the gold."

"Yeah, me too. Thank you, Dennis you've been a big help. And thank the rest of your team for me, please."

"Sure thing," he said and disappeared.

"Curt, let me try one out on you," Gaby said.

"Okay, shoot."

"What if Balakova really didn't know the scrapped container was in his warehouse because he never put it there?"

"I'm not following."

"What if the gold was shipped somewhere else and when he told his people to send it to the scrap yard or out to sea, one of them sent it to a place they arranged for us to find it? While we're all over Balakova this other person could go to the original site and recover the gold while Balakova was dealing with us, or even better, after The Mechanic had dealt with him."

"That pretty face hides a devious mind. It makes some pretty good sense, though. So what do we do now?" Curt asked. "We don't know what the first site was or which of his people did it. Seems to me they're all dead except that dirty CIA spook."

"No not him. I'm thinking it sounds a little like a queen sacrifice in chess—the kind you would only do late in the game when you knew it would guarantee victory. I might know who was behind it."

Curt blinked. "What the hell does that mean?"

Gaby sighed exhaustedly.

"Oh, I don't know. Maybe just my imagination. I'll tell you what, Curt, I've had about all the excitement I can handle in a day. I think I'll take up this problem in the morning."

"I'm with you," he said. "And for what it's worth, I think you did a hell of a job, especially for your first time out."

"Thanks Curt. I think I'll stop by the hospital and check on our murderous benefactor and then crash into a hot tub. You have a good evening."

Gaby got directions to the Park Plaza and pulled out of the parking lot, her mind working hard and coming up with nothing but muddy results. Something was nagging at the edges of her awareness but she just couldn't bring it to the surface.

What in the world was the deal with Alex Pushkin? One minute he wants to pledge his troth and the next he bolts. Not so different from some men she had known, but not in character for Alex. She didn't feel as if she had been used by him. Should she? Based on their last exchange, it was more the reverse. What was his real mission? To distract her? He had been singularly successful at that but he didn't have to ask her to run away with him. What if she had said yes? Where would she be now? Tahiti? Dead? Besides he really had aided the investigation. Oh, the hell with it. Clear your mind and start over tomorrow.

Gaby circled the hospital lot twice before she parked at the door. She didn't have anything designating her rental car as FBI but she was in no mood to worry about parking tickets.

Eventually she made her way to the Intensive Care Unit and asked for the physician in charge of George Gordon. She was told that Doctor Aguilar was his surgeon and that he was in OR number two. He would be out to speak to the family when he was done.

She found the Waiting area where she saw Katherine Wallace sitting with her arm around her nephew. They were huddled in one corner of the otherwise deserted room in front of a television running a game show at low volume.

"Hello again, Matthew," Gaby said to the boy. "Do you mind if I sit here?"

Katherine gave her a shrug and a look of resignation. Matthew only reacted by cutting his eyes toward her briefly and then resuming his lifeless study of the TV screen as Gaby sat in a chair near them.

"Doctor Wallace, have they told you anything?" she asked.

"No. He has been in there over two hours but a nurse just stopped by to say it shouldn't be much longer."

"Doctor Wallace . . . may I call you Katherine?"

The woman managed to say, "You can call me Kate", without making it sound friendly.

"Kate, I'm here to help you both, believe me."

"Unless you're a surgeon or a travel agent, I don't see how you can do that," she replied.

Gaby tried the boy.

"Do you remember me, Matthew?" It had only been a matter of hours but he looked as if he was unaware of much of anything.

Finally he nodded. She was lost for clever and disarming small talk so she tried a little bribery.

"Can I get you something? How about a Coke?"

He didn't exactly say yes, but he looked receptive to the idea. Eventually Kate agreed to a cup of coffee and Gaby asked him to come with her to the vending machines. He looked at his aunt and she gestured that it would be all right.

On the way, Gaby searched again for something innocuous and comforting to say but he spoke before she had a chance.

"Are you going to put my dad in jail?"

"That's not up to me, honey. Right now I'm just hoping he's going to be all right, just like you are."

She assuaged her conscience by getting him a Hershey bar with his coke and got two cups of syrupy coffee to take back. When they returned, a man in green scrubs was standing over Kate. She had her hands in her lap clenching and unclenching them furiously. Gaby called the doctor aside and explained her position.

"It's a fifty-fifty proposition," Aguilar said. "The man should be dead. I honestly don't know what kept him alive all that time. The wounds weren't so bad by themselves but because of the delay of treatment he lost an incredible amount of blood. There was probably kidney and liver damage and the bullet he took in the spine didn't sever it but it caused a very bad bruise. I can't tell just how extensive the insult was. We'll just have to wait and see, but if he survives the night, he'll probably make it. He'll almost certainly be paralyzed to some degree. There could even be some impaired brain function."

She thanked him and went over and sat on the opposite side of Kate Wallace from Matthew. Kate was trying to cover her crying with a tissue. First Gaby said something encouraging about Gordon's survival, then as she was moving toward the exit she had a sudden inspiration.

"I'm truly sorry to bother you. I know this is a bad time. I promise I'm not trying to find out anything related to Mister Gordon's situation. At the moment I'm more concerned about the people who kidnapped Matt and brought all of us down here.

"You said before that George got the address of that container shipment from a man in Mississippi. Would you happen to remember what that address was?"

"Of course not. Oh, wait. He had it on a piece of paper when he came back to the car."

She began rummaging in her purse. In a few seconds she found a scrap of paper and handed it to Gaby.

"Fabulous! Thank you, Kate. I'll keep my fingers crossed for your sakes."

Gaby was out the door before she looked at the paper. It was not the address where they found the scrapped Molotov box.

Chapter 29

It took some time for Gaby to interpret this new view of the facts. She was at the pay window of a fast food joint on Biscayne when it came to her. Before she got her change, she decided that it wouldn't wait for morning. The Mechanic had killed nine people and put another out of the way with his assault on the Matrosskaya and that was a big vacuum in any organization. Those left behind would be in a panic and moving quickly.

Gaby had the phone in her hand to call for the surveillance team but decided she didn't need the embarrassment if she were wrong. She put the phone back and picked up her Miami map. It took a while to locate the spot. She wasn't far away from the second address.

As with all out-of-towners in all large cities, she found the street names confusing. Like why would Northwest 71st street be on the east side of town? It was dark by then and she drove by once, closer than she intended to get, on the almost deserted street. All she could do was hope she wasn't spotted because when she passed, there was a van in the loading area. Gaby mumbled a curse through tight lips and cruised a block away, parking at a corner where she could just see the rear of the van in her mirror. Quickly she dialed one of the two local numbers stored in her phone, both of them belonging to Curt Bell.

"Curt, I'm sorry to bother you at home but I'm afraid our day isn't over yet," she said.

She explained what she thought was happening and Curt picked up on it immediately after the discussion they had had earlier. His excitement came through the earpiece. He told her to sit tight and he would join her with backup.

Gaby looked all around the car feeling suddenly very exposed and alone. She pulled her service pistol out, flipped the safety off and placed it in the passenger seat next to the greasy paper bag. Jesus, what was she thinking coming here by herself?

She took two of the forgotten French fries and ate them. Her mouth was dry and they felt like lead washers when they hit her stomach. Gaby looked at the bag with the hamburger inside and remembered what she had told Alex about fast food. She downed a mouthful of Pepsi and in her nervousness almost missed the holder when she tried to replace the cup. Come on, Curt!

Gaby was at the point of wishing that she had not quit smoking, a desire that she had been unaware of for more than two years, when she saw the taillights in the van come on. It backed into the street to turn in her direction and she saw that there were not one but two identical white vans pulling out. She got a flash of two men in the front of the lead truck before she had to duck down in the seat to avoid being seen. She heard the second one pass and raised up slowly. She started the car, intending to leave the lights off but forgot that they were on automatic. Cursing the technology, she dowsed them quickly and turned to follow the trucks while she hit the redial button.

"Curt," she said into the handset. "Where are you?"

"I'm still twenty minutes away," he said. "But there are two units of ours and one police cruiser that should be there in a couple minutes."

"It's too late," she said, unable to keep some of the rising panic from her voice. "They're on the move and I'm following. Two white vans traveling east on 71st at about 35. I think they're going to turn south on Biscayne. I know it's the right one because the rear end is almost dragging the ground. I'm trying to keep my distance but give me a second and I'll give you the license plate of the trailing vehicle at least. I can't quite make it out. I know they can't outrun me with those heavy loads but if they were to notice me . . ."

All at once the Van in front of her hit its brakes hard and went into reverse. Before she could react, she was right on top of him, standing on her brakes. She turned the wheel instinctively to avoid the rear of the truck but it kept coming as she swerved and forced her car sideways right into the rear bumper and doors. It bounced off in a scream of rubber for ten feet but Gaby didn't know it. She hit her head on the side window at the first impact and never saw what happened next.

Gaby regained consciousness in odd, painful stages. First she was aware of the motion and nausea, then just the dim light that hurt her eyes and finally the noise and pounding in her head. She spent a disoriented minute reacting to these things as a dumb animal, unable to understand.

As her surroundings came into focus she saw that she lay on a narrow bunk attached very solidly on three sides to the enclosure walls. The room was no more than eight feet square, with a small desk on the opposite side whose lamp was the only source of illumination. Her hands were cuffed to the bed's frame and it had no give at all when she pulled on it. Caught by the men she was pursuing. Great, Gaby, just great.

The word 'boat' came into her mind before she had even formed the thought that she was on one, her subconscious having had much longer to work on the question. The noise she heard through the walls, no, bulkhead, she thought. The noise was the steady roar of diesel engines close by. It was not at all surprising to her that the men had taken the gold to a boat. She had already guessed that and was on the verge of explaining her belief to Agent Bell just before the crash.

Gaby yanked on her handcuffs and the bar through which it was twisted a few more times with identical results. The cabin was a little dingy and smelled of too many voyages and too few airings. It held no props either helpful or otherwise, nothing at all she could use to her advantage even if her hands were free. There was nothing she could do but wait, frightened and irritable, for someone else to decide her fate. An hour passed and the pain was becoming manageable by the time someone came in to check on her. And he made an impressive entrance.

Even in the rather shabby surroundings there was something regal about his bearing. He had a sharply angled, lupine face with thin lips and a narrow nose surmounted by intelligent blue eyes that almost glowed with light of their own. She knew him as soon as he came in though she had never seen him or his picture.

"The Comrade Colonel," she said steadily, much cooler than she felt. "I had hoped we would meet but this isn't exactly the way I pictured it."

His eyes showed amusement but his expression barely changed as he unhurriedly turned the desk chair around and took a seat. There was a languorous economy to his movements that was somehow grandly theatrical at the same time. Both his polo shirt and casual slacks were crisply pressed and perfectly tailored for him. The man crossed his legs like a senior executive at a business conference and smiled briefly.

"Agent Bernard," he said, "I am very pleased that we have these moments to become acquainted. You are of course correct. I am Andrey Sergeyevitch Dashenko."

Dashenko's grammar and strict pronunciation were probably as good as Aleksandr's but the hint of extra vowel sounds came through in his accent. He leaned closer, his face only a yard or so from hers.

"I feel I know you already Colonel," she said.

"And I you. May I call you Gabrielle? It is too familiar perhaps but I have never known anyone of that name and it has a delicious sound."

"Please do," She said. "Part of my training is to gain the confidence of kidnappers or other criminals I plan to arrest."

This time he even laughed a little.

"Well said, my dear. Well said. Whether it is bravery or bravado it suits you.

"I must say that you have been a surprise to me almost from the beginning and I am a man unaccustomed to surprises. My plans have been redirected twice in this endeavor and in both cases due to you."

"That's quite an honor for me, I suppose. What have I done to deserve it?"

"The first time, I regret to say that I overestimated your intelligence."

"Oh?"

"Yes. I projected that with the information provided you would be able to trace the first Molotov box, which for our purposes is the only significant one, to the Vista warehouse in Miami, the one I wanted you to find. The destination was planted at the Nashville Street Wharf in New Orleans, but you gave up when your family sources failed to discover it for you. Your poor performance required me to, to cheat the sequence of events by sending the location to Aleksandr."

Gaby shook her head in reluctant admiration.

"Jesus, I had it wrong. You didn't choose me for the assignment because I was a woman. It was because of my family in New Orleans wasn't it? I'll bet you really are a heck of a chess player."

"In fact this was very nearly another mistake, although one which I could not have foreseen. The fact that you are a woman was immaterial to my plan but Lieutenant Pushkin now believes that he is in love with you. Now that I see you, I can understand. In retrospect, you were a very poor choice on my part.

"Revealing myself as the source of the information was the most expedient way of getting the FBI to increase its vigilance in Miami. I believe I am correct in my judgment that it was for this reason you became suspicious enough to search for the second location, the one I would have preferred remain unknown for the moment."

"Probably," she admitted. "The Bureau would certainly have uncovered it eventually but the idea that there was another—agency at work made it more urgent."

"Yes. In this I underestimated your abilities. I apologize."

"I can't take full credit for that but Russians have been underestimating Americans since Khrushchev."

"I am sorry that we have no time for a debate on this subject," he said with his expression of amusement intact. "The Soviet Union underestimated how effective your system could be, not your people. Surely you can understand how our government could have made the mistake. Soviet Communism was based on a utopian idea of sharing, encompassing the finer, more praiseworthy instincts of humanity, while capitalism is based on a system of Darwinism and naked greed. Which was the more negative and cynical? Ours was an experiment doomed only by the flaws in the human animal."

"We try not to look upon human beings as animals, Colonel. On the other hand, you've managed to embrace those flaws rather completely. Or are you telling me that you plan to distribute the gold you've stolen among the suffering poor in Russia?"

"I am a pragmatist above all else, Gabrielle. When Communism ruled, I was the best Party member that I could be. Now I am the best Capitalist."

"Betraying your friends is not part of our code."

He laughed softly again.

"But of course it is. Your code, if it exists at all, simply does not embrace the possibility of being caught at it. Besides, the betrayal was not mine. The gold belongs to me as much as anyone. It was I along with Yaponets who arranged to liberate it originally. When he was incarcerated by your organization, it was through the treachery of our trusted friend, the departed Mister Balakova, who then usurped the control of Matrosskaya from him along with the gold."

"And Alex, he's a part of all this?"

"He has played a role of which he was not always aware. But yes, Aleksandr is, as of now, fully involved."

"He must be very proud of his father."

Dashenko's thick brows came together in an almost continuous line over his eyes.

"What do you mean?"

"I notice your last names are different but he does use 'Andreyevich' sometimes. Has he always known? That you are his father?"

"I must say, Gabrielle, you have surprised me again. He told you this?"

"No. He didn't have to. Until he disappeared today I had no reason to suspect it but then I got to thinking about his nautical ambitions and how his daddy was in the Navy and all that. When I saw you just now, I knew for sure. He has your eyes, doesn't he, Colonel?"

"I can see why he has formed such affection for you. You are intelligent and perceptive as well as beautiful. Quite extraordinary. I have never met a policeman with your . . . qualities and I daresay the same is true of my son. It was that attachment as much as anything that caused all the difficulties my plan has encountered. I am sorry that you and he will never produce my grandchildren. They would undoubtedly rule the world. And I am very sorry that we cannot spend more time together."

He rose from his chair and replaced it under the little desk, taking care that it should be symmetrically positioned.

"There are still details which must be attended to," he said.

Gaby tightened her diaphragm so her voice wouldn't quake as she asked; "Now I suppose you have to murder the mother of your unborn descendants?"

He paused when he was in the corridor with the knob to the louvered cabin door in his hand and turned back. There was a sly look on his face as if he could see the terror plainly through her calm facade. After a moment he shrugged.

"I don't think that will be necessary. You will in all likelihood spend several unpleasant weeks in Havana, but your death would accomplish nothing. The fact that you have seen my face harms nothing, as I am a rather public figure with a large body of photographic records. The damage you can do is already done."

The door was closing and she called, "Not if I can help it!" loudly just before the latch clicked shut. From the other side she heard his laughter again along with a farewell. He laughed big, just like Alex.

When she knew he could no longer hear, Gaby let out an explosive gasp and her next few breaths were shudders. She had fought hard to keep Dashenko from seeing how frightened she was, but panic was very near.

She began to work on the bed frame for another few seconds but the angled iron was so firmly attached that it quickly became absurd. And in her brief experience in law enforcement she had learned a few simple tricks about opening handcuffs but all of them required better tools than fingernails and teeth. Also it was clear to her that even if she were able to

ROR

free herself there were sure to be armed men and she knew nothing about boats or even marine radios.

Havana. No doubt the Colonel had contacts there from the Soviet days who would help to either transport or sell the gold they carried. Any pursuers wouldn't be allowed to penetrate Cuban waters. She tried to picture a Caribbean map. Havana shouldn't be far. A hundred fifty, less than two hundred miles anyway, she thought. They should be there soon. Then Gaby heard a different noise.

She couldn't make it out. She was just too close to the engines.

The boat began a series of hard turns and her arms were nearly wrenched out of their sockets as her body was thrown to the floor. She shrieked with the pain, grabbed the bedrail and held on. The turns continued with the noise. Somehow, pursuit had found Colonel Dashenko.

She had no trouble hearing the explosion. It resonated through the hull and the deck tilted to its craziest angle yet. The ship righted itself and the diesels were screaming at an even higher pitch when the door burst open. Alex Pushkin stumbled in.

He looked angry, frightened and apologetic all at once.

"Gaby, I am so sorry," he said. "I never thought this would happen."

"Are we hit?"

"No, not yet but your Coast Guard is firing on us."

"Alex, you have to get me out of here. If we start to sink . . ."

"Yes. I have brought the key."

He released one hand long enough to get it around the bed frame and latched the cuff back on.

When she protested, he said, "Sorry, but the others . . ." by way of an aborted explanation. Then he pulled her in his wake out of the cabin, stumbling all the way up the passageway and a flight of steps to the deck above.

Just as she cleared the hatch, the water on the starboard side where she stood and the night sky above it erupted in an incandescent geyser no more than 30 yards off their beam. Four crewmen that she could see were firing those damned ubiquitous Kalashnikov rifles at the smaller of the two boats in pursuit. It was close enough for her to read Harbor Patrol in giant red letters on its side. In the distance was a much larger, darker shadow out of which came three spotlights. It could only be the Coast Guard cutter that was firing cannon at them.

Alex threw her roughly against a wall near the bridge. He warned her to stay low and went forward. So far he didn't have a weapon that she could see. The Russians on deck were firing tracer bullets that made sparkling zigzags on the calm surface of the ocean not yet disturbed by their passage. Owing to the absence of impact noises, Gaby guessed the crew of the small craft was either not firing at all or firing over their heads waiting for them to see the absurdity of resistance. Finally someone on the other side lost patience or his marksmanship was both poor and lucky because the Russian crewman firing the most enthusiastically went down. That brought a thunder of shots out of the dark from both directions. One of them hit Gaby in the leg.

She cried out for Alex and he ran to her looking wild and frightened. He saw the blood, went briefly inside and returned with a first aid kit, pulling out tape and gauze. Hastily he yanked her skirt up almost to her hips and began to wrap the wound just above her knee. He worked in silence until he was done, then told her where to apply pressure. There was as much pain in his voice as there was in her leg.

"Gaby," he said, "if only you had come with me last night, this would be so different.

"I swear to you I did not know about the Colonel and the Matrosskaya until we arrived in Miami. He came to me while you were in the courthouse. He was using both of us just as you feared on that first night. But for me he has been . . . I could not . . ." Finally, he just said, "I am sorry."

He tested the repair work of his bandage and just looked at Gaby for another few seconds, pain, anger and regret painted across his features by the light from the passageway behind her. Above the binding, he placed the flat of his palm on the smooth skin of her thigh for just a moment. He opened his mouth to say something more but closed it in a moment as though he had gone suddenly mute.

More gunfire erupted and a slug buried itself near Gaby's head. Alex grunted out something that sounded like a curse. He reminded her to keep pressure on the wound, leapt to his feet and disappeared aft, calling out something in Russian.

The shooting by the crew stopped; then the engines stopped. The chase was over.

Chapter 30

Eight days crept by in a cycle of pain, medication and bad food. The bullet had been a ricochet that tumbled in at less than full velocity but with maximum tissue damage. It had nicked an artery and only by sending her back to Miami on the Harbor Patrol boat at full speed were they able to avoid more serious complications. She was accompanied all the way to the hospital by a tall Coast Guard petty officer who was reputed to be the best health services tech on the east coast. He did everything right and saved at least her leg and possibly even her life.

The prognosis was good, but Gaby discovered that three days was the absolute limit of her endurance as a model hospital patient. After that she strove to become the irritant in the belly of this antiseptic beast so that it would expel her back into the world.

Her first visitors had been her parents. It was only after ten minutes of reconciliation and tender concern that her mother made a comment that implied that the injury was divine retribution for choosing such an inappropriate life for herself and disappointing the family. Lacking the energy to fight, Gaby more or less agreed with her.

Curt Bell made the first of many appearances the same day.

"The hero awakes!" had been his opener. He was holding a flower arrangement that he placed next to the other three that she had not noticed until then.

"Some hero," she said. "Bamboozled by a team of Russian cowboys and then shot by my own people while lying helpless on the deck of their getaway craft."

"Not the official view, my darling. Not the official view at all."

She had known Curt just a few days but he had a contagiously sunny attitude that sprinted right up to the borderline of saccharine, and stopped abruptly. The Bureau really had some superb employees.

"Metcalf has called every day and you even got get well wishes from the Director himself."

"You're kidding."

"Nope. He suggested to Metcalf that he would entertain a nomination for a commendation—meritorious service star and all that stuff. You are the real deal."

"I wonder if that means I'm not suspended any more? You stay unconscious for a day or two and good things happen. That reminds me, how in the world did they find me anyway?"

He smiled and brushed at his fingernails.

"What, you think you're the only one that can be a hero? When you were cut off, the last thing you said was that you thought they were going to turn south on Biscayne Boulevard. I guessed that you meant they might be trying to get to the harbor or one of the larger marinas. It wasn't much of a logical leap, really. If you have something you want to transport in Miami and you don't want anyone to know about it, The Atlantic Ocean is a popular choice. It took me a while to get to the right man in the Coast Guard but once I did they were great. Even so, we barely caught up with you. Another half-hour and they'd have been in Cuban waters and the Coast Guard wasn't going to shoot it out with them."

"Were you on one of the boats?"

"Absolutely—Dramamine patch and all."

"Hell, you're probably the one who shot me."

"There was a line forming," he said with a grin.

"Seriously, Curt, I owe you one. Thanks."

"Someday—and that day may never come—I will call on you for a service . . ." Bell said in a bad imitation of Marlon Brando in The Godfather.

She chuckled and called him a nasty name.

"Were Metcalf and Cannon involved?"

"I didn't have time to call them. They might even have read about it in the morning paper. I did speak to Metcalf at the hospital the next morning though. He and Cannon flew out immediately for DC, probably so they could spin the story a little better. Metcalf told me—rather candidly, I thought—that it would be better all around if he made a hero out of you and a genius out of himself for sending you."

"That's so sweet of him. How about Dashenko and the Matrosskaya?"

"Everybody we know connected to them is either dead or in custody. Of course we don't know what we didn't know about them. There are certainly others, but it's safe to say that they won't be giving us any serious trouble for a while."

"We have Mister Gordon or whatever his real name is to thank for most of that. Did he make it?"

"Yeah, that amazing son of a bitch is going to live, but he won't be playing the piano again any time soon. He took a slug in the back that partially wedged between two vertebrae. The doctor says the pain must have been off the scale right up until the time that his spinal column decided to shut down. He got shot twice out by the driveway where we were, did his own field dressing, took out three more guys with automatic weapons and climbed the stairs to get to his son before the loss of blood got him. Damned impressive. I'm kind of glad we don't have to worry about him any more. Looks like he'll be paralyzed from the shoulders down."

"I shouldn't be that way I guess, but I'm almost sorry. Kate Wallace and that boy really loved him. Strange situation."

"We still don't know who the guy really is—or what his story is. Personally I think that Mooney guy knows but he won't say squat about The Mechanic. Could be he is afraid something about Gordon's story might be incriminating to him too, but I think he is just plain afraid. I don't understand what he thinks the guy can do to him now, though.

"How about your leg?"

"It's coming along—not fast enough to suit me but it's coming along. Apparently the artery was repaired but there was some nerve damage as well. I'm supposed to start physical therapy tomorrow and there will be a nasty scar but I'll be okay.

Curt flicked his eyebrows upward twice. "Care to show me your scar?"

Gaby groaned. "Get out of here, Agent Bell. Don't you beach bums down here have anything to do when I'm not giving you work?"

"Darn, you're right," he said. "I've got windsurfing at two and then the Hawaiian Tropic Bikini Team is coming in for a security consultation."

He wished her well and left but he was back every day of her stay with a magazine or a bar of chocolate.

The physical therapist was a tiny Columbian woman with a grip like a stevedore and the work ethic of a heavyweight fight trainer. Also, the sight of the jagged incision when the bandages were removed almost made her cry and the support stocking she was given to wear over the stitches was nearly as ugly. Both Gaby's leg and her scandalous vocabulary of foul language got a complete workout twice a day for the remainder of her stay.

The afternoon of the eighth day Gaby was allowed to move to a hotel. It was suggested that she stay over for another day so she could participate in the delivery of The Mechanic into the custody of the US Marshals who would accompany him to a more secure facility. She instantly ordered room service and her taste buds heartily endorsed the change.

The next morning she limped into the Miami FBI office for the ride to the hospital with Curt Bell. Everyone stood and applauded. Heads popped out of offices and others joined in. Gaby fought off the tears but the blush was inevitable. She waved and nodded at everyone and hurried as best she could to Curt's office. Several people whose names she couldn't recall offered congratulations and wanted to shake her hand. It was embarrassing but nice.

On the way back to the hospital Curt kept the mood light with his good-natured gibes about her new status in the Bureau and how he was going to enjoy having friends in high places but Gaby thought mostly about Aleksandr Pushkin. She hadn't visited him and her presence was not needed for his arraignment. It was unclear whether impersonating an Interpol operative was actually a technical infraction of US law. It would have been difficult to prosecute him for obstruction since he had materially aided the investigation. Neither of these charges would have ever been brought because the Bureau stood to suffer embarrassment for no particular gain. Only his presence on the vessel containing three tons of gold brought the indictments that might see him spend time in an American jail. Afterward he would certainly be deported and there might be other difficulties awaiting him at home. For the trial, she would be there to testify in favor of leniency if his lawyers asked, and they were certain to do so. She would go and visit him this afternoon, she decided.

"What was this all about anyway?" Gaby asked. "I mean how did it start? You must have interviewed The Mechanic by now."

"No, but Dashenko was surprisingly forthcoming about that since he had nothing to do with it. Malenkov went to Memphis to inspect the damage to the container and apparently it was just coincidence that he ran into The Mechanic in that freight yard. Then Balakova put a contract out on him because he was afraid that he had discovered the existence of the gold."

"So it was all just a mix-up?"

"Completely. They were hiding the gold after all this time, moving it once in a while and waiting on the price to rise but Dashenko is convinced that their secret was still safe and Balakova just overreacted. He, Dashenko that is, decided that he could turn the situation to his advantage and I guess he nearly did. You know, the truth is we don't have much on either him or Alex at all. He's kept his skirts pretty clean, and most of the charges against Alex will never see a courtroom because of the embarrassment to the Bureau."

"Poor Alex. This must be a nightmare for him. I don't think he even believed he was breaking any laws until the last minute and then I guess he thought it was too late.

"By the way," she said, "I never thought to ask where all that gold came from. Did Dashenko tell you that?"

"Oh, yeah. No he didn't but I meant to tell you. Way cool! We got onto somebody at CIA and they told us that a large amount of gold bullion was unaccounted for at the reserves in Moscow after the Soviet collapse. We're only guessing of course. The gold had been re-cast so there was no identification on it, but that's really the only place it could have come from."

"My God! Looting the Kremlin? That fits with what Dashenko told me. He was probably still in KGB then and arranged with Ivankov to clean out the treasury when no one was looking. So, what happened to the rest of them?"

"The rest of what?"

"Curt, are you kidding me again? You know that when Alex and I first went to that yard in Memphis the manager told us that there had been thirty white containers just like the one we found here only two months before."

Bell looked sideways at Gaby and blinked in disbelief. He used a word she hadn't heard him use before.

"Are you telling me there are thirty more boxes just like this one? That would be what—a hundred tons of gold? Jesus! You never told me that!"

"It was in the reports."

"Well I didn't see it and all I can tell you now is that they're not in either warehouse. And you think all of them were full?"

"In that CIA report, how much gold did they say was missing?"

"A hundred twenty to a hundred thirty tons, but they weren't too sure about the accuracy and it never occurred to me that all of it would have disappeared to the same place. We're having customs recheck every ship in the harbor."

Gaby had to laugh.

"They're not going to find it there," she said.

"Why not?"

"Colonel Dashenko is running ahead of us again. Curt, there's a good chance that he's sitting on a billion dollars in gold. Maybe two. Damn! When he gets out, that Russian is going to have a heck of a retirement fund waiting for him unless we watch him closely. He's using a contingency plan. That son of a bitch really is a genius. Alex might just get his boat after all."

"You were kind of sweet on Pushkin weren't you?"

She started to protest and thought better of it. She was sure it didn't take an FBI detective to figure that out.

"He asked about you, you know," said Curt.

"He did?"

"A hundred times. Even with his lawyer he wouldn't make a statement until we told him that you were going to be okay."

With that Gaby was lost in an unsatisfying series of what-ifs and Curt left her to her thoughts until after they had parked and entered the hospital. She did some quick math. The price of gold was still depressed but it always comes back. What would Alex's cut of two billion dollars come to anyway?

A gray Bureau of Prisons van and a Marshal's car were already in front of the drive-through pavilion.

Katherine Wallace, Matt Gordon and two uniformed policemen were in the room when they got there. Gaby spoke to the relatives but understandably got little response.

It was her first real view of the man she had chased half way across the country and back. He didn't look very deadly now. He was an ashy gray and he appeared to have lost a lot of weight. The civilian clothes they had dressed him in looked at least a size too big. Even his eyes were cloudy, as if he were barely aware of his surroundings. Gaby really wanted to talk to him, curious about how someone got to be like him, but especially with the family present it didn't seem to be a good idea. She would save that conversation for later.

"I'm sorry," Gaby said. "It's time to go."

It wasn't exactly a heartwarming goodbye. The boy was close enough to get his shoulder patted by his father and his sister-in-law gave him a weak smile. Gaby thought Katherine still wasn't sure what she was supposed to feel about the man.

"Remember what I told you," was all George Gordon said.

The room got even more crowded in a hurry. An overweight orderly was there to pick him up and place him in the wheelchair. It was not one belonging to the hospital. It was purchased by the government to transport handicapped prisoners. A nurse showed up to wheel him out but Curt waved her off and placed him in handcuffs. The hospital people looked at Curt as if he was being monstrously cruel but the prisoner might have been the most prolific killer in history, many of them with his bare hands, and those seemed to be in working order.

Curt pushed the chair down the hall with the retinue in his wake minus Kate Wallace and the boy. They elected not to see his final moments of limited freedom.

The trip down in the elevator was uneventful. Though they expected no trouble, the policemen made a show of inspecting ahead of them and waving them on. George Gordon rode slumped in his seat as if in a medicated daze.

At the front door of the hospital the police surveyed the people around the entry as Curt wheeled the prisoner down a ramp. At the bottom they were no more than a dozen feet from the open door of the van.

Gaby saw a flash out of the corner of her eye from the top of a building across the street like the morning sun reflecting off of glass. George Gordon fell forward out of the wheelchair at the same time that Curt Bell's left leg buckled with a loud thud and he collapsed to the ground.

Gaby started toward them confused. Then she heard a sound she had never heard before but recognized immediately as the whine of a bullet bouncing off the pavement.

"Gun!" she shouted and moved as best she could on her injured leg into a defensive crouch, drawing her weapon. Several bystanders began to scream at the sight of Curt's blood. He was just able to drag himself into cover behind the van. Gordon had rolled forward to safety when he hit the ground. She couldn't tell if he had been hit. Both policemen were behind the car. One was talking into a radio.

"Did you see the shooter?" he called out.

Gaby pointed and squinted at the tops of three buildings of equal height. "I just got a glimpse of something. One of the buildings over there, I couldn't tell which."

"Stay here," said the cop, and the two of them charged across the street while the Marshals spread apart to get a full view of the possible threat. Gaby was trying to cover them but there was no further evidence of shooting. She turned to Curt and pressed both hands on the fabric over his wound. He had been shot through the hip and was in shock. A gurney from the Emergency room came for him and they carted him away.

In sixty seconds there were four cruisers with lights flashing blocking the street. The marshals pulled back to the van. One of them looked inside.

"Where's the crippled guy?" he asked.

Gaby's heart leapt upward in her chest.

"He was right there by the door," she said stupidly. "Didn't you watch him? I had an agent down."

Gordon had seen the flash off the rifle's scope just as she had. Gaby used the nastiest curse she could think of with as little volume as her adrenaline would allow. In the gutter next to the open door she picked up Curt's open pair of handcuffs.

"When he fell down, I thought he was shot again. Paralyzed, my ass!" she said. "I guess the crippled guy got up and ran off while we were dodging the bullets meant for him."

The first policeman reappeared crossing the street holding a silenced rifle by a piece of newspaper wrapped around the grip.

"Did you get him?" one of the marshals asked.

"This guy was dead already," the cop replied, indicating the man who had used the rifle he held, "in an alley over there. Looked like his neck was broken. We saw a car driving off that was probably his partner. His partner must have double-crossed him."

Gaby looked at him with a sour expression. "That wasn't the shooter's partner; that was this guy," she said and held up the open pair of cuffs.

"Who was the shooter?" one of the marshals asked the officer with the rifle.

"ID said he was from Brooklyn. Name was Lucchesi, Carl Lucchesi."

Epilogue

A storm had passed over the grassy expanse just hours before. Ragged clouds in the easterly direction it thundered layered the sunrise with breathtaking and varied colors. It had washed the last smells of fire and death from the moist air, leaving it recharged and fresh. Kate breathed deeply and took a moment to enjoy it without thought before she got her things out of the rental car. Except for one jogger and a passing cyclist, she and Matthew would be alone in Wainwright Park.

The battered green Taurus was gone from the parking place where it had been on the day of George's assault. She had not told anyone about it, so she couldn't ask whether they had found and confiscated it or if it had been towed after a few days as a matter of course. God only knew what sort of horrible equipment he had kept secreted in it and she had no interest in improving the case against him. It was ridiculous, she admitted to herself, that she should feel protective toward George Gordon and she wondered again about Stockholm Syndrome or whatever odd psychological path she traveled to get to where she was. She only knew how she felt and acted on it. And she knew that Matthew was still alive only because of the frightening skills and tenacity of his father.

From the back seat Kate got the canvas bag she had brought from George's trailer hideaway what seemed like weeks before. Draped through the long straps were two beach towels of reasonable quality and exorbitant price she had purchased from the gift shop in the lobby in anticipation of the wet conditions. One of them, folded twice, went on the bench at the picnic table where she would sit. The second she used to dry the seat on one of the swings where she led Matthew.

He had to be led everywhere now. The boy had regressed into some stage of consciousness where he was docile but nearly disconnected from his environment. He would eat when food was put before him and he would bathe when she pushed him into the bathroom but he offered little in the way of communication.

In a voice usually reserved for three-year-olds she urged him to sit and play for a while. He accommodated her without enthusiasm and stared off in the distance, rocking more than swinging in a barely moving arc.

Tonight she would take Matt back to Memphis. Perhaps he would do better in familiar surroundings. The idea that lighthearted vacationing in the sun would solve his problems was clearly a failed concept. It would take all her patience and the skills of some of her more specialized colleagues to bring Matt back to where he had been just a little over two weeks before. She promised him that they wouldn't stay long as if the opportunity to play on a park swing was a chore to be endured rather than a privilege.

If being at home and seeing his friends didn't help, maybe she would take Matt and start a practice somewhere new. The money George had given and promised would allow her to do that easily. Tragedy had given her personal life meaning but at the moment, no satisfaction. Kate would exert all her efforts to heal those wounds just as George had known she would.

She returned to the table and sat facing the ocean, waiting for something but not knowing what it was. Her watch told her that the assigned hour of 8:30 was at hand. She looked all around her. Matt was still moving in a parody of a child on a playground swing, the jogger was laboring in another circuit of the running track and the woman on the bicycle was gone from sight.

In the distance she could just hear the rumble of a motor coming around the point on the water. It was an electric blue powerboat just like the one she had seen docked at the rear of the Russian's house down the way. She shaded her eyes against the low red and yellow sun and tried to see who was in it.

When the boat was just opposite her, the driver cut his engine and rocked to and fro on the gentle waters of Biscayne Bay less than two hundred yards from where she sat. A dark figure outlined by the brilliance of the morning stood by the wheel and seemed to be looking her way.

He made no gesture and after a few seconds she waved to him in acknowledgement. The figure responded with one raised hand. He stood that way for a few minutes unmoving. Finally he waved his hand slowly a few times and when he sat down again she heard the engine restart.

The bright blue craft made a slow turn out toward deeper waters, and then bore back to the north on the Intracoastal Waterway that led in a convoluted path all the way to Canada.

Kate watched it until it disappeared around some trees in her line of sight as a dot on the horizon. There were other vessels far out in the Bay and she watched them for another moment. There was no reason to hurry. She checked on Matthew again and pulled a dog-eared paperback she had almost forgotten from her bag and opened it to the bookmark. At the moment, Frodo was lost in the Dark Land.

FINIS

LaVergne, TN USA
19 May 2010

183229LV00002B/30/P